KJ BURRAGE

RENEGADE'S DIPLOMACY

DRAGON SOUL DUET BOOK 2

Paperback ISBN: 978-0-6459722-4-5

Published by Valiant Heart Publications

Cover designed by Chicklen.Doodle

instagram.com/chicklen.doodle/

Before You Read

Renegade's Diplomacy is written from multiple character points of view. British English is used. At the back of this book, you will find character, location and language indexes for your convenience.

Content

Renegade's Diplomacy includes themes and discussions including alcohol consumption, anxiety and depression, blood and corpses, amputations, death, mentions of executions, mentions of grief, physical abuse, slavery, violence and torture.

RENEGADE'S DIPLOMACY

goodreads.com/author/show/22623993.K_J_Burrage

amazon.com/author/kjburrage

instagram.com/kjburrage_writes/

For those who have travelled dark paths and

have found hope again.

Proud of you. Keep Going.

CYNEDIR
FRAEHILN
NAVILLA
GYTALL
TALSULLAH
AURELIA
CORRELLAIN
MT WEIRHELM
HEMMRYN VALE
FAHLORE FOREST
IRANI
VANCARDE
DEAD MAN'S FOLLY (MT WILLABAHL)
SAEMORE
TARRAMINE
ALVARAINE
TACEBIA
VALLEY OF YREW
CHARKARA
NEZAHA
YARYN
EUQUALL
SANGELL
HALVAINE

Contents

CHAPTER 1

Uhl'hari

EDVERN

Edvern's power laboured to sustain the heat of the funerary pyre. His body trembled with fatigue, yet he stood vigil. There was no honour guard to witness Kyros' passing into the afterlife, just him, a bastard son of a disgraced dragon rider. Nothing could tear his stinging eyes away from the hard scales curling and dropping from the red dragon's corpse. Kyros deserved better.

His lips parted in a prayer of thanks, breathing the arid smoke deep into his lungs. As if in a dream, he stepped into the firestorm, the roar of the fire surrounding him.

The flickering flames answered his prayer, twisting and growing hotter with every word. They beat down on him, but he did not burn. Dressed in only his smallclothes, he knelt, smearing his knees with soot.

Wingspan spreading impressively behind her, Alynta prowled towards him. The dyrathakin had grown. In the place of the small, foxlike dragon was a creature the size of a large wolf. Edvern could only stare in amazement; she was no longer a kit. Through their bond, their shared power thrummed.

"Alynta ..." Edvern choked, reaching out with a shaking hand to touch her, to see for himself that his dyrathakin was real, that he wasn't alone.

Alynta rubbed her soft head against his bare chest, pressing her body close to his. Her elongated ears paused over his heart. Overcome, Edvern wrapped his arms around her neck and drew her close, burying his nose in her fur.

"You've given him dignity with your flames. Now we must continue his fight," Alynta said. Her voice deepened with her new body.

"To my dying day, I'll honour him with my life." Edvern's throat bobbed.

Kyros had left him a new calling. Toppling Moira, his despotic grandmother, was no longer good enough. The dragons of Aurelia must be freed.

In knowing that Kyros had traded his life for him, Edvern's resolve for vengeance increased. Many of the old tales spoke of how a falling dragon could protect their rider, rolling to soften the blow. The great dragon had deemed him worthy of life, and by talons, he would fight until his last breath to honour him. Moira Tallermayne would pay for the mistake of letting him live long enough to escape.

A cold wind tore through the valley between the mountains, but he didn't feel the chill. He lifted his hand, and the inferno gutted, the tall flames falling like a crimson curtain before dying. Only ash remained.

Edvern turned his head to look at the tongues of fire and feathers that formed his wings. Heat radiated off them. Instead of panic, a creeping numbness rose within him at the sight of his extra body parts.

The sword he held in his injured hand echoed with his fire magic. Pain throbbed through his hand. What use was a magic weapon if the wielder was weakened?

Edvern shook with the memory of Yahler, Moira's sadistic torturer, taking his second finger. Swallowing bile, he fought to subdue his growing panic. Would his amputation hamper his ability with the sword? He would have to learn to write with his left hand. And tying his own shirt or lacing boots would prove to be a challenge.

Yahler was a bastard. When he had hacked off Edvern's finger, he ensured the cut was not clean. To stem the flow of blood, Edvern had sacrificed material from his smallclothes. If he wanted to stave off infection, he would need to cleanse and cauterise the wound. It was a task he had been dreading, avoiding it even though it had to be done.

The fingers on his uninjured hand curled, summoning tongues of fire to his palm. The flames burned bright until the orange glow gave way to a blistering blue. Clenching his teeth against the pain, he brought his wound to the fire. Blood sizzled and charred, but he remained resolute to see the task done.

"Eddi ..." Alynta leaned closer into his chest.

Ear against her side, he could hear and feel her comforting rumbles. Good hand clutching her fur, he looked up through the haze of sweat in his eyes. The ground tilted as his head spun. Gritting his teeth, he stood on shaking limbs. "I'm well. It had to be done."

"You are strong, my Eddi." Alynta's ears twitched.

Edvern scoffed.

Izorah, his father's blue dragon, prowled closer, muzzle to the ground, eyes downcast. In the approaching dawn's light, her scales shone. *We go. The riders will come looking for us.*

Edvern inclined his head. Kyros had been honoured, and his ancient dragon soul had departed. He could only hope that one day, when he left the mortal world behind, he might fly upon Kyros' back once more.

A soft smile tugged on Edvern's lips. Kyros was free. Although losing him tore a hole in his heart, he was glad the dragon's torment was over.

Izorah nudged him. *"I would be honoured if you would take me as your dragon."*

A memory long forgotten, when the waking world was still new to him, surfaced in his mind. He remembered being bundled up tight, warm and secure, and lying between scaled claws. A voice, rich and feminine, filled his soul, promising that one day, once he learned to walk as a grown man, he would fly with her.

"You've already taken me to be your rider," Edvern said. "You've always known."

Alynta rose, stretching her large body, and flapped her wings. Her tail swished as she watched Izorah and Edvern. There was no jealousy in the dyrathakin's eyes, only acceptance. "In Ancient Nezaha it was not unheard of for a dragon to pass from parent to child, especially if the father died prematurely."

Izorah nodded. *"From the moment dear Rikar placed you, a days-old babe, within my grasp, I knew you were mine."*

Many would be horrified that a father would place his babe within the talons of a beast, fearing that a dragon might think the child a tasty snack. But to Edvern, it seemed only natural that he had known Izorah from his very beginning. Even though Rikar could not have known the sentient capabilities of dragons, he had trusted Izorah.

"Then it is so. You're my dragon, and I'm your human." A lump lodged in Edvern's throat. Guilt collided with his budding excitement. He had a dragon, a beautiful, wise dragon, and yet Rikar had to die for Izorah to be his.

"You're hardly human." Alynta sniffed, her long, bushy tail flicking once more. She had sensed his morose thoughts through the bond and was redirecting his mind.

Thankful for the distraction, Edvern looked down at himself, to the cuts, scrapes and blood on his naked flesh. His tongue grazed along his sharpened fangs as he turned his head to look at his still burning wings. He sighed. "I suppose this means I can't go in public anywhere. What am I, anyway?"

"Uhl'hari," Alynta said, her nose twitching and tongue tasting the air. "A hybrid of human and dragon soul. Though unlike Raziel Yavari, you have me."

"If you say so." Edvern wasn't sure that this explanation was a thorough definition of whatever he was. "Where are we going to go?"

"Near water," Izorah rumbled. *"I've a place to meet a friend."*

Raising an eyebrow, Edvern pivoted to stare at her. She revealed nothing as she lowered her forelegs to the ground in a clear invitation for him to mount.

"Friend?" Edvern asked, incredulity creeping into his tone.

"You didn't honestly think that we are the only rebels in the dragon rider camp?"

"Yes," Alynta said, baring her fangs. "No one has helped Eddi. Not before you."

"There are others. It's difficult for us to meet, and I wasn't the only one who helped Eddi," Izorah replied. *"Come."*

Edvern glanced towards Alynta, and she nodded her regal head. Wasting no more time, he clambered onto Izorah's back. He enjoyed the burn of her searing hot scales on his palms and thighs. Exhausted, he lay along her back, resting his cheek on her neck.

"Lyssandra," he murmured. The last time he had seen the Saemorish diplomat, she was fighting off the poison Symmeon had given her.

What is lost has a way of finding its way back," Alynta said. "I doubt you've seen the last of her."

The dawn was painted with pinks and oranges as he lifted his face skyward; his mind was consumed by a dark-haired beauty, by haughty eyes and pinched, kissable lips. Wherever she was, he hoped that she had made it to safety. Breathing a prayer that Aryis would guide her home, he let the darkness claim him.

Edvern was cold and wet. Shivering, he stared up at the tall trees that loomed over him like sentries. A hard knot in his stomach loosened as he realised there was no sign of his strange wings of fire. His fingers had been left in the frigid stream, numbing the pain. He sat, bemused to see a clear boundary showing where the snow had been melted away by his power.

Submerging both of his hands in the river, he drank. When he had taken his fill, he splashed his face and considered the merits of washing the grime and blood from his skin.

"Alynta ... Izorah?" Edvern swallowed against the rawness of this throat. He stumbled to his feet, shuffling forwards, his muscles groaning in protest.

"My Eddi." Alynta prowled among the trees. Size had not been the only way she had changed. She moved now with the confident gait of a skilled predator. In her maw she carried three plump rabbits.

Wagging her tail, she dropped the rabbits and bounded forward, knocking him over as she nuzzled him. Determined to get onto his lap, as she had done when she was smaller, she tumbled onto the ground beside him.

"You've gotten too big for my lap." Edvern laughed. He buried his fingers into her fur as he pressed his nose into her back. Closing his eyes, he held her close. "What are we going to do?"

"Down with the dragon riders."

Coming from Alynta's lips, the sentiment seemed simple. It had become their mantra, their call to arms. But within his soul, doubt began to take hold. How long before Moira caught up with them and slaughtered everyone he held dear?

"If we die," Alynta said, "then we'll still have one another. Death shall not separate us."

Edvern swallowed and let the truth spoken by the dyrathakin sink into his heart. They were forever bound. While Moira Tallermayne may tear them asunder in this world, she could not reach them once they were dead. Together they could face any obstacle.

Alynta rubbed her face against him once more. "This is what it means to be dyrathakin and Uhl'hari. We are paired souls who draw strength from one another."

"Your fire did something to me," Edvern said.

"My fire is your fire." Alynta's long, forked tongue licked Edvern's face in a slippery kiss. "We transformed one another."

"I still think you did the majority of the work," Edvern replied.

"My first flames were not only to honour Kyros but to fan the fires of your soul."

"I still have missing fingers." Edvern didn't mean for his tone to be full of bitterness.

Alynta drew back and hissed.

"Sorry." Edvern wiggled his remaining digits. "I'm worried. How am I going to do anything for myself? Tie my boots, dress or fight."

"I cannot give you those back," Alynta replied.

"You gave me wings ..." How Edvern hated the thought of them, knowing that with them, he could never find a home among the humans.

"What is not there may not heal." Alynta scratched her head with her talons. "*I* did not give you wings; you did that yourself. They were already within you."

Turning his eyes away from his damaged hands, Edvern looked through the trunks of the trees. In time he would learn to live life without his fingers. When he lost his first finger, he learned to adjust. He would need time. Something they didn't have. "Where's Izorah?"

Alynta shrugged, rolling off Edvern's lap. She nudged her kills. "She went to find her friend. Shall I catch some fish for our dinner too?"

Edvern stumbled to his feet, searching for a branch long and sturdy enough to make a spear. It would be difficult, but his body needed to learn how to accomplish tasks. "I'll help."

"I've seen human hunting." Alynta gave him an indulgent look, and Edvern wasn't sure he appreciated it. "You build the fire."

Hands loose at his sides, Edvern watched Alynta as she waded into the cold stream. She seemed at ease with the temperature of the water, her fur flowing around her like an orange halo. When she didn't look back to see what he was up to, Edvern drew in a deep breath, exhaled and did as his dyrathakin suggested.

Searching among the trees, Edvern gathered as much firewood he could and brought it back to their makeshift camp. While he worked, he kept half an eye on the skies, looking for Izorah's return or enemy dragons. He tried to work out where he was, but he had no idea how long Izorah had flown and in what direction. There was no way of knowing how long he had slept. When he asked Alynta, she merely looked up at him and said, "A day, or maybe a few." And went straight back to her fishing.

The temperature in the forest was frigid. Hugging his arms around his torso, he closed his eyes and willed for his wings. It took some concentrating, but he felt them flow from his shoulder blades. The air around him swelled with glorious heat.

The challenge of moving about with wings was an unexpected complication. He lost count of the times he forgot about them and clipped them or tripped. Wherever he touched the trees, he started fires. He became quickly accustomed to throwing snowballs at the fires he started as he walked.

He had the sneaking suspicion that Alynta was watching him blunder about, making a fool of himself while she fished. She may not have given any indication that she thought it was funny, but Edvern was hot and angry by the time he had collected the firewood.

His new body was a danger to everyone. Shoulders hunched, he sat on a felled log to watch Alynta fish. Sweat from his wings streamed down his back. By the time it dripped to the ground, it was frozen.

"Uhl'hari," Alynta said, lifting her snout from the stream. "There must be a way that you can control whether or not you set the world on fire."

Feeling a headache forming, Edvern rubbed his brow with a groan. The dyrathakin was of course right. There had to be a way he could live with the wings without being a danger to everything around him.

"I'll meditate later," Edvern replied, his temples throbbing with the thought of mental exercises. "Let's get supper ready."

"I'm grateful for your wings," Alynta said. "Your strange hairless body would freeze without them."

Pursing his lips, Edvern dipped his head in acknowledgement. The cold was a killer. It was fortunate that he carried his own personal heating supply with him. He cleared an area for the fire, careful of where he dragged his wings, then sat to prepare the rabbits for supper.

Skinning the rabbits or gutting the fish seemed an insurmountable task. He had no knife or weapon. Frustration bubbled up in his gut; his hands were useless! Forgetting that he also had fangs, he bit his lip and tasted the coppery tang of his blood. He cursed and spat.

"I can feel your pain, Uhl'hari," Alynta said. She had stopped to study him with her large lavender eyes. "Be patient. You'll adjust in time. You're a son of a great dragon master."

"Another lie," Edvern snarled. "He'd be disappointed in me."

Alynta hummed. "You're wrong. Let me know when you are ready to talk."

Leaving the rabbits to the side, he considered using their fur for clothing. He would have to ask Alynta to hunt a good deal of rabbits to make anything useful. Perhaps her offerings tonight might make him something to cover his feet. It would be better to head into a human town and steal some clothes, but how could he do that unseen? An almost naked man was sure to raise questions.

Alynta padded up from the riverbank, her fur soaked through. She had been able to catch thirteen fish and proudly laid them out so that Edvern could select his for cooking.

From her tail to her velvety paws, she shook her coat. Then she drew a breath and lit their campfire before curling up to watch Edvern skewer two fish.

His hands shook, and it was slow, but he managed.

Alynta gave him a told-you-so glance.

"We're going to need supplies," Edvern said, watching as the fish blackened over the flames.

Alynta snorted. "What for?"

Gesturing to his body, Edvern said, "For a start, I need clothes. I have no knife, no weapons."

"You have teeth," Alynta replied.

Edvern ran his tongue along the points of his canines. He was not sure how the dyrathakin would take his reluctance to use his fangs to rip up meat for eating. It would be barbaric to do so; he wasn't an animal. He thought perhaps on this matter silence was the better option and held his tongue. It was quite possible that Izorah's friend might be able to do something about his sorry situation.

Ravenous, Edvern pulled the flesh of his fish apart and ate. While Alynta fell onto her own dinner, her lavender gaze didn't leave him. The whoosh of dragon wings came overhead as he buried the bones and carcass of his meal. The air gusts extinguished their fire, but he could clearly identify Izorah with another dragon.

Izorah landed first. She prowled forward, a dragonish grin parting her scaled lips, displaying her fangs. Triumphant amber eyes gleamed with pride. "Look who I found, rider."

A large navy dragon, with a silver underbelly, stretched his wings. He blew warm air over their smouldering campfire to reignite the flames. The slumped form of an unconscious human lay across the drake's neck.

"He could do with a bath." Wide nostrils flared as the dragon lowered his face to peer at Edvern.

"Hello to you too, Lyrus," Edvern said. Although the pair were fond of one another, he was still surprised that Izorah returned with Uncle Alaxen's dragon. Tilting his head, he tried to get a better look at the human with Lyrus. "Who's that?"

"It is as you say. He does understand us." Lyrus shuffled closer, his eyes studying Edvern intently.

"Now you can ask for belly rubs any time you like." Izorah nipped at Lyrus, rumbling and pressing herself close to him. The male dragon returned her gestures with a low hum as he rubbed the side of his face against her.

"Lyrus?" Edvern ignored the pair. "Who's your prisoner?"

"Prisoner?" Lyrus lifted his leg and cocked his head wickedly. *"This is no prisoner. This is my rider."*

"Uncle Alaxen?" It took three heartbeats for Edvern to process who Lyrus' rider was. "Why is he unconscious?"

Lyrus' grin faded as he shrunk back. *"I may have hit his head when I kidnapped him."*

"It was a complete accident," Izorah said, coming to Lyrus' defence.

"You can't go around kidnapping dragon riders!" Edvern's stomach dropped. Alaxen wouldn't be pleased to have been kidnapped.

Flicking his tail, Lyrus looked wholly unimpressed. *"I don't see why not. Riders have been controlling and harassing dragons for centuries. I happen to like this one and plan to knock some sense into him."*

Edvern faced Izorah. "He might try to kill me."

"I doubt that," Izorah said. She studied her claws as if they were fascinating. *"You're being dramatic."*

"Dramatic!" Edvern cried. "He's a Tallermayne."

For some reason, Lyrus seemed to think that was funny. He rumbled with laughter, lifting his snout to the sky.

"Nonsense," Izorah said. *"Alaxen has been helping the rebels for years."*

Edvern blinked and turned to look at his hapless uncle once more. Well, the man he grew up believing was his uncle. Lyrus had left Alaxen with his weapons. Draped over the navy drake's shoulders were travelling bags and supplies. He doubted getting himself kidnapped by his dragon was a part of his uncle's plan.

After kicking a patch of earth free of debris, Edvern laid his head down and didn't say anything more. Lyrus gently placed Alaxen near the fire, using his talon to straighten his head. The large male dragon curled up beside his rider, scaled chin on his front claws.

From her spot, Alynta watched on, her lavender eyes lighting up the dark. She took up some of her catch and laid them at the claws of the dragons. She nudged Izorah with her snout and coiled around her foreleg. They conversed with one another, the dyrathakin sending him concerned glances when she thought he wasn't looking. Smoke billowed from Izorah's nostrils.

"I would appreciate it if you didn't talk about me," Edvern muttered.

Lyrus opened his maw wide and yawned before running his tongue along his teeth. *"I don't see why not. Riders talk about their dragons all the time."*

"I'm not a dragon rider."

Izorah huffed, while Lyrus rumbled with laughter. He nudged Izorah with his snout before turning his glowing eyes towards Edvern. *"Here's a dragon; there's a human. Pretty sure that qualifies you as a dragon rider."*

"You should sleep, Eddi. Lyrus and I will keep watch," Izorah said. She lifted her face to the sky, scenting the air. *"I don't sense any danger. Sleep well, rider o' mine."*

Under the watchful stares of the dragons, Edvern rolled over. Dragons were stubborn creatures, and he wouldn't win an argument with them. He closed his eyes, feeling Alynta slinking close to the ground to huddle up next to him. His fingers caught in her fur, and he drew her closer to listen to her steady heartbeat.

Soon he was dreaming of burning cages and running beside a fleet-foot diplomat. Hunting dogs barked in the distance, and he could feel her trembling against him. The crystal river was nearby so he took her to its bank, abandoning her, while the dogs turned to nip at his heels.

Alynta
Fire Dyrathakin
Drawn by Eddi
cute cheek spikes
bone spikes
tail feathers

Men are cruel and carnal creatures. Stemming from the depths of their depravity, bastards plague the good name of Saemorish ruling families. Let the fruit of such dalliances be removed from their mothers. Girl children born in such disgrace should be tutored in the arts of diplomacy, the boys either put to the slaughter or trained for the frontlines of war. Tasks such as these should not be given to trueborn heirs.

"THE PROPER PLACE OF ILLIGITIMATE CHILDREN"
A POLITICAL PAMPHLET

LADY IDA BALROSA

CHAPTER 2

Royal Bastards

LYSSANDRA

Nausea roiled hard in Lyssandra's belly during the first hour of her flight home to Saemore. Dread and anxiety melted away from her mind as Antonella sung soft Euquallian songs in her lilting accent. Her friend rested her chin on her shoulder, her breath ghosting over Lyssandra's cheek as she sang. Underneath her thighs, Lyssandra's beautiful green dragon hummed and rumbled, providing a comforting vibration. A smile parted her lips. Elisaria was singing along.

"There it is! The palace of Tarramine!" Antonella cried; her voice was whipped away by the wind.

I'm home, Lyssandra thought, resisting the temptation to take out the letter the Black Prince had written in his own hand. He who once was the enemy was now relying on her to deliver his missive to King Jahon. To call her king to action would be her most difficult challenge yet. Under the leadership of Moira Tallermayne, the Aurelians were terrifying foes. Saemore and Nezaha needed to reach an understanding.

"I can't wait to put my feet on solid ground." Antonella leaned over the side of the dragon to peer down at the king's palace.

"I, for one, cannot wait to walk among Saemorish people again," Lyssandra replied.

How she longed to hear her native language spoken. Edvern, bless him, spoke what little he picked up clumsily.

"Antonella! Please!" Lyssandra cried, biting her lip to stop herself from grabbing her friend as she leaned precariously over the side of the dragon. "Don't do that."

Antonella laughed, while all Lyssandra could do was stare in bewilderment. Beneath them rolling green hills gave way to towns and villages. Overlooking the cerulean sea was the king's palace, its white turrets capped with green stones, gleaming in the winter's sun. Saemorish architecture was said to be the most beautiful in all the known world. From the sky the palace looked like a quaint dollhouse.

Lyssandra patted Elisaria's scaled neck. She was returning home with a dragon; she should use it to her advantage. "Do you think, my beautiful girl, that you could make a grand entrance?"

Elisaria cocked her head to the side, nostrils flaring as her gaze turned towards Lyssandra. The dragon's smile was all fangs.

Gliding on the cool downdrafts, Elisaria descended at a leisurely pace. Lyssandra inhaled and then released her breath. There had been many times she had feared she would never see her homeland again. Her homecoming brought with it a sense of premonition that meeting the Black Prince had irrevocably changed her destiny.

There were many ways that a diplomat might enter the city of Tarramine, but never had she anticipated the gut-wrenching apprehension and jubilation of landing with a dragon in the palace gardens. It was every diplomat's dream to return to the king's capital as a hero of the nation. Few ever attained the glory they sought.

The motions of a dragon in flight were smooth, but landing was another story. The ground underneath Elisaria's claws trembled. Biting back a cry, Lyssandra was jolted forwards by the impact of the dragon landing. Her fingers clung to the scales of Elisaria's neck. Behind her, Antonella latched on to her to avoid falling off and suffering embarrassment. The green dragon huffed.

"That wasn't funny," Lyssandra said, hoping that the dragon would take her scolding to heart. She didn't want to worry about how Elisaria planned to land every time they took to the skies.

Guards in the Saemorish emerald and gold swept into the garden, their pikes lowered, and Lyssandra did her best to gracefully dismount from the dragon's back. It was with a flash of annoyance that she observed how fluidly Antonella leapt to the ground.

Elisaria regarded the palace guards with cool indifference. She yawned, flashing long, white fangs, stretched, then lay on the ground to curl into a ball. One amber eye remained open.

"I have an urgent message for King Jahon. Take me to His Majesty at once," Lyssandra said, her hand hovering where she had stowed the parchment for safekeeping.

Lyssandra resisted the urge to tug on the stiff collar of her coat. The soldiers recognised her Saemorish accent but eyed her clothing with suspicion.

"How is it you've come by a Nezahrian's uniform?" A young man, three years Lyssandra's elder, swaggered forward. Piercing hazel eyes regarded her as he stopped three paces away. A smirk, reminiscent of his father, curled on his lips.

"The clothes that I escaped in were no longer satisfactory. Surely, you'd not have me return to Tarramine in soiled rags, cousin."

"Captain Konrad Stamos," Antonella purred. Sweeping her curls over her shoulder, she smiled coyly at him.

Konrad's mouth twitched, his eyes lighting up as he beheld her friend. A soldier behind him cleared his throat, his expression shuttered and his face transformed into a stern mask.

It was Lyssandra's turn to enjoy another's discomfort. Konrad, the illegitimate son of the crown prince, had won favour in his grandfather's court. At a tender age, he had been taken from his mother's arms and given to the weapon master. Forged to be a tool for his father's coming reign, Konrad lived a rougher lifestyle than his trueborn siblings. But he had his father's charisma. Silly girls had the infuriating habit of falling at his feet.

Antonella and he had a rivalry that spanned years. The last time they were together, her friend humiliated him in a card game and took his earnings plus his uniform. Konrad was forced to stumble half-drunk back to the barracks without his clothing.

"It is always a pleasure, Lady Antonella Fenin." Ever the gentleman, Konrad dipped his head. "The king wishes to speak with you. Your dragon …"

Chuckling at Konrad's stumbling words, Lyssandra turned to pat Elisaria's snout. "She's fine to wait here."

"*Here?*" Konrad looked around at the other soldiers and then to the carefully cultivated paths and pristine gardens. "Wouldn't it prefer more suitable … lodgings?"

"The dragon can look after herself. As I have previously stated, the matter is urgent." Lyssandra picked up her skirts, raised her nose and glided past him. He fumbled and followed, not before giving Antonella a sidelong glance. Lyssandra couldn't help but notice the indulgent look on Antonella's face as she regarded him back.

"You might take the opportunity to change," Konrad offered. He cleared his throat. "And brush your hair."

Before Lyssandra could stop herself, she lifted her hands to the wisps of hair that had worked themselves loose during the flight. Konrad smirked. His fingers rested on the handle of his sword while his gaze remained on Antonella.

"The matter is urgent," Lyssandra repeated.

"King Jahon is displeased with Nezaha, and my father ..." It was almost imperceptible, but Konrad shifted his weight, casting his eyes towards the other soldiers. "He's looking for any reason to go to war."

Pinching her lips, she regarded Konrad in silence. Like many talented young men, he never suffered from a lack of confidence. Something was wrong.

"If you think it wise that we change, we'll do so," Antonella said.

The spark of light returned to Konrad's eyes. "There are no words in the tongues of man to adequately describe how pleased I am to see you well, Lady Fenin."

Lyssandra looked askance to Antonella. Her friend's face heated with a rosy blush. Konrad's eyes left Antonella and slid to her as if he was trying to gauge her reaction. Even if he didn't deign to show it, she knew he valued her opinions. It had been that way since the first time they met as children.

She had been playing in the gardens on a rare free day when Crown Prince Torsten came out of the palace. Intimidated by the trueborn royal, she hid herself. It wasn't long before the prince's men strode into the gardens, hauling a frightened Konrad behind them. He was filthy, his feet covered in festering sores, and dark rings sat beneath wide hazel eyes. To her dying day, she'd never forget Konrad's haunted look as he beheld his father for the first time. She could tell he knew he was a royal bastard, and he'd either live or die at his father's command. That was how it was for boy bastards.

Torsten had said nothing, merely grunted and turned back. Mercy was granted, and Konrad was allowed to live. Their paths had crossed frequently when they were children. To survive, he used his charm and easy demeanour as a shield. Under the weapon master, he grew to be athletic and shrewd. Once he reached manhood, he rapidly rose among the ranks of the king's guards.

"Are you not happy to see me well, cousin?" Lyssandra asked, stepping aside to allow Konrad to open a side door. She did her best not to bristle. Try as she might, she hated that she was prohibited from using the front entrance of the palace. In Correllain, under Ellrahera's tutelage, it was easy to forget her ill breeding. She hated the capital, where polite society deemed her undeserving of respect.

Gallant as ever, Konrad swept the door open, ushering them inside. His usual calm mask of indifference slipped. "I'm glad that some of our diplomats survived the massacre. Would we be expecting others?"

Sweeping past him, Lyssandra lifted her chin. "No."

Shifting again, Konrad turned to the other palace guards. "I can escort the ladies from here."

Remembering the night that Correllain burned, Lyssandra didn't hear the guards' footsteps on the carpet as they left to their various posts. It seemed like another lifetime ago that she had made her daring escape. She had been broken apart and made into a newer, better version of herself.

"Saemore is balancing on the edge of a knife," Konrad whispered, his voice echoing on the polished stone walls. He was taking them through the servants' passageways, which meant he wanted to talk away from opportunistic ears. He swallowed, hazel eyes once again seeking out Antonella. "Whatever your news, please be careful. I heard the final protocol was enacted. You shouldn't be alive."

"Take us to get suitably dressed," Lyssandra said, because there wasn't anything she could do about her disobedience. It had been her duty to die, and she had dared to live. If the king was aware that Ellrahera had enacted the final protocol and she had not participated, she would have to prove the benefits of her living. Prove that her life could benefit the crown.

Appropriate clothing was a weapon, one that Lyssandra fully intended to wield.

Lyssandra finished brushing out her hair, eyes drifting to stare at herself in the mirror. The silk gown the servant woman had brought her was her preferred shade of emerald. The cut of it was simple but elegant. In Correllain, she had dozens of dresses just as beautiful before everything she had known had been torn from her hands.

"I'm glad I no longer smell of dragon," Antonella said, coming from the side room. Her gown was a lovely jade.

"I don't think a dragon smells of anything in particular." Lyssandra strode towards her discarded Nezahrian uniform, her soft skirts swaying around her ankles. Bending, she scooped them up, refusing to look at herself in the mirror. "How long?"

"Pardon?"

"How long have you been courting my cousin in secret?" Lyssandra demanded. She ran her hand down the bodice of her dress.

"Nothing has happened between us." Antonella's voice crept up an octave, as well it should. She was playing a dangerous game.

Lyssandra's slippered feet were silent as she went to the side table to look at the jewellery left out for her. She curled her lip at the silver earrings and pendant. While she appreciated pretty, delicate things, the silver marked her as a diplomat, an outcast. It was a reminder that she was something less than the other ladies at court. No matter how hard she worked, she would never have the right to wear gold. She picked up the first earring between her fingers. She couldn't refuse to wear the silver; it would be an affront to the king.

"You're courting him, but you haven't bedded him."

In the mirror, Antonella's expression was uncomfortable. "It's been at least a year." Antonella cringed, eyeing Lyssandra as if she suspected she might fly into a rage.

"He is the crown prince's bastard," Lyssandra said. She shouldn't have to give words to her warning. "It's not up to him to decide who he beds or weds."

Dropping her chin, Antonella refused to let her eyes meet Lyssandra's. "I know," she whispered. "But ... I love him, and he loves me. He's a good man."

"And good men are hard to find." Lyssandra's mind wandered back to Edvern. Her stomach clenched with the mere imaginings of what he might be going through in that very moment. She had found a good man, and she had let him go.

Silence followed Lyssandra's solemn declaration until a serving maid entered to let them know the king had summoned them.

Drawing herself to her full height, Lyssandra followed the servant, chin raised and shoulders back. At her door they were joined by Konrad and two unknown soldiers.

Konrad walked ahead, a silent escort. She could feel the judgemental eyes, heard their whispers following her. The daughter of disgraced Princess Fiora had returned to the palace. Passing the wing in which rumours said her mother languished, she straightened her shoulders. It took all her strength not to glance to the side. She wondered, did her mother have attendants that whispered news of her bastard daughter in her ear? With the way the gossipy commons called Fiora 'the Spider', she thought it likely.

Antonella's fingers brushed her hand, and Lyssandra's lips twitched. Her friend understood her feelings without the need for words to be spoken.

They were both orphans by circumstance and favoured by Ellrahera for their abilities.

Lyssandra kept her eyes on the emerald of the marble floor as they were ushered into the throne room.

Court was not in session. King Jahon sat upon his throne, a handpicked selection of advisors around him, their cruel eyes observing everything and missing nothing. She saw their raised eyebrows and the twist of their lips. She was uncomfortably reminded of her lesser status.

Konrad's father, Crown Prince Torsten, was at his father's right-hand side. He looked down his nose at their entrance, his bitter expression turning into disgust. Two paces back, she heard Konrad's soft sigh as if he was steeling himself for battle.

Lyssandra had been trained from the time she could walk, so she fell into a graceful curtsy and held the position until the king decided he would acknowledge her presence.

The king must have been displeased with her. He left her in position, sweat beading on her brow, until one of his advisors bravely cleared his throat. Gritting her teeth, Lyssandra kept her gaze on the mosaics on the floor.

"My sister Princess Ellrahera is dead, and yet two diplomats have returned to the hive." King Jahon's habit of letting petitioners know he had no patience was famous throughout the kingdom. "Are you becoming like your vicious mother, child? She was a scandalous woman, my youngest sister, a spider in a web until one of her schemes entrapped her."

"I'm your most devoted servant, Your Majesty." Lyssandra's eyes burned. She had heard the story of the Spider of Saemore, a cautionary tale given to young, impressionable diplomats. It was her secret shame that she was the cause of the princess' downfall.

"Stand and tell me what you want," the king barked.

Lyssandra rose to her feet, clasping her hands demurely, chin still lowered so that her eyes were downcast. "We have important intel, my king."

"Why wasn't the final protocol performed?" Torsten snarled. His eyes drifted over Konrad, and not for the first time, Lyssandra wondered what it was her cousin felt standing so close to the man who had sired him. Was it pride or shame that beat in Konrad's heart? As a child he'd been careful about revealing his feelings. Nothing had changed.

"Princess Ellrahera and I had different perspectives on the situation," Lyssandra said. Her words needed to be chosen carefully. The king valued courage and forthrightness, but if he judged your words to be insolent …

Rising from his throne, King Jahon moved with the difficulty of an ageing man. She caught the grimace on his face.

Prince Torsten's eyes gleamed as he observed his father's painful steps down the dais. He was a snake ready to strike. Once the king succumbed to the eternal sleep, he would take power quickly. He was impatient to have the crown upon his head.

The king approached, and Lyssandra's blood froze. She had always hated being in his presence. In the past Ellrahera had stood between them. This time the buffer was gone.

"Careful, girl," the king purred. "It's only that you have brought me a dragon as a gift that I won't have you beaten for your disrespect."

Gift? She had made no mention of a gift. Resisting the urge to flee, Lyssandra pressed her sweaty palms into her silk skirts. "Your Majesty, the situation with Aurelia is volatile. There's a village on our border, Hemmryn Vale—"

"We don't need a geography lesson, girl," one of the advisors said. Lyssandra lifted her head at his words, piercing him with a contemptuous gaze. From his gaudy rings on his fingers to his rounded stomach and outrageous furs, this man was incapable of feeling compassion for the common people. He could never know what it was like to fight for survival or watch those he loved suffer.

"The Aurelians attacked."

"We heard you murdered a Tallermayne," Prince Torsten said. "You're responsible for the slaughter."

"I have it on good authority that Princess Ellrahera knew the Black Prince was coming to Correllain ... yet she let him come. She refused to treat with him, and he burned the city to the ground." Although the crown prince terrified Lyssandra, she couldn't allow him to bully her into submission.

"It was on my command." The king reached out and gripped Lyssandra's chin, pinching her skin.

On my command.

Ellrahera was a royal diplomat; the king's wishes were law. He was the one to command the final protocol, and Ellrahera was bound to obey. He was the one who refused to treat with the Black Prince and let the city of diplomats burn.

It was a new side to the final protocol that she had never expected to face. Brother commanded his sister to commit suicide for the crown. Ellrahera was a trueborn princess, a daughter of a king. And yet even she wasn't safe ...

Lyssandra wished she had Edvern's courage. He would have spat in the king's face, called him a coward ... He would have done something. Anything would have been better than standing as still as a statue, unable to respond.

Her stomach cramped, and she felt bile rising. For what purpose would a king give the command to do nothing? He had the power to stay the Black Prince's hand. There was little doubt in her mind that the order to kill the young Nezahrian prince had come directly from him. The murder of Prince Hedriel was a deciding factor in the brutality the Black Prince had bestowed on her people.

"Edvern Tallermayne is alive," Antonella whispered. She sent a pleading glance to Lyssandra, begging her to corroborate the story.

For a fleeting moment, Lyssandra allowed herself to feel the sting of betrayal. But she understood why Antonella spoke. Withholding information was treason, and they were already in danger of being accused. Surely Antonella didn't know the depths of Lyssandra's feelings for him.

Flexing her fingers, Lyssandra drew in a deep breath. On her exhale she released her anger. She had hoped to keep her king unaware of Edvern's status. Now she had to work carefully to get what she wanted.

Standing in this room, she was the only one who would defend Edvern. Whether death at the hands of his countrymen or hers, she knew she had to do her very best work to save him. He deserved that in the very least, to live free, even if that meant she had to let him go.

"Alive, you say." The king released Lyssandra's chin and stroked his beard. "How?"

"When Correllain was attacked, I managed to get out of the city. I made my way to Gytall to claim Edvern as was planned. Edvern had already fled. Lady Moira forced the removal of foreigners from Aurelian cities, and so I've had to battle to find my way home," Lyssandra said, thinking it was better to speak before Antonella could intervene. She was taking control of the situation. "I had the good fortune of meeting him on the road."

"With how the Aurelians have treated our borderlands, perhaps an execution and not a wedding is in order," Torsten said. "Where is he now, girl?"

"It seems the Aurelians have recaptured him," Lyssandra replied. The words felt heavy to speak. Her stomach plummeted at the thought of the torture and pain he would endure at the hands of his own people. And if he survived that, what torment would Torsten and the king heap upon his shoulders? Cautiously, Lyssandra pulled the Black Prince's letter from the deep pockets of her gown. She held it up in offering to the king. "Nezaha hopes to mount a rescue mission."

"A rescue mission?" one of the advisors spluttered. "Preposterous!"

"We've all heard the rumours about Edvern Tallermayne," Antonella said. "The Nezahrians feel they have a claim to him."

Torsten sniffed. His cruel eyes swept over Antonella, assessing and dismissing her in the same heartbeat. Lyssandra admired the way her friend didn't falter. She could not imagine the Crown Prince becoming her father-in-law. Not that Antonella had a chance with Konrad. It would never be allowed. Lyssandra suspected that Torsten fully intended to use his bastard son, a shield of blood and bone, for his trueborn progeny. He would be kept a bachelor with no children to carry on his bloodline. He was born from corruption; Saemorish nobles held to the superstition that the children of their ill-conceived sons would destroy the true bloodline.

Bastards were curses.

It was the reason so many bastard sons never reached their first birthday.

Her sweaty hands trembled as she continued to hold out Raziel's letter. She dropped her arm. The king was disinterested in anything that the Nezahrians had to say.

"Edvern Tallermayne was purchased with my gold." It was with the king's words that she remembered her disagreement with Edvern in Hemmryn Vale. He had said the same thing. He had been nothing more than an item to purchase. Knowing how her rulers would use him, she understood his disgust.

"If we work with Nezaha, Your Majesty, we'd be one step closer to ensuring we have a chance of taking Edvern into custody." Lyssandra hated herself as she spoke those words. It felt like a betrayal. But Nezaha needed help getting Edvern to safety. If she had to be creative with the truth, she would. "Edvern Tallermayne is a talented fighter and ..."

"And ..."

Lyssandra bowed her head, praying that Edvern would forgive her lie. She would do whatever she could to provide him with some protection. "He's bonded with a dragon."

She was not sure if the dyrathakin was dragonish enough for King Jahon. But she said what she must to buy herself some time, to work out a way she could save Edvern.

"We'll weather Moira Tallermayne," the king boomed. His smile was enough for Lyssandra to step back. He turned his back to her and returned to the sanctuary of his throne. "We'll prise the dragon from Edvern's cold, dead fingers."

Lyssandra wanted to protest, to tell the king how bullheaded he was being. She bit her lip instead, letting the pain stall any hasty words spoken in anger. Her warning would fall upon deaf ears.

"I admit the loss of my sister was a blow," the king said, settling himself on his golden throne. "But while Nezaha and Aurelia are content with tearing each other to pieces, we'll be building our armies. Nations on extended military campaigns suffer. Once they're vulnerable, we'll swoop in and finish them both. With your dragon ..."

Lyssandra blocked out the rest of the king's speech. Had she been so arrogant as her sovereign in the past? He was so sure he was in the right that he refused to listen to anything she might have to say. Studying the king as he sat before her, posturing and lecturing, she wondered if this was what Edvern had seen in her when they first met.

She was so lost in her thoughts that she didn't register that she was dismissed until Antonella touched her elbow. Lyssandra dipped into a low curtsy. She cut a beautiful figure, refined and graceful as any of the court ladies, and yet she was beneath the king and his council's notice.

Lyssandra's mind continued to wander as they were led by the soldiers from the king's presence. There was much that she longed to say to Antonella, but this wasn't the time. The walls of the palace were alive. There were eyes and ears everywhere, willing to betray the daughter of a disgraced princess.

At their door, Konrad released the other soldiers of their duty, and he entered their room. After Lyssandra stepped over the threshold, he closed the door and locked it.

"This is hardly appropriate," Lyssandra hissed. She hated locked rooms.

Konrad smiled at her winsomely, and she cursed his dimples that no doubt got him far in life. "There's nothing wrong with me visiting my dear cousin."

"Now see here!" Lyssandra snarled. She turned on her heel and stalked towards him. "I am not playing games."

"Neither am I." Konrad tilted his head, and his voice deepened with something that Lyssandra couldn't quite define. He studied her as a cat studied a bothersome mouse. She hated that look.

"There's something you ought to see," Konrad continued. "Or rather, someone."

"Who?"

Konrad's eyes flicked over the walls, and he shifted in his place. He inclined his head. "My father underestimates my affection for you. Your time is running out."

Lyssandra knew his words were for her friend. Not her.

"If you want to leave the palace alive, be ready at midnight."

"Midnight?" Why must any nefarious schemes be worked upon at such an ungodly hour? Lyssandra was hoping for a comfortable bed in the palace tonight.

Konrad stepped further into the room, his gaze on Antonella alone. Sensing that this was a moment they ought to have in private, Lyssandra moved away. She knew she shouldn't watch with such rapt attention. But

...

Konrad reached out and touched Antonella's cheek with reverent care. She leaned into his hand, her lips parting in a soft sigh.

"Stay safe, milady."

"I will," Antonella whispered. "Are you coming with us?"

Konrad leaned forward, his lips pressing against Antonella's. Their kiss seemed to stretch out for all eternity, and Lyssandra wasn't sure where to look.

Her friend deserved happiness, and it hurt to think that if she chose this man, if she loved Konrad, she might never have that opportunity.

Konrad pressed his forehead to hers. "I've not decided."

He leaned forward again, his arms wrapping around her. This time the kiss was hungry, determined. Antonella's body melted against him, pressing so close to him that they might have well been one. Sharing this illicit kiss, they showed no shame.

Konrad stepped away, straightening his uniform. "Midnight."

And then he was gone.

CHAPTER 3

Dead Man's Folly

MOIRA

Moira's cloak snapped in the breeze as she stood among the smouldering ruins of her encampment. Breathing in the arid smoke, she curled her fingers around the locket at her throat. Regret weighed heavily on her shoulders. Was it guilt or grief that caused her to cling to a small lock of hair, proof that once upon a time, she had a beloved daughter? It was a grave weakness, relying on the piece of metal around her neck, but it was her daughter's memory that kept her grounded. She loathed her habit. Dropping her hands to her side, she knew that her riders needed to see her in control of her emotions. She should have poured herself a goblet of wine and enjoyed Edvern's screams of agony as he burned. Lifting her head, she swallowed thickly, surveying the ruins of tents and equipment and the bodies of her riders.

Quashing all thoughts of Tamah, Moira swept through the rubble, stopping before the dog cage. She had underestimated her enemy; delaying Edvern's death had been a costly mistake. In her mind she could still hear the agonising cries of her riders as the camp erupted into flames. She would have to weed out the weak and replenish her numbers. And soon.

Witnesses told her of a winged creature, a demon that came in the dead of night. The beast was followed by a familiar dragon.

Not only had Edvern corrupted his father and uncle, but he also conspired with dragons. Moira had hoped that with the bastard gone, Izorah would choose another rider. But the blue dragon proved to be stubborn and sided with Edvern. If not for their recent loss of dragons, Moira would have butchered the stupid beast.

When they thought they weren't in earshot, her riders whispered theories that Edvern was a mage. Given his Nezahrian heritage, it was a possibility. He had proven he could twist the minds of dragons to his will.

Since her husband's death, she had full control of the dragons, even though she was only Tallermayne by marriage.

As a discarded daughter, she had come to Gytall with nothing. She had to fight for everything she'd gained. Never resting, she had trained at all hours. Shedding the frailty of her humanity, she had become the heart of a dragon. Fierce, proud and merciless.

She cast aside her family name, Valmorle, an ancient and proud line. She returned home to her father, burning him and his second wife, along with their precious sons. Every single one of them had died bathed in Kyros' flames. Valmorle was no more.

Free of her family, she returned to Gytall a rider who equalled the Tallermayne legacy. During her marriage to Fennix, she controlled him, and by the time he was killed, she had firmly placed herself as a leader among the dragon masters.

Edvern's defection weakened Moira's power. Everything had crumpled the moment he had fled Gytall. He was a challenge to her power. It wasn't long before whispers of dissent spread.

The rebels had sensed the shift as well. In Gytall they started meeting openly. The news of Edvern's murder and funeral divided public opinion. Some guessed rightly that it was fake, an excuse to declare war. Others thought she had slit the boy's throat herself, many rejoicing in the spilling of Tallermayne blood. When she returned home, she would have to send her wolves among the sheep and frighten them back into submission.

"We should have beheaded him when we had the chance." Master Yahler approached her, stepping on parts of tents, supplies and bodies without a glance. When one was as feared as he, one did not have to worry about respecting corpses.

"Mind where you are stepping," Mistress Whilmana snarled. The head of interrogation looked around the dead, the whites of her eyes prominent. As they walked through the camp, she picked her way through the deceased, ensuring that even her cloak did not touch them. Whilmana came from an ancient bloodline, and she still adhered to the old ways.

"Dead men don't talk," Yahler replied. He shrugged, his lips twisting into a cruel smirk.

"If you are careless, the dead have a way of getting their revenge." Whilmana's reply was cutting. Many within their ranks hated her. She was a quiet woman, rarely speaking to fill a void. It was her calm indifference and calculated cruelty that first impressed Moira. Faced with Whilmana, few kept their dark secrets.

Yahler stepped in line with Moira, his eyes raking over the place of Edvern's cage. "Say what you will about the bastard, but he wasn't going to break."

"In the end, they all sing." Whilmana crossed her arms against her chest. "All that is needed is the right type of pain."

"You failed to break him. Mark my word, he was determined to die silent." Yahler's thick lips quirked into a wry smile.

Not in the mood to listen to her masters' petty arguments, Moira turned away from the pair. Bickering, they followed her to what remained of her personal tent. Their hushed voices ceased when they reached the patch of scorched earth.

For the first time in many years, Moira was at a loss of what to do. A painful lump caught in her throat as she stared with vacant eyes where her tent used to stand. She was tired, so very tired, but could not let her failure cause her to stumble. If Fennix were alive, this would never have happened. He would have killed Edvern before he could walk in order to protect Rikar.

Her mercy had been her undoing.

Moira lifted her chin and straightened her back. Edvern's victory was only a minor setback. He may have wrenched the control of the dragons of Gytall Spire out of her hands, but she had two other ancient dragon strongholds of which she was mistress.

And what did Edvern have?

One dragon. He didn't even have the clothes upon his back. In this weather he would soon freeze to death. She hoped it was slow and painful.

"Grand Lady?"

Moira started.

"Shall we go after Edvern?"

Yahler's question was a good one. She considered for a moment what they knew. The boy's disappearance had heralded the decline of the control she had over the dragons. That could be no coincidence. When they had lost the precious glass egg, she had her riders meticulously sweep the spire to see what else he had taken.

It hadn't been much. He pilfered supplies such as clothes, weapons and food. All stolen from his dead father. Cursed goods. Qavi, lord of the shadows, did not bless those with cursed goods.

"Leave him," Moira snapped. "I need to consult the old snake from the library ... If anyone knows, it'll be him."

The dragon's legs buckled as she landed heavily in the training grounds of Gytall Spire. Impatient with her creature, Moira kicked its sides with her spurs. The dragon snorted, raking its talons along the ground, leaving icy shards in its wake.

Dismounting, she studied the new armour she had commissioned for the beast. Perhaps Edvern had been right. It was too heavy.

"You'll get used to it," Moira said.

The teal lifted her snout. Her long tongue slithered out of its maw, tasting the falling snowflakes. Disgusted by her choice in mount, she missed the glory days when Kyros had ruled the skies.

"Take her back to the caverns," Moira barked to a nearby novice. Without another glance, she turned away and strode inside the spire. Novices rushed forward to peel off the dragon's armour. She could hear as her dragon protested, bellowing and huffing as it was pulled away from its game with the snowfall.

Gritting her teeth, Moira let her dragon have its tantrum. Intent on her destination, she stalked through the corridors. It was unusual for her to enter the library; research and reading were tasks she assigned to her riders. The types of answers she needed would not be found in the thousands of dusty tomes but rather in the aged mind of Nabert, the library master. If he failed to answer her questions, they risked losing further control of the dragons. She would not bear the humiliation of losing more.

She paused at the heavy oak doors that sealed the entrance to the library. She dragged in a deep breath, pulled her shoulders back and took a moment to collect her racing thoughts. If Master Nabert sensed she was less than confident, he would use the opportunity to unsettle her.

Pressing her hands against the doors, she pushed them open and stepped into the austere space of the library. The bright light that greeted her was almost blinding; old Nabert needed plenty to read his precious words.

The library was cavernous, filled with old texts from floor to ceiling. Rows of bookshelves, built from the heaviest timbers, were accessed by ladders. Glancing up, she admired the stained-glass dome. The crystalline face of Ullryk Tallermayne and his dragon looked down at her. Warm colours from the glass illuminated the library. The windows were portraits of Saskah, the beautiful Aurelian princess who helped Ullryk defect and later became his wife. Her large drake was depicted with chin resting on Saskah's shoulder, his silvery wings outstretched. It was, of course, foolish propaganda. Dragons did not care for their masters.

Moira's footsteps echoed as she walked the mosaic tiles of the library. The scent of ancient leather and musty parchment kept the air in the library stifling. There was only one older apprentice sitting at the table.

"Kirra, go study somewhere else."

Pushing back her short blonde hair, Kirra collected her books, her chair scraping on the floor in her haste to obey. She dropped two scrolls but did not move to retrieve them as she fled. Kirra Deltmine was on the cusp of graduating to master, but she wasn't there yet.

From between a set of bookshelves, Nabert shuffled forward. He scowled, adding more creases to his wrinkled face.

"Mistress Tallermayne," Nabert said with a half bow. "To what do we owe the pleasure?"

Breathing in through her nose, Moira was determined to ignore the fact that after all these years, Master Nabert still refused to call her 'lady'. His famed loyalty to her late husband was the only reason she kept him alive. That and his head was full of arcane information that he refused to pass down to the younger generation. Such was his deep understanding of the histories and magics; she knew he still had his uses.

"Have you started the research I commanded?"

"Indeed, I have." Nabert inclined his head, a sly smile curling on his thin lips. There was always a price to pay before he would divulge anything of real use.

"You've not come forth with any information."

"You weren't here, Moira." Nabert swept his arms out wide. "Nor did you call for me. Why are you concerned about our glorious nation's mysterious past when you never cared before?"

"Glory will come on the battlefield." Moira gritted her teeth. Older than her, Nabert had served briefly under Fennix's grandfather, then his father before Fennix. He had retired a decade ago when his dragon had died in battle. He had served with distinction, and because he had never married, he was allowed to linger in his beloved dust-covered cave. He had unofficially earned himself the title of library master. Ullryk help anyone if they hurt his precious books.

"Well?"

Nabert had the nasty habit of seeing how far he could push her. He had never made it a secret that he disapproved of her marriage to Fennix. It didn't help that Moira had fairly earned his ire. Adelia Valynt, the woman Moira had ruined to marry Fennix, had been his favourite niece. Three months after Adelia was shamefully removed from Gytall, Moira married Fennix.

The Valynt family had never forgiven Moira.

"Superstitions and beliefs sometimes stray too far from the original teachings," Nabert said. A slight sneer parted his lips, and Moira knew he was going to enjoy what he told her next.

"How so?"

Nabert's predatory smile widened, like a spider observing its trapped prey within its web. "The belief that Tallermayne blood is the main component to controlling dragons is utter dragon piss. That theory has been disproven many times."

Moira did not react. She'd not give the library master that satisfaction. She was aware of Nabert's next argument. He wasn't the only one who resented Moira for her marriage into the Tallermayne bloodline. Fennix mourned the loss of Adelia. He had loved that woman from afar to his dying day. She never found out if he knew it was her who had been his lover's downfall. He had remained aloof during their marriage. He kept his own council and doted on his sons.

"Nonsense. The power and dominion over dragons has been passed down for centuries through the Tallermayne bloodline."

"You're not Tallermayne. Fennix is gone. Where are his children? They don't stand with you." Nabert had the audacity to tilt his head and study her as if she were little more than a curiosity. She hated how he effortlessly made her feel like a young woman again. Withered hands adjusted his fading robes. Moira caught a glimpse of Fennix's personal banner when he was Grand Lord of Gytall, and she, merely his consort. She clenched her teeth. Nabert saw her gaze, and a mocking smile touched his lips. He never changed his allegiance from Fennix to her when her husband was killed.

But Fennix was dead and gone, and she was the Grand Lady. Nabert, like any other occupants of the spire, owed her his loyalty.

"If I were you, I'd start speaking in plain words," Moira said.

Nabert wasn't fooled by her sweet tone. The shrewd light in his eyes sharpened. "If I were you, *Lady* Moira, I would be concerned about Edvern's adventures. Very concerned, indeed."

Stepping around the old man, Lady Moira perused the bookshelves. Her fingertips brushed the leather of the spines, and she breathed in the smell of old parchment. She kept her steps languid, her heels clicking on the stone floor. It was an intimidation tactic she had used proficiently for years. She was a predator, Nabert the prey. In Gytall she had all the power. She could stalk and goad her quarry at her leisure. There was no rush to strike.

"What do you know about Edvern?" Moira asked. She spoke softly, not deigning to look at the library master. "I didn't think news would have reached you before me."

"Something happened. I thought so," Nabert said. He shifted slightly to the right, keeping Moira in his full line of sight.

"You'll spill your secrets, old man; it would be a shame to stain your precious tomes with blood."

"When you've lived as many painful years as me, threats begin to lose their power." Nabert chuckled, his robes rustling.

She moved towards one of the chairs at the desk that Kirra had been studying at. She waited. Nabert, thinking himself wise, would break the stalemate and speak. All she needed was patience.

"It seems almost impossible that you would remain so ignorant. Fennix kept the truth from you. Rikar came seeking answers a month before the attack in Charkara. I dare say Rikar shared what I told him with Alaxen."

There was one thing Moira couldn't abide by, and that was gloating. She balled her fists at her side. Nabert had a special power to rile her, to make her so angry that she lost her sense of reason.

"What truth would that be?"

"Rikar was no Tallermayne."

"Don't be ridiculous!" Moira snapped. "I was there when I gave birth to that ungrateful wretch. He came forth from my own womb!"

Moira sucked in a breath, her mind awhirl, trying to make sense of what Nabert was hinting at. Pinching the bridge of her nose, she turned to look at the old man. She hated librarians, articulate fiends, who were full of double meanings and riddles.

Nabert seemed amused. "Fennix was a master at illusions. It stuck even after death."

"Rikar was my son."

"Employing Fennix's once lover as the baby's wetnurse was cruel but also a serious miscalculation. Adelia smothered your son, and Fennix sent her away. But not without asking me to find him a newborn child for him to cast an illusion over. There was always a part of him that loved Adelia. He chose her over the child he had with you."

A lesser woman would feel the sting of grief at this news. Instead, the thought of her dead child brought a strange hollowness to Moira's belly. She braced herself for the pain. But it did not come.

Rikar was not her son.

That was a cause for celebration. Perhaps Moira had always known there was something rotten about Rikar. She had never been able to put her finger on what it was, but she had always felt a sense of disgust with him. A mother's intuition.

"If Rikar is not your son, Edvern is—"

"Not my grandson."

"Follow the logic through," Nabert suggested. "Edvern isn't your grandson, yet he has pried control of the dragons out of your grasp, even though he doesn't possess a drop of Tallermayne blood. Nor is he adopted or married to one. Common sense would dictate he did something else to sway the balance of power in his favour."

The edges of Nabert's mouth curled up. Moira wanted to scream. She had spent so much time and energy maintaining her power, yet this librarian knew her source of power was an illusion. It was dangerous knowledge.

Moira's fingers found the handle of her hunting dagger. Tracking her movements, Nabert's eyes fell on her weapon. He smiled at her then, and she knew he had been aware that telling her this information could only mean one thing for him.

He straightened, pushing his shoulders back with a groan. "Shall you paint my tomes with my blood now, my lady?"

"No one can ever know the truth," Moira said. It was all an apology the old man would get. She was the Grand Lady of the spire.

Nabert tilted his head, his eyes narrowed, amusement gleaming in their depths.

Moira stayed her hand. The fact that Nabert didn't plead with her wasn't a surprise. She had dispatched enough of their own ranks to know many dragon riders didn't beg for their lives.

"The people call you the second coming of Halsabith. Lord Qavi knows you've left enough broken bodies in your wake."

"Halsabith is a foolish children's tale."

"Is it?" Nabert tilted his head, eyes going to the glass windows. His gaze lingered over the depiction of a cloaked man, face hidden, crowning a young woman with a wreath of light. "I have never feared you, Lady Halsabith," Nabert said. "But I would be a fool not to fear Lord Qavi's judgement. Atonement can be granted through an act of defiance in the face of Halsabith."

"Another silly tale. I am not her."

"The people condemn you, and by extension, all dragon riders. The mob will take you and all who stand in their way. Your death will not be a kind one. The great darkness is coming for you."

Moira's fingers tightened on her dagger. "Don't mistake me for kind, old man."

"Children's story or not, best to die before madness takes you." Nabert shrugged, opening his hands wide, inviting her dagger to embed itself into his chest. Her hand shook with the need to punish someone, to let her anger leech out.

Lunging, Moira drove the dagger into the old man's torso. His eyes widened as the breath was stolen from his lungs. She stepped back, watching dispassionately as he sunk to his knees.

Nabert did not utter a sound. He stared up at her, a sly smile widening his lips, blood coating his teeth. She stood over him as he bled out, the red pool of blood slowly spreading over the library floor.

Nabert rallied, his lips quivering with a final message. "The cursed queen's reign is ..." He choked on the rising blood, his old eyes calm. "Over."

Rage coursed through Moira. Untameable power coiled in her belly, searing hot and merciless. She lashed out, her dark power consuming her body and soul. The old librarian's cunning mind warped under the influence of her might. She caught control of his brain ... pouring fear and pain into his thoughts that no mortal man could defeat.

Nabert died screaming for mercy.

CHAPTER 4

Scorched Earth

RAZIEL, THE BLACK PRINCE

The scorched earth ran red with blood. From his vantage point on Faelowyn's back, Raziel spotted dozens of unfortunate riders and dragons, their bodies broken and scattered. Faelowyn drifted over Moira's encampment, her nostrils flaring at the putrid scent of charred flesh.

Raziel moaned, not in pity for his foes, but for the unknown fate of Edvern. The blessed one had been within his grasp, and he had foolishly let the boy goad him into an argument. A wiser man would have ensnared Edvern in his power and hauled him to a safer location. The boy's stubbornness and anger could have been dealt with in Tacebia, surrounded by an army. Now it looked like he was dead, and Raziel laid the blame on his own shoulders.

Faelowyn banked, circling over the camp. She was reluctant to leave the site, hopeful that she might spot a clue as to Edvern's whereabouts. A sentiment that Raziel shared.

"There!" Faelowyn shifted directions, and he caught sight of a dragon limping away from the carnage. Even at the height they were soaring, he could tell she would never fly again.

"Let's see what we can find out from the Aurelian scum." Raziel ground his teeth, running his trembling fingers along the hardness of Faelowyn's spine.

"We'll make her talk."

Raziel shivered. Faelowyn's tone held her eagerness for vengeance. She dove sharply, and he held on with the confidence he had gleaned from many hours in the air with his bonded dragon.

The grounded dragon paused in her morose trek, tilting her head to the sky to regard them with something akin to resigned apathy. Her orange scales were covered with a thick layer of ash and soot.

"Have you come to slay me?" she asked, swaying her head back and forth as Faelowyn landed before her. *"Not much left for you to nibble on, I'm afraid."*

Raziel took a closer look at her. Indeed, her tail hadn't been hacked. The wounds were made with precise straight lines. They were manmade. White bone was visible along her jaw, where a chunk had been bitten away. Blood dripped from her bared teeth. More disturbing, she was walking on a bloody stump. Her front left claw was missing. Something terrible had happened to this pathetic Aurelian.

"We're searching for news of a rider who was last seen on Kyros' back."

"Indeed. He's dead. Ullryk's great beast is dead." The dragon slumped where she was on the ground, curling her tail against her body. She laughed and coughed. Dark clotted blood bubbled on her fangs, and bitterness seeped into her tone. *"The humans attacked me when I let my rider fall to*

her death. I should have removed their limbs earlier. Born in servitude, but at least I'll die free."

"You have a strange view of freedom," Faelowyn commented.

"When you are born in dark caverns, live in the cold depths, hungry and brutalised ... death under smoky skies tastes like freedom." The dragon wearily closed her dull yellow eyes. Death was near.

"Kyros' rider?" Raziel asked. He couldn't help but let hope seep into his words.

"Edvern Tallermayne ... ah, yes." The orange dragon's eyes opened. *"Tenacious as they come. Surprised to see him alive after his theft."*

"Tell us what happened to him," Faelowyn demanded.

"They waited for Kyros to die and took him prisoner. They do what humans do, whether Aurelian or Nezahrian. Torture and pain ... then rescue came from the skies. The dragon who took him started the fires." More hacking laughs. *"And then those dragons, tired of the reign of terror thrust upon us by humans, joined the burning."*

Considering how staunchly proud Aerin had been of his kills, Raziel shouldn't be so shocked at a group of dragons turning to slaughter. From the very first strands of the dragonsong, nothing like this had ever happened. He had truly underestimated how deep the discontent ran in the Aurelian dragons.

"There are whispers that whatever Edvern stole has significantly weakened the control of the dragons in Gytall."

Of course he knew the power placed inside the dyrathakin eggs. He had already made arrangements with a few of his loyal war wraiths to retrieve the remaining two.

"Please ..." The orange dragon's words were fading. *"Moira has taken a new dragon. Young, not yet strong enough to wear armour and carry a human to battle ... chosen purely for her vibrant scales."*

"What would you have us do?"

"The hatchling doesn't wish to fight." The orange dragon let out a long, soft sigh. *"Free her."*

The dragon's pained expression stirred a strong emotion within Raziel. He pitied his dragonish enemies. Swallowing, he hardly dared to look at Faelowyn. "Did you see where Edvern's rescuer went?"

"No ... find Kyros' body ..." And with those final words, the orange dragon breathed her last.

Side by side, Faelowyn and Raziel stared contemplatively at the corpse.

"Should we burn her?" Faelowyn asked. *"She's Aurelian, and she let her rider die."*

Raziel stepped forward, his hands tracing over the cooling scales of her body. "We've all done things that make us monsters. She's suffered enough in life," he said. "In death we should honour her and burn her body."

He stepped away, and Faelowyn set the dead dragon alight. Her scales curled, consumed by the fire as they fell away. Attuned to the dragonsong after so many years as Faelowyn's partner, he heard the echoes of the dragon's soul depart. Instead of victory over a dead enemy, her demise filled him with shame and a deep sense of sorrow.

They did not stay to watch her complete burning.

The orange dragon's suggestion to visit the place of Kyros' death was sound advice. If the great dragon had been burned, strands of his unique song might be still heard.

Humans could not hear the songs and souls of the departed, but part of the Father Dragon's soul was embedded within Raziel. Extending out his power, he could potentially sense the final strands and song of Kyros, the Red Plague. It took practice and concentration to track the death place of a dragon, but it was a skill that Raziel's predecessor had forced him to learn until he had perfected the technique.

Contrary to popular belief, the dead could talk, if you had the wits to hear their final moments.

Kyros' last battleground was a barren stretch of scorched earth. Nothing physical was left of the Red Plague.

Years of enmity, and this was how it ended.

Faelowyn landed, and Raziel felt the remnants of Kyros. He brushed away his feelings of hatred and listened. He heard the notes of his first rider, Ullryk. The red dragon had been thinking of him as he died. Ullryk. A blessed one who had been shunned, born from a poor family. Ullryk was special; he heard Kyros' voice like no other.

Kyros had feared the Nezahrian emperor, who had discovered the control he could exert over dragons. The wild ones fled, leaving those with riders at the mercy of Nezahrian forces. But Kyros did not go with them. He stayed with Ullryk; it was he who convinced his rider to defect before it was too late. Others followed and supported the small kingdom of Aurelia, who had come under the rule of the Nezahrians.

For a time, they had victory, but Ullryk grew old and perished. New humans rose in the order. Ullryk's own descendent, Edvern the Red, betrayed them. Where Ullryk had taken the dyrathakin eggs to hide them, Edvern the Red dug them up to use them as a weapon. Ullryk's descendant changed the tide of the hostilities. The defence of the Aurelian border morphed into outright attacks on Nezaha. The power in the dyrathakin eggs were used to subjugate the dragons inside Aurelian borders.

Taking control over their dragons, the riders twisted the partnership into something more inhumane than the Nezahrian emperor could have ever dreamt. The throbbing power of the dyrathakin stone tormented him day and night. His mind was no longer his own, his thoughts corrupted, and the madness crept in. The chains came next, and war. Kyros held to who he was ... remembering his glory days.

There were long years of self-hatred. Then came Edvern, a small babe; he had sent another dragon rider who could hear faint echoes of his will to fetch him. Hope was resurrected for dragons as he grew. He would be the one to release dragons from their imprisonment.

Raziel felt the moment the ancient dragon knew he was dying. The last flight and fight. The fall … protecting Edvern with his life. Edvern's soft voice singing him into his eternal rest, followed by blackness as his soul returned to the Father Dragon's nest.

His body was burning, and there was peace in knowing for all his faults and failures, the Uhl'hari was released.

Raziel blinked, staggering away from the scorched earth that had served as the red dragon's funerary pyre. He sucked in a breath, and he knew he did not have to ask Faelowyn if she had felt Kyros' story unfolding.

"Goodbye, Plague," Raziel whispered to the wind. "Find peace. Find your rider."

"He didn't deserve our hate," Faelowyn said. *"He wanted freedom for dragons."*

Raziel swallowed, and from the corner of his eye, he considered what he might do for his dragon. *Anything,* he thought. *I'd do anything to keep her safe.*

"He took Edvern from us," Raziel replied.

"He was afraid that we would use, hurt and betray him." Faelowyn looked to the sky as if she could see the looming shadow of the mysterious dragon who had rescued Edvern.

Raziel let the silence stretch between them. Then he turned, mounting Faelowyn. "Perhaps he was right to be concerned that we might have ill-used Edvern."

After unfurling her wings, Faelowyn leapt into the air, and they soared once more among the clouds. For a moment, Raziel relaxed, letting all thought of war wash away. Here, thousands of miles above the cold, frozen earth, he could find small moments of peace.

Bloodshed was coming.

He owed it to the dragons of Aurelia to try and free them. Recalling the orange dragon's plea, he allowed himself to feel the despair and helplessness. Kyros had been right. Nezaha's blessed ones had abandoned the dragons of Aurelia ... He had prolonged their suffering. The red dragon had acted as he saw fit to help his own kind. And to bring dragons hope, he had conspired to kidnap a temple babe to become their champion.

A smile curled on Raziel's face. Born of Nezahrian heritage, blessed by the temples but raised by the enemy, Edvern might be the very weapon that was needed.

"Kyros wanted Edvern to grow among the dragons so he would love them," Faelowyn admonished him. Raziel winced at the sharp tug of his conscious. *"Edvern will fight for them because he is one of them. He's not a weapon to wield."*

"The two aren't mutually exclusive," Raziel said. "I'll ensure that he's protected."

"And after the war is finished?"

The conclusion to the war was a foreign concept to Raziel. Nezaha and Aurelia had been fighting for centuries. Could it be that he could become instrumental in its climax?

"If the war is over and peace established, I'd ensure Edvern is properly educated in who he is ... then ..." The blessed ones had always been embroiled in conflict. "Then we'll decide from there what paths he might take."

"Once you have him, could you let him go? Crushing a hatchling's wings is ill-advised," Faelowyn said sagely.

"We should return to the men and tell them what we have discovered." Worry clawed at Raziel's belly. If Edvern had bonded with a dragon, it would be Aurelian bred. How far had Aurelia snuck its claws into his blessed one?

Faelowyn was right. Edvern's path would naturally be different. Previously, he would have huffed at the idea that Edvern might want to stay with the Aurelian dragons. Now it seemed likely. Raziel could only hope that the dragon he was bound to would be wise, caring and willing to protect him at all costs.

CHAPTER 5

Revenge is Rising

EDVERN

Sharp stones pressed into the vulnerable flesh of Edvern's stomach as he groaned and rolled over. Groping for the comforting warmth and softness of Alynta, he was disappointed to find the dyrathakin was not with him. A cool wind caressed his wings as he sat and stretched them. Curiosity got the better of him, and he traced a finger along the fire of his feathers. They were blisteringly hot, yet his hand came away unburnt.

"You've gained control of your powers."

Edvern jumped to his feet, his head spinning and throbbing.

Leaning against the scaled side of Lyrus, Alaxen sat observing him with hooded eyes. Bruised and broken, Edvern felt insignificant against his uncle. At six foot five, Alaxen was a giant among men. Years of hard training had honed his broad-shouldered frame into a muscled weapon.

As a boy, he remembered lining up to measure his hands and feet against his uncle. Even in the wilds, Alaxen's blond beard was trimmed and neat. Everything about his uncle screamed that he was Moira's heir, the next Grand Lord.

Edvern was little better than a beggar.

Mouth dry, he had no idea what he should say to his uncle, so he settled on, "Good morning."

"Morning, yes. Good? We'll see." Alaxen bent his head over several pieces of wood, his whittling knife moving in quick, precise movements. He abandoned his project to study Edvern. His dragon, Lyrus, curled his head around so that he could stare up at his rider. Izorah snuggled close to Lyrus' side.

"Are you hungry, Eddi boy?"

Edvern licked his chapped lips. Despite Alynta's hunting and fishing, he was hungry. He flicked his gaze out into the shadows, sensing rather than seeing Alynta prowling and observing Alaxen at a safe distance.

"I'm a man grown," Edvern replied.

Holding out a biscuit, which was standard dragon rider issue, Alaxen huffed and shook his head. There was nothing special about riders' rations, but the palm-sized biscuit was enough to make Edvern's stomach rumble.

Alaxen broke his biscuit in half and offered it. "Grown or not, come eat. Fire magics consume lots of energy."

"Aren't you surprised?" Edvern asked, nerves making his guts clench. In Aurelia only dragon riders were allowed to hone and cultivate their gifts. "About the fire?"

"Your father's death and your expulsion from Gytall didn't kill the power and potential I sensed within you."

Edvern stepped up to him cautiously, taking the biscuit with his uninjured hand. "You're calmer than I had anticipated, Lord Alaxen."

"Let's not stand on graces here. I'm still your uncle, a man who raised you." Alaxen grunted again, his shoulders rising and falling. He studied his gloves for a long moment before he continued. "You weren't the only one who felt imprisoned."

"But you were a lord," Edvern said.

Alaxen lifted an eyebrow. "A lordship doesn't guarantee freedom or safety."

Edvern looked away. There was a part of him that had always known the truth of Alaxen's statement. But that didn't stop his next words. "Safe enough. You abandoned my father. Abandoned me."

It had hurt. Standing with his family, yet alone, witnessing as his future was burned with his father. His father's last breath was a clear line in the sand. Alaxen had taken him from the execution site and dumped him in a dark corridor.

"Edvern." Alaxen's voice was soft, his grave eyes pinning him. "Rikar and I made a promise many years ago that we would protect our sons before ourselves."

Edvern glared back.

"If I protested too loudly, my sons' lives would have been forfeit," Alaxen said. "I advocated for him. I used whatever power I had as dragon lord to try and sway the other masters to pressure Mother to show clemency. It was enough for her to exile me and take my sons."

"You've not seen Kendrick and Bastian?"

Alaxen shook his head. "Not since your father's execution."

Edvern swallowed. The lump in his throat felt like a fireball. His chest constricted, and his hands flared with flames. He lifted them to his face … The ration biscuit was incinerated. Two tongues of flame flickered where his missing fingers should have been. He tried to bend them to his will, but they refused to move.

Alaxen didn't flinch. Edvern surmised that years of service under Moira Tallermayne had taught him to hide his emotions. Thinking too liberally tended to get one killed.

"You'll need to learn to manage outbursts," Alaxen said, taking up another ration biscuit and holding it out to Edvern.

"I know," Edvern replied. He calmed his breath and willed the flames to still and extinguish themselves, then took the ration biscuit. He nibbled along the edge, watching his uncle from the corner of his eye. "Can't go setting villages alight."

Alaxen rammed the rest of his biscuit into his mouth and rolled onto his feet. Back turned to Edvern, he rummaged through his packs.

"Where were you going when Lyrus waylaid you?" Edvern asked.

Alaxen's shoulders stiffened. He turned, a dragon rider's uniform in his hands, and ignored the question. "Frankly, you reek. Wash up, and I'll take a look at your hand."

Edvern looked down at his body. Standing in only his smallclothes, he had been determined not to be embarrassed by his vulnerability. "I cauterised the wound."

Alaxen raised an eyebrow and pointed towards the stream.

Knowing he wasn't going to win the argument, Edvern slunk towards the water. He paused, looking at his wings, wondering how they would react to getting wet.

From the shadows, Alynta stalked towards Alaxen; she observed him from a careful distance. For his part, Alaxen studied her intently, remaining still as a statue.

"I was expecting more questions from you," Edvern said.

Eyes still on the dyrathakin, Alaxen replied, "You're creatures of Nezahrian mythology. I had the advantage of having access to documentation that you, a novice, never had."

Edvern gestured to his body. "Can you tell me what I am?"

"Nezahrian temples have a hierarchy. Children born with tapered ears are called the blessed ones. They're believed to be born of ancient lines and are blessed with strong powers. Nezahrian parents leave their newborn 'blessed ones' at the temples. Often, they grow to become judges, sages and in some cases, warriors or spies."

Edvern nodded. His tutors had taught him about the Nezahrian blessed ones. At one point he had been one of them. Whoever his birth parents were, they had left him at the temple. Did they think of him still?

"The Black Prince, or Raziel, is the Yavari, the military leader responsible for Nezaha's war machine. Every few centuries a blessed one is chosen by the current Yavari to be their heir. They're given long life and have extraordinary powers. Raziel chose you to be the next Yavari."

"Yavari ..."

"Is a title, not a family name. Loosely translated, means sword."

Edvern gestured to his body. "And this ..."

"From the blessed ones also come those who are chosen by the fire fox. Your familiar chose you to be the one to siphon her power with. Someday you may outrank Raziel Yavari."

"What am I?"

"Other than an emissary between human and dragon, I don't know."

"You aren't repulsed?"

"No. When Rikar brought you home, you were his son. I accepted my brother's decision." Alaxen's eyes swivelled to Edvern. "He spoke of the powers of compulsion protecting you, but he would never have harmed you, Eddi."

"I know," Edvern whispered. His feelings about his adoptive father confused him, but he knew Rikar had been as honourable as his Tallermayne blood had allowed him.

Tallermaynes, by definition of their nature, were not compassionate people.

An uncomfortable silence stilled over them, and Alynta continued to prowl forward. She stopped shy of Alaxen, staring up at him with tail lashing. "Lyrus would like a belly scratch, rider."

Shocked that she would reveal she could speak with the voice of a man to his uncle so soon, Edvern choked back a laugh.

"Lyrus wants me to scratch his belly?" Edvern was impressed how his uncle's expression didn't shift into utter disbelief. Alaxen turned to his dragon, who rolled over, thrusting out his chest.

"He's been waiting all morning," Edvern said with a nonchalant shrug.

"This is convenient," Lyrus said as Alaxen moved towards him and started to scratch his belly. *"I like having translators."*

Without turning his head to glance at Alaxen, Edvern dipped his toe into the water. His stifled chuckles morphed into a yelp and a string of curse words that would make even dock workers blush. He stumbled back onto the riverbank.

"Better get it over with," Alaxen commented from the relative warmth of his dragon's side. Was it Edvern's imagination, or did his uncle sound amused? He quashed the insane urge to poke his tongue out, steeled his shoulders and stepped in.

Edvern sucked in a breath, then walked forward until he was submerged in the water. Arms wrapped around his chest, he turned back to the bank. Alaxen was standing, watching him with his unwavering gaze.

"Catch!"

Edvern had trained rigorously as a youngster, and wanting to show up his older cousins, could always be found in the middle of games of older boys. He caught the item easily. It was a bar of soap. He saluted, plunging it into the water.

He rubbed a lather on his hands, and the scent of Aurelian mountain roses wafted in the air. He felt a surge of unexpected guilt. Who was he to use a nobleman's soap, a luxury most Aurelians couldn't afford?

It took three rounds of intense scrubbing before he felt clean. He washed his hair four times before grime and blood were no longer dripping down his shoulders.

Before wandering away, Alaxen had laid out the uniform neatly, including clean smallclothes. The sizing was too small to be his uncle's. Kendrick's uniform. Dressing, Edvern had to wonder what his uncle thought of his state. An ill-used oarsman on a slave galley would have been in better condition.

"Thank you," Edvern mumbled.

Alaxen nodded curtly, coming over and surprising Edvern by helping him tie the cuffs of his shirt. "You've lost some definition."

Edvern shook his head, letting his uncle finish dressing him. "It's been a lean winter."

"That it has," Alaxen said. "It's been a terrible three years."

"Three?"

Alaxen lifted his gaze. "Rikar started making plans many months prior to being caught."

"Because of me," Edvern said. It wasn't a question, rather a statement. He knew the truth of his words. And Alaxen had known of Rikar's guilt and never betrayed him. "Because of what I am."

"Rikar made his choice the day he took you from the temple," Alaxen said. "Do you know he's not your—"

"Yes," Edvern said quickly, remembering the imagery Symmeon, one of the Black Prince's men, had shown him through the soul touch. "He wasn't my father; you're not my uncle."

"He protected you unto death, Edvern," Alaxen said sternly. His growl had little bite though. "He did more than what many fathers would do for a natural born son."

"I was lucky, I know," Edvern admitted, looking down at his hands. "I feel conflicted."

"Not unexpected," Alaxen remarked. His dark eyes roved over the missing fingers. "It was either smuggle you out of Nezaha or leave you on the altar to perish. Your father chose life for you."

"The Black Prince said I was stolen from Charkara."

"Three of your father's masters flew rogue. By the time he reached you, the Nezahrian city was falling." Alaxen shook his head. "The Black Prince lost the battle."

Edvern sucked in a breath. That was a detail that the soul touch had not shown him. A weight settled on his shoulders, and he wished for nothing more than to curl up on a bedroll and sleep. Preferably forever.

"Give me your hand."

Edvern glanced up at Alaxen, who seemed content to wait. He went to give his uncle his left hand, but Alaxen shook his head ruefully. Uncertain, he paused, not wanting to expose his terrible injury further. But as his uncle waggled his fingers, he complied.

Alaxen weaved his fingers between what remained of Edvern's own. He squeezed tightly, and with his free hand, he held Edvern's elbow. "Deep breath."

Before Edvern could open his mouth to ask what his uncle meant, his knees buckled under him. Only Alaxen's strong grip stopped him from falling. A wave of raw power swelled in his arm. Overwhelming pain tore through his body. He clenched his jaw, unwilling to put a voice to his agony.

Alynta growled, and he was powerless to turn his head to her. He could do nothing for her distress. Lyrus had risen and placed himself between Alaxen and the dyrathakin. He was aware of the two of them having words, but through the haze and fog of the power, he could not make out their conversation.

Alaxen released Edvern, and with two hands on his shoulders, guided him to sit.

"What ...?" Edvern was not impressed with how pathetic he sounded.

"I sped up the healing process of your muscles and tendons," Alaxen said gruffly. "There was infection in the wound. Deep breaths."

Edvern struggled to steady his breathing. His lungs burned, and his head swam. "I couldn't keep the wound clean." His hands fell to his lap, face burning with shame. "She kept me caged like a dog."

Alaxen's eyes roved over the dark fuzz that was left on Edvern's scalp. "You've shorn your hair."

"Not of my own choice," Edvern muttered, hanging his head. "I thought to join mercenaries but was tricked into signing away my freedom."

"Edvern ..." Alaxen's voice was soft as he reached out a heavy hand to place it on the crown of his head. A gentle push of power made Edvern's scalp tingle. Hair, dark and soft, grew from the roots at an unnatural speed. "You'd have been wasted as a mercenary."

Hardly believing the miracle that Alaxen was able to produce from his body, Edvern lifted a hand to touch the new hair. His eyes burned, and he felt ridiculous. It was just hair. He no longer looked like a runaway slave.

Lifting his hand to his uncle, Edvern asked, "Can't you do anything more?"

Alaxen shook his head. "The human body is incapable of regrowing limbs. I'm sorry, Eddi."

Disappointment gripped Edvern's guts. He tried to not let it show, but he suspected he failed when Alaxen sighed and turned away.

"You're very lucky to have a healer," Izorah said. She looked to the dyrathakin and continued, *"Calm yourself, little beastie. Your master will recover."*

"How did you become a healer?" Edvern asked. "Where did you learn?"

"I was born a healer," Alaxen said. "Who do you think healed your ears so no evidence remained?"

"I thought Aunt Thleah ..."

"No." A soft smile touched Alaxen's lips. "She held and coddled you while I worked. The compulsion over Rikar wouldn't allow him to participate."

Edvern blinked. "I thought your power was in stealth. You can only have one power."

"Wrong. It certainly isn't common to be blessed with two natural powers." Alaxen nodded, and seeing that Edvern looked stable, released him. Lyrus stepped aside so Alynta could scamper to him. As she passed Alaxen, she gave him a dirty look.

"Impossible."

"As impossible as you having wings?"

Edvern decided to change the subject and answered the question with another question. "Were you compelled to protect me?"

"Not in the way you are thinking," Alaxen said. "You held a sway over Rikar as a small babe, but as you grew into adolescence and were able to protect yourself, the power decreased. Rikar said that the compulsion would flare when you were in high distress or afraid."

"Did it take away all his choices?"

"Not at all. We worked with the compulsion to do as we thought best. For example, when you were particularly naughty, as all young boys are every now and again, and afraid of punishment, the compulsion wouldn't allow Rikar to chastise you."

"So you'd ..."

"I'd step in."

Everything made more sense. "But there were times he punished me."

"The compulsion lashed out terribly." A shadow fell over Alaxen's expression. "Your grandmother thought Rikar's reluctance in punishing you was a weakness. There were times she gave your da an ultimatum: him or another dragon master of her choosing. Talons, he'd do anything to keep Whilmana away from you."

Edvern swallowed, glancing down at his hands. "The power punished him. How?"

"Debilitating pain that sleep couldn't relieve, headaches, vomiting, nightmares and visions. On a few occasions, paralysis. Hiding these symptoms from our mother was problematic."

A memory filtered through Edvern's mind. He'd marched right up to Moira and told her he hated her. His father had no choice but to punish him. After, Rikar had lain beside Edvern, exhausted, and wept. "I wish he told me while he was still alive."

"He didn't want you to have the burden of knowing, Eddi."

"That doesn't answer the question," Alynta said. She sat on her haunches and glared up at Alaxen primly. "Are *you* compelled?"

"Noble one, Rikar was compelled by something within Edvern. I was compelled through my own nature."

"What do you mean?" Edvern asked. Even Lyrus lowered his head over Alaxen's shoulder to better hear the answer. Absentmindedly, Alaxen scratched the softer scales under his dragon's chin. Lyrus purred.

"I had my own reasons for starting a humble rebellion eight years before you were brought to us."

"So long ago?"

"Choosing my friends and foes was a slow and deliberate task. My power of stealth allowed me to weed out those who would be staunchly loyal to Moira. Dragon riders are suspicious by nature; a little manipulation and those who were a threat to the rebellion were branded as traitors. Moira has been burning her own people for many years."

"You had no reason to rebel against Moira. You're the next Grand Lord. Why risk your position?"

"Life is full of risk. Healers once held great influence and respect," Alaxen explained. "Now we're perceived as weaker because the magic within us wants to restore and rejuvenate ... sometimes even our enemies."

"You've helped Aurelia's enemies before. Does Lady Moira know?"

Alaxen shook his head. "She might have been happy to hear I had two powers, but learning my secondary power was healing might have also brought her shame."

Edvern looked down at his hand and then back to his uncle. "Well, thank you."

A sad smile tugged on Alaxen's lips.

"I've so many questions."

"Ask."

Despite Alaxen's invitation, Edvern hesitated. "I suspected Aunt Thleah had healing powers. Was she ... did Moira kill ... her?" He could see the pain in Alaxen's eyes, a well of sorrow he had seen before. Growing up in the nursery with his older cousins, he had known that Alaxen and Thleah had a marriage unlike most Aurelian nobility. Once upon a time, Alaxen had been happy. "Forgive me."

"We were a love match," Alaxen said. "We married in secret, and when we could no longer hide it, we told my mother. Thleah wasn't welcome within the dragon rider circles, but we had each other. I fear every day my sons will be killed next."

"Moira wouldn't ..." But Edvern stopped at the twisted look of torment on Alaxen's face. Nothing was certain. Although Bastian and Kendrick were trueborn sons of the Tallermayne line, his uncle still believed them in danger.

Lyrus widened his nostrils and blew hot air at Edvern. *"Tell him why we are here."*

"We plan on taking down the dragon rider order," Edvern said.

"We?" Alaxen raised his eyebrows.

"The dragons and I," Edvern clarified. "Lyrus wanted you to know."

"Lyrus *wanted* me to know." Alaxen looked between the dragons and Edvern. It didn't take him long to figure it out. "You can understand them? Speak with them?"

"Yes," Edvern admitted.

Alaxen swore and started to laugh so hard that tears began to roll down his cheeks.

"He's distraught!" Lyrus cried. The darker dragon lifted his head, swaying it side to side. *"There's something wrong with him! He's going mad."*

"I don't see what's funny." Edvern was inclined to agree with some of Lyrus' assessment, but he turned to the male dragon. "Calm down."

Alaxen wiped his tears away and looked up to Lyrus, whose large amber eyes were wide with alarm. "My mother and those before her have searched for a way to know the minds of dragons, to pluck knowledge of the past from their brains. And here you are with that exact ability."

Edvern shook his head in disbelief. "Kyros was the first dragon to speak with me."

"Poor old Kyros." Alaxen bit his lip. "I tried to persuade Father to set him free. But he was too valuable."

At the mention of Kyros' name, Edvern felt sick. "Valuable?"

"He was an old dragon," Alaxen said. "The knowledge that he had was the reason he was Mother's favourite. And the prestige of riding him."

"In the end he ..." Edvern's words faded as the memories of the damage done to the red dragon played in his mind. With all of his might, he wished he could turn back the hands of time and change Kyros' fate. It seemed unfair that he perished at the claws and talons of his fellow Aurelian dragons.

"Moira couldn't have known how old he was," Edvern said. "The records of dragons' ages are unkept."

Alaxen stared back at him, and Edvern was drawn back into his last moments with Kyros. He had been too anxious at the time to process the old dragon's thoughts. Kyros had given him a name of one of his riders who he had loved.

"He mentioned another rider ... Ullryk ..."

"The Liberator," Alaxen finished for him. "That old gent was around when Ullryk Tallermayne fled the tyranny of Nezaha and established his own order in Aurelia. Perhaps if you're on good terms with him—"

"He's dead." Edvern's voice sounded flat. It was as if he were detached from his body and someone else moved his lips. Standing abruptly, he turned away from Alaxen and the eager dragons. His feet took him to the very edge of the forest. "He's dead, and it's all my fault."

"Eddi..." Alynta whispered. She padded to Edvern's side and rubbed her furred head over his trousers. "Kyros died free, with your hands upon his scales and a rider of his choosing."

"To die free is a blessing most Aurelian dragons don't dare dream about," Izorah said.

"I am truly sorry to hear of his passing." Alaxen's shoulders drew back. He seemed stiff and formal once more.

Edvern knew they did not have time to dwell on the dead. The red dragon would have him steel his heart and start plotting. He knew from experience the grief would still be there when it was a more appropriate time to mourn. He was certain it would never leave his heart. "Are there any suggestions for what is next?"

Lyrus nodded his head. He looked towards Alaxen and back to Edvern. His tail swished back and forth. *"Ask my rider about the rebels."*

Alaxen caught Edvern's gaze flickering over to Lyrus and back to himself. "What is it?" he asked.

"Lyrus wants me to ask you about the rebels," Edvern said.

"I have some contacts," Alaxen replied. "We'll have to be careful. I'm sure my absence has been noted."

"We already have the egg from Gytall," Edvern said. "We should be stealing the eggs for Cynedir and Navilla."

"Egg?"

Edvern turned towards Alaxen, forgetting he was a little behind on some matters. He gestured towards Alynta. "Behold the dyrathakin from the glass egg of Gytall."

Alaxen's jaw dropped, and Edvern enjoyed the rare occurrence where he was taken off guard.

"We need to steal the dyrathakin eggs, free the Aurelian dragons and take our country back."

Again, Alaxen looked towards Edvern for clarification. "They want to free dragons and steal eggs."

"Sounds fun," Alynta said. Her voice deepened. "Revenge is rising."

"Revenge is rising," Alaxen parroted. "I like the sound of that."

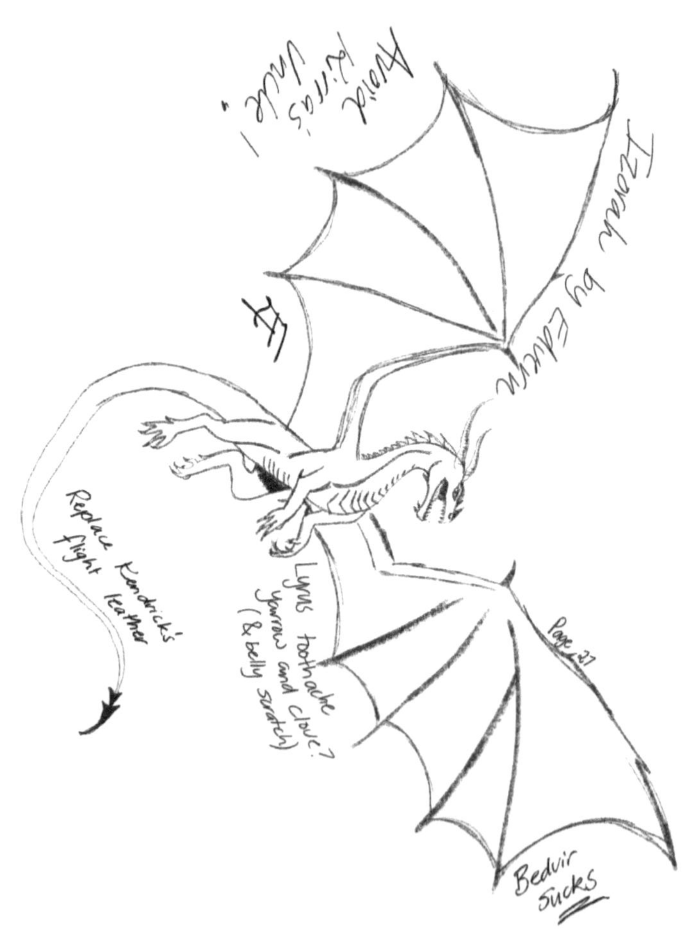
Avoid Kirra's Jade."
Izbook by Edwin
Replace Kendrick's flight feather
Lyra's toothache - yarrow and clove? (& belly scratch)
Page 27
Beduir sucks

CHAPTER 6

Tarramine Dungeons

LYSSANDRA

As the hour of midnight approached, Lyssandra could feel unease coiling through her belly. It had been painfully clear that the king was displeased that the final protocol hadn't been successful. He wished for all the diplomats to be rotting corpses, and she had the audacity to escape.

To keep her mind occupied, she exchanged her long, sweeping skirts for fitted trousers and a cotton shirt. Konrad's sense of secrecy left her in little doubt that if they were caught, they would be in danger of the headsman's axe. Wrapped in a black woollen cloak, she waited for her cousin.

In the light of the oil lamps, Antonella's face was the picture of calm. She toed off her delicate heeled shoes and pulled soft leather boots over her feet. They exchanged glances, and although neither of them had dared to speak of it out loud, Lyssandra knew her friend's mind was occupied by the horrors of Correllain.

The Black Prince had been telling the truth.

The order for the final protocol had been given prior to the attack. Ellrahera was prepared but had done nothing to defend Correllain's citizens. Try as she might, Lyssandra could not forget the cries of the dying. While Ellrahera held some responsibility, she blamed her king.

Surely, the prime diplomat couldn't have known the hour of the Black Prince's coming. Otherwise she would have gathered her diplomats beforehand. It was the only reason that Lyssandra and Antonella had survived.

Antonella's nails tapped a rhythm on the wooden side table, distracting Lyssandra from her thoughts. She stole a look at her friend as she whispered the lyrics of an old Euquallian ballad. It was a song of two star-crossed lovers. A discarded daughter and a soldier. The parallels between the song and her friend's budding relationship weren't lost on Lyssandra.

Konrad loved her friend. If they escaped with their lives, he'd be a good match for her. But in the world of the living, love wasn't enough.

"Konrad's life was purchased from the brothel master," Lyssandra whispered. "He's owned by the crown. If he leaves Tarramine without permission ..."

"Your people are obsessed with debts and owning." Antonella's voice was tight with emotion.

"Not all of us were fortunate enough to be born free in Euquall." Lyssandra wished she had the restraint to curb her words. She shouldn't have said it. But deep down, somewhere near her gut, she felt the simmering anger at Antonella for putting Edvern in danger.

There were some things that Antonella couldn't fully appreciate. Her friend was born to a wealthy family in Euquall and had the protection of parents. Whereas Lyssandra understood how fragile her safety was. She had never seen her mother, much less enjoyed the security of her royal status.

Raised in the bastard nursery until it was time to prove her value, Lyssandra refused to think of the fates of those ill-gotten children deemed useless.

Antonella stared, her brown skin paling and her eyes alight with fury. "I rather think that proves my point."

Conceding the argument, Lyssandra dipped her head. She would no longer speak a word in defence for the royal household or her countrymen. Her adventures had opened her eyes to the evil that lurked beneath court pleasantries.

"You shouldn't have told the king about Eddi," Lyssandra said.

"I was doing what I thought was right!" Antonella cried. "To keep silent is treason."

"And now my Eddi is in danger." Lyssandra's cheeks bloomed with a searing heat. Her heart raced. Tendrils of green wrapped around her shaking fingers, the power seeping from her. Winter roses in the vase were revitalised, their red petals filling with vibrant colour. Fruit in the bowls sprung roots from their seeds.

"Your Eddi?" Antonella drew in a breath, shaking her head. "Lyssandra … you can't have feelings for this boy."

"He's my *friend*. And now his life is in jeopardy because of you!"

Whatever Antonella thought to say to defend herself was lost at the sound of the door's latch.

"Control yourself!" Antonella hissed, her eyes going towards the roses that continued to flourish.

Lyssandra swallowed past the lump in her throat, her power snapping back. She looked askance at the sprouting fruit. This time with the loss of her power, the fruit did not rot, nor the winter roses wither.

The dragon! Edvern had told her that a human's power would grow after bonding with a dragon.

Raising her eyebrow, Antonella threw a cushion over the bowl of fruit as the door opened. Stony-faced, Konrad slipped into their room; in his hand he held a glowing oil lamp. Not a word was spoken between them as the midnight bells tolled. Inhaling, Antonella glided over to Konrad, and Lyssandra turned away from the sight of Antonella in his arms.

It had been a few years since she had last seen her cousin. She could understand Antonella's attraction to him. In all the time she had known him, she had never seen the soft, genuine smile on his face as he looked at Antonella. He saw into her very being and cherished her. Despite her misgivings, she decided against telling her friend the dangers of love. Love was not meant for women of their station.

But there was little harm in letting Antonella bask in the beauty of Konrad's attentions for a little while longer.

"We cannot tarry," Konrad said. He placed a firm kiss on Antonella's forehead. "If we are to do this, we have a small window of opportunity."

Feeling a little out of sorts, Lyssandra crossed her arms against her chest. "You haven't exactly told us what you are up to."

Konrad inclined his head, eyes drifting over the cushion covering the fruit bowl. Take away his dark soldier's uniform, and he looked very much like a prince. "You'll have to trust me, cousin."

"Forgive me if I'm not exactly the trusting type."

Konrad saluted, opened the door and ushered them out. "Heads down. Move quickly."

Lyssandra stood in the middle of the room, unsure how far she should trust Konrad. Should she try and escape on her own? Would he betray her?

"Our chance to escape is now, Lyss," Konrad said. "Come, don't you remember last time we hawked together?"

Shame washed over her as she recalled their last hunt. She had been twelve, struggling with a fast that Ellrahera had demanded of all her diplomats. In a moment of weakness, Konrad witnessed Lyssandra stealing food from one of the princess' saddlebags. When the theft was discovered, he was blamed. The boy sired in a brothel was the obvious suspect. Prince Torsten dragged a kicking and squirming Konrad to the whipping post, where he was severely punished while his smug sisters watched on. He protested his innocence, but he never gave her up when they pressed him.

Tears welled in Lyssandra's eyes. "I'm sorry."

Glancing over his shoulder at her, Konrad shrugged. "A child of the brothels needed frequent beatings."

"One moment." Lyssandra turned and threw the cushion off the bowl of sprouting fruit. She selected an apple and tucked it inside her cloak.

"I don't think this is a good time for a snack." Konrad raised his eyebrows at the evidence of her power.

"Just in case." Lyssandra reached out and gripped Antonella's hand. Come what may they would weather the storm together. It seemed that the cruel world was spiralling out of control, and she hated the feeling of helplessness.

"Come. Stay close to me," Konrad said as he led them from the room.

Although she disliked Konrad's secretiveness, Lyssandra knew she had no choice. She followed her cousin into the dark halls. Only the pale silvery light of the moon and stars lit part of the corridors, which was obviously Konrad's intention. The plush carpet muffled their footsteps as they followed the orange glow of the lamp.

Lyssandra's brain was bursting with questions, but she bit her tongue as they crept through the dark palace. She noticed with some alarm that the halls gradually became darker and colder as they continued their quest. A sidelong glance in Antonella's direction told Lyssandra her friend felt the same unease.

It really shouldn't have come as a surprise when Konrad drew them closer to the dungeons. Lyssandra paused, but it was Antonella who voiced her concern.

"Konrad, what are you dragging us into?"

Konrad looked down at her, a feral grin on his face. Gritting her teeth, Lyssandra held herself back from slapping him. "One way or another, we are headed to war. If we don't make a choice now, we'll soon be forced."

"Konrad ..."

"My father is angry," Konrad said. Shadows danced over his face under the light of the lamp. "The final protocol was unsuccessful. And I—"

"You're a fool," Lyssandra muttered.

Konrad whipped his head around to glare at her as if he had forgotten she was standing with them. He shifted his weight, and looking thoughtful, he glared towards the dungeons. "The king is holding a prisoner that the Nezahrians would be relieved to have returned. If Saemorish nobles such as us are instrumental in his safe return, the Black Prince may be persuaded to show mercy to our people."

"Konrad ..." Antonella shook her head.

"I'd betray a thousand kings just to have one night of freedom with you."

Lyssandra blinked, turning away from her cousin and friend. If they were going to do this, they would all be traitors. But if she stayed, she would die. The Black Prince was her only chance of survival, and she'd grasp that hope with two hands. Hopefully the Nezahrians would be placated with the return of an important prisoner. Talons knew her people had suffered enough on the borderlands. And with Aurelia gathering strength ...

"A hostage is a good idea," Antonella said.

"Who is it?"

"We aren't returning the prisoner to Nezaha as a hostage. We're freeing him, asking nothing in return," Konrad said, his voice taking on a tone that suited his rank as a captain. "If this is to work, we need to be seen as liberators and a friend to Nezaha."

"Fine." Lyssandra sighed, not liking where her night was heading. "Who are we breaking out of prison?"

"Shhh ..."

Lyssandra was about to snap at her cousin for hushing her when she spotted shadows playing on the far wall and the clank of armour. Without speaking a word, Konrad pushed them both towards the gateway to the dungeons. Lyssandra allowed herself to be led down into the bowels of the palace.

The sound of their timid footsteps echoed in the darkness. The constant dripping of moisture gnawed at the last thread of calmness in Lyssandra's mind. She had never thought herself a coward, but the last few days had tested her. She longed to scream her lungs out.

Konrad strode ahead, his strong fingers gripping Antonella's hand. Under the stern guidance of the weapon masters, he had grown to be fond of his rules and regulations. Now he was breaking every oath that he proclaimed to believe in. All of it for Antonella and his wayward heart.

"Is it far?" Antonella's voice was laced with anxiety.

"No."

"Where are the prisoners?" Lyssandra asked. The dungeons were too quiet. While she never had a reason to venture into the lower levels of the palace, she had imagined that the king would have prisoners. The lack of human voices was eerie.

Konrad cleared his throat, a grimace twisting on his lips. "The king is holding a high-profile prisoner. He ordered all others executed, from the petty thief to the worst of the bunch."

"Seems a tad extreme," Antonella said.

"The guards have only one man to watch," Konrad replied. "It cuts down on distractions."

"Distractions?" Lyssandra couldn't imagine callously ordering the executions of so many prisoners at once. She had heard the rumours of the name the commons whispered: Gravedigger King. Jahon was infamous for his stringent laws and full prisons.

In her lessons, Ellrahera had admonished her; it wasn't the king that was responsible for the high imprisonment rates. It was simple administration of the realm. Tucked away in Correllain, the dreadful realities of the lower folk in Saemore seemed so far removed from everything she had ever known. Meeting Bea, the old widow of Gytall, and then Edvern forced her to reevaluate everything she had been told. Should not the care and needs of the people be considered a priority to the crown? And now, standing in the dank confines of the dungeon corridors, the life and liberty she once knew seemed like a dream.

Lyssandra didn't like what she was discovering about herself and her kinsmen.

"Let me do the talking," Konrad whispered. They rounded a bend and were welcomed by the sputtering glow of torches. A pair of bored guards sluggishly straightened to attention. "Good evening, gents. How's our guest?"

"Surly as ever," the elder guard grunted. He turned inquiring eyes over both Antonella and Lyssandra. "This ain't the place for ladies."

"Good thing they're no ladies," Konrad replied.

Lyssandra longed to stomp on his toe.

"Diplomats then?" the younger said, scratching two-day-old stubble on his chin. "I hardly think His Majesty—"

"You're to give us time with the prisoner," Konrad growled. He stepped forward, just enough so that he loomed menacingly over the guards. "Do I need to remind you who I am?"

"No reminders needed, sir," the younger assured Konrad. "But we have our orders and—"

"And now you have new ones," Konrad said. "There's a delicate matter the diplomats need to discuss with the prisoner."

"What would that be?"

Konrad shrugged. "It's not my place to know the workings of the realm. Only to obey."

"Ha, you'd know all about knowing your place, sir." The older guard shifted, despite his confident words. He was caving. Lyssandra decided to help him step over the edge.

"We've travelled with great haste on the king's command," Lyssandra said. She ignored Konrad's glare. A ridiculous memory surfaced in her mind where her cousin had accused her of cheating and told her she was a poor liar during a card game. She straightened her shoulders. "I assure you we're not in the mood to be trifled with, so I kindly suggest you do as your king has commanded and let us speak with the prisoner."

The two guards looked Lyssandra up and down, weighing in their minds, she supposed, how much of a threat she was to their careers and their lives. In the end the younger shrugged and stepped aside. "Don't get paid enough for this."

The older guard followed him. "We're not going far," he warned.

Konrad planted his feet where he stood defiantly in the middle of the walkway, hands loose at his sides. The guards approached and were forced to step either side of him, eyeing him doubtfully.

"Ow! Something bit me." The younger guard's hand went to his hip.

"Probably fleas or worse," muttered the other guard. "Something bit me as well."

"Poor hygiene, gents," Konrad said with a shrug, crossing his arms against his chest. "I wonder what you two did to be assigned the dungeons by your officers."

The guards made no reply, the curl on their lips showing only disgust for Konrad. For his part, Konrad didn't break their stare.

"I'd think they would give a captain more respect," Antonella said, worrying her bottom lip with her tooth as the guards finally marched away.

"They belong to a rival captain and don't expect I'll last long. I've had to come up with more creative ways to instil a sense of respect."

Lyssandra did not let her eyes leave the backs of the guards. *Respect?* They had shown anything but. She knew better than to underestimate her cousin. To keep his position, he needed his subordinates to show appropriate deference to his station. A captain who did not have the men's respect was a dead man. It wasn't until the yellow light of their torch was gone that she spoke. "Are you going to explain, cousin?"

"I thought they'd never leave," a soft, young male voice whispered in the dark. A thrill of horror snaked up Lyssandra's spine. She knew that voice, the soft intonation of a nobleborn Nezahrian. "I grew weary of their crass humour."

"Prince Hedriel?" Lyssandra stepped forward, crouching to peer through the dark. It was indeed Hedriel, the prince Nezahrian spies had confirmed was dead. But here he was, alive. Two years ago, he'd been a boisterous yet gracious host when she had arrived in Nezaha with Ellrahera. He was scrawnier than she remembered.

Squinting in the dim light, she could see his hair had been savagely cut. His clothing was torn and his skin caked with grime. Dried blood was crusted on his knuckles.

"Don't look at me with such pity, Saemorish," Hedriel said. The sting of his words was lost by the tremble of his voice and his vague, sunken eyes.

"Have you slept?" Konrad asked, lowering his tone.

Hedriel shook his head, shuffling closer to the bars. This wasn't the first time Konrad had ventured down here. It seemed the Nezahrian prince already trusted her cousin. "I've tried ... the nightmares."

"The Nezahrians believed that Prince Hedriel and his escort were ..." Antonella hesitated, staring at the young prince. She bit her lip and let her words fade away.

"They beheaded everyone but me," Hedriel murmured. "They left me alive ... Happy sixteenth birthday to me ... All I wanted was a big red stallion."

Lyssandra didn't want to ponder about the fate of the young prince. The king's plans for Hedriel were not benevolent. The Nezahrians believed him murdered by Saemore, resulting in the attack of Correllain.

"We're breaking him out," Konrad said.

"What?" Hedriel spluttered, looking torn between scared and hopeful.

"We're all pawns to be used until we serve no purpose," Konrad said. "I would prefer to live on my own terms. No more rigid rules and punishments. I'll just be Konrad, son of a prostitute."

"Your father will be king one day," Lyssandra said.

"All the more reason to leave now," Konrad replied. "What happens if one of my mediocre brothers ascends the throne? How long do you suppose I would survive?"

Antonella reached out to him. Their fingers met, curling around one another, and Lyssandra knew there was more to Konrad's decision. Love had a way of forcing men to find their courage.

"The guards—"

A twin set of thumps interrupted what Antonella was about to say.

Konrad's malevolent grin in the torchlight told Lyssandra everything she needed to know. The bites had been the prick of small, almost invisible needles.

"As I said, I have my way of demanding respect." Lifting a hand, Konrad revealed the silvery point of his weapon. A slim needle. "Poison. Learnt from the best."

"You killed them!" It was comical the way Hedriel's eyes bulged, but his gaunt face and pinched expression were far from funny.

Tilting his head to the side, Konrad stared at the Nezahrian prince in amusement. "It was a mercy, I assure you. Once the king finds out ..."

Lyssandra clenched her fists and closed her eyes. She had come too far to back out now. The moment she had escaped Correllain and survived, she had been too deep. Those in power had hoped that all the diplomats would die that day.

Besides, she was fond of the Nezahrian prince. The youngest of the emperor's nephews, he had never been expected to ascend to any position of power. He was a handsome, happy child who was eager to please. He was his mother's joy. His siblings were considerably older, and they had been overprotective of him since the day he had entered the world a squalling babe.

"Do you have the courage to escape?" Konrad asked.

Looking around his cell, Hedriel shrugged his shoulders, a ghost of his former cheeky smile on his face. "It can't get any worse than this …"

"Good." Konrad lifted what looked like a piece of black cloth from his cloak. "You're going to have to wear this."

The mirth drained from Hedriel's expression. He looked away, refusing to let his eyes linger on Konrad or the cloth. "You want me to wear a hood?"

"Yes." There was little pity in Konrad's tone. "We need to get you out of the dungeons without being recognised."

Lyssandra thought it was a little crude for a plan. How many people in the palace knew that the prisoners had all been murdered?

"You can do this," Antonella said.

Hedriel swallowed. "I guess you have to bind me too."

Konrad just gave the prince a stare that clearly said that was an obvious conclusion. He nodded as Hedriel rose upon his knees to stand. "I'll retrieve the keys and make sure they're … no longer a threat."

Leaving the torch in Antonella's hands, Konrad went to check on the guards. With eyes full of dread, Hedriel watched him go.

Lyssandra drew closer to the bars. She reached out and grasped his fingers, and the young prince turned his tortured expression to her. "I'll be with you, every step of the way."

"I remember you," Hedriel said. "You were supposed to marry Dalain."

"Yes," Lyssandra said slowly. "Plans have changed."

"You accepted a dance with me. You wore a gown with silver leaves. On the train there was a stag." Hedriel tilted his head to look at her. "The empress would not see you. We stole sugar cakes and ate them on the balcony."

"You remember correctly." Lyssandra hadn't been bothered by the empress' refusal to see her. She'd sat with Hedriel on the balcony until the early hours of the morning. Dalain had found them and chased them to their bedchambers, saving Lyssandra from a sound reprimand from Ellrahera.

Hedriel licked his bruised lips. "I'm not made for war."

"They're wrong." Lyssandra's fingers ghosted over Hedriel's bruised knuckles. She had heard that gentle, comforting touches calmed frightened people. Whatever her countrymen had done to Hedriel, she was of no doubt he had a good reason to be afraid. "No man or woman is made to be a prisoner. Once we're out of here, I'll tell you about my time in an Aurelian dragon den ..."

As predicted, her own adventure sparked the prince's interest. "Promise?"

"I promise." Lyssandra gripped his fingers tighter. "You are a prince of Nezaha. You can do hard things."

Konrad returned with the keys and made quick work of the lock. Hedriel's hand shook as Konrad fastened the hood over his head.

"I'm with you," Lyssandra whispered. She grasped Hedriel's wrists, feeling his tremours as Konrad bound him. He offered no resistance as he was led from his cell. She couldn't wait to leave the palace of Tarramine. In the camp of the Black Prince, she would wash away the guilt and shame of what her king had done.

CHAPTER 7

Alaxen's Command

EDVERN

Flying with Kyros had been wonderful and natural. Edvern doubted that there were any words in the human language that came close to describing the sense of oneness he had with Izorah. He sensed her heartbeat coming to sync with his own. Every soft touch of the wind currents on her wings he felt brushing against his skin. She became an extension of himself.

The air whipped around them, and he bit the inside of his cheeks. He longed to leap into the open sky. Izorah's soul was a pleasant hum, just out of the human ability to hear but no less there.

With Kyros he tasted freedom, but that was a mere appetiser to the rush of euphoria he felt with his bonded dragon. He caught his uncle observing him throughout the flight and wondered if he felt the same with

Lyrus. Resisting the urge to cry his victory, he grinned back and leaned over Izorah's slender neck.

Lyrus flew closer than what Edvern thought necessary. Sensing how the male dragon's attention greatly pleased Izorah, he said nothing. There was no doubt in his mind that once the war was over, they would build their own nest together. A time would come in which he would need to allow the dragons to be left to their own devices. Instead of jealousy, his heart sung with joy for his dragon.

The breeding and hatching of new dragons were considered a part of building the formidable Aurelian Army. It was a military secret, and so Edvern was not sure how dragons preferred their nests. Or how many eggs he should expect in a clutch. He shook his head; it was a conversation for another time. For now, they were at war. Hatchlings would come after.

If there was an after.

Alaxen lifted his hands. His fingers moved in quick succession. It took two repeats of the same movements for Edvern to realise they were part of the military language. Yelling wasn't practical when flying in formation. His uncle had signed, "Close to Cynedir."

Lyrus rumbled, head tilting to look down below.

Alaxen made more gestures.

"What is he saying?"

Seeing his uncle signing to him brought unexpected pain. Rikar had spent hours teaching him the signals from a young age. They had played games together until he was proficient. He later used the signals to communicate to Kirra places where they might meet. The library at midnight had been a favourite spot.

"Edvern?" Alaxen signed his name.

The dragons were relying on him to translate their words to Alaxen, so Edvern looked to his ruined hands and buried his emotion. He signalled back the best he could with his injury. "Cynedir not safe for you."

Alaxen gave him an approving nod. His signals were far from perfect, but his message was received. He'd have to practice. Alaxen ran his gloves along Lyrus' dark blue scales, and his face twisted with regret. "Fly on the outskirts. Caves on the seabound side of the Island of Rock."

Edvern nodded and lifted a hand to show his uncle that he understood. Alaxen was a master at strategy, but so was Moira. There was no guarantee that the masters of Alaxen's old command would be able to help them. No security in knowing they were safe. For now, subterfuge was their only option.

Cynedir was said to be the most beautiful and liberal of the spires. It was also unique in design. An enclosed bridge connected the two islands; the spire split so that both islands had a tower on each. It was said to be a marvel of Aurelian engineering built by Ullryk's daughter, Yenni.

Edvern wasn't surprised that Alaxen had chosen the Island of Rock. It was the most secluded part of Cynedir. The tower was built on the island's coast, a small trading village at its base. The rest of the land was full of rock formations. Local myths said it was a place where the water wyrms had come ashore during a battle and cursed the island. The isolation and uselessness of the island's land meant it was not patrolled frequently. They could hide the dragons within the rock formations and make their way on foot. The trek was secluded, and they could anonymously enter the trading village before making their way to the spire.

Alynta ruffled her feathers, growling under her breath. A large fluffy dragon was sure to get the attention of any dragon riders still in Cynedir. He wasn't willing to reveal her if Lady Moira remained ignorant of the dyrathakin's existence.

Lyrus took the lead, banking to the side. Without prompting, Izorah followed, and they sailed into the updraft, flying higher. Edvern tilted his head to the side to see that Alynta easily kept up with the larger dragons. She was diving through the misty clouds, her orange fur damp with moisture.

Edvern's heart skipped a beat as they flew high and parallel over the towers of Cynedir. The great spire city below was nothing more than a grey mass. He found himself a little disappointed; he had hoped that magnificence of Cynedir was visible from the sky.

"When this is over," Alaxen signalled, "come back to Cynedir ... with me."

Edvern turned his face away, not wanting to be the one to tell his uncle that he planned to burn the Tallermayne empire to the ground. Sometimes it was best to leave the illusion alive. It confused him that Alaxen would outright invite him to visit, especially considering he failed to when he had been forced to flee. The thought stung, and Edvern tasted bile on his tongue.

"Follow me."

Edvern dragged his attention back to their flight and nodded. There would be time later to contemplate his uncle's proposition.

Looming ahead, the grey formations of the Island of Rock protruded from the dull blue of the ocean. Edvern breathed in the salt air and watched the waves crashing on the shoreline. The dragons headed for the furthest shore and landed, a spray of pebbles scattering under their collective weight.

Edvern swung down from Izorah's back and stood, staring out at the far horizon. As far as his eyes could see was water. Ships built for the fury of the sea bobbed out in the far depths. Of course he had seen illustrations of the ocean before, but he realised he had very little context of the vastness of the world. Cynedir was nothing like Gytall.

"Won't you be recognised?" Edvern asked.

"There are enough rebels within Cynedir that I'm reasonably sure of our safety," Alaxen replied. He swung down from Lyrus, giving his navy dragon a hearty pat. "Nevertheless, it would be best to stay on your guard. If you could ask your furry dragon fox to fly hidden ..."

"I am a dyrathakin, and I speak the words of humans," Alynta said, snorting back her irritation. The hollows of her nostrils flared orange. "Ask me yourself."

Alaxen looked down at her, lips set to a grim line. He nodded curtly and cleared his throat. "My apologies, noble one. Might you find shelter away from the curious human gaze?"

"I hate that I'm always relegated to the shadows," Alynta grumbled.

"It won't always be like this," Edvern replied. He longed to stretch out his fingers and brush them down her wings. "After all, it was you who rescued me."

"I'll do as you ask, golden fur," Alynta said, swinging her head towards Alaxen. "But I'm not happy about it."

Together Edvern and Alaxen watched the dyrathakin bound over the loose stones. Alaxen lifted his hand to his beard. "Did she call me by the colour of ..."

"Your facial hair?" Edvern finished. "I believe she did."

"Well, you humans often refer to us by the colour of our scales," Lyrus rumbled. Alaxen stroked the drake's neck, and Edvern thought how strange it must be to ride a dragon who you couldn't talk to. *"There's no difference."*

Edvern hummed.

"What did he say?" Alaxen asked.

Edvern had the sneaking suspicion that he would be forever a translator for the pair. "Said humans call their dragons by the colour of their scales."

Alaxen paused his ministrations. "I can stop if it bothers him."

"No. I don't mind," Lyrus said. *"I liked it when he called me pretty when we were younger."*

A smile curled on Edvern's lips. He couldn't imagine Alaxen calling anything pretty, let alone his huge drake. It seemed a shame that after Aunt Thleah's death, Alaxen shut himself off. To him, his uncle had seemed so stern, serious and unshakeable. But there was a softness to him that Edvern was ashamed to admit he had never bothered to understand.

"So, this is your home?" Edvern asked, mostly to fill the uncomfortable silence.

"Before I married and sired sons, I dreamed of flying away over the ocean to foreign lands. If you wish to abandon the mission, I'll think no less of you. But once we put things into motion, there will be no going back."

Dragging in a deep breath, Edvern whispered, "I'm committed."

"Good," Alaxen said, laying a firm hand on Edvern's shoulder. "To stand and fight for the future is noble."

Edvern looked to the horizon over the glistening water. His feet started walking in the direction of the working docks. He heard his uncle sigh and fall into step with him. Kicking the pebbles, he said, "There's nothing noble about me."

"Nonsense. Alynta and I chose you." Izorah bumped Edvern's shoulder with her snout, then turned to follow Alynta. Likewise, Lyrus lowered his snout, looking into Alaxen's face, blowing warm air around his uncle. Then he turned and sauntered after Izorah, rumbling at her to wait for him.

As Alaxen wiped dragon spit from his face, Edvern had to bite his lip to stop himself from laughing.

"They're mated, aren't they?" Edvern asked, although he was confident he already knew the answer.

Alaxen inclined his head. "Lyrus is very much attached to her, unlike the female he previously nested with."

"Why would he—"

"Without talking to him," Alaxen drawled, "I'd assume that it was because a nesting pair are spared the attentions of riders. Of course, his eggs hatched well before my own birth."

Edvern peered out over the sea once more, then in the direction of Cynedir. "Where is the egg of Cynedir hidden?"

Alaxen turned towards the village. "The audience chamber."

"That may pose a problem," Edvern murmured. He never liked stealing in open rooms where there were little options to take cover. "I suppose there're no secret tunnels?"

Looking over his shoulder at him, Alaxen raised his eyebrows. So no secret tunnels, and they had to get to an open space.

"Is it guarded?"

"We might get lucky," Alaxen said. Edvern didn't like the answer. His uncle didn't believe in luck.

"I'll start beseeching Qavi, the lord of the dark, for his favour," Edvern muttered.

"The dark star is for those living in darkness looking for hope," Alaxen answered. "Not would-be thieves."

"It doesn't hurt. I've survived this long."

Alaxen grunted.

They walked in silence, Edvern happy to be left to his thoughts. A quick glance in his uncle's direction told him that Alaxen felt the same way. The steady cascade of the rounded stones scattering under their boots soon grated on Edvern's ears.

"Do we need a plan?" It seemed foolish to be heading into the stronghold of the enemy without considering how they might do what they needed and escape with their heads still on their shoulders.

"I've the bare bones of a plan," Alaxen said. "Don't you worry."

"It might have escaped your notice, Uncle, but I'm not a child. Don't you think I should be in on the plot?" Heat prickled in Edvern's shoulder blades. His nostrils flared, and he heard Alaxen's footsteps hesitate.

"Of course, I'm sorry."

Edvern waited for his uncle to continue. When Alaxen made no attempt, he halted and turned to face him. He frowned, hands upon his hips. His new power burst into life, and his fiery wings made themselves known, ripping yet another shirt.

"You must learn to control yourself, Eddi." Alaxen huffed at the ruined shirt.

Edvern sucked in a deep breath and held it until it hurt. He closed his eyes and willed his extra appendages to fold away. He struggled to open his eyes again. His head was aching. "What is it you don't want me to know?"

"Tenacious as your father." Alaxen's eyes had a faraway look. "Not all of my spies—Rikar made enemies by taking you in. Many of my men didn't like your father."

Edvern's lips twitched. "My presence isn't welcome."

"No, it won't be." Alaxen's answering grin held something wicked. "I've got my contacts, but I need to go alone. Once I know more, we can plot and scheme."

They reached the docks as the sun was setting. Hood up to cover his face with shadows, Alaxen led the way. Edvern trailed after him, listening to the sailors gossiping. They said little of worth, discussing the daily catch and the poor winter fare.

A part of Edvern hoped that Alaxen would walk up to the spire and knock on the door, and they'd be welcomed in. He heard it said within Gytall that Alaxen's three captains were fiercely loyal to his uncle. But he was no fool. There was no guarantee that Alaxen's captains were in the city, or that if Moira had learned of Alaxen's defection, that they were still alive. Caution was wise.

"Stay here," Alaxen said, shuffling Edvern into an alleyway. He reached over and pulled Edvern's hood further to hide his face and hair in shadows. "Stay out of sight and out of trouble."

Edvern would have loved to argue. He didn't know Alaxen's contacts, and it wasn't worth upsetting his uncle when he had enough to worry about. Nodding, he leaned against the wall and crossed his arms against his chest. "Your captains?"

"I hope so," Alaxen murmured. "If I don't return by nightfall, go to the docks and ask for the burnt soldier. My men will find you. Tell them you are a spy I had on the border; you've got fresh intel for me. If you tell them this, they'll prioritise keeping you safe."

"Very well, I'll lie low until dark," Edvern said. "What name should I give your men?"

"A name is unnecessary," Alaxen said. "The password will be enough to give you protection. I'll be back soon."

Edvern waved him off and couldn't help being disappointed watching his uncle leave him behind. He stayed on his wall, the cold of the stone starting to seep through his cloak. His muscles were stiff, and he longed to sit by someone's hearth to warm his hands.

"Still better than being Titas' slave," Edvern muttered. He wriggled his numb toes in his boots and sidled along the wall to watch the people of Cynedir mingle from the entrance of the alleyway. People watching had been a pastime of his when he lived in Gytall. When they knew no one was watching, people did whatever they pleased.

From his vantage point, Edvern caught sight of a grubby girl, no older than seven, steal a string of dried fruit while her brother caused a distraction. There was a barman handing a customer coin under the table. Another customer was cheating at cards, while a maid sipped from her mistress' glass as she filled it.

He missed being surrounded by ruffians in a warm pub, where he could fade away in the haze and be nothing and no one.

Edvern's eyes were drawn to a pair of well-dressed men huddled around a blazing brazier. Sweat beaded on their brows. One of the men undid his shirt buttons and rolled up his sleeves. From the scattered mugs around them, they were well into their cups and were less guarded. Even where he stood, Edvern could hear snippets of their conversation. Hearing Moira's name, he decided to get closer.

Drawn by an invisible force of yearning, he dawdled past them, catching part of their conversation.

"Would have been more believable if Lady Moira didn't make such a grand spectacle," one of the men said.

"Aye," his friend agreed, fingering the blade of a wicked dagger. "If her bastard grandson had truly been murdered, she would have thrown him on the rubbish heap. My niece wrote to me about the performance they made of the funeral. The king was there, and Moira lit the pyre herself."

"If you want my opinion"—the first man guffawed, waving his mug about, the froth of his drink spilling as he did so—"he's out there somewhere ... Lady Tallermayne wanted a just cause to punish Saemore."

Lyssandra. Edvern's mind went back to the dark-haired diplomat. Cold dread settled in his stomach. With the attack in Hemmryn Vale, Moira had proved her reach extended into Saemorish territory. The diplomat may be back on home soil, but that didn't mean she was safe. They had still been miles off the Saemorish capital, Tarramine, when the Black Prince intercepted them.

"I like to think he's out there causing trouble for the Tallermayne bitch."

There was a round of laughter, and Edvern turned away, but the next softly spoken words stayed him a little longer.

"We can't afford another war."

"It's coming whether we will it or not."

Edvern had loitered too long, and they noticed him. Eyes bleary with drink, one of the men stared. He tugged down his hood, willing his body to move, to pretend he wasn't listening, but he remained frozen.

"Eavesdropping, boy?" The man who spoke dragged thick fingers through his golden mane. Looking closer, Edvern could see he was well-kempt, and his beard was meticulous. "One would think you'd know better."

"He looks like he could do with a drink," his friend said, lifting his beer and saluting. "Come here."

"He looks cold and in want of a meal, Oskar."

"Thank you, I ..." Feeling a little reckless, Edvern murmured, "I'm looking for the burnt soldier."

"A crispy soldier man, eh?" the one called Oskar said, his cold, dark eyes sharpening. He stood to his full height, took three quick steps and wrapped his powerful arms around Edvern's shoulder. Edvern found himself dragged closer to the heat of the brazier. A few patrons stopped to watch but quickly returned to their own conversations, determined not to get involved.

Eyeing the macabre tattoos that ran up Oskar's arms, Edvern bit down on his tongue. He'd been incredibly foolish. This man wasn't as drunk as he wanted the world to believe, and now he was being maneuvered against his will.

"Oskar is always looking for another drinking buddy." Shoving a mug into Edvern's hands, Oskar's friend chuckled. "You'll find he's too friendly by far when he's in his cups. Now what you say about joining ol' Gus' workforce, eh? Get you mucking out some stables; at least you'll be warm."

Edvern felt himself paling. He'd die before finding himself trapped in slavery again.

"I want to hear more about this burnt soldier," Oskar insisted.

"What's a handsome Nezahrian lad like you doing here of all places?" Gus asked. Edvern could feel the shrewdness behind the man's squinting. "What name do you care to give us?"

"No name," Edvern replied, hoping he could muster enough confidence to fool the men into releasing him. "A name isn't needed."

"We'll call him Thom," Gus declared, guzzling down his beer. "Come lad, drink up. If it's a toasted fighting man you want, we're sure to get you just what you need."

Edvern could not think of a way to find out with certainty if these men belonged to his uncle without compromising himself further. Thankfully the men continued their drinking, unperturbed by Edvern's silence. Oskar did not release Edvern.

The beer in his hands was too tempting. He lifted it to his lips and drank deeply, keeping one wary eye on his captors. The quality of the beer in the inns in Gytall had been low, so the bitterness did not stop him from gulping down the drink. Out of the corner of his eye, Oskar observed him.

They were staring at his hands. Or more precisely, his missing fingers.

"Run amuck of the law, lad?"

A knot formed in Edvern's stomach, which had very little to do with the acidic beverage he had consumed. "Aurelian law cares not for justice or truth."

"He has the measure of the land's lawmakers!" Gus hooted. "It makes no difference. Guilty or innocent, the burnt soldier's men all swing if they're caught."

"We can look to a swift burning, Fergus," Oskar grumbled.

"Speaking of the burnt soldier, here he is."

Edvern dropped his mug onto the barrel, wincing as he saw Alaxen stalking towards them. The 'drunk' men straightened to attention. From the look on his uncle's face, getting arrested was the least of his worries.

Saying nothing, Alaxen approached until he was shoulder to shoulder with Fergus.

"You've been named a traitor," Oskar said to Alaxen, his voice a whisper.

"What Oskar means to say, General, is welcome home." Fergus nodded at Edvern, who winced at his uncle's unblinking gaze. "We got you a present."

"Eddi." The stern expression on Alaxen's face did not shift. Edvern resisted the urge to hang his head in shame. "Have you not learned your lesson? Drinking? Now?"

"I'm sorry," Edvern mumbled. His cheeks burned as Oskar let his arm drop away from his shoulder. "They gave me a drink, and I ... I'm sorry."

"Humph." Alaxen clamped a heavy hand on Edvern's shoulder. "You have my thanks, gentlemen."

It hit Edvern then. Oskar Hertforde and Fergus Kalbrynt. Two of the three of his uncle's loyal captains.

His knees buckled.

"You'll want to move quickly, General," Oskar said, turning to eye his companion.

"Moira sent a spy in our midst. He killed Donnell, so we tied bricks to his feet and watched him drown." Fergus studied Edvern curiously, as well he might. He was one of Kirra's uncles. Edvern bit his tongue and hoped that she hadn't written to her family about them. But all thoughts of his dalliances fled from his mind as the name Fergus spoke resounded in his ears.

Donnell.

Alaxen's third loyal captain. Dead.

"We're running out of time. More of her kind are arriving by the day."

Alaxen nodded, his face giving no sign whether or not he grieved Donnell's death. "I've found refuge for the night. But I have business in the spire. I need the path cleared of threats."

"Your will be done, General. We'll eliminate Moira's soldiers, but you'll need to be quick." Fergus peered at Edvern. "You went back for the boy?"

"Any who oppose Moira are welcome in my ranks," Alaxen replied. "He's a dragon rider with his own dragon."

"Perhaps you ought to be more discerning, General." Fergus lifted his goblet to his lips and drank.

Crossing his arms against his chest, Alaxen waited for Fergus to swallow and place his goblet down on the table. "Edvern—"

"It's not about the boy," Oskar growled. "We've got reason to believe that someone close to you is a traitor."

"You know how we deal with traitors in our ranks, gentlemen."

Edvern shivered, watching as his uncle's face turned to stone.

"Don't have the evidence," Fergus grumbled.

"Evidence first," Alaxen said. "Then you've my permission to act in the manner you feel necessary."

Fergus and Oskar exchanged glances. It was Oskar who spoke. "You may not like what we find. We believe that Donnell uncovered the truth."

"I trust you," Alaxen replied. "Be careful." Edvern knew he was missing something by the way the older men exchanged glances.

"Word is something else is stirring," Fergus said. "I, for one, don't want to be in Cynedir when it rises."

"We're recalling as many of our riders from missions as we can." Oskar shook his head. "Not many are returning to us alive, and many that do are reluctant to fight."

"Wait and gather as many as you can. Make your move against Moira when you sense the time is right." Alaxen turned his attention to Edvern. "Come, we have a warm meal waiting and a bed."

Alaxen turned to go.

"Sir!" Oskar called after him. "Good luck."

Fergus raised his cup. "See you on the other side of this."

Edvern dragged himself after his uncle, determined not to look back at the captains. He could feel their stares on his back. Now that they had mentioned tales of another creature, he did see a strange uneasiness in people's eyes when they looked towards the water. How had he missed it?

A nearby merchant was watching the water. Edvern seized his opportunity, grabbing a bottle from his store. As he pivoted, he caught sight of what the merchant was staring at. Ice bobbed on the top of the water.

Alaxen stopped further ahead and called his name, his eyes narrowing as he spotted Edvern's prize. Edvern jogged to catch up with his scowling uncle. "Sorry."

"Port towns can be dangerous," Alaxen said, nostrils flaring. "Stop taking risks, or I'll flog you myself. Do you have any idea what would have happened if you spoke so rashly to one of Moira's spies?"

"I've an inkling," Edvern muttered darkly. He uncorked the bottle and took a swig. At Alaxen's dirty look, he dropped the bottle to his side. "I can look after myself."

"I know you can. Rikar did an excellent job raising you." Alaxen frowned at him. "He'd be disappointed that the drink is controlling you."

"I'm in control."

Alaxen shook his head. "I know the signs. After I lost your aunt ... the world was a dark place for me. It took me almost losing my sons to my own stupidity to wake me up."

"You loved her," Edvern replied. "And it must have been hard ... You had two sons ..."

"She loved you too," Alaxen said.

Edvern cursed. "The compulsion."

"No," Alaxen replied. "A stronger force than compulsion."

"What is stronger than magic?"

"Maternal instinct."

Edvern's mind went back to his seventh birthday, when Thleah had given him his very first sturdy pony of his own. Of her teaching him how to ride from the moment he could walk, to hawking and hunting with her. She who believed he could learn his letters, never giving thought to the tutors' convictions that he was stupid. To nights that she stayed up with him when both Alaxen and Rikar were absent.

And then one day, she was gone. No one spoke of what happened to her.

"How? I mean ... it's ... I shouldn't ask."

Alaxen sighed. "My mother took her life."

Edvern wanted to choke back his shock and failed. The expression on Alaxen's face was blank, but he could see the grief and turmoil.

"She was executed." Pain radiated from Alaxen. After all these years, the grief within his uncle was still raw.

"Why?"

"The rumours that Thleah's family had Nezahrian contacts were true. She wrote a letter, completely innocent, asking about the welfare of extended family in the borderlands. It was considered too close to Nezaha so ..." Alaxen shrugged. There was more to the story, but now wasn't the time to pry. "They killed her before I could fly home."

Edvern closed his eyes. His aunt's sudden death and funeral was a blurred memory. "I'm sorry ... I don't know if I told you at the time."

"You did," Alaxen said. "Many times during the funeral. Rikar took you from the temple; your distress disgusted my mother."

Edvern let the subject drop, and they continued along the docks. The room that Alaxen had found was an old run-down bakery. The warm meal that had been left out for them had gone cold. Nor had their sanctuary been given for free. He scowled as Alaxen counted out two gold and three silver coins and slapped them down on the counter.

After scooping up his bowl, Edvern found a space on the old shop floor and started to eat. Although cold, the soup was at least decent quality. There were even a few chunks of venison floating among the winter vegetables.

"They could have left us some bread," Edvern muttered.

"It's been a lean winter," Alaxen replied. He frowned into his own bowl, however, chasing the last square of potato around the bottom. "Be thankful."

"I think that pork pasty you gave me in Gytall was my last decent meal," Edvern grumbled. "I know I sound ungrateful but ..."

Alaxen closed his eyes as if he was in great pain. "I'm sorry, lad. I should have provided you with more provisions."

Edvern said nothing but stared into his bowl. He huffed, taking out the bottle he had stolen. He took a swig, trying to savour the taste. Unsurprisingly, the beer was watered down. He offered the bottle to his uncle.

"It's perfectly fine to desire better food," Alaxen said, reaching out to take the drink. He studied the bottle before taking a gulp. He swallowed, grimacing. "It's normal. Many fine young warriors go through the same thing on their first campaign, and I dare say they still eat better than you have."

"Have you ever eaten bark?" Edvern lifted his head, a smirk playing on his lips.

"Can't say I have."

"Don't recommend."

Alaxen huffed back a laugh.

A bowl of cold water was left on an uneven side table. Edvern could have sworn he saw shards of ice floating on the surface. Striding over, he dipped his finger in, and the water bubbled. It didn't take long for it to cool, and both Edvern and Alaxen washed.

Edvern unfurled his wings, his fire lighting and heating the room. Running his tongue along his teeth, he idly wondered what use they were to him. He was aware of Alaxen watching him closely.

"We don't want to be cold," Edvern said.

"No," Alaxen agreed. "We don't. Just don't get too comfortable spreading your wings in front of anyone. Even me."

"Take the rug, old man," Edvern replied, lying down on the hard floor. He closed his eyes. "I'll be the fireplace."

"Old man?" Alaxen looked affronted, but he still stretched himself out on the rug. "You're enjoying your power a little too much."

"I enjoy being warm." Edvern yawned, wrapping himself in his wings of fire that did not consume. Closing his eyes, he welcomed the quiet dark.

The question of good and evil is something each of us in turn must grapple with. What may have a pleasant outcome for some may bring disaster to others. We're all villains in someone's story. Sometimes heroic deeds are impossible, and the way forward is villainy. The question is, can you live with the decisions you've made?

A RULER'S HANDBOOK ON ETHICS

KING PENTROS OF SAEMORE

CHAPTER 8

Renegade's Diplomacy

LYSSANDRA

Cool night air caressed Lyssandra's cheeks as she stepped from the servants' tunnels into the king's courtyard. From the lack of dust disturbance, it had been quite a few years since they had last been used. Escaping the stale air of the dungeons was a relief. She coughed weakly, her grip tightening on Hedriel's shaking hands. How was he managing to breathe under the thick hood?

She wanted to plead with Konrad to show mercy, to take the hood off. Although he was a palace guard, he was not unnecessarily cruel. If he thought it was important that the prince keep the hood over his face, he had a reason.

Most courtiers preferred games of chance and gossip during winter, so the courtyard's torches remained unlit. Very few would venture out into cold gardens after dark.

"It's over," she whispered to Hedriel, whose fingers danced over one another in clear agitation. The stress of his imprisonment had affected him. What would the Nezahrians think, seeing their youngest prince in such a sorry state?

Hedriel turned his head towards the sound of her voice. She could barely make out his muffled reply. "We're still on *your* king's land."

Good. There was still a bite of defiance in Hedriel's tone. She'd keep baiting him, forcing him to remember who he was.

"Move," Konrad said, pushing her gently from behind.

"Take the hood off him, Konrad." Antonella lifted her hands to the thick cords around the hood. Hedriel flinched at her touch, and shivers ran down his body.

Konrad sighed dramatically. "We're wasting time."

"Sorry," Hedriel murmured, his voice muffled by the hood.

Konrad loosened the hood, his lips pinched. The hood fell away, and Lyssandra could have drowned in Hedriel's haunted round eyes.

"Hey! You there!"

Hedriel stiffened, his eyes bulging at the sound of a stranger's voice. Lyssandra grabbed his bicep, her fingers digging into the prince's flesh.

A courtier, dressed in ridiculous burgundy velvets, drunkenly stumbled from a door. She recognised him as one of King Jahon's advisors. A pair of dice dropped from his slackened fists and rolled until they landed on a pair of sixes. Lyssandra's lip curled. Trick dice. She had no time for cheats and liars.

"What are you doin'?" the courtier, asked falling to his hands and knees, searching for his dice.

Lyssandra grinned, the toe of her boot stepping on the dice. "Escorting a dangerous prisoner. Go back to your rooms."

"Lyss …"

She took no notice of Konrad's soft warning or the soft hiss of his sword sliding from its sheath. Holding up her hand, she halted him. Too long she had remained on the sidelines, silent. Now she'd make her stand.

"He's mine."

The courtier tilted his head to look up at her, a dumb expression on his face. "You look like your mother." He turned to Hedriel, his pitiless eyes gleaming in delight. "Your Highness, I had the pleasure of besting your father on the battlefield."

It took everything within Lyssandra not to boot the pompous nitwit in the face. Within her, her power coiled.

"Get out of our way," Lyssandra said. Her sweating fingers slipped into the folds of her cloak, finding the apple she had hidden earlier.

"What do you suppose the reward is for capturing traitors within the king's own palace?" The drunk courtier staggered to his feet, leering at Lyssandra and then Hedriel. As he lifted his hand to take hold of her, she stepped forward, grabbed his right wrist and twisted. With a howl of pain, the courtier dropped to his knees.

"Stand back," Lyssandra snapped, hearing Konrad's footsteps behind her. The last thing she needed was to accidently kill one of their own. "He's mine."

"Whore's child. Diplomat—"

Without thinking about what she was about to attempt, she rammed the apple into the courtier's mouth. There would be no mercy. Not this time.

"Time for negotiations is over," Lyssandra said. The world around her faded away. "Call this renegade's diplomacy if you will."

Choke him, her power cried. It twisted beneath her skin, answering her summons. *Silence him.*

The flesh of the apple splattered as the seeds began to sprout. Her fear and desperation fuelled and guided the power to do her bidding. Twisted roots slipped around the man's neck, forming a wooden noose. Before he could scream, they constricted, cutting off his airways.

"I've never seen a cultivatist use their power quite like that," Hedriel muttered, sounding intrigued.

The courtier tumbled over, his fingers scrabbling at the roots in a bid to save himself. He was pinned to the cold garden path, his eyes bulging from their sockets.

"Cultivatist?" Lyssandra murmured. She couldn't tear her eyes away from the horrible scene before her. The roots warped over one another, delving into the stones of the garden path. The tree matured in a matter of moments, the trunk thickening, and despite the cold, thick green leaves covered the branches.

"Power of plants and growing things …"

"Effective, but perhaps a tad enthusiastic," Konrad said. He sheathed his sword, slamming it into his scabbard. He reached out, his fingers brushing over a blossom. The small white flower shuddered and grew into a large red apple. "A little more warning about what you could do would have been appreciated."

Lyssandra's hands shook. She was a monster. Her gift was meant for growing, not taking life.

Ah, sometimes it takes a monster to kill a monster, the little voice in her head whispered.

"This is all still new," Lyssandra whispered.

When Konrad touched Lyssandra's elbow lightly, she swallowed, balling her fists at her sides. She gritted her teeth, determined to look at her victim, even as his bones began to crack and the roots pushed him into the ground. He wasn't innocent.

"Renegade's diplomacy indeed," Konrad murmured appreciatively. "You've saved all our lives tonight."

Hedriel shivered, and after reaching up to the branches of the trees, he plucked an apple. He bit into the fruit, the juices running down his chin. "I hope the Gravedigger King likes his new orchard."

"We have to go." Antonella grabbed the young prince's hand, and Hedriel stumbled after her.

Lyssandra took one last look at the now still courtier. What would the palace guards think when they found the corpse?

"Lyss!" Antonella hissed. "Come."

Lyssandra closed her eyes, determined to forget the twisted grimace on the man's face. Bile burned in her throat, her power coiling around her in triumph. She turned and ran into the dark gardens.

In the past, Lyssandra would have debated the cost of taking Hedriel with them. She would have weighed the benefits of what the Nezahrians would give in return. Hedriel could not stay behind, even if he slowed them down.

"You'd think we'd be able to find your dragon," Konrad remarked as they rounded yet another bend, only to find no dragon in sight.

"Dragon?" Hedriel lifted his chin, and a spark of life flared in his dark eyes. "A wild dragon?"

"No," Lyssandra said, worried that someone might overhear them. "A dragon who defected from the Aurelian camp."

"Defected?" The smile on Hedriel's face was infectious. "That's *never* happened before. This could be the end of the Aurelians."

"It's one dragon," Konrad drawled.

"More than one," Antonella told him, laying a delicate hand on his arm. "The Nezahrians have eight in their camp now."

"It's a start," Hedriel said. "Fancy that; I'm alive during the fall of Aurelian brutality."

"Not much help if we can't find our ride out of here," Konrad muttered, his breath creating small puffs of air.

They continued through the gardens, the only sound loose stones under their feet. The outer wall loomed above them.

Feeling a puff of warm air on her cheeks, Lyssandra glanced up. Her green dragon was perched on top of the garden wall. Elisaria's piercing stare reminded her of a hungry bird, hunched over, ready to dive for a crumb. Leathery wings half unfurled and shook loose a thin layer of ice.

The dragon rumbled a low note, lowering her head to scent her. Obliging the dragon's apparent want for attention, Lyssandra went to her and ran her hands along her hard scales.

"She likes you," Hedriel commented.

"She chose Lyssandra," Antonella said.

The Nezahrian spluttered. "A Saemorish diplomat! That is unheard of."

"As unheard as of dragons defecting to Nezaha and abandoning their Aurelian masters?" Antonella asked.

Hedriel didn't seem to hear the hint of scolding in Antonella's voice. He smiled wickedly, rubbing his bruising fingers together. "Aurelia will soon be no more."

Only a few short months ago, the thought of Aurelia's total annihilation would have brought Lyssandra joy and comfort. Hearing Hedriel speak those words gave her a hollow sense of dread. She couldn't blame the young prince for his glee. The riders of Aurelia had caused his people unpardonable, unforgivable damage.

But Edvern had grown up Aurelian ... and there was kindly old Bea and even the potter Zanniel, who had done what he could to help her escape. There was kindness and worth still among the people. Treasured souls that should have the opportunity to live out their days in peace. And what of the Aurelian dragons ...?

"We have to go," Konrad said.

An unexpected calm washed over Lyssandra as she stared back over her shoulder at the palace still shrouded in darkness. Deep within her soul, she knew this was the last time she would see this place. Her destiny had changed, and it was time to step into a new future.

"Yes," Lyssandra said, lifting her chin. "Let's go."

Flying under the skyful of stars brought peace into Lyssandra's soul. She would never admit it, but murdering that man in the cold courtyard shook her. If it was true that the Father Dragon had blessed her with powers over living things, surely he didn't mean for her to use it to kill.

She could still hear the sound of bones cracking, of flesh being ground under pressure. Red was all she could see, crimson puddles at the base of the tree while fruit ripened within its canopy.

Antonella understood her shock. Her friend wrapped long fingers around her upper arm. She didn't have to say anything. They had flown with all haste towards the camp of Tacebia. As they approached Elisaria rumbled. She interpreted the sound as one of displeasure and disappointment. Swinging her head around, Lyssandra spotted a small red dragon flapping frantically towards them.

"Marsyna, you shouldn't be here," Lyssandra said.

Unconcerned by Elisaria's warning growls, Marsyna flew circles around them. Her eyes glowed like embers in a fire as she stared at Hedriel.

For a fleeting moment, Hedriel's fatigue and suffering melted away as he lifted his hand, reaching out to the young dragon.

Marsyna continued to fly around in dizzying circles until a booming roar halted her game. Charging through the cold air was a familiar brown dragon, the one they called Aerin.

Lyssandra did not need to be an expert in body language to read that Aerin was angry. The drake's tail lashed around, his teeth were bared and the light in his eyes was almost feral.

It wasn't the sudden appearance of the dragon that was the cause for Lyssandra's greatest surprise. Perched on the brown dragon's back was a grim-faced Dalain. Lyssandra had been of the impression the brown dragon was an angry beast, not at all inclined to play nicely with humans. And here he was, barrelling towards them with a prince upon his back.

"Marsyna!" Dalain bellowed over the wind.

The young crimson dragon hovered. She had done wrong, and she knew it. Her posture reminded Lyssandra of a dog with its tail between its legs.

Whatever wrongdoing the young dragon had committed was forgotten the moment Dalain caught sight of Hedriel. The two princes stared at one another.

Hedriel gave a wordless cry of delight, and the brown dragon swept upon them, twisting so that the princes were side by side.

"Hedriel ... you're alive."

Hedriel nodded. "It appears I am, cousin."

"They sent us your head," Dalain murmured. "Oh, blessed Father Dragon, this is the best news I have received this week."

"He'll need a good feed and a rest," Konrad said. "I'm afraid he's not had the best of Saemorish hospitality."

At the sound of Konrad's voice, Dalain's attention was lifted from his cousin. The elder Nezahrian prince regarded Konrad coolly. He looked him up and down, marking his uniform as a ranking guard in the Saemorish palace.

"This is Captain Konrad Stamos," Hedriel said. It seemed at least one of the Nezahrian princes remembered his manners. "He helped me escape from the dungeons in Tarramine, along with Lady Lyssandra and Antonella, of course."

Distrust and gratitude warred over Dalain's face. Lyssandra had never noticed how expressive he was. "Then you have my thanks."

"I was hoping we could provide them with shelter and aid ... once their king ..."

"Lyssandra and Antonella are already known to Uncle Raziel," Dalain said. He looked back to Konrad. "What's one more foreigner?"

"You have my thanks, Your Highness," Konrad said, with an elegant dip of his head. Lyssandra always thought it such a shame that he was born a bastard. He would have made a better king than his unruly trueborn brothers. He might be a pain in her rear end, but he did have a stable personality and could see issues beyond his own nose.

"Marsyna, land!" Dalain commanded, returning his attention back to the young crimson dragon. The red dragon pouted but did as she was told. Aerin snapped at her tail as she slunk past.

"We're not far from camp," Dalain said once he was satisfied Marsyna was being obedient. "Follow me down."

Aerin tore down to the earth in a swift descent, while Elisaria's approach to flight was gentler. She landed among the humans of the Black Prince's camp without causing a fuss. Aerin, however, seemed to delight in scattering the humans in a chaotic mess. Dalain dismounted, and the brown dragon yawned lazily as the older prince patted his snout.

"Aerin, this is my cousin," Dalain said.

Lowering his nose, Aerin breathed in deeply. His claws scraped the ground as he snarled at the younger prince.

Hedriel had already dismounted Elisaria, having jumped from her back the moment her claws hit the earth. Grinning in wild abandon, he ran, stumbling and crying, to his cousin. Lyssandra had to admire the way he ignored Aerin's agitation. He stopped just shy of Dalain, toeing his boots and wiping his tears. He glanced awkwardly at the gathering men. Whispers of shock and bewilderment drifted through the armies of Nezaha.

But Dalain ignored the men and royal protocol. He swept Hedriel into a tight hug, kissing the top of his filthy hair. "Little cousin, I'm so sorry ... I'm sorry."

"It's okay." Lyssandra heard Hedriel's muffled voice from where he was pressed firmly into Dalain's chest.

"Are you hurt?" Dalain gripped Hedriel's shoulders, stepping back to study him at arm's length.

Licking his fat lip, Hedriel shifted. "I'm hungry and dirty." Hedriel's words were punctured with a loud yawn. "I could sleep for a season ... I'm so tired."

"You!" Dalain snapped his fingers at a pair of soldiers. "Take Prince Hedriel to my tent. Get him water to wash, food to eat and a medic."

"No, tell me about your dragon. Where did he come from?" Hedriel pulled himself out of Dalain's grasp.

"Aurelian deserter," Dalain boasted. "He brought a gift of dead riders to Uncle Raziel as a peace offering. It seems when his little sister decided to fly off, he—how did Raziel phrase it?—'he'd make do with you'."

"I was hoping he was a wild dragon from the mountains, come to protect Nezaha."

Aerin rumbled, lifting his head, and snorted hot air. Both princes paused to look up at the brown dragon, who was glaring at the humans. Dalain shrugged and turned back to Hedriel, firmly clasping his shoulder. "You need to get some food and rest. I'll have someone escort you to my tent."

Hedriel nodded his thanks, but Marsyna blocked his path with a low growl.

Frozen on the spot, his eyes wide as a full moon, Hedriel watched the crimson dragon as she slunk forward, her belly close to the ground. She didn't halt her slithering until she pressed her snout to his belly. The young prince seemed dumbfounded. When he didn't lift his hands to pat her, Marsyna nudged his side with a playful purr.

"Dalain ..."

"Marsyna, he's a boy still," Dalain said.

The brown dragon snorted, plumes of smoke bursting from his nostrils. Marsyna nudged Hedriel again.

"What's happening?" Antonella asked.

"She's chosen Hedriel as her rider," Dalain replied.

"But ..."

"It seems that Aurelian dragons are stubborn." The crowd parted, and striding towards them was the Black Prince himself. "Just as Elisaria picked a foreigner and Aerin picked a prince, Marsyna has chosen one who is still a boy."

"Uncle!" Hedriel looked torn between going to the Black Prince and staying with his dragon.

"Hello, Hedriel," the Black Prince said. His hand came down to rest on the head of Odharn, who padded at his side. The one-winged dragon shivered and rumbled at the contact. "This is Odharn. Faelowyn has taken a liking to him."

The Black Prince gestured to Hedriel. "Odharn, this is Hedriel, another of my kin."

Odharn cocked his head to the side and tentatively took a step forward, scenting the air. When no one made a move to stop him, he took a few more steps. Under Faelowyn's care, Lyssandra could see the growing confidence of the little one-winged dragon she and Edvern had rescued.

"He's ..." It seemed Hedriel was uncertain what word to use to describe Odharn. "Adorable."

Lyssandra held back a cough. Scrawny, minuscule, or skeletal were all better adjectives. She exchanged a look with Konrad, her movements alerting the Black Prince to the stranger in their midst.

"Uncle," Hedriel said. "Might I introduce Captain Konrad Stamos? He broke me out of the Tarramine dungeons."

"Our great and noble empire is indebted to the kindness of Captain Stamos," Raziel said.

Lyssandra was beginning to read the man's cues. His face seemed to be carved like a statue, carefully neutral as if he held the weight of the world's secrets in his mind. But she caught the twitch of his lips. He was fond of Hedriel.

Hedriel, on the other hand, was staring askance at Marsyna. "I won't make a very good dragon rider," he said. "Is there nothing to be done, Uncle?"

Aerin rumbled, baring his fangs and swaying his head side to side.

Looking up at the large male drake, Hedriel stepped back.

"It seems, Your Highness, we must submit to the wisdom of the dragons," the Black Prince said. "Arguing with them is pointless. Do not bother yourself with Aerin. He's a scaly bag of hot air. Now go, rest. I'll come and see you a little later, and we'll talk."

Hedriel nodded, finally lifting his hand to touch Marsyna's snout. He smiled thickly to Dalain and allowed the two soldiers to escort him to his cousin's tent.

"Behave yourself," Raziel said, admonishing Aerin, but his eyes never left Hedriel.

The brown dragon snorted indignantly.

"I've more good news. Edvern is alive."

At the Black Prince's proclamation, Odharn lifted his head to the sky and let out a raucous squeal of delight. Flapping his one wing, his body lifted off the ground, and he spun in tight circles.

"Alive?" Lyssandra couldn't help the note of hope in her voice, and Konrad glanced sideways in her direction. "Where is he?"

"It seems he has escaped Lady Dmoira," the Black Prince replied. He looked fondly to the small green dragon, quietening him with a simple hand gesture. Odharn landed, panting.

"*Escaped*?" Lyssandra's heart was ready to burst. "Where is he now?"

"That remains a mystery." The Black Prince shook his head. "He had help from another dragon."

"Which means he has protection," Konrad murmured. "This is good news."

"Stamos ..." Dalain looked Konrad up and down. "You're one of Torsten's boys."

"One of many," Konrad answered stiffly.

"Not an easy man to grow in the shadow of," the Black Prince commented.

"With all due respect, my father had nothing to do with my upbringing." The smile on Konrad's face was forced. "Now that I have freed one of your princes, might I know what you intend to do with me?"

"You could either join us ..." Dalain shrugged, seemingly unconcerned that he touched a nerve. "Or you can leave peacefully. We, of course, will supply you with some rations."

"Very well. You have my sword as long as you don't attack any Saemorish towns or cities."

"How noble," Dalain said dryly.

"Prince Dalain, I lived in a brothel for the first six years of my life," Konrad said. "There's nothing honourable or noble about me."

Odharn rumbled, flapping his wing.

Raziel's lips twitched as he turned away. "Odharn disagrees. Take time to rest, Captain Stamos. We shall convene a meeting soon. Lady Antonella, feel free to go with your Saemorish captain. Lady Lyssandra and I have notes to compare."

And just like that, Lyssandra had been accepted into the Black Prince's inner circle. Hardly daring to look over her shoulder at Antonella or Konrad, she followed after him. Raziel didn't wait until he reached his tent before he began telling her everything he knew. She hung off every word he spoke.

He who had been her enemy had become her strongest ally. The Black Prince's goal aligned with hers: Edvern's safety. Past enmity no longer mattered. Together they would find Edvern.

CHAPTER 9

Serpents of Ice

EDVERN

Pain lanced through Edvern's body, the bone-chilling cold of the empty bakery waking him. Blinking the sleep from his eyes, he sat, searching for the cause of the steep temperature drop. Frozen water dripped from his wings, leaving him lying in a wet puddle.

Kneeling before him, Alaxen was ashen, his hand outstretched on his shoulder. Strong fingers pressed firmly into his skin. "Talons, I was afraid when I couldn't wake you."

"Uncle ..." Edvern let his wings dissipate.

Hauling Edvern to his feet, Alaxen wrapped him in a thick blanket. "Dry yourself. Quick."

"What's happening?"

"I heard strange tales as a boy." Alaxen rose and turned abruptly on his heel, striding towards the door. "We need to go. Now."

"What stories?" Edvern rubbed the itchy blanket across his cold body, surprised by his uncle's urgency. Alaxen was a good leader to have in emergencies; he never acted out of panic.

"In the far north, there are tales of sudden temperature drops brought by angry seas."

Edvern closed his eyes. "The sea is not a thinking entity." Alaxen's outstretched fingers froze over the knob of the door.

Alaxen gave him a look that clearly said he was being daft. "It's what's in the sea that's angry. Something has stirred them."

"Them?"

"Myths and legends always hold a grain of truth." Alaxen's voice softened to a whisper as he swept the door open. "I don't intend to stay long enough to gauge how much truth the stories hold."

Edvern came to stand beside his uncle, staring out at the dark streets of the village, not believing what he saw. The ground was covered in a thick blanket of snow. There was no light, not even the rowdy inn down the road. The moon and stars would have to guide their way.

"Come."

Alaxen waded out in the snow. Gritting his teeth against the chill, Edvern followed, tugging the blanket tighter around his shoulders. They struggled through the streets until they reached the docks. Not a soul moved. Swirling mists shrouded the water, and when he strained his eyes, Edvern could see the ocean churning. Large shards of ice bobbed on the surface of the water.

"It is as I feared. They've returned. Let's get the egg and leave," Alaxen said. "We need to go before true panic sets in."

"Panic?"

Alaxen gave Edvern a pitying look. "Once dawn breaks and citizens realise that an unnatural cold has gripped their island ... Many will have died during the night ..."

Edvern didn't know what came over him. His feet took him along the dock's edge to look over the opposite side of a large cargo ship. The constant slapping of the waves against the haul of the vessel had him on edge. There was another sound accompanying it ... a grinding.

Staring down through the mist, he could see ice scraping alongside the ship. The largest piece was the size of a large man. He continued to look down and caught another movement.

Edvern sucked in a breath, taking half a dozen steps backwards. There were several scaled creatures below. He caught sight of a grey tail as it flicked and dipped under the water.

"Water wyrms," Alaxen said.

"Pardon?" Edvern's voice squeaked. He knew many stories about water wyrms. He had even decorated his book with fantastical figures of the legendary beasts. But no one had seen one in hundreds of years.

"Dragons of water and ice," Alaxen replied. "Ask the dragons to be ready. We cannot tarry any longer."

Edvern steadied his breathing, and closing his eyes, he called for Izorah and Alynta. They didn't need his words to understand his panic and need.

Grabbing his shoulders, Alaxen forced Edvern's feet to move towards the spire of Cynedir.

Edvern may not have enjoyed reading his history lessons, but he remembered well the cautionary tales of Aurelia's natural disasters. The great floods three centuries ago had swept away whole villages. The waters had risen quickly, and it was believed many of the dead had drowned each other in their haste to escape. The fires at the palace a century ago had a similar result. The sheer number of nobles and servants during the annual ball meant the swarm of people trampled those who had fallen.

Swallowing, Edvern nodded to show he understood the gravity of the situation. He grimaced, trying not to think of the young and the old. It was the way of the world. The vulnerable fell first. He wanted to ask Alaxen what they could do, but he knew the people would either survive or they would die.

They made their way around the base of the lesser tower. Alaxen opened the back door, and they stepped into his old command post. Their footsteps echoed in the dark.

They met no one on the stairs, but Alaxen didn't stop to look over his shoulder.

"I hate the hopelessness," Edvern commented, his breath misting in front of him.

Alaxen looked sharply at him. "You'll get used to it."

"We shouldn't have to."

"No," Alaxen agreed. His voice lowered to a growl. "We shouldn't. But the world is a cruel and wicked place, and we are merely pawns."

They crept through the quiet of Cynedir. Edvern didn't like the silence of the spire. He should have sensed a rider or two. Unless ... He looked towards Alaxen. Had his captains cleared the riders out of the towers so they had a clear path to the dyrathakin egg?

Alaxen stalked ahead, looking in every direction. Now that they were steadily climbing the stairs, he couldn't hear his uncle's careful footsteps. Pressing his shaking hands against his thighs, he wanted to ask how much further to the bridge.

"Halt," Alaxen whispered. "Someone's coming. Not Oskar or Fergus."

Edvern froze. His head cocked to the side. Did his uncle fear that his captains were unable to ease their way through the spire? He listened but couldn't hear approaching footsteps. But he trusted Alaxen. If his uncle sensed danger, there was danger lurking. It was always good practice to have a skilled master of stealth. Alaxen was one of the best. He could feel the firm press of his uncle's power, knowing that they'd remain concealed from any sentries until they were upon them.

They stayed still until Edvern's muscles screamed in protest. Finally, Alaxen nodded, and they proceeded with caution. When they stepped onto the enclosed bridge, the temperature dropped further.

Edvern placed his hands over the walls. He could see where ice had formed, melted and frozen over again.

Alaxen joined him. The air pressed in around them. "They tried to melt the ice."

"Where do you think the riders are now?" Edvern whispered. "There should be some in the bridge."

"Dead or gone." There was a finality to Alaxen's tone.

Alaxen walked further onto the bridge, his imposing frame swallowed up in the darkness. Not wanting to be alone in the eerie silence, Edvern hurried after him and tripped. His uncle's hand gripped him, stopping him from tumbling over. He looked down to see what he had fallen over.

His cry of shock stuck in his throat. A boot. He ran his eyes along the limb to the torso and face, realising with a shock he knew the man. Fergus. Underneath him the ice was red. Raising his eyes, Edvern peered along the stones to spot several riders spread along the bridge. Their skin was waxy in death, eyes wide with terror, mouths agape. The captains had remained faithful, fighting to make their way through the spire clear. The cost had been high.

"Death doesn't discriminate against the high and the low," Alaxen said, seeing where Edvern's gaze was. "It comes for us all."

Edvern should have asked his uncle about his power's reach, practiced estimating the distances between them. The moment he stepped out of his uncle's ring of concealment, he realised his mistake. Outside the stealth power's influence, the air was lighter, easier to breathe. He felt naked and exposed. Something was lying in wait in the dark.

"Edvern!" Alaxen grabbed his upper arm to drag him back into the circumference of his power's reach. Too late.

"Die, Aurelian bastard!" A black shadow rose from among the corpses. Before Edvern's brain could comprehend what was happening, their would-be attacker was running for them, a long, curved sword raised, ready to decapitate them.

Alaxen's hand tightened around Edvern's arm, thrusting him out of the way. In a heartbeat his uncle had his sword in his hand, stepping between Edvern and their attacker. Sprawled along the stones, Edvern felt his skin sear with heat and his wings burst from his shoulder blades.

The flickering fire of his wings was enough to illuminate the bridge and reveal their attacker. The wiry man may as well have been made from shadows. Only a curl of brown hair was visible from the hood and scarf he wore. The relief that they were only facing one Nezahrian war wraith was soon replaced by fury at the sight of the dyrathakin egg tucked under the man's arm.

"Thief!" Edvern barked. The irony was not lost on him that he was in Cynedir to steal the egg. "That doesn't belong to you!"

"None of your concern." Curiosity gleamed in emerald eyes, the voice young and muffled behind the scarf. The war wraith lifted his sword to gesture at Edvern's chest. "Your Aurelian companion will kill you."

"Stand down!" Alaxen barked, moving to intercept the war wraith. He raised his sword, meeting the assailant's blow with ease.

"General Tallermayne, what a displeasure, seeing you here."

"Get out of here, Eddi," Alaxen grunted, his sword flashing in the firelight.

Pressing himself along the wall, Edvern weighed his options. The bridge was narrow, the height of the roof only inches from the top of his uncle's head. He considered fleeing, but where would he go? And he wasn't going anywhere without the dyrathakin egg. Joining the battle between the Nezahrian war wraith and his uncle would only complicate matters for the combatants. But if he was fast enough, he might be able to grab the egg and pull the war wraith off balance.

"Eddi. Go!" There was panic in Alaxen's voice.

Bracing himself, Edvern crouched and waited for the few seconds he could get between his uncle and their attacker. He felt Lyrus' presence the moment he flew into range.

"Duck!" Edvern screamed.

Alaxen's dragon landed on the bridge the moment Edvern bent his knees and launched himself at the war wraith. He crashed into the spy's side, clasping his hands around his middle. Wind escaped his lungs as he hit the stones, and stars danced before his eyes.

Above their heads, Lyrus bellowed for his rider. The whole bridge shuddered under the dark blue dragon's rage. Stone exploded as Lyrus smashed his tail into the wall of the bridge, trying to get to Alaxen. Rock and dust flew into the air.

So much for being stealthy, Edvern thought grimly, glancing up through the hole that Lyrus had created. He curled his legs and kicked the war wraith in the chest. His fingers found purchase on the green dyrathakin egg and wrenched it out of his arms. It didn't have the same warmth that Alynta's egg had. A second later the war wraith tackled him.

One moment he was sprawled along the firm stones, the next he was airborne. The stupid Nezahrian had hurled them through the gaping hole that Lyrus had made in the bridge.

Although terror-filled eyes locked with Edvern, the spy continued to hold on to the egg. Edvern pressed the priceless artefact to his chest.

The war wraith brought his free hand up, slashing down. Dragonstone! The bastard had a shard of dragonstone. Blood blossomed over his arm, skin burning. Edvern yelled, refusing to let go. His wings unfurled, and he clumsily lifted himself and his attacker into the air. His lack of experience did not prepare him for the task of flying with a human burden.

Gritting his teeth, Edvern lifted the struggling man, his muscles straining under the load.

"Take the egg!" Edvern yelled, aware that Alynta was at his side. The war wraith's eyes widened as Alynta's wings brushed past. The dyrathakin's clever claws grabbed the egg, dislodging the Nezahrian spy.

Having enough of death, Edvern reached out and latched his fingers on to the spy's wrists to stop him free-falling into the water. The weight was too much.

"Go!" Edvern might have shouted before he hit the water; he wasn't sure.

Pain exploded throughout his body, followed by a stunned stillness. His mind screamed commands, but his body refused to obey.

Water rushed into his open mouth, and the salt stung his eyes. Around him the ocean hissed and spat, but his wings were not extinguished. Under the haze of the water, Edvern lost sight of the war wraith. Despite the man's act of violence, his fingers stretched out for him. He hadn't meant to be the spy's doom; he had wanted to remove him as a threat.

Something touched his leg, scraping along his shin. Edvern jerked, and his limbs started a frantic fight to reach the surface. The water around him reverberated with a cackle that sent shivers of dread up his spine.

His body was bumped to and fro before a pair of luminous yellow eyes emerged from the depths. The long, sinewy creature had the face of a dragon. Two long horns sat upon its head while a line of serrated fins ran along its back. The creature's thick body tapered into a finned tail and was covered in hard dragon scales.

"Why are you here?" The creature's voice hissed and spat through Edvern's mind.

"I think it's I who should be asking you," Edvern replied.

"Insolence." The creature dragged out the word, its sickly eyes watching Edvern with the utmost interest.

Edvern said nothing, because truly what could one say to such a beast?

"How long can you hold your breath?"

"Longer than you think, water wyrm," Edvern said, praying this dragon would not drown him. He could think of a thousand ways he would rather die.

"We are the dragons of water … free from any influence …"

"Did you freeze the isle on your own?" Edvern's eyes lit up despite the danger he knew he was in. *"Or are there more of you?"*

"We remember … always remember." The creature's voice was joined with a myriad of others. The water moved with the water wyrms so that Edvern could not tell where one began and where it ended. *"Humans have been our enemy from the dawn of dragonsong and praise."*

"As you can clearly see, I'm not quite human."

"You were with them," the water wyrm said. *"Close enough. Dragons of fire and sky were the first to bargain our freedom. But we never did."*

Edvern shook his head sadly. *"Then kill me if that is indeed your goal."*

He didn't wait for the serpent to lunge. He held out his hand and prayed his power might be able to help him. The pulse of fire was weak but pushed the serpent backwards. Kicking his legs, he fought to reach the surface.

The outraged sounds of the water wyrms below were deafening. Edvern's fingers broke the surface, his head coming up to gulp in a lungful of fresh air.

Astride Lyrus, Alaxen was screaming his name while Izorah flew low over the water's surface. He saw the water gurgle underneath her.

"No!" Edvern cried, although the sound came out a rasp.

The water frothed, and a water wyrm jumped, biting Izorah's tail. With a shrill cry, the blue dragon was jerked backwards. Edvern screamed as she was dragged under.

From Lyrus' back, Alaxen leapt into the water only a few strokes away from Edvern, leaving his dragon free to help Izorah.

His thick, muscled arms grabbed Edvern around the middle, giving him extra time to grab gulps of air. There was time to look up into his uncle's stoic face, devoid of any fear, before something clamped down on Edvern's ankle.

The pain was like needles of ice, and Edvern couldn't help but shriek. Alaxen's arms tightened around him, and he thrashed.

"Remember ... training ..." Alaxen yelled into his ear.

Edvern stilled, and they were both plunged under the water. His fingers found Alaxen's. He tried to pry his uncle off him so that only one of them would die. But his uncle held on, refusing to let go. His wings beat and struggled, trying to lift them both to the surface. For a moment playing tug of war with the water wyrms seemed to be working.

Exhausted, Edvern felt the moment that his wings of fire failed and extinguished. His cries were cut off as they were once more plunged into the dark depths.

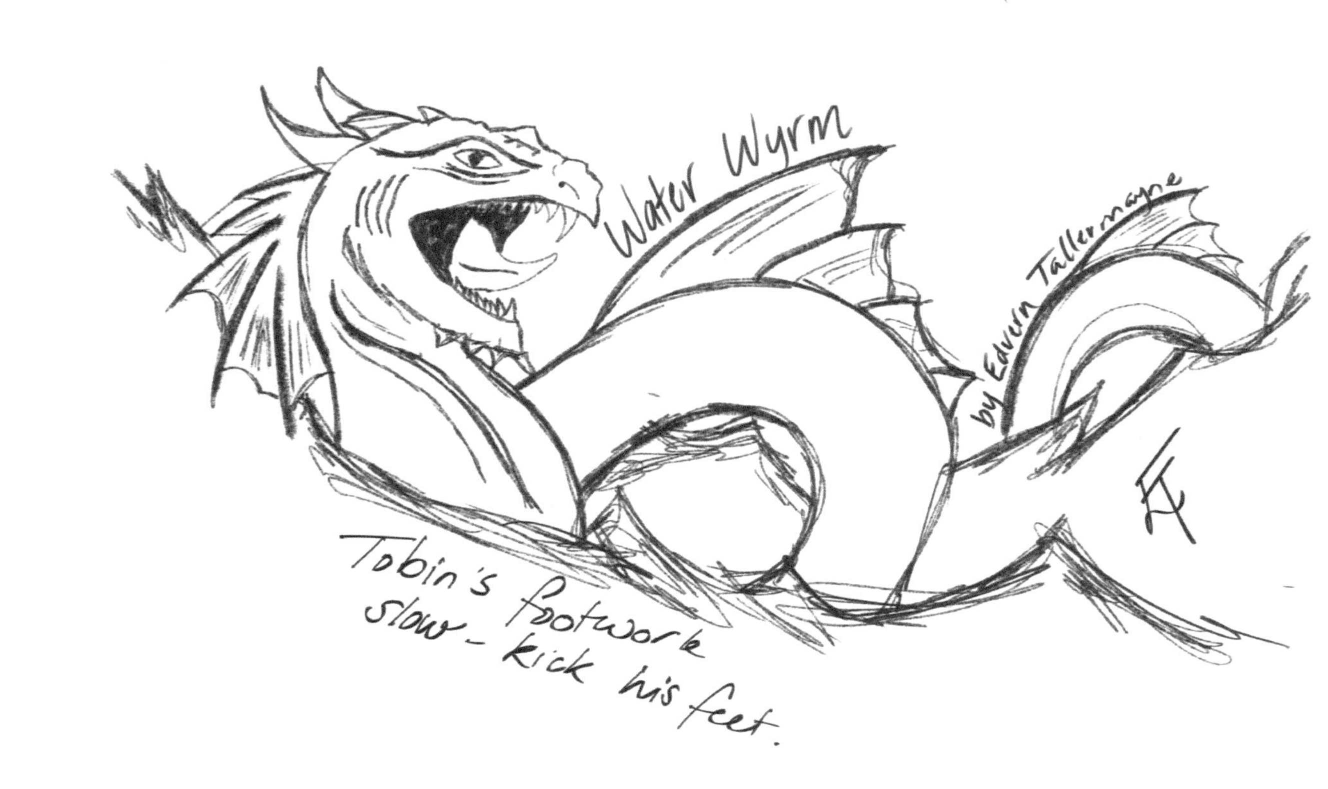

Water Wyrm
by Edvern Tallermayne
Tobin's footwork
slow - kick his feet.

*Halsabith was a traitor to her own kind, executing and
murdering people in the thousands at the mere suspicion of
betrayal. No mercy was granted, not even to her sons.
In the last year of her reign, a great snowstorm blanketed the
land, a warning of what was to come.*

HALSABITH, THE CURSED

LORD TYFORDE, ROYAL HISTORIAN

CHAPTER 10

Traitors

MOIRA

The tea service was cold. It had been left hours ago by a nervous servant, who looked ready to faint at the sight of Nabert's body. Chips of ice crystalised on the rim of Moira's favourite teacup. Sighing, she stirred a generous dollop of honey into her tea. The pleasant chime of the porcelain echoed through the library as she tapped the spoon on her cup. By now that servant would have spread the news of the beloved library master's death.

"Those steadfastly loyal to me won't let your fate bother them," Moira said to Nabert's stiffening corpse.

"Many of those who remember their oaths to me have doubts." There were times that Moira could still hear and see Fennix. When she was at her weakest points, his memory haunted her. *"You've only yourself to blame."*

"You're dead!" Moira spat, tearing her eyes away from the corpse. Fennix's ghost was fond of placing the blame for everything that was wrong in her life at her feet. "And so is he."

She shifted in her overstuffed chair and rubbed her throbbing temples. A cold fog had crept into the library, swirling along the stones of the floor. Her breath misted before her. The chill of winter was unnatural and sent an ache through her bones.

Halsabith. Nabert had warned her the people were speaking of the long-ago queen in the streets. The uneducated would blame the weather on her rule. They'd rebel.

She was no fool. Nabert had started the whispers, hoping the people would turn to Alaxen, a Tallermayne by birth and virtue. After all, she was only a woman who married into the bloodline.

Her seat of power in Gytall was lost. She needed to act quickly to mitigate the damage and give her riders the impression she was still in control. The thought of retreat was bitter.

When she first came to Gytall Spire as a betrayed girl, her emotions were on display for all to see. Murdering her father, his new wife and her horrid stepbrothers had healed the hurt. Their deaths were a soothing balm to her aching soul. Still, it had taken years and discipline to harden her heart to become untouchable.

Moira's hand went to her gold locket at her throat, the metal cold at her touch. Tamah's death was the last time she had allowed herself to feel the true strength of her emotions. She had remained unyielding and stoic beside her husband when the news of Tamah's capture was relayed to him. Behind closed doors Fennix had flown into a rage. It was her fault, he said. She had created a daughter so full of bloodlust that she would not listen to her father's advice.

He had seen the trap laid out for them; he had warned Tamah that the Nezahrians were lying in wait. Tamah had written back, calling him a coward.

That night, without a farewell, Fennix flew after his daughter. Moira didn't stop him.

Fennix's desperate rescue attempt was futile. He died at the Nezahrian lake, murdered when the Nezahrian emperor did not honour his own terms of parlay. With her father dead, Tamah was dragged through the capital of the Nezahrian empire, humiliated and executed. What little of Moira's heart remained shattered. It was to the skies that she screamed her grief. But at dawn, when she woke, she buried her sorrow.

With her beloved daughter gone, there was nothing left in the mortal realm that could be used to hurt her.

"I should have seen the truth," Moira murmured, running her fingers along the rim of her teacup. She pressed it to her lips, sipping the frozen tea. She did not taste the sharp ginger or the sweetness of honey. "Talons! I should have killed him!"

Moira slammed her teacup down on the tray, the utensils clattering. She was angry with herself, at her husband, at the grinning library assistant and Rikar.

Rikar was not hers. He was a fraud. He was born of a weak bloodline. No drop of his father's Tallermayne blood flowed in his body. It was for this reason that he failed. Those who were not born to be dragon riders were doomed.

Fennix had lied to her, protected the wretch of a woman who dared say she loved him and concealed the murder of her son. Where was the true Rikar now? Had his father thrown his body to the dirty river?

"It doesn't matter," Moira said. "The worms have him."

Her eyes lingered over an ancient tome that could either be her salvation or her ruin. Following her murder of Nabert, she had torn apart the library, searching for clues. Books littered the ground where she had flicked through them and discarded them.

She caressed the book, running her fingers over the rough ridges of the well-worn leather. The yellowing parchment of the book was written in ancient Nezahrian. She was unable to read the illegible foreign scribbles, and it had been a source of frustration since she found it.

Two blathering servants had been sent to fetch a sage to come and decipher the text. That had been some hours ago. Moira cursed, glancing towards the door. She did not want the humiliation of sending for the sage a second time nor the drama of being seen going to them. And so, she was resolved to wait for the old man to arrive.

Moira stood, hating the way her body ached with fatigue. She paced the floors, with only the ghosts of her past to keep her company.

Two hours later the sage unapologetically arrived. Moira bristled in annoyance at the audacity of the man not to come when he had been summoned. She was the Grand Lady and was to be obeyed without question.

Standing to her full height, she took in the sage's drab robes of brown and the tie of black rope cinching it around his generous waistline. The hair on his head was a thin whisp of silver. He pressed his palms together and bowed at his middle, his keen eyes never leaving hers.

"You called, my lady, and I came."

"I don't have time for your games," Moira snapped. She turned away and let her hands run over the dusty parchment. "I need a translation."

"A translation. At this hour?" The old sage raised his eyebrows. He looked pointedly to Nabert's stiffening corpse. His expression became pinched, but he mercifully said nothing. Nabert and the sages had a complicated history. There would be celebrations in their austere temples tonight.

"It would have been earlier if you came when you were summoned," Moira replied.

The sage lifted his eyebrows. "I am a servant to the people of Gytall. Their needs come before the spire's."

Moira held back a scoff. It was control over the populace that the sages cared for. "I'm working for the good of the people of Gytall. Hence, the summons."

"I see." The sage seemed unaffected by her proclamation. "Then you are fully aware of the misfortunes the cold snap has wrought on the poor and afflicted."

"Don't pretend to be a saint that cares for the unfortunate. You bleed gold from the people as well as any leech might," Moira said. "Give me my translation."

"I fail to see the urgency." The old man's eyes went back to the body. "Perhaps you should move him."

Moira waved his concern away. "The dead need nothing from me. Edvern has been missing for too long. Anything we can learn is helpful in planning his defeat."

"I thought Edvern was murdered," the sage said, a shrewd light in his dark eyes. "Seems you have a murderer loose in your spire."

Moira bit down on the urge to scream. The old man knew the body that was burnt was not the bastard. The sages who had been given leave to prepare the body for burial had been under strict orders to never speak of what they knew. "Get to work before I send you to a cell for all your—"

"My lady, you do realise that dozens of people are dying in the town?" Not only did the sage interrupt her, but he also had the gumption to chide her as if she were a child. Her. The Grand Lady who ruled over him and every other soul in Aurelia. "What will you do when the cold reaches your tower?"

"The dragonstone makes the spire warm," Moira said, although she knew her words rang false. "We're safe here."

"When people die in great numbers, revolt is never far away," the sage replied, his tone holding rebuke. "The afflicted in Gytall already call to Lady Aryis to send Qavi to come for Halsabith."

"That is the temple's concern, not mine," Moira said. "I need you to start translating."

The old man chuckled, walking forward with shuffling steps. Moira stamped down the impulse to grab him by his robes and drag him across the room. She gritted her teeth, reminding herself that killing too many of those who worked in the temple was never a good idea. Now and then she required their assistance, and the people had odd ideas about these aged men.

Finally, the sage made his way to the ancient manuscript. He ran his gnarled fingers over the writing, making a contemplative humming noise as he did so. "Wherever did you get this, my lady?"

"That's not important."

The sage lifted his head, surveying her with eyes that saw too much. "Perhaps it is, perhaps it is not. This is a Nezahrian text."

"Hence the reason I sent for you."

The old man tilted his head. "As I was saying, my lady, a Nezahrian text from the time of Ullryk Tallermayne, the Liberator."

"How do you know?" Moira asked, heart pumping fast in her chest.

Ullryk!

Maybe he would have some wise words to save them.

The sage did not hide his sly grin. He tapped a finger at the bottom of the parchment. "These two Nezahrian glyphs make his monogram. Very few samples of his signature survive."

Moira sucked in a breath, her fingers falling to the long dagger at her side. "What does he say?"

"Let's see." The sage picked up the parchment, eyes roving over the glyphs and symbols. It seemed to take an age for him to translate the small document. "Three spires for the three eggs taken from Nezaha. Three tokens that ease the communication with dragons. If held in ..."

The sage stopped, his brow wrinkling and his mouth opening and closing, but no sound came forth.

"Yes?" Moira wanted to shake him.

"Forgive me, my lady, but this text is difficult," the sage murmured. "The best translation I can make is if held in powerful hands, the eggs may be used to exert will over dragons."

"Control?" Moira's mind was already screaming at her that Edvern was responsible for her loss of power in Gytall. The moment he had stolen from her ...

The brat had stolen a glass egg.

"What else does the text say about the eggs?"

"They're guarded by ..."

"Yes?"

"A stone heart?" The sage shook his head. "Poor translation, I'm afraid."

But Moira already knew where she could find these eggs. Statues. Each of the spires had a stone dragon with a glasslike egg in their mouths. The moment Edvern had fled with her priceless work of art, her control slipped.

Nabert, that pesky librarian, had been right. The power to control dragons didn't come by their Tallermayne blood; it was from the glass eggs that were stationed in each spire.

Edvern had one egg, and she had no way of knowing if he knew about the power he held. She still had Cynedir and Navilla Spires under her control. Gytall was lost, but she had the advantage still.

The sage folded the parchment, handing it back to her. "You must assemble your riders and tell them this news."

The smile forming on Moira's lips melted. The sage had made a fatal mistake. Those she ruled could never know the secret to her power. Her fingers curled around the handle of her blade.

A flash of fear crossed the old man's face as he watched her unsheathe her weapon. His mouth opened to scream, but she sprung forward and lunged, burying the long dagger into his heart. She opened the channels of her power, letting unfathomable fear of death invade the old man's mind. Terror replaced the sage's haughtiness. Her power let him linger, not out of pity, but so he might suffer a little longer. He crumpled to the ground like a discarded doll and died in silence.

At least old Nabert now had some company.

Stepping away from the corpse on the floor, Moira tucked the parchment into her breast pocket. It was imperative that she take control of her remaining spires. The eggs had been guarded carefully; to break the dragonstone was to become cursed.

"Rider!" Moira yelled, knowing that a rider would be lingering nearby in case she required them. "Rider!"

A satisfied smile touched her lips as she heard booted footsteps running to see what she needed. The library door opened, and Kirra entered, jogging to her side, eager to hear the next order.

Moira schooled her features to unbothered as the young woman halted in her tracks to look down at the dead sage. A shadow passed over her expression. A moment later it was gone.

"Waken the riders. We're leaving."

Kirra's brow furrowed; she looked down again at the dead sage. Then back to Moira's face. "My lady, people are dying. The river and seas are freezing over. Reports of monsters ..."

"We must protect the lives of our dragons," Moira said. Kirra had given her the perfect excuse. "We're flying out in an hour. Meet me in the tunnels."

"As my lady commands," Kirra said, bending into a deep bow.

Moira didn't watch her go.

The dragons were restless. Deep in the tunnels of Gytall, they rumbled, scraping their scaled bodies along the coarse rock as if they knew what was to come. The weak and rebellious would meet a swift end. Many of the targeted dragons were already chained down.

Only the strong, controllable dragons would be spared. The remainder would have to be put out of commission. If she was going to be forced to flee, she was not going to leave resources behind. Her enemies would have nothing to scavenge.

Whilmana and Yahler flanked her, their blades drawn and ready. Attuned to the powers of destruction, they were suited to their roles of executioners. They would not be swayed into showing mercy.

Moira's fingers caressed the pommel of her sword. Her guts clenched as she remembered her wedding day when Fennix gave it to her. She would take a new weapon; she would leave her faithless husband's gift behind. Tonight, she would free herself of the Tallermayne name. She would begin afresh, taking the first steps in regaining control and becoming the most powerful woman in Aurelia's history.

"My lady."

Moira turned, a harsh word stilling on her lips. Kirra ran towards her, a piece of parchment clutched in her hand. The young rider halted before her, taking in the sight of the dragons. She eyed the chains and cuffs with a frown.

"My lady, this message was intercepted."

After snatching the letter, Moira scanned the neat handwriting in the dim lighting. Yahler brought a lit torch closer. Water wyrms had made their way back to Aurelia. They'd attacked Cynedir, bringing with them ice and death. Corpses lined the street.

The resurgence of the wild dragons of the water made sense. Crumpling the paper, Moira knew it was these monsters who were causing grief in Gytall. Death was at their door. Her instincts to retreat had been correct. Reason would predict the water wyrms' next target: Navilla.

She needed to prepare for their assault.

Tucking the parchment into her armour, Moira felt her mind race. Water wyrms were reclusive and hadn't been seen in centuries. It was known they held little interest in humans and dry land. So why had they returned?

"Perhaps they sense Halsabith reborn," Fennix's voice whispered in her ear. She could almost feel the teasing touch of his fingers running along her spine. *"You're the reason they're here."*

"Mount your dragons," Moira said. "There's been a situation in Cynedir."

"My lady?"

Moira hated it when her orders were questioned. "What?"

"The other dragons ... the ones without riders." Kirra tilted her head to the side, her eyes fixed on a young dragon chained down.

A cruel smile spread across Moira's lips. She didn't need to look towards Yahler or Whilmana. They knew what needed to be done. Moira enjoyed the dawning horror on Kirra's face as they stepped forward.

"No! You can't." Kirra moved in between Moira's loyal riders and the dragon.

"Out of the way, girl," Moira barked. "Or die a traitor."

Moira could see the bitter realisation in Kirra's eyes. She already knew that her defiance meant her death. Resignation and fear crossed the younger rider's face. Resolve followed as she raised her weapon.

"Very well then." Moira leapt forward, the steel of her blade clashing with Kirra's. She might have been old enough to be the girl's grandmother, but decades of training and experience made her stronger. At the pained expression on Kirra's face, Moira allowed herself a grin. The riders around them yelled and cheered. Some decided to side with Kirra. Fools! The fight was not destined to last long.

Moira pressed her advantage, forcing Kirra against the damp tunnel wall. She slashed her blade down, amputating the girl's exposed wrist. Dark tendrils of her power surged towards the girl, unbidden and untameable. She felt it coil through Kirra's thoughts, sapping her courage and replacing it with fear.

Kirra wailed, dropping her weapon as she sprawled to the floor. The desperation to live, to fight, rose within the girl. Rallying what little control she had over her own mind, she called to the waters. Underground, Kirra was at a disadvantage. The walls of the caverns merely produced droplets. She scrambled for her weapon with her left hand, which shook in her attempts to fight Moira's power.

Moira prowled forward. The young rider was still belly down, reaching for her weapon, when she pressed her boot in the middle of her back.

"Please ..." Kirra sobbed, her courage gone, replaced by terror that left her paralysed. "Please."

Moira's heart had hardened many years ago. No amount of pleading or grovelling would reach her. The point of her sword hovered over the young woman before plunging down. The blade met little resistance as it stabbed through flesh and muscle.

There was a moment of hush through the battle at the first kill. Watching the blood blossoming underneath Kirra, Moira allowed herself to enjoy it.

Death had a majestic beauty.

She stepped over the dying rider, leaving her blade glinting in the firelight as she approached the bound dragon. The hatchling hissed pitifully, his haunches wriggling as he attempted to escape. She held out her hand; Yahler offered her another weapon.

A roar answered the young one's cry for help. Moira's sword halted, and she grinned up at the sound.

Xyran, her late husband's loyal dragon. He was a rare beast. His ancient lineage could be traced back to Saskah, the Aurelian wife of Ullryk. The bond he had forged with his first rider had been so strong that Saskah's power had fused with his own dragonish might. In the hope that he might take another rider, Moira hadn't forced the large silver dragon to retire.

He had an extraordinary ability to resist magical attacks. At first it bothered her that she had a dragon who was shielded from her powers. Over time she saw the benefit of harvesting his power for herself. The difficulty was learning how to siphon the power from him. When Fennix passed, the brute had become demanding and aggressive. Without the support of his human rider, his power began to wane. Still, she coveted it. He was weaker now.

If she could not coax the dragon into giving over his power, she would relish the triumph of taking his life. She would do so personally. The scaly bastard probably knew of her husband's betrayal.

"He's mine!" Moira yelled.

The other riders were keen to step out of the way of the approaching dragon. Xyran wasn't a dragon who enjoyed company; he rarely allowed himself to be seen. For some of the riders, this would be the first time they met him.

Moira took in the long talons, the sharp fangs and flashing eyes. His nostrils flared. He looked at the slain rider, to Moira, and then to the youngling. He shook his crowned head, lowering himself to peer down at her, and bellowed.

"Shall I return you to your rider?" Moira asked, grinning despite the rank smell from Xyran's breath.

The dragon cocked his head, lips curling as if he understood her. He bellowed again, clawing the hard ground. She saw his belly glow with the forming of fire ... and she acted.

Reaching out with her free hand, she loosed her power against him. The black tendrils of fear wrapped around the beast. He resisted. Moira dug deeper into the well of her power, body shaking as she delved further into what she had studiously honed over many decades. It was time to fully reveal her might.

A phantom hand gripped the dragon's heart and squeezed. Xyran bellowed in fear and rage ... His shields buckled, and fear took him.

Blood poured from Moira's nose and ears from the sheer exertion. She could hear shouts, laced with fear, of the riders behind her. To bend a creature's organs to one's will should result in the magic wielder's death. None had mastered the skill and survived. But Moira was stubborn and angry.

"You knew!" Moira yelled. "You knew what your rider did! Did you also kill my Tamah? Did you kill my girl?"

The dragon's bellowing ceased, the giant body shuddering under the influence of her power. He stumbled forward a couple of steps before blood burst from his mouth and he collapsed.

Eyes full of fire and hatred glared up at her as he lay dying. For the briefest second, she saw the ghost of her former husband. He knelt beside his beloved beast, hands resting on his scales. Brushing the image away, she snatched up a spear from a nearby rider.

Moira peered down at the dying dragon, ignoring the thumping pain in her skull. Lightheaded, she allowed herself to glory in the drake's blood. This was the night she would wipe out the knowledge of Fennix Tallermayne. None who were loyal to him would leave Gytall alive.

CHAPTER 11

Homecoming

EDVERN

Thud, thud. Thud, thud.

Even as his heartbeat floundered, Edvern's ears were filled with the sound of a steady rhythm of another heart. Cold darkness enveloped him, dragging him down, down, down into a watery grave. Death was waiting to greet him.

Thud, thud. Thud, thud.

Strong, corded muscles pulled him close to a broad chest. Ice stung his flesh like a thousand stabbing knives. The waters parted, his face breaching the surface. He sucked in a lungful of air while all around, shrieks of anger and terror erupted.

The arms tightened around him. He could feel the creatures underneath churning the currents.

"Ready!"

He wasn't going to die alone. Alaxen was with him.

Water crashed over their heads, plunging them back down into the dark depths. Edvern's hands covered his uncle's. He shouldn't be here. He couldn't be responsible for another family member's death.

Alaxen hung on. It was his steady, calm heartbeat that Edvern could hear. His uncle remained uncompromising and unafraid.

Thud, thud. Thud, thud.

The water frothed around them in a dizzying fury. The screams of outrage from the water wyrms echoed in his ears. Alaxen freed one of his hands, and Edvern thrashed in panic, fearful to die alone. His uncle's one-armed grip on him constricted. Kicking his legs, Alaxen clawed his free arm at the water.

They broke the surface again. Edvern's lungs screamed as he choked on the briny air. He glanced up. An unknown dragon hovered above, his jaws and front claws savagely attacking the creatures just below the surface.

Reaching up, Alaxen grabbed the claws of the dragon's back foot. Water cascaded from their bodies as the green dragon pumped his wings and they were airborne. Drenched, Edvern shivered as the wind whipped and stung his flesh.

His lips parted to speak, but he found he could not coax the words from his throat. They flew higher, the dragon holding them securely in his forelegs. The dragon ducked his head to peer at them, rumbling in satisfaction.

"Bring us up, Tynum!" Alaxen cried.

The dragon complied, placing them gently on his back, never breaking the pumping of his wings.

Lifting his head from the dragon's neck, Edvern tried to scream for Izorah and Alynta. All he managed to do was cough up water.

"We need to land!" Alaxen yelled, his arms loosening from Edvern's waist.

Another voice answered, along with the deep rumble of the dragon. Edvern searched his memory; he knew this dragon. It wasn't one he was able to visit often. He had a rider of a higher rank.

"Hold on, Edvern. Tynum will find somewhere warm and dry." Alaxen pressed his mouth close to Edvern's ear.

Tynum.

He knew the name. He and Lyrus had similar abilities and strengths. Tynum. A forest-green male with dapples of grey. He was large, with a broad frame, a rounded muzzle and a keen sense for hunting. He and his rider had left Gytall a few seasons back to join Alaxen at Cynedir.

The air was soon full of the sound of frantic wings. He sensed Alynta's presence joining them first. Unable to open his eyes, he felt the brush of her mind over his. Mind still sluggish, he was not able to reply he was well.

The second presence he felt was Izorah. She was struggling. With all of his might, he tried to reach her mind. It was a minor injury that would heal quickly. But she could not go far. She flew underneath Tynum, bellowing for Edvern. The giant male released them so that Edvern could lie on Izorah's back.

Once free, Alaxen rubbed his arms. His skin was like ice.

Slowly, the terror seeped from Edvern's mind. The understanding that he was safe washed over him, and he curled his fingers into a fist. A gentle flood of power twisted up his hand to his arm. Warmth radiated with it, and soon his body ceased its shivering.

"Uncle?"

"Ah, you had me worried for a moment." Alaxen's hand brushed over the cut made by the dragonstone.

Hissing, Edvern pulled away. In the moments of horror under the water, he had forgotten the burning sting. Alaxen held him firm, his power running along the cut, soothing as it went.

"Dragonstone ..." Edvern said, quite unnecessarily. "He would have broken the statue to get the dyrathakin egg."

"Breaking the dragonstone would have been his only way to take the egg. The burn should dissipate shortly," Alaxen said gruffly.

Pride and another unknown emotion swept through Edvern. The egg hadn't come easily for the war wraith. Alynta's egg had come for him, warming his fingers the moment he had touched it.

Alaxen shivered, and Edvern belatedly remembered his uncle had been in the freezing ocean too. Wiggling his fingers, he grasped on to Alaxen's wrist and let his power flow into his uncle's frozen flesh.

Alaxen made only an arbitrary noise of protest. Edvern smiled, knowing that the relief his uncle felt was enough to silence any argument.

Alynta flew opposite them, her mind awhirl with anxiety. She flew dangerously close to Izorah's left-hand side, the stolen dyrathakin egg clutched in her front paws.

Steadying his breathing, Edvern made eye contact with Lyrus. He flew lopsided, and the pain he was feeling was palpable. Scratches, raw and red, adorned his face and down his throat. Membranes on both of his wings were ripped.

"Are you hurt?" Alynta demanded. "Eddi, are you hurt?"

"A little." Edvern shrugged. "I'll be okay."

"We're not going far." Tynum's rider finally spoke, forcing Edvern to peer over at her. He had trained briefly under Mistress Taseria, who, like his uncle, was a skilled tracker. For his father's sake, she tolerated him. Her behaviour towards him changed noticeably when Rikar was absent from Gytall. She hadn't been in Gytall long, however, before her skills had her stationed in Cynedir. "Alaxen can heal him when we get our feet on the ground."

"Mistress Taseria ... did the captains call you back to Cynedir?"

Taseria lifted her chin, refusing to answer Edvern. He sighed, somewhat resigned to being ignored.

"Did you see what happened to the Nezahrian war wraith?" Alaxen asked.

"Fluffy here helped him," Lyrus grumbled. He eyed both his rider and his mate in turn.

Alynta's lavender eyes shone. "I couldn't let him drown. We'll need him later."

Lyrus huffed, and Alaxen stretched out his gloved hand to his dragon companion. They didn't touch, but it was a simple gesture of comfort.

"What's the news from Gytall, Tas?" Alaxen asked.

"The water wyrms aren't the only disgruntled wild dragons we've come across," Tynum said. His voice was gravelly and dejected when he spoke into Edvern's mind.

"What other dragons have you seen?" Edvern asked.

Taseria's brow furrowed as she frowned deeply. "How did you—"

"Edvern has astute observational skills," Alaxen replied before Edvern could formulate a response. The lie came easily to his uncle's tongue, and he felt Alaxen's grip on him tighten. A warning to be careful.

"You don't trust my rider," Tynum said. His nostrils flared. *"She's a good human, as riders go."*

"In uncertain times we must all be careful," Izorah replied.

Tynum wasn't placated, but the forest-green dragon dipped his head. Perhaps sensing her mount's increasing displeasure, Taseria stroked her hands down the scales of her dragon. "We saw lizardlings in the forests of Talsullah."

"Lizardlings?" Edvern could not help but raise his eyebrows. These were creatures of silly children's stories. Living in packs, the small dragons worked together to confuse unsuspecting prey and lure them into traps. They used their numbers to subdue their intended victims, often dividing their meal while the prey was still alive. His cousins had told him all sorts of tales about lizardlings hunting small bastard boys, so much so he had nightmares for weeks.

"Don't look so alarmed." Alaxen sounded amused. Lyrus flew closer, and the older man stood confidently on Izorah's back. He leapt towards his dragon, and Edvern sucked in a breath. It was a risky manoeuvre, one that only riders who trusted their dragons would do. Alaxen jumped as if gathering the courage to leap into the open sky was nothing more than walking up a flight of stairs. "You have a dyrathakin and just fought water wyrms ... it stands to logic that lizardlings are real."

"All legends have a grain of truth," Izorah said.

"Blessed talons have mercy on us all," Edvern whispered. "How many?"

"Their number is unknown, General Tallermayne," Taseria said, turning her head to address Alaxen rather than answer Edvern directly.

"You're Uhl'hari," Lyrus rumbled. *"Why fear them?"*

Edvern's chest tightened at Lyrus' faith in his abilities. He certainly didn't feel like a great leader or warrior. Who was he to lead dragons into freedom?

"The fight for independence is never easy. It's fraught with danger. Whether he lives or dies, a man who is sure of his convictions shall live on." Edvern wished he had Alaxen's confidence.

The quote was familiar to Edvern, as well it should be. His father had spoken to him at length about the strength and tenacity of Ullryk the Liberator. He felt confused now. To the Aurelians, even those who now hated the dragon riders, Ullryk had been a hero. Kyros, who Edvern loved, was Ullryk's dragon, who according to his confessions, was the instigator of the rebellion. The Nezahrians viewed him a traitorous villain ... Could it be possible he was both? Could a man be a hero and a villain simultaneously? What would Ullryk make of him, a boy raised as a Tallermayne, now a creature with wings of fire?

Silence descended on the group, each of them caught up in their own private thoughts. Eyes inevitably were drawn below. The waters between the islands and the mainland, normally calm, churned. Water wyrms breached the surface of the water, their bodies undulating between large hunks of ice.

No one said a word. Winter in Aurelia could be a bitter, difficult time. Even growing up in the relative safety of the spire, with a father who made sure he was provided for, Edvern knew less fortunate folk perished in the colder months.

The coldness from the water wyrms would increase the number of the dead. Of this Edvern was certain. He wondered how long it would take for the dragon riders to investigate Cynedir.

Something had to be done.

Thankfully, the rising mist was enough to blanket Tynum to fly ahead and scout the area. He hadn't gone far when Edvern caught sight of several dark shapes rising from Gytall Spire in the distance.

The air around him fizzled, and his skin tingled at the sensation of fingers gliding over his skin. He glanced to his uncle, knowing that his power was cloaking them from being detected.

The shadowy forms of dragons continued to rise from the spire. Edvern felt sick. Either they were flying to battle or they were leaving the common folk to their fates. He wasn't entirely sure which one was worse.

"Well, that solves the problem of landing undetected," Alynta commented. "Lyrus can't go any further."

It wasn't long before Tynum and Taseria returned. The female rider glanced at Alaxen; a look of understanding passed between them. Edvern wondered how many missions they had flown side by side to achieve such communication.

Alaxen turned towards Edvern. "We'll land in Gytall and find the rebels. Harden your heart. There may be little we can do for the people."

Edvern bit down on his lip, staring at the disappearing specks on the horizon.

Cowards.

Gytall was a city guarded by a dragon rider's spire. Even in the depths of winter it was a bustling hive. So landing in the middle of the market square to find it abandoned and shrouded in mist was unnatural. The sound of people's voices haggling for a bargain was swapped for wailing.

Alaxen had warned him to harden his heart. But Edvern found it impossible to do so. Where were Larah and Ellie? Were they safe?

Alynta padded ahead, sniffing at bodies tinged blue. She recoiled away, as if she was surprised to find the people unresponsive.

This, Edvern decided, was the ultimate picture of desolation. He had been shocked and saddened at Hemmryn Vale. A part of his heart had been torn from his chest when he worked shoulder to shoulder with the Saemorish to move their dead. This … this was worse.

From where he had been tending to Lyrus' injuries, Alaxen glanced at him, his eyebrows furrowing and his thick lips turning down into a stern frown. He expected his uncle to say something. But he remained stoic in his silence.

"Talons," Taseria said with an exhale. She stood huddled against Tynum's chest, soaking in the warmth from his scales.

If the cold came from the water wyrms, who were mostly confined to the water, perhaps he could reverse some of the damage. It was too late for many in Gytall, but maybe, just maybe he might be able to make a small difference.

Edvern didn't dare look back at his companions as he made his way to the muddy riverbank. His feet seemed to know where he wanted to go, and before he could stop and think on the wisdom of his actions, he was standing up to his knees in freezing water. His fingers tingled with heat, power begging to be released into the world.

Palms up, he spread his arms. Tongues of flame licked up his fingers, wound around his arms, down his torso and into the water. The river hissed and spat as ice and fire magic collided. He lifted his face, sweat pouring down his temples. The air hummed as the wet mist curled around him ... The water at his feet bubbled as Alynta joined him.

Edvern let his hand drop to his side, his fingers touching the dyrathakin's spikes. He blinked, looking up at a blue-grey sky. All around him the snow and ice were melting.

Nudging him with her nose, Alynta escorted Edvern back to the shore, where everyone was watching him with various levels of disbelief.

"You've reversed winter," Izorah said, her weight pressing her claws deep into the mud of the riverbank. Lifting her snout she scented the air. *"The water wyrms have retreated."*

"We need to get people away from the waters," Edvern said as Alaxen offered his hand. He allowed his uncle to pull him from the mud. "Aren't you going to chide me?"

"No, you're not a child. Come, I want to check on my spy." Alaxen raised his gloved hand to Edvern's shoulder and gave it a squeeze. Unable to formulate a response, Edvern allowed his uncle to lead him through the slums of Gytall.

"Do you think she's still alive?" Taseria asked. "She's not been much use to the cause of late."

"I must look for Bea," Alaxen said.

"Bea?" Edvern enquired. He knew no one of that name.

"She would have been inconsequential to you," Alaxen said, the hard planes of his face softening a little. "But she watched over you for me after your father passed. Bea is ... she's valuable to me."

"That's how you found me at the temple. This Bea?"

Alaxen inclined his head.

"This way."

Edvern bit his lip, looking in the opposite direction to the slums that Alaxen seemed keen on entering. "Uncle … I … There's someone I need to check …"

Taseria opened her mouth to speak, but Alaxen silenced her. "Your seamstress girl?"

"How …?"

"I had my eyes on you, Eddi."

Edvern refused to be cowed. "Yes, the seamstress."

"Go."

Edvern didn't need to hear any more. Nodding his head, he turned and disappeared through the closest alleyway. Larah and Ellie lived nearby in a little room under the seamstress' shop.

Edvern's shoulder blades burned, and his fingers itched as he walked through the city. Gytall was a tomb of decay. In his chest his heart felt like a stone. His throat closed over, and he fought back an urge to scream.

As a boy he had dreamed of leaving Gytall forever; now the city had fallen drastically, abandoned by its dragon rider patrons.

His eyes burned, but he forced himself to look at the defrosting bodies. He had left Gytall, left his home and … What was the point of all his power if he failed to help the vulnerable?

Edvern stopped before the seamstress shop. Shattered glass littered the frames of the dark windows. The quaint sign of a silver needle painted onto a red background lay abandoned at the threshold. The door was splintered, torn from its hinges. Sensing no danger, he entered. He called forth a ball of fire to his hand to light his way.

Bolts of fabrics and delicate lace lay strewn over the polished floorboards. Pearls lay scattered like fallen snow. The stockpiles of fur that he had helped Larah fold, ready for winter, were gone.

"Hello?"

Silence greeted him.

"Larah, it's Eddi. Are you here?"

"Eddi." Alynta padded forward, her long ears swivelling. "No one's here."

Edvern swallowed, his heart sinking as he passed the fine golden cloak still draped half-finished on a dummy. People became desperate when they felt the cold fingers of death approaching. He could only imagine that the shop had been raided for the only thing of worth to the people of the city: warmth.

In a daze he moved to the back rooms and descended the stairs to the cellar. When he lifted his hand to the door, he found it locked. This couldn't be real …

A burst of flame and the lock mechanisms melted, and the door swung open.

There he found her, curled up in the corner, her long lashes caressing her pale, gaunt cheeks. Her sister, Ellie, lay in her arms. Sweet Ellie, only sixteen, was stiff and blue in death. Her eyes were closed, hand clasped with her sister's.

Hand shaking, he reached out to Larah. He could see frozen tear tracks on her face. She was cold. So, cold.

Falling to his knees, Edvern wanted to cry out, but nothing came. Just a terrible numbness.

"Did you love her?"

"No," Edvern said, cusping her hand in his. "I think I loved the idea of her. She was kind. She was goodness in a world full of tribulation. When I had no value, she believed I had worth."

"I think that is love of a sort," Alynta said. "She wasn't your nesting partner …"

Edvern nodded, the movement wooden. He let some of his power slip from his fingers to her hand. Slowly her body warmed. "Of all the people in Gytall, she deserved a blessed life."

He stood and went back to the dark shop. From the dummy he grabbed the golden cloak, the finest fabrics and some ribbons. Then he returned to the sisters' side. Their bodies were stiff and hard to move as he laid them down, hand in hand. He smoothed their skirts, and with trembling fingers he braided silk ribbons in their flaxen hair. His eyes burned with unshed tears as he remembered how he often had fantasised with Larah about running away with them. He'd talked about marrying her, buying her gold fabrics and showering her with jewels. He'd promised a better world. And he had failed them.

Alynta, sensing his need, had gone around the shop, finding a pair of candles. Carefully she set them beside the two young women.

Kneeling beside the corpses of the kindest girls of Gytall, Edvern flexed his fingers to light the wicks. He stumbled through the lament for maidens. When he reached the end of his prayer, he leant forward, brushing his lips against Larah's.

"Goodbye, Larah. I'll be eternally thankful for the light you shone in my life. Go in peace." He touched her hand, resisting the urge to shake her awake, and turned to Ellie. A memory of the sisters singing, dancing and twirling around the tables of the tavern washed through him. The first time they met, it had been the spring after his father's execution. Ellie had found him drunk and desperately unhappy. She'd pulled him to his feet, spinning him into the dance until they were both laughing and gasping, breathless. Larah had taken him home, fed him fresh sweet buns, and they kissed under the light of a full moon. "I'm sorry, Ellie. Save me a dance in the afterlife."

He stood, the ground seeming unstable underneath his feet. Then he gestured and let his flames take them into the Father Dragon's arms.

The shop caught flame as Alynta and Edvern stepped over the threshold and into the street, only to find a little old lady, bent over with age, hobbling towards him. A tattered dragon rider's cloak was wrapped around her bony shoulders.

"Wearing that cloak is tantamount to impersonating a rider," Edvern said. "Trust me, ma'am, you don't want to anger the dragon riders."

"Bah!" the old lady said, shaking her head. Her silver bun wobbled as she did so. "When my Dirk was alive, you should have seen the nonsense we got up to under this cloak."

Edvern swallowed a laugh of surprise. He could imagine well what a youthful dragon rider might get up to. The trouble was he couldn't imagine this woman as young.

Alaxen arrived, looking a little put out. He glanced towards the burning shop and frowned at the woman. "Bea, I've been looking for you," he said, clasping the old lady's shoulders to bend and kiss her cheeks. "This is Edvern."

"I know who 'e is," Bea snapped. "You had me running all over Gytall, watching him for you when that woman burned his da."

The idea that the old woman had chased him around Gytall seemed ludicrous. Perhaps he was too predictable. He frowned, hating to think this woman knew what mischief he had gotten into and with whom. Alaxen stared pointedly at him, and his cheeks heated, knowing she had reported a good deal of his behaviour.

"Who of the rebellion is in Gytall?" Alaxen asked, his voice dropping to a whisper.

"I'm afraid I'm alone," Bea said. "I stayed here to die. I suppose you had something to do with reversing winter?"

Alaxen looked pointedly at Edvern and to the shop. Edvern waved his hands, and his flames snuffed out.

"I see," Bea said. "Anyone like some stale biscuits and tea?"

"Taseria is searching for a meal," Alaxen said.

"Ah, you have Taseria with you. Be careful." Bea sniffed. "She'd be lucky to find anything to her exacting standards."

"Taseria is a valuable member of the rebellion," Alaxen said. From his tone it sounded like he'd had this argument before. "Now, are you going to invite us to your home or not, old woman?"

"My hovel is damp and dreary. But whatever I have, General, is yours," Bea said. "I'm sure Edvern is looking forward to a pork pasty."

Edvern stopped in his tracks. Had Bea followed him before his father's death? Surely he didn't eat the pastry treat often enough for her to divine that it was his favourite. How long had she been spying on him?

Bea grinned up at him toothily.

CHAPTER 12
The Imperial Army

LYSSANDRA

Like moths to a flame, Antonella and Konrad gravitated towards one another, uncaring if they got burnt. Every morning Lyssandra pretended to sleep, her heart heavy as her friend rose and fussed over her hair, hoping to impress Konrad. In the loneliness of her tent, envy consumed her.

Lyssandra was under no illusions as to her character. She might have worked hard for Ellrahera's approval, but she was vain, entitled and prone to jealousy. She wanted what Antonella had, and it hurt. Their circumstances were dire, yet Antonella and Konrad were blissfully happy.

Now that they were all traitors to the Saemorish crown, they had to take what joy they could from the world. She didn't expect Antonella's good fortune to last. Nothing did.

I deserve to be happy too, her mind grumbled. If Edvern were hers, she could learn to be content. And if she couldn't have him, she only wished for his safety.

But he wasn't safe. And she was all alone.

Lying on her back, she recalled in vivid detail the morning she had woken in his arms. The scent of him, fire and woodsmoke, consumed her dreams. Pressed against his side, she'd been protected from the cold. He slept peacefully, his even breaths tickling her neck as he pulled her subconsciously closer. When he awakened, he allowed her to continue lying on his arm even though it was numb. He hadn't wanted to disturb her. The considerate dolt.

Snarling, she viciously kicked aside her blankets and pulled on her new Nezahrian fur-lined boots. Cursing her ill fortune, she tugged on the laces.

All she could do was bury her budding feelings for him. Since she had returned to camp, Prince Dalain had been a perfect gentleman. He never mentioned their broken marriage contract. He hadn't forgotten ...

She brushed her fingers down the soft cloak that Dalain had gifted her to ward out the cold. It was one of his, lined with luxurious fur. The gold clasps were his as well. How she wished she knew what the gift meant. Throwing it over her shoulders, she crept into the sleepy camp.

It was little past dawn, the morning air biting against the skin of her cheeks. She was grateful for the cloak. Staring out over the forest of tents, she saw no sign of Antonella or Konrad.

Tacebia was easily the largest military camp she had ever seen. For as far as the eye could see, canvas tents dotted the flat plains. Nezahrians built their military cities in circular patterns. Everything had its order and place. Raziel's war tent was central, easily identifiable by its black and crimson banners. A large circumference was left so that Faelowyn could always be close to her rider.

Large paths separated the camp into quarters, each section with its own name. Another ring of space divided the essential supplies and officer tents from the main army and service tents. These pathways were not only so that Faelowyn might move, but it provided quick and easy access for spies and messengers from whatever direction they came in.

Lyssandra didn't like to think of herself as a coward. But moving around the Nezahrian camp alone as a foreigner was uncomfortable. She couldn't blame her hosts for their scrutiny or doubts of her intentions. She was a diplomat of an enemy nation. It was not enough for the Nezahrians that she had rescued Prince Hedriel.

Reaching the cook's tent, she was relieved that it was empty. She grabbed a bowl, helping herself to the watered-down rations, which looked like last night's leftover stew. Overcooked vegetables were welcome after the thought of stripping bark off trees.

Her thoughts returned to Prince Hedriel as she fled and passed the tent he shared with Dalain. Her feet stalled, her guts telling her she ought to visit him, to say something to alleviate his suffering.

No words would ever be good enough.

Far from placating the Nezahrians, returning the prince had only inflamed their fury. The story of Hedriel's mistreatment spread like wildfire through the camp. And then there was the screaming.

She wondered how many of them had been awoken in the night by Hedriel's cries. Being disturbed by the sound of the young prince amidst his nightmares was jarring. It was a terrible thing to be privy to.

The first night it happened, she had grabbed her borrowed robe and dashed into the dark barefoot. She saw the Black Prince still dressed in his armour, running through the camp ... Symmeon on his heels. Raziel's general saw her and shook his head. She stood in the dark until Hedriel's cries ceased, then returned to her bed, heart heavy.

"Lady Stamos! Good morning."

Lyssandra started, surprised that the object of her thoughts had caught her gawking. "Good morning, Prince."

Grinning at her, Hedriel strode over, hands in his pockets to peer into her bowl. He made a face at her. "Stew again. Why are you walking around with it?"

"I do not wish to intrude on—"

Hedriel snorted. His grin widened, telling her that he knew exactly why she didn't want to stay in the cook's tent.

"You look well this morning."

It was the wrong thing to say. Hedriel's face fell. "I think if Marsyna hadn't taken me as her rider, Raziel would have sent me home already."

"No shame in that," Lyssandra said. "We're not all born soldiers."

Hedriel fell into step with her, and they walked a little way. During the daylight hours, she had watched him move around the camp, winning the hearts of soldiers. He mingled among them, Marsyna at his shoulder. The young dragon would dip her head for pats, blowing playful bursts of smoke. Hedriel clasped hands, smiled and chatted as if he wasn't haunted by the Saemorish prison cell. He might not have been a soldier, but Lyssandra thought he made a mighty fine politician. The soldiers loved him.

"I've a spot I like to sit when I'm alone," Hedriel said. "I'll show you."

Lyssandra accepted his invitation with a dip of her head, letting the prince lead her to the edge of camp. Hedriel took her to a large felled log and sat. With her back to the camp, she could look out over the grass fields where the dragons had made their own place to congregate. From here she could watch Faelowyn hold court with her small band of dragons. The large black matriarch was currently curled in a patch of sunlight, Odharn nestled at her side. The green dragon looked like the runt of her litter. From the rumbling purr that came deep from his chest, Odharn was asleep.

"She'll never have a chance to return to her own family," Hedriel said. "She was exiled by her kin."

"Odharn seems so small," Lyssandra said, turning her face away. Was Hedriel comparing her betrayal of her king to that of Faelowyn's dragonish family drama?

"He is." Hedriel inclined his head at the log, and Lyssandra felt obligated to sit beside him. "Faelowyn was once a wild dragon from the high mountains. In leaving her place there, she gave up the hope of family. Looks like she's building a new one."

Lyssandra peered at the two dragons, Faelowyn shifting to tuck the slumbering green dragon closer to her body. When they first met, she had been concerned that the black dragon might reject Odharn for his missing wing.

"He lost his mother." Lyssandra clasped her hands in her lap. The memory of how she demanded that Edvern leave the crippled dragon to his fate burned in her mind. "The Aurelians speared open her throat while she bellowed for her baby. I tried to convince Eddi to leave him behind ... He wouldn't."

"And now?"

"I was a fool for thinking dragons unfeeling beasts," Lyssandra admitted, her cheeks warming with a rush of shame. "Even watching Eddi conversing openly with them, I should have seen it sooner. He was dedicated to Odharn's care from the moment we conceived the plan to escape."

"Happy is the person who knows they're a fool while they are still young." Hedriel's lips tugged into a wry smile. "Or so my mother tells me."

Lyssandra set her bowl down, her appetite gone. "If anyone can get themselves out of trouble, it's Edvern Tallermayne. He's smarter than he thinks."

Hedriel huffed in response. "I hope you're right."

"I'm rarely wrong." Lyssandra lifted her gaze, telling herself she was stupid for imagining all the ways Edvern could be captured. Her eyes drifted towards Faelowyn once more.

Hedriel's eyes followed her gaze. "You have your mother's tenacity."

"What would you know of my mother?" Lyssandra asked.

A wistful smile tugged on Hedriel's lips. "The perks of being the youngest prince in the family. I overhear all sorts of titbits. Did you know your mother, Princess Fiora, had a chance to be the minor wife of Emperor Ze'hyrn? She gave him something better than gold, so he offered her the honour of sharing him with Empress Ionah. Your mother declined."

Lyssandra turned away, confused at her annoyance. "Other than a dragon, what is better than gold?"

Hedriel's smile was feral. "Tamah Tallermayne's demise."

"Edvern's aunt?" Lyssandra had heard the stories before. How Tamah had become impatient and flown into a trap set by the Nezahrians. Edvern's grandfather flew after her. He'd sent his dragon home as a condition of a parlay. Although he came in the hope of a peaceful exchange, it was said he was ripped limb to limb. Fennix's body was left to rot in the great lake of Yrew. This, of course, had been before she was born.

Hedriel laughed and slapped his thigh, a wicked light in his eye. "They call your mother the Spider of Saemore, do you know? At her suggestion the emperor sent Moira a lock of her dead daughter's hair."

"That's grim." Lyssandra didn't know how she felt about the Tallermayne family now. Was Moira's hatred of the Nezahrians justified? Her daughter was coaxed into a trap. And when her husband flew to Tamah's defence, he'd been killed, despite coming in peace. If you asked an Aurelian, they'd say Tamah's trial and execution on the steps of the emperor's palace had been murder.

"Remind Empress Ionah who you are."

"The empress?" Startled out of her reverie, Lyssandra couldn't help the look of horror blossoming on her face. When she accompanied Ellrahera to Nezaha to broker the marriage contract between herself and Dalain, she'd been an unimportant cog in the negotiations. Ionah hadn't even summoned her. "The empress only wanted King Jahon's support and loyalty, not a bastard daughter for Dalain."

Hedriel shrugged, his expression almost indulgent. "Despite your ill-breeding, you're royal blood. An almost princess who would have been easier to manipulate than a pure woman."

"Why barter for my hand in marriage?" Lyssandra demanded. The question had bothered her for months.

"The Nezahrian court is full of intrigue." Hedriel tilted his head and shrugged. "The emperor wanted inside Jahon's head. What better way than a pliable girl who'd be thankful for a prosperous marriage?"

Lyssandra blinked, dumbfounded. The Nezahrians had thought she would be easily swayed into their way of thinking, that she would betray her country and her king. Her stomach cramped. She had done exactly as they predicted.

"The Great Emperor believed that the benefits of marrying you to Dalain outweighed the costs of giving his son a bastard daughter."

"And the empress?"

"Better a lower woman than a grasping, manipulative noble. I, of course, have my own ulterior motives for waylaying you." Hedriel grinned, flashing his perfect teeth. Lyssandra didn't like the knowing tone his voice had taken. "The Imperial Army will arrive by midday. Be prepared."

Emperor Ze'hyrn rode ahead of his Imperial Army on the most magnificent white stallion Lyssandra had ever beheld. Unaffected by the number of fighting men and women of Taccbia, he acknowledged no one. The olive skin of his face was unblemished, giving the illusion that he was ageless.

The winter sun reflected off the emperor's golden armour, blinding any who dared stare at him. Draped over his broad shoulders was a fine crimson cloak, which was heavily decorated with gold embroidery. Dozens of blood-red rubies adorned the heavy crown that sat upon his brow.

Growing up among the diplomats, she had been witness to the pomp and ceremony that came with power. King Jahon looked like a foolish bauble in comparison to the emperor.

Ze'hyrn of Nezaha was accompanied by his wife. Lyssandra could only stare dumbstruck at the sight of Empress Ionah. The empress' mount was a stallion black as night. The hooves of the beast were easily the size of her dinner plate. Ionah sat tall and regal in the saddle, her simple crimson gown split so that her practical riding trousers were visible. A crown whose tapered spikes resembled dragon fangs sat among coils of dark hair, heaped high on the empress' head.

Her sword was strapped to her side, its handle embellished with Euquallian patterns and swirls. The pommel held a diamond, clear and brilliant and as big as Lyssandra's fist. There were very few ruling queens that wore armour, but the empress' black and gold scale mail was beautifully crafted. Lyssandra had no doubt that it was functional.

It was plain as day that she was Prince Dalain's mother. She shared the same smooth brown skin and high cheekbones as her son. Like a hawk, her dark gaze took in everything around her.

Lines of Raziel's men and women parted for the imperial company, and as the empress drew level with Lyssandra, she looked down. A flicker of recognition lit the empress' eyes, and a shiver curled up Lyssandra's spine. She dropped to her knees, anything to take her gaze away from the woman who at one time was to be her mother-in-law. Beside the empress, Lyssandra was an insect.

Lyssandra's fingers found Antonella's as her ears strained to hear what was happening around her. Her friend squeezed her hand while Lyssandra debated the wisdom of joining with the Nezahrians.

No words were spoken by the royal couple. They continued to where Raziel and Dalain were waiting.

Hedriel joined Raziel as Prince Dalain went forward to greet his parents. She noticed with a frown Dalain's stiff posture. The emperor's bland expression showed no hint of joy at the sight of his son. His greeting was distinctly cold.

Ionah was different. Her whole countenance changed the moment she saw her son. Lifting her gloved hand, she reached out for him. "Dalain, darling."

The lines around Dalain's mouth softened, and he took his mother's hand, allowing her to draw him closer. She ran her fingers down his cheek, tutting as her fingers trailed over the stubble on his chin.

Raziel stepped down to greet his monarchs. In his shadow Hedriel followed, his head bowed.

The emperor's piercing gaze skipped over Raziel and landed straight on to Hedriel. "Come here, boy. Stand before me like a man."

"Ze'hyrn, is that how greet your nephew who has been miraculously returned to us?"

Hedriel shifted, his eyes darting between his aunt and uncle. The emperor huffed, crossing his thick arms against his chest. "You hurt, boy?"

"No, Great One," Hedriel murmured.

"The rest of your party?"

"Dead, Emperor."

"The Saemorish plans?"

Hedriel's panicked eyes looked over Lyssandra's shoulder. Konrad stood behind her. She wasn't entirely sure how Hedriel hoped how Konrad might help him.

"Only time will tell, Great One," Hedriel settled on saying.

The emperor turned to see where Hedriel's gaze had strayed to. Lyssandra found herself falling into dark, cold pools.

He's performing. He cares very little that his nephew has been returned, Lyssandra's mind whispered.

Lyssandra looked to the prince again. Hands shaking, Hedriel averted his gaze from the emperor.

Hedriel knows his uncle didn't want him returned. Lyssandra bit down on the inside of her cheek, wishing her brain would stop supplying her with these horrible thoughts. *Is the emperor disappointed that Hedriel is alive?*

The empress reached out with a gloved hand and gripped Hedriel's chin gently. "I believe there are Saemorish here who are responsible for the return of our beloved nephew, husband. I greatly desire to speak with them."

The emperor snorted, his attention off his son and nephew. He took half a dozen steps before he spoke again. "As you will, my dear. Come, Raziel, to the strategy table. Attend to your studies, Dalain."

Without a last glance, the emperor strode away. Watching him, Dalain relaxed his shoulders. He turned ruefully to Hedriel, whose downcast eyes were fixed upon the ground.

"Dalain, sweetling, your father ..." Whatever the empress was going to say about the emperor was drowned out by the sound of an Imperial Army. Men dismounted tired steeds. Officers shouted orders in a bid to organise ranks out of the chaos.

Standing on shaking legs, Lyssandra turned to speak to Antonella and Konrad when she caught sight of a little shadow. She should have thought about Markos' whereabouts the moment Hedriel warned her about the Imperial Army's impending arrival. The Black Prince and his advisors had been busy, and talons knew what the boy had been up to.

"Markos," Antonella groaned.

Markos had obviously been adventuring with his free afternoon. His clothes were askew, his cheeks ruddy, and his curls were covered in twigs, moss and dirt. Somehow, he managed to get his way between the ranks of the army and almost to the empress' gigantic stallion.

A guard dressed in impeccable finery grabbed his wrist as he went to touch the reins of the empress' horse. The little mischievous face twisted into an indignant frown. Most of the men of Tacebia camp had given him space to play with their animals, as he seemed to be blessed with an ability to tame anything.

Lyssandra cried out in dismay. The empress' bodyguard couldn't be expected to be told about the little imp. He would act to protect the monarch.

"His shoe is going to slip!" Markos cried out as the guard lifted him so that his feet dangled in the air.

Thankfully Dalain was nearby, still staring at his father's back in irritation. He didn't even turn his face towards the bodyguard. "Let him go."

Empress Ionah's red lips parted in surprise to see a grubby little boy wriggling in her guard's hold. "Another one of Raziel's finds?" she asked.

Dalain sighed. "Yes. He's a stolen blessed one. Put him down, Grimm."

The guard looked from his prince to the empress. At Empress Ionah's small nod, he gently lowered the boy. The moment his legs touched the ground, Markos darted between the empress and her stallion to hide behind Dalain's legs. Two large eyes watched the guard from behind the prince.

"His shoe is going to slip," Markos repeated. "His front hoof is hurting."

"Your Majesty?" Grimm murmured.

"Check it," Empress Ionah said.

The guard grunted, grabbing the reins of the black stallion. He smoothed a hand down the horse's neck and then bent to encourage it to give him his leg. He stared down at the hoof, brow furrowing. "The boy is right."

The empress smiled, but the warmth of her expression didn't reach her eyes. "Take him to my tent once it is erected. Bathe and feed him. Then I'll test him further."

"Mother, I think Raziel is the one best to make judgements on the care of the child," Dalain said.

The empress smiled again, her expression thawing. "Sweetling, I'm best to decide what is for the good of the realm."

"I don't want a bath." Markos' fingers tightened around Dalain's leg, his knuckles going white. There was no dissuading the empress. Dalain was forced to allow one of the empress' men to take Markos and escort him to her tent.

Lyssandra swallowed thickly, wishing she had the courage to implore the empress to be kind. Court was no place for a child, and Marcus had been through enough in his short life.

Heart still hammering in her chest, Lyssandra could only bow her head once more as the empress turned to approach her with the swoosh of her skirts. "I find myself surprised to see Fiora's girl here, since the contract between Saemore and Nezaha was callously flung to the side. Saemore has not shown themselves as a friend to Nezaha."

Closing her eyes, Lyssandra drew in a steadying breath, her mind scrambling to find the correct words to appease the empress. Alas, all her training had fled her mind.

"Are you without words, girl? Won't you even look me in the eye?"

"No, Empress." Lyssandra shook her head, wishing to be anywhere but under the empress' direct gaze. Feeling she had no choice, she lifted her eyes. "It seems our countries find themselves at an impasse."

The empress' laugh was hollow. "I wouldn't call the current political tensions between Saemore and Nezaha an impasse. It's war, child."

Lyssandra flinched, for the first time wondering that as a daughter of a disgraced princess, did her life hold any value that could be used against her king? Would her death be celebrated in the streets of Nezaha just as Rikar Tallermayne's had? She clasped her hands in front of her, lowering her chin a fraction.

"First Saemore betrays us in favour of our mutual enemy Aurelia, and then they take one of our own and slaughter a peaceful delegation."

"The people of Correllain might say that vengeance has already been meted out." Lyssandra cursed her disobedient tongue. She had worked hard throughout her training to curb its unruliness. Sometimes it seemed to still have a mind of its own.

"Hmm ..." The empress sounded unimpressed. "Walk with me."

Sending a furtive glance behind her, Lyssandra caught Antonella's eye and then Konrad's. *If anything should happen to me*, Lyssandra longed to say, *run*.

Lyssandra had very little choice but to fall into step behind the empress. Her guards followed a respectful three paces behind them. Lyssandra still felt it was too close.

"Tallermayne family: what can you tell me?"

"The Tallermaynes?" This was not the question Lyssandra was expecting. The empress' tone was clipped. It was the voice of a woman already planning battle strategies, and Lyssandra was her chosen informant. She could only assume it was well-known that she had met many of the Tallermaynes before. "Edvern is not like the average ..."

"I don't need to know about Edvern. He's not a Tallermayne. He was stolen—"

"Edvern will always see himself as one of them." Lyssandra wasn't willing to let the empress' sharp tone cow her. She had promised herself she would not be the cause of more hurt to Eddi. "You can't change that about him. Once you get underneath his mask, he's ... sweet. I refuse to be used against him."

"*Sweet.*" The empress spoke the word as if tasting it on the tip of her tongue. She paused, the planes of her face harsh as she studied Lyssandra. Under the empress' scrutiny Lyssandra felt like a bug to be squashed under the toe of a boot. "And the other Tallermaynes. What has Edvern told you about his *family*?"

"Whatever you disliked about Rikar Tallermayne, Edvern will always remember him fondly."

The empress lifted her eyebrow, and it took everything for Lyssandra to carry on.

"His relationship with Alaxen seems ... conflicted. Alaxen raised him, and from what I gather, struggled when his wife died."

"Some chit with connections to Nezaha." The empress sniffed. "It was quite the scandal when we found out they wed."

"Moira hates Edvern ... She'll harm him."

"Unsurprising. She's an evil, overbearing woman. And his cousins?"

"His cousins?" Edvern spoke little of his cousins. Lyssandra was under the impression it had been some time since he had seen them. She had met them both on numerous occasions. A few years ago, Alaxen Tallermayne had been keen to foster diplomatic relations with Saemore. It seemed he was pressuring his sons for this life rather than that of a rider.

Bastian had been quiet and stern, while his younger brother Kendrick liked to talk. He also liked action and had caused quite a headache with his father during negotiations.

"Edvern didn't speak much of his cousins, other than to say he was raised alongside them. I doubt they would have been thrilled to be in the company of a bastard younger cousin."

"Are the cousins trustworthy?"

Lyssandra blinked. This wasn't the type of questioning she was expecting. Empress Ionah's interrogation had a purpose. "I didn't dislike either of them."

"I didn't ask for a diplomatic answer, girl," the empress snapped. "I was inquiring if they would betray Moira."

"Their uncle and father both have," Lyssandra pointed out. "Bastian is studious, diligent and rarely jests. Alaxen wanted him to try his hand at diplomacy. He was a force to be reckoned with in negotiations."

"Is that so?"

"Moira put an end to Alaxen's aspirations for his sons. Bastian is a strategist for the riders." Ellrahera had been gleeful when she heard the news that Bastian would no longer be included in diplomatic talks.

"His current occupation and exile in Irani are known to us," the empress said, with a listless wave. "I want to know the younger Tallermaynes' potential value to us."

"Moira has alienated every single member of her living family." Lyssandra's memory went back to the day she saw the Tallermaynes together last. She could see the pallor of Edvern's face, his uncle ushering him away. Kendrick had covered his vulnerability at witnessing his uncle's execution with a joke. His older brother had rammed an elbow into his ribs. Lyssandra had not missed the tears in Kendrick's eyes, nor the trembling in Bastian's hands. "Kendrick is ... not unaffected as he would have everyone think. Whatever course Bastian decides to take, he'll follow his brother. Even into the grave."

"It may be the key to tumbling Moira Tallermayne from her throne is through her own bloodlines." The empress' stern eyes turned away from Lyssandra to stare out into the forest. "If Edvern is truly what I hope he is, the winds are changing. He'll have an enemy in all courts until he can establish himself."

"Edvern wants no throne or power," Lyssandra said. And she knew in the depths of her heart that this statement was true.

Empress Ionah's eyes left the tree line, her red lips tugging into a smile. "And that's why the Father Dragon will give it to him. The emperor will keep him alive long enough to use the power he has been granted ..."

The depths of the empress' eyes were cold. Lyssandra heard the threat clearly. As long as Edvern's power could be exploited by Nezaha, he'd be safe.

"Of course, Great One." Lyssandra bowed her head in deference. Better the empress thought her a simpering fool than someone who had their own convictions. Pressing her hands together, she was determined to start building Edvern a network of supporters within the Nezahrian camp.

The empress' lips parted. "I see we understand one another."

CHAPTER 13

Return to the Spire

EDVERN

Numbness crept through Edvern's body when Taseria gave her reports on the number of citizens who had succumbed to the cold. It did not subside during their meagre meal, or when Bea ordered him to sleep.

Lying on sackcloth flung over brittle straw, he watched his uncle diligently whittle while taking the first watch. Edvern had no idea what his uncle was making. There were half a dozen pieces no larger than pebbles.

The dragon riders were not the only ones who had abandoned the once great city to its fate. The sages had also slipped away in the night. Taseria found survivors in the temples looting whatever treasure or scraps they could find. Her revulsion had been clear as she described to Alaxen how she shooed away the 'diseased rats pilfering Aurelia's wealth'.

Taseria's repugnance turned to loathing when Edvern commented it was the failures of the dragon riders and sages that were responsible for the people's suffering. Who were the real rats of Aurelia? He had little love for the sages; he could not fathom them leaving Gytall when their purpose was the well-being of the people. Their care and their taxes were all a farce. When Alaxen had grunted his agreement, Taseria left to fly the perimeters, despite the fact Moira was long gone. Alaxen let her go.

Hands stilling on his project, Alaxen spoke into the dark. "Your body needs rest."

Lifting his head, Edvern could see his uncle's expression change from stoic to troubled. He rose from his sack. "I'll take the next watch."

"You've not slept." Alaxen looked over to Bea; the old woman slumbered like a stone.

Edvern stepped past his uncle. "Neither of us will tonight, yet both of us pretend sleep and watches are necessary. I'm getting air."

"It wasn't your fault, Eddi boy." Edvern halted by the door, unable to look back at his uncle. Alaxen's throat bobbed. "Those poor girls ... It wasn't your fault."

"I left."

"Staying would have been your doom. Moira planned to have you assassinated."

Edvern swallowed, trying to dislodge the terrible imaginations of Larah and Ellie's final days. They'd barricaded themselves in the basement. They must have been terrified. Without another word, he opened the door and stepped into the cold night air.

His hands found their way to the dyrathakin egg securely tied to his belt. In his fingers it remained cold and lifeless. This dyrathakin was not meant for him.

"Darkness has descended on Gytall," Edvern whispered, looking to the sky and finding Aryis shining brightly. But it was to her consort he spoke. The prayer was not an ancient formula of correct words, but those from his own heart and mind. "Lord Qavi, lord of the darkest hour, if you're listening, come soon. The people are scared. I'm scared. I beg your guidance and Aryis' wisdom."

Alynta appeared at his side, slinking from the shadows. She lifted her snout, scenting the air.

"You won't find what you're looking for here," she said.

"The water wyrms will come again." Edvern leaned his head back against the wall of Bea's home.

"It is a sign that dragons are declaring war," Alynta said. "On whose side they are on ... I do not know."

"I have to go back," Edvern whispered. "To the spire, to walk those halls one last time."

"It's why I have abandoned my hunt for the night." Alynta pressed herself closer to Edvern's side.

Having nothing to say, Edvern rose and began the long walk home. His life had been overshadowed by Gytall Spire and those who ruled. He didn't know why he felt a great need to return to the hornets' nest, only that he must. If Moira had left dragons or prisoners behind, he needed to free them. He could not bear the weight of responsibility for yet more unnecessary deaths.

The wind was bitingly cold as they made their way through the deserted streets. He tossed his cloak aside and let his wings unfurl. Heat prickled his skin, and Alynta brushed herself along his side to get closer.

As the iron gates of the Gytall Spire loomed over them, Alynta bounded off. She prowled along the perimeter, nose to the earth, ears alert.

Edvern halted to wait for the dyrathakin's verdict.

"What do you sense?" Edvern asked as Alynta returned, her ears flat against her head. She quivered under his touch. "What is it?"

"I sense nothing," Alynta replied. "Absolutely nothing. Not even a heartbeat of a rat."

Edvern didn't have the words to make the dyrathakin feel better. "I have to do this," he murmured, stepping forward. He pressed his palms to the iron of the gate and stepped inside. Alynta squeezed through the opening after him, a soft whine escaping her. Grateful for her presence, Edvern offered her a tiny smile.

Frost on the dying grass crackled under the soles of his boots as they made their way through the silent training yards. At the base of the spire, he paused and lifted his chin to the very top of the tower that had cast a shadow over his existence.

"It may take more than the death of one human to free dragons. But she will fall," Alynta said. She flicked her long tail, her eyes glinting in the dark. "Evil always fails."

A smile tugged on Edvern's lips. Alynta had not yet learned that in the epic battle between good and evil, evil sometimes won. Besides, the heroes weren't the heroes in everyone's story. Sometimes they were the villains. He wondered in how many stories he featured as the villain.

"I couldn't afford a sweet-smelling candle for my father … Tonight the spire is my offering to my dead." Edvern moved forward, his heart filling with dread. He eyed Alynta. If the dyrathakin was correct and there wasn't even a rat … the best he could do was destroy the symbol of dragon rider oppression in the doomed city. It should not remain standing while the people fell.

"A great blessing indeed," Alynta said, prowling forward.

Edvern followed her into the dark, along the stone pathways and around the gaping entrances around the back. Moisture dripped from the tunnel walls as they entered. Sucking in stale air, he held on to hope and strained to hear the low rumblings and groanings of the dragons. The tunnels remained unnaturally quiet.

Sensing his unease, Alynta pressed her warm body closer to him. Together they moved forward, drawing what comfort they could from one another.

"Maybe they took all the dragons with them," Edvern whispered. It felt blasphemous to speak loudly. He doubted this fact. Not all dragons at the spire had a rider. The aggressive, those on the brink of retirement and the hatchlings were riderless. Moira's questioning hinted that she was losing control of the dragons. If this was true, it would be too risky to move dragons without the aid of a rider.

Flames licked up Edvern's palm, lighting their way.

It was a small yellow dragon with talons of brass that he spotted first. His amber eyes were open wide, his mouth slack and tongue lolling. Edvern halted in his tracks, blood soaking the toes of his boots.

"Sweet talons, something has ripped out his throat."

Edvern stepped forward and almost slipped. He looked down, drawing the fire to illuminate what he had tripped over. A human hand severed at the wrist. Female.

Turning on his heel, he spotted the young dragon rider lying face down. Impaled through her back and into the unforgiving stone, her body was pinned by a dragon master's sword.

"She tried to protect him," Alynta said.

It was a stark reminder that not all dragon riders were evil. Not long ago he had been an immature boy dreaming of the day he would join their ranks.

"There's hope that if this rider rebelled ... others might do so as well."

A quick gesture of Edvern's wrist, and flames danced along his fingers. The ground was littered with corpses, dragons and riders both. It had been a bloodbath. If Alaxen hoped that rebels were still among the riders of Gytall, he would be disappointed. Moira had purged her ranks.

Edvern chewed his bottom lip, then stepped forward, his boots echoing in the dark. Placing his foot on the first dead rider's back, he gripped the sword and tugged it from the body. With a wet squelch, the sword slid out; it seemed almost eager. Fire danced along his fingers and touched the blade. Under the light of his flames, he read the inscription: *unyielding in power.*

His power flared at his fingertips, heating the sword. He knew the words well. Knew this blade.

"Lady Moira was down here."

Edvern kicked the dragon rider over onto her back. Even in death there was a grim expression of determination on Kirra Deltmine's face. He froze, hardly daring to believe he was looking in his once friend's dead eyes.

"Do you know her?" Alynta asked.

"It seems like another lifetime ago. We were almost friends." Edvern turned away from Kirra's corpse. They could have been something more than friends. A strange sense of nothingness washed over him; guilt followed this acknowledgement. "Goodbye, Kirra."

Edvern's throat constricted as his gaze swept over the young dragon. He could have wept at the sight of the heavy chains holding the drake down. A thick, ugly collar had been clamped over his neck and forelegs. Trembling, he reached out and touched the dragon's snout. This had been an execution. This poor dragon had no way to protect himself.

He didn't want to continue, but his feet disobeyed him. Walking forwards, he saw another dragon, famous for his aggression, lying in his own spilled innards. By the light of Edvern's wings, his once magnificent silver scales were dim. Spears pierced his sides; a lance was embedded in his eyes. It seemed these injuries were not enough to quench the thirst of Moira Tallermayne. He had been gutted, sliced from the base of his neck to belly.

"Xyran." The dragon's name fell from Edvern's lips.

After a series of battles and losing his grandfather, Xyran struggled to take another rider. Deemed as troubled and unstable, he had been left to rot. Although Xyran would lash out at dragon riders, he never tried to harm Edvern. The silver dragon was affectionate to the hatchlings and was docile when he was among them.

"He tried to protect the young one," Alynta said.

"What have I done?" Edvern whispered in the dark. His vision blurred with his tears. He lifted his hand to stroke Xyran's snout. But as his tears dripped down his cheeks, his hand fell uselessly to his side.

"Eddi …"

"Moira will kill any potential allies as soon as they rise up." Edvern walked faster, taking in the bodies of riders and dragons alike. He hated how his voice started to take on a note of panic.

"Standing against evil takes fortitude," Alynta said. "This is not your doing."

"I set things into motion." Edvern shook his head, closing his eyes against the sight of the piles of bodies, both flesh and scaled.

"If you didn't steal my egg, you would never have hatched me," Alynta replied. "For the chance you have given me, I am grateful. We must take whatever comes, the good and … the bad."

Edvern had been told that there was strength that came in knowing you had looked into the face of despair and survived. His father called such people Qavi-blessed, those who had seen evil days and remained undaunted.

Swallowing a mouthful of bile, he paused, allowing his trembling to subside. Once calm he moved on, his strides taking a sense of purpose. From his lips he whispered the prayers he remembered, looking upon each slain dragon in the face. He would honour them with his life, or his death, if necessary.

There were ten slain dragons in total. The remnants, those that Lady Moira and Aurelia did not want. Edvern looked back through the tunnels, determined not to forget a face or name.

"Farewell, Vallyn, Torack, Xyran, Divien, Halle, Tarmine, Idarah, Coraxin, Zorun and Randael."

The sound of Edvern's voice faded away, and there in his empty chest, pain blossomed. Was there anyone in the known world who would mourn the loss of these dragons? Grief, the terrible monster she was, rose and welled within him. A scream of rage tore from his lungs. He screamed until his throat burned and his voice gave out.

He looked up, counting fifteen humans. Dragon masters and those yet to reach the rank. The men and women he had grown up with, those he had trained among. He whispered their names, committing their souls to the Father Dragon as well. Kirra Deltmine's name he left to last.

Beside him, Alynta lifted her own muzzle and let her own grief mingle with his in a symphony of mourning. Edvern had no way of knowing how long he stayed on his knees in the dirt and gore.

His wings crackled under the pressure of his lament. Flames licked up his arms, spiralling out of control. It was only right that the dragons burned, the humans who came to their defence with them.

Heat and power radiated off him, and the underground chambers shook. Once the fire tasted the blood and stone, the inferno took hold. It should have been impossible, but the fire only intensified.

Edvern's world became a wall of flames, heat, sizzling blood and bodies. Unsteady on his feet, he stood and watched as everything was consumed with his unquenchable fire.

Knowing that his own power would not harm him, Edvern turned away and calmly stalked from the spire's tunnels.

By the time he reached the entrance and made it out onto the grass, the dawn sun had risen, and fire was climbing up the spire. People had gathered outside of the gates to gaze upon the inferno. At the very front, Edvern spotted Alaxen.

He cared very little what he looked like, emerging from the burning tower, his wings of fire trailing behind him and rider's sword dripping blood in his hand. He continued toward the gate, his hand falling to his side to touch Alynta's coat.

Alaxen's eyes tracked his every movement, then returned to the greying skies. Following his uncle's gaze, Edvern spotted their three dragons wheeling. Now that his business with Gytall was finished, it was time to leave.

"They're all dead," Edvern said in an undertone.

Alaxen nodded, the news not unexpected. His uncle's eyes fixed on the sword; his breath hitched.

"The water wyrms of ice will return. You need to leave Gytall tonight," Edvern called out to the crowd. He ignored the murmurs that rippled around him. They could each decide for themselves what was best for them. With his warning, his job in Gytall was done.

At Alaxen's side, Taseria pushed open the gate. Without pausing, Alynta squeezed her body through, and Edvern joined her on the other side.

"We need to go," Edvern said without pausing. "Now."

"We need to return to Bea's home. I'm not leaving her behind, not like this," Alaxen replied. The stern lines of his face were unreadable as he looked over the people of Gytall. Good people were capable of great cruelty and violence when they were desperate. "Then we fly towards the Nezahrians."

"The Nezahrians!" Edvern scoffed. "Uncle, they would rather skin you and roast your innards than listen to you."

"I have faith they'll not harm you."

"Faith? What good is *faith*?" The next words bubbled from Edvern's mouth before he could stop them. "You must find another way ..."

"You *command* me, boy?" Alaxen drawled, his gaze hardening. Nearby, the dragons landed. They swayed, their rumbles giving sound to their dark amusement at the standoff. Lyrus snapped his jaws at Edvern for his rudeness.

Taseria whistled, shaking her head and took a few steps away. She clapped Alaxen on the shoulder as she passed him. "Trust me, Lord Alaxen, leave this one behind. Tie him to the gates. He'll cause only trouble."

Edvern rounded on her. "Tell me. Other than be born a bastard, is there something I have done to offend you?"

"Your whole kind reeks of filth." Taseria spat on the ground, spittle landing near the toe of Edvern's boots. "Rats don't belong on the backs of dragons."

Alynta bared her teeth, but Edvern laid a comforting hand on her head. "You're welcome to stay behind."

"Enough!" Alaxen snapped. "Keep your tongue civil, woman. Edvern is my nephew."

"Keep your distance, Edvern Tallermayne." Snapping her teeth shut, Taseria curled her lip as she eyed Edvern up and down. Her expression shuttered as her gaze lingered on his wings of fire and the dyrathakin at his side. She turned her back without another word.

Edvern swallowed thickly, averting his gaze so that he was staring at Taseria's retreating form, then to the bedraggled crowd watching on curiously. "Why do you keep her around?"

"She's skilled," Alaxen said, brushing his hands through his hair. "She can be antagonistic, but she's a member of the rebellion."

"The Nezahrians will kill you. I need you by my side. Alive. We have the egg from Cynedir ... We need the one in Navilla."

"The eggs are useless without the Uhl'hari to hatch them."

"We can't go to Nezaha. And I can't do this without you!" It was true. They didn't have the strength to challenge Moira yet. Edvern knew this. But he hated the idea of returning to the camp of his enemy. An enemy he had been taught from the cradle to fear.

While he had some assurance that the Black Prince would not harm him, he knew that Alaxen's and Taseria's lives would be forfeit. If they came with him to Nezaha, they would be stripped from him.

"You need Raziel Yavari. And as loath as I'm to admit, so do our people. Our only hope is that he would consider what is at stake because of you."

As Alaxen spoke, Edvern turned to cast his eyes over the burning inferno of Gytall Spire. The grief he felt discovering the bodies of the riders and their vulnerable dragons dulled to a numbing throb. It couldn't be real, he decided. It was a bad dream. Surely Moira would not continue her assault against her own people.

Grey ash fell from the sky, swirling around their heads. Edvern's lips seemed to be frozen together, unable to utter a parting prayer. Without saying another word, he turned his back on his childhood home and walked away.

They found Bea tottering about her cottage, packing worn packs with whatever salvageable goods she had. She moved sluggishly, her gait uneven as she barked orders at Edvern. Concerned for the old woman, he hastened to obey, eager to keep his hands busy. From the corner of his eye, he observed her.

"Bea, are you well?" Taseria asked the question that was on everyone's lips.

"It's the damnable cold," Bea grumbled. "Freezing my bones and cooling my blood. Pack my best tea, Ed. Not that old, battered teapot. My nice teapot! Who taught this boy how to pack?"

"He's packing like a rider. We're fleeing for our lives," Alaxen growled. "Not for a merry trip to a summer house."

"Dirk had three summer houses," Bea replied, hobbling forwards with the use of a cane. "This old lady wants Dirk's good teapot and tea."

Edvern looked up from where he was attempting to pack a suitable rations bag, each teapot in a hand. He looked from the old woman to his uncle, trying to decipher which teapot he should pack.

"Pack Lady Hillyard's teapot." Alaxen's frown deepened at the sight of Bea's cane.

Edvern obeyed, pinching his lips together to stop laughing at the look of defeat on his uncle's face.

Bea reached out with her walking stick and rapt his knuckles. "Careful with it. It's a relic!"

"Word of my betrayal has reached other riders," Alaxen replied. His tone was gruff and low. It was one his uncle used when he thought subordinates were being unreasonable. "We need to move quickly."

Grumbling, Bea turned around and left the room. "Need to find Dirk's other cloak …"

Edvern looked back towards his uncle to see if there were any further instructions. Dark eyes shimmering, Alaxen stared at the open door where Bea had disappeared.

"It's near," Taseria whispered. "I'm sorry."

Alaxen remained frozen, his expression broken. "We'll get her somewhere safe and warm."

"We can't very well take her into battle," Edvern pointed out.

Alaxen's shoulders slumped. "Sometimes the loss is so great, the heart can never let go. After all these years, my soul still screams for my Thleah."

Edvern wasn't sure if Alaxen was talking about Bea or himself. There was something haunting about Alaxen's countenance. He intimately understood Bea's grief. What was it like, loving someone so dearly their loss rent an unfillable hole in your heart?

Alaxen started out of his reverie, his eyes returning to Taseria. "Thleah left me two sons. They're stationed in Irani in the palace of the king. The longer I delay, the more danger they're in."

"The palace is a cushy job with no danger," Edvern said.

"They're my sons, Edvern," Alaxen replied. "They're all I have left. My mother wouldn't hesitate to …"

Edvern bit his tongue, wanting to spew back that his cousins could hang for all he cared. They had done nothing when his father was in trouble. None had stood for Rikar. None had stood by him.

Alaxen's face was so full of pain that Edvern felt as if a bucket of iced water had been dumped over his head. His cheeks flushed with shame, and he hoped that he would never love another as fiercely as Alaxen loved Thleah and his sons. His uncle's love was his curse and downfall.

Bea returned, wrapping in her tattered dragon rider's cloak around her shoulders. "Your cousins are both skilled dragon riders. You're going to need as many as you can gather."

Edvern grimaced.

"Your cousins can't help you if they're dead." Bea waggled her cane at Edvern.

"We rescue Bastian and Kendrick," Edvern said. He turned back to face Alaxen, who wore the expression of an overindulgent parent. Taseria was glowering at him. "And then what? Dump me on the Black Prince?"

"Eddi," Alaxen murmured.

"Don't call me that." Edvern glowered. He stomped over to Izorah and climbed onto her back begrudgingly. His blue dragon swayed her head back and forth and bit at his heels. "And I'm very much aware that I'm on my own."

"When not properly tamed, fire mages can be terribly unruly," Bea grumbled. "I'd much rather die in my own home."

Alaxen took Bea's elbow and led her to Lyrus. He was quite the gentleman as he helped the little old lady mount his drake. Edvern felt another rush of shame. He was the youngest rider; he was supposed to help the vulnerable in their party. It was his uncle who had thought of Bea's needs before his own.

"We can do better than an old, cold cottage," Alaxen replied.

"Call it as it is," Bea said. "My hovel isn't much. It has the structural integrity of dragon dung."

Anyis Lady of Hope

*What could possibly be more delightful than using one's
opponents' moral codes against them? Find the weakness in
authority and exploit those serving under its thrall.*

A LADY'S GUIDE TO DIPLOMACY

CHANTILLY YARROW

Chapter 14

War Wraith

Lyssandra

Soft chords of an Euquallian tune faded as Lyssandra entered her tent. Not wanting any further Nezahrian attention, she'd fled the moment Empress Ionah dismissed her. A soft sigh escaped her lips as she sunk down onto her pallet.

Having grown up among the etiquette of diplomats, Antonella returned her attention to the Nezahrian fiddle that lay across her lap. Long, elegant fingers plucked at the strings. She would not press for details until Lyssandra was ready. Konrad, however, a soldier at heart, had no such compunctions.

"What's our status?"

"Status?" Lyssandra blinked at her cousin, watching as he shifted from one foot to the other. Talons, he was already plotting, preparing for a fight. "We're safe ... for now," Lyssandra admitted. "The empress wanted to know about the Tallermaynes."

"The Tallermaynes?" Konrad paced the length of their tent.

"Eddi?" Antonella asked, brow furrowing as she plucked another chord.

"His cousins."

Konrad frowned, pausing his track through their tent. "From the intelligence we received in Tarramine, the Tallermayne brothers aren't actively involved within the spires. Weren't they sent to the Aurelian king's palace?"

Lyssandra nodded her head. "Our sources confirmed they were sent to Irani. I spoke with Kendrick Tallermayne the morning he left."

"I have a distinct feeling we are missing a piece of the puzzle," Antonella murmured.

"I'm sure we'll find out sooner or later," Lyssandra replied, smoothing her hand down the soft material of her cloak.

"And Markos. What are we going to do about him?" Antonella pressed the palms of her hands together.

"There's not a lot we can do," Konrad said. "He's Nezahrian born. A blessed one, who was supposed to have been given to their temples. To the Nezahrians he was stolen."

"I'll speak with Raziel," Lyssandra found herself saying before she could think her words through. "If anyone can convince the empress to give Markos up ..."

Antonella sighed heavily, her shoulders hunching. "I think we all knew Markos was destined for the temple the moment the Black Prince found him. It's just a matter of which temple they send him to."

"I'll have words with Raziel anyway." It was the very least that Lyssandra could do.

"Up! Up! Up!" The rays of the dawn sun had not yet crested the horizon when Prince Hedriel burst through the flap of the tent. Bread halfway to her mouth, Lyssandra paused, taking in the prince's dishevelled appearance. She blinked the sleep from her eyes, dreading whatever her early morning messenger might say.

"Good morning, prince," Lyssandra said, lifting her hand to stifle a yawn. "To what do we owe the pleasure?"

Puffing, Hedriel waved away her greeting. He straightened his shoulders. "Lady Stamos, I fear I must speak with you."

"I suppose you have a good reason for bursting in on us," Lyssandra replied, dropping her breakfast to her lap. "A prince ought to show more decorum."

Hedriel flushed, averting his gaze as Konrad rose from Antonella's pallet shirtless and alert. "You of all people should know some things cannot be helped."

"What is it?" Konrad snapped.

"Begging your pardon ..." The red in Hedriel's cheeks deepened, his eyes boring into the canvas of the tent as Antonella rose. She was only half dressed. "One of my uncle's war wraiths has returned and ..."

Lyssandra raised the bread to her lips, bit down and chewed slowly. Talons, it was much too early to play mind games.

"And?" Antonella prompted, pushing her curls away from her face.

"I think it might be wise for Saemore to have a representative present." Back stiff, Hedriel still refused to make eye contact.

"Any idea where this war wraith has come from?" Lyssandra could see Konrad's mind working through the puzzle. Their safety relied heavily on the imperial couple's acceptance of them. Ill news for the Nezahrians might mean a swift execution for them.

"Overheard Edvern's name along with the town of Vancarde."

Lyssandra leapt from her place, breakfast forgotten. She nodded briefly to Konrad and Antonella before pulling on a cloak over her rumpled clothing. If the Black Prince had any scrap of news about Eddi, she wanted to hear it. Especially before any of his potential enemies.

Hedriel followed her out into the cold morning, but Lyssandra didn't slow. She continued through the camp, determined to reach the Black Prince's tent. The fate of her friend worried her so much that she did not pause to consider she might find herself in imperial company.

By the time she reached the tent, Lyssandra began to have second thoughts. Faelowyn curled around the base of the tent, Odharn snuggled at her side. Lifting her large, crowned head, the black dragon watched their approach. She rumbled, plumes of mist lifting from her warm body. Odharn's hind legs and tail twitched as he slumbered, his breathing deep and gravelly.

"He's dreaming of flying," Hedriel whispered at Lyssandra's side. "See how his eyes move under his eyelids."

Despite her nerves, Lyssandra's lips curled into a smile. Odharn huffed in his sleep, and he rolled, pressing closer to Faelowyn's side. The black dragon yawned and closed her eyes.

If the black dragon was at peace, then surely the news couldn't be bad. Right?

"My uncle, the emperor, cannot abide dragons," Hedriel said, his shoulders relaxing. "If they're out here, he won't be within."

Prince Hedriel left the rest unspoken. The emperor might be missing, but that didn't mean that the empress wasn't with the Black Prince.

All thoughts of treading lightly fled the moment Lyssandra stepped over the threshold of Raziel's war tent. A roaring filled her ears, her breath catching in her throat while the world tilted on its axis.

Ignoring the empress, who sat primly drinking, Lyssandra approached. The war wraith stood apart from Raziel and Symmeon, who were studying maps.

"I believe the pair of you have met." Raziel cleared his throat.

Lyssandra could not find her voice to reply. The war wraith inclined his head, his dark scarf concealing his face. But there was no hiding those emerald eyes ... His golden curls were now dark, and he looked menacing in his black leather uniform. But there was no denying who those eyes belonged to.

"Zanniel?"

An elegant hand, sans the colourful paint, drew down the scarf. The smile remained the same, all but confirming his identity as the potter of Vancarde.

"My lady." The voice sent shivers down her spine.

"Your hair."

"I am a blessed one. Nezahrians still have the ancient magics. I can change my appearance at will." Emerald eyes blazed with power as Zanniel's hood fell back. How had Lyssandra missed the tapered ears?

"Raziel's messenger has been telling us the most interesting tale of Vancarde." The empress' tone was sharp. Clearly, she remained unamused by Edvern and Lyssandra's misadventures. "The loss of the Tallermayne boy was unacceptable, Raziel."

Lyssandra's gaze could not be torn from the smug expression on Zanniel's face. "I'm sure Zanniel's anecdotes are delightful," she said, gritting her teeth. Blood rushed back to her cheeks, humiliation washing through her.

"You should be honoured that I'm revealing the identity of one of my spies, Zanniel Oberion," Raziel said. He nodded at Symmeon, who shifted his weight and glared at the war wraith. There was something she was missing. "Especially considering his counterpart was murdered in Vancarde."

"Counterpart? Murdered?" Goodness, it was too early for mind games.

"To be fair, Black Prince, Lyssandra might have already been in my bed or in jail at the time of death."

Lyssandra drew in a deep breath, meeting his eyes and refused to be cowed. And then her stomach clenched as she thought of how she had been lured into the bed of one of Nezaha's legendary spies. Was that what he had been telling Empress Ionah and the Black Prince? War wraiths were crafty indeed, famous for their ability to infiltrate and their high-profile assassinations. She had no clue that Zanniel was anything more than a simple-minded potter. She had severely underestimated him.

"Your uncle was the captain of the guard." Lyssandra could have cursed herself. She sounded like an inexperienced girl, naïve in the ways of the world.

While his expression remained the same, Zanniel's eyes hardened. Something dangerous lurked just beneath the surface. "I played my part of the wandering nephew very well. The captain gave me a credible story, and I kept his many sins secret."

"You knew?" Lyssandra's voice changed to have a strangled note. "You knew the dyrathakin egg would hatch."

"And if it didn't ... one less Tallermayne in this world. And Nezaha had an egg to find a more worthy candidate."

Some strange emotion roiled in Lyssandra's belly. Zanniel didn't give Edvern the egg out of compassion, in the hope that they would escape and survive. It had been an experiment, and if she and Edvern lost their lives, the spy would have made alternative plans.

She stormed up to him, her hand raised. Before she could slap him as he so richly deserved, he reached out and grasped her wrist. "Careful, Princess."

"I am not a princess," Lyssandra hissed. "I'm a ..." *No longer a Saemorish royal diplomat*, she thought as the words died on her tongue. She lifted her chin, staring at him and then the empress. "I'm a criminal, a fugitive."

"You're a foolish girl, that's what you are, who could be fooled by a few kind words," Zanniel said. "I told you to give Edvern to the Black Prince."

"I wasn't handing my companion over to die!" Lyssandra snarled. "I'm not a heartless monster."

"We wouldn't have killed him," Symmeon said, finally breaking his silence. He winced at Lyssandra's glare.

Lyssandra turned back to the Black Prince. He was watching the exchange as if it was providing him with an immense amount of entertainment. She cursed him.

"We didn't know what your plans were ..." Lyssandra stressed. "If you hurt his dyrathakin ..."

"We would never harm a dyrathakin," the empress said, lifting a goblet of a thick red wine. From across the tent, Lyssandra could smell the heady scent of wild berries. Her head spun.

"Rikar's letter quite clearly said to go to the Black Prince," Raziel said. "If he was smart ..."

"Edvern never read them," Lyssandra cried.

"The fool."

Lyssandra wretched her hand out of Zanniel's grasp. Before the spy could react, she stomped on his toe as hard as she could. The caps of his boots were made of metal, and the sole of her foot protested. But determined to show no signs of discomfort, she snarled in the spy's face, "Watch your tongue. He's my fool."

"Oh, I see," Zanniel said, one elegant eyebrow lifting.

"No. It's not like that," Lyssandra said, her traitorous mind telling her she very much wanted it to be like that between herself and Edvern. She wanted more than a drugged kiss, where she was almost insensible.

Zanniel's lips upturned into a smirk. "If you say so. Here, what can you tell us about the style of this scrap of information?"

Taking the parchment from Zanniel's fingers, Lyssandra carefully unfolded the missive and cast her eyes over the loopy handwriting. She read through the letter in silence twice over, noticing her reactions and thoughts. The style of the letter was consistent with her observations of Kendrick Tallermayne. Could the letter in her hand be authentic?

While the death of our uncle has greatly shaken members of our family, be not mistaken in thinking this letter was written in a moment of weakness. Directly after Rikar's execution, our grandmother, Lady Moira Tallermayne, deployed us to the royal palace of Irani. The position of palace guard has provided me and my brother some welcome relief from the rigors of dragon rider life.

When we arrived in Irani, we found ourselves with plenty of leisure time. I promptly applied myself to the research of the local area, of its art and history. The palace, of course, was Ullryk the Liberator's home, built as a gift to his Aurelian bride, Princess Saskah. The great liberator is quoted in saying his giant red dragon preferred the open skies and lush gardens of Irani. There's a book of poems written by him for his beloved Saskah. She loved the old lore, and so the gardens were built to celebrate the ancient temples and palaces of the region. The gardens survive to this day and provide a fascinating distraction. A perfect spot to visit if you are so inclined.

Bastian and I have done well for ourselves in Irani. We are looking forward to the night of the king's birthday ball. The event is to take place on the fourteenth week of winter on the night of the full moon. Alas, word on the king's guards' lips is our Euquallian neighbours will not be fond of our king's surprise.

Bastian and I have made arrangements to welcome friends if they desire to meet with us during the ball. If this does not work, we are content to make other plans.

Apparently, our puppet king sees himself toppling Moira and has commenced the beginnings of a rebellion. A startling influx of militia has entered Irani, and we have found ourselves increasingly on the outer. The presence of detained Euquallians fill us with grave concerns, especially for one General Eupheana. Bastian and I haven't seen any evidence of their continued living status in days.

All communications with our father, Lord Alaxen, ceased. Neither Bastian or I have had any word of our father's health or the political undertones of the spires. And so, I beseech whoever reads this to convey to him our good health and continued loyalty.

Further interesting information has been plied from our fellow guards. Edvern Tallermayne, my bastard cousin, has fled Gytall. While I applaud his daring, I fear that he may be in possession of information that could cause irrevocable harm. Deliver him to Nezaha, and let the Black Prince sort my wayward cousin out.

A militia family from Vancarde has come forward to make an official complaint to the king, stating Edvern was their bond slave and escaped, taking den dragons with him. Two dragons had to be put down.

With all sincerity,
Kendrick Tallermayne
Copy Nine

Aware that the empress and Raziel were observing her reactions, Lyssandra read over the letter a number of times. It seemed so very odd. When Princess Ellrahera was alive, it was she, the prime diplomat, whose opinion held weight. Her thoughts were to remain private and unheard.

She folded the parchment, her fingers lingering on the creases.

"Lady Lyssandra?" Symmeon hazarded.

"The Aurelian king is plotting a rebellion. The Euquallians are prisoners, and if we want to free them so they can't be used, the gardens during the ball is our best bet," Lyssandra said. "It isn't worded cleverly, but one could surmise that Kendrick and Bastian are working on a way to get the Euquallians out. Their plan hinges on outside communication that they have no guarantee of making."

"I had the same thoughts," Zanniel replied, his gaze sweeping over to the empress, who was very still. Lyssandra could see the dangerous gleam in the ruler's eyes. She was prepared to go to war and spill blood for her fellow countrymen. Eupheana of Euquall was her younger sister.

"His description of Lady Moira's actions towards her own family members tracks," she said. "Kendrick's sources are sound. Edvern escaped servitude and was sentenced to die in the dragon dens. We escaped. It was a military family he upset. Which, of course, Zanniel has already confirmed."

"Still can't understand why Edvern would sell himself into slavery. It seems desperate," Zanniel mused.

"Don't judge Eddi harshly. He was injured and under the impression he was to be employed to look after his ailing master until death ... They forced him to sign the documents while barely conscious." Lyssandra shook her head, remembering what Edvern was willing to tell. "It's easy to make a lapse of judgement when starved in the middle of winter."

"He could have come to us," the empress said, fussing with the fabric of her skirts.

"He doesn't speak a word of Nezahrian," Lyssandra said. "He's never left Gytall, and he had no money, no friends ..."

"He'll need to learn our language," Zanniel said. "It's imperative."

Lyssandra had had enough. Glaring at Zanniel, she demanded, "My sources said that there was news of Edvern. Are you or are you not wasting my time?"

Something Lyssandra said struck a nerve. The teasing light in Zanniel's eyes faded, and his expression froze. Symmeon's curt laugh was interrupted by a suspicious cough. She turned to face him, catching a touch of dark amusement in the curl of the older man's lips.

"Edvern has been seen," Raziel told her.

"That's wonderful news." For the first time in days, Lyssandra felt a stirring of hope. "He's alive."

"When I last saw him." Zanniel didn't particularly sound thrilled. "He's back to his old tricks."

Lyssandra blinked, cocking her head to wait for the rest of the story. Sometimes minimizing interruptions meant that people revealed more than they ought to. She assumed that Zanniel, being a Nezahrian spy, knew that.

"Raziel sent Zanniel to Cynedir to find the second dyrathakin egg," the empress said. She hid a smirk from behind her goblet. "He infiltrated the spire and had the egg in his possession."

"Before Eddi took it right out of his arms," Symmeon continued, saluting Zanniel with his own mug. "Imagine being bested by an untested rider."

"Edvern has the dyrathakin egg?" Lyssandra repeated. "Will it hatch for him too? Did you see Alynta?"

"I saw his dyrathakin," Zanniel said tightly, "and his bonded dragon, along with the company he is keeping."

Lyssandra lifted an eyebrow.

"He was with Alaxen Tallermayne. There was another rider in the area as well." Zanniel spat on the ground, his lips curling. "I managed to kill one of Tallermayne's captains ... Fergus ... The other two remained unaccounted for."

"Don't mind Zanniel," Symmeon said. "He's a little sore that he had to be rescued from drowning."

Lyssandra let the smile touch her lips. "Edvern saved *you*?"

She let the silence answer her question.

"The dyrathakin did, my dear." The empress took a sip of wine, her elegant brows rising at the blush on Zanniel's face. "Although Edvern did attempt a futile rescue of his enemy war wraith."

Lyssandra allowed herself a heartbeat to enjoy Zanniel's embarrassment.

"Your Majesty," Lyssandra said, turning towards the empress. "You suspected happenings in Irani, that your sister was in trouble? Is that why you were asking about the Tallermaynes?"

"Eupheana can look after herself. But yes, girl, I had the letter in my possession. What are the motivations of the Tallermayne boys? Are they helping Euquall so my sister is in their debt or something more nefarious?" Empress Ionah said. "What is it you think, daughter of the Spider?"

Lyssandra swallowed, thinking the name a little rich. She was a diplomat, not a spy. She worked in the light, not with the shadows. The empress would never believe a Tallermayne would help someone out of empathy.

"Maybe they're tired of war," Lyssandra said. "Or maybe they want to annoy King Oluvin or do something to stop their king's rebellion against their grandmother."

"The King Oluvin is a fool if he thinks he can use my people as hostages."

"Tallermaynes never do anything good," Zanniel muttered.

Lyssandra regarded him and shook her head. "Maybe they're just like you and me, searching for a way to survive the impossible circumstances they've found themselves in. Like you, they inherited this war. Maybe they want a shot for freedom."

Symmeon grunted, knuckles running along the map. "Question is, what does Oluvin want with Euquall?"

"The ships," the empress said. She sat up straighter, understanding lighting her eyes. "My father's royal navy and trading ships have large hulls with room for an army to move swiftly. It is indeed true that Euquall has metal weapons that spew fire and destruction without the aid of a dragon."

Cold dread washed through Lyssandra. She had heard rumours of the Euquallian king testing fire-breathing metals and powders. The empress was all but confirming the rumours. "King Oluvin hopes to ransom your people for this knowledge."

Empress Ionah inclined her head. "If my father, in his wisdom, has not buckled to pressure from my husband for these secrets, he will not give into Oluvin."

Lyssandra's heart raced. Here was an opening to find Edvern powerful allies if needed. "If we were to free the Euquallians, your people, would your father consider joining us in the fight against Moira Tallermayne?"

The empress plucked up her wine goblet, swirling it gently. "He may consider. But he must be approached with great care. My father, although a king of a small population, does not take well to threats or bribery."

"And the Tallermaynes?" Lyssandra asked.

"The young Tallermaynes would make for valuable prisoners," Ionah said. "Ze'hyrn would see them publicly beheaded as traitors. But those boys have dragons and seem to have information on who within Aurelia can make the cursed country collapse."

"They sound loyal to their father," Symmeon grunted. "If we can work out what side Alaxen is on ..."

"Alaxen has kept Edvern safe," Raziel said, glancing down at his hands. He turned his dark eyes towards Zanniel. "What do you make of them?"

"Alaxen risked his life to save Edvern," Zanniel muttered reluctantly. "He jumped into the freezing water in the middle of water wyrms."

If Alaxen wanted Edvern dead, he would have let him drown and be pulled apart. No one would blame him for not attempting a rescue.

"It is my opinion that Edvern Tallermayne is just the type of idiot to try and rescue his family. It seems to be a family trait," Zanniel said.

"Edvern is kind," Lyssandra replied, hiding her hands behind her back, hoping her nerves did not give too much away. She recalled the feeble attempts of Edvern's cousins trying to comfort him during his father's execution, how quickly Alaxen removed him from the scene. "The Tallermaynes aren't monsters."

"Ullryk's blood, Tallermayne blood, belongs to the powers of Nezaha. Centuries may have passed, but Ullryk's line will be brought to heel and

Aurelia ground into dust," Symmeon snarled. "My family is dead because of Tallermaynes. Why should I not destroy them?"

"Was it Bastian or Kendrick who murdered your loved ones? Or were they still little boys playing with toy soldiers twenty years ago?" Lyssandra asked lightly, turning to look back at the letter. "The cycle has to end, Symmeon. Your pain doesn't give you the right to hurt the next generation of Aurelians."

Symmeon scoffed.

Lyssandra's mind went back to the devastation of Hemmryn Vale, the dead and dying in the street. The deed had been committed by the Aurelians. But to do the same to the people who lived within Aurelia's borders ... did that make them no less evil?

Lyssandra had never thought of herself as a monster. But if Edvern's life was at risk, if her loved ones' lives were in danger, who knew what atrocities she might be capable of? If there was a way for her to survive the coming fight without becoming a villain, she needed to find a way. And quickly.

CHAPTER 15

A Lovely Death

EDVERN

The palace of Irani was the pride of the Aurelian people. Through the swirling mists, Edvern peered down in wonder at the king's residence. Set like an emerald jewel in the middle of grey barrenness, the boundaries of Ullryk's eternal summer spell were clear. The grounds of the palace were lush and vibrant; but the king's comfort did not extend to the town of Irani. While their puppet king enjoyed luxury, the people of the town were still living in the depths of winter.

Their mood was sombre as they flew high and further south. Edvern could see that his uncle was doing his utmost not to look down at the place his sons were stationed.

"You're going back for them," Edvern signed.

"I'm doing my best for both you and my sons." Alaxen's jaw tightened. "Below there's an abandoned hut."

"I sense no life. It's as he says: the hut is abandoned," Lyrus said. He turned and banked to land first. *"Rebel riders use this place from time to time."*

Edvern swallowed his bitterness, hating the way that envy coiled in his stomach. This was a part of himself that he despised. From the time he had been a small child, he had to battle his envious nature.

On the ground Alaxen had already dismounted and was helping a muttering Bea from Lyrus' back. When the old woman's feet were on the ground, he set off towards the hut, motioning everyone to stay quiet.

"Aren't you going to let him know it's safe?" Edvern asked Lyrus. He slipped from Izorah, his fingers automatically twining in Alynta's fur as he watched Alaxen scout the area.

Lyrus blinked lazily at him, lifting his snout slightly to scent the air. *"My rider likes to feel useful."*

"Humans need to have a sense of accomplishment," Tynum added wisely. He rumbled as Taseria reached up to scratch the sensitive skin under his jaw. *"Humans are simple creatures to train."*

A laugh burst from Edvern's lips, which he turned into a choked cough at Taseria's annoyed look. He stared straight ahead, struggling to keep the amusement from his expression.

"No one is home," Alaxen proclaimed when he returned. "There are hunting traps and a collection of firewood in the front garden."

Grumbling about her old bones and tired muscles, Bea hobbled toward the hut as fast as a woman of her age could move. Alaxen and Taseria followed her, speaking in hushed whispers. Not wanting to face another cold night, Edvern strode around the hut in search of the firewood. It had been left where his uncle had said, axe impaled on the chopping block. After a quick inspection of the pile, he selected the best pieces and took his bundle inside. Taking a piece in her jaws, Alynta followed on his heels.

As Edvern kicked open the door, Taseria and Alaxen's conversation ceased. Looking over his shoulder, Alaxen pointed to the room to his right. "Bea's through there. Go build a fire for her."

Edvern hefted his bundle and nodded.

"We won't go hungry. There's some dried meat and pickled vegetables," Taseria said.

Edvern suppressed a wince. He hated both options but was smart enough not to complain. He would be grateful that his belly would be full tonight. Too many of the common folk suffered during the lean months.

Taseria turned from the door and rummaged through another crate full of fabrics and materials.

"Do we have a plan?" Edvern asked, annoyed that he was being left out of the discussions. Alaxen needed to realise he wasn't a boy anymore.

"We're looking for anything of use to get us into the palace," Alaxen said. "Any ideas how we can break in?"

"I'd need to scope out the walls," Edvern muttered.

"Too risky." Alaxen shook his head. "You look Nezahrian, which may be dangerous in these parts. Taseria can go on the reconnaissance mission."

"I'm not a young dragon rider, General," Taseria snapped, turning from her position at the crate.

Edvern looked between the two dragon riders and decided that he didn't want to be involved in their argument. He stepped past his uncle with his bundle of wood, and Alynta silently padded after him.

In the next room, Bea was sitting in a pile of furs, her husband's cloak wrapped around her shoulders. She watched him move around, and Edvern felt a prickle of unease at being judged by the old woman.

"Well, get on with it," Bea said. "Build me a fire."

Edvern inclined his head and decided it was best to say nothing at all. He knelt on the floor, his knees popping in protest. Arranging the wood as he had been taught from boyhood, he glanced up at Bea before letting his power warm and curl about his fingers.

One heartbeat was all it took to light the fire, the power addictively warm and pleasant on his skin.

"My Dirk was a real Aurelian," Bea said. "He twisted water to his will."

Edvern swallowed back any hurt he might feel. A land of islands, Aurelia was deeply connected to water. Powers associated with water were a mark of national pride. He let the old woman's comment go.

"Do you miss him?"

"Every day my soul still screams for him. When I lay my head down at night, I hear his voice," Bea answered. She closed her eyes, looking old and weary. "I'll see him again soon. Of that, I am sure."

Edvern turned back to the fire, unsure how to answer her.

"Don't be so coy. Death at my age is a relief."

"I cannot begin to imagine," Edvern muttered. "I hope I never love like you have or Uncle Alaxen."

"Don't be a fool, boy!" Bea snapped. "You have your whole life ahead of you. The strongest force in this world is selfless, pure love in its truest form. Even if I had known that Dirk and I would only be given eight years, I still would have married him and suffered."

"I'll see what I can do about getting you something to eat." Edvern stood, brushing his hands on his pants. "Would you like me to make you some of your tea? It's been a long day ..."

Edvern let his words fade. In the back of his mind, he had a memory of his aunt explaining that sometimes old folk needed more consideration and patience. Alynta slunk towards Bea and lay down beside her, resting her chin in the old woman's lap.

"Tea would be ..." Bea blinked, rubbing her wrinkled hand against her eyes. "Yes, that's kind of you, boy."

"Alynta, are you coming?"

Raising her head, the dyrathakin blinked her large lavender eyes at Edvern. She blew warm breath through her nostrils, the fur of her belly briefly glowing. Instead of fire, Edvern felt soft waves of warmth from his dyrathakin.

Bea's lips parted in a contented sigh. "I see Dirk. He's coming for me. I feel his warm arms around me."

"I'll stay. Bea needs me." Alynta closed her eyes as gnarled fingers brushed her fur.

"Very well." Edvern tiptoed from the room to join Alaxen and Taseria. They were pulling supplies from trunks when he entered.

"I thought I would hunt for food. There's gear outside," Edvern said. "Bea would like some tea. It might cheer her up. She says she can see Dirk."

"No. I'll make the tea." Alaxen rose and shook his head, his eyes full of sorrow. He threw a bar of lye soap, which Edvern caught. "Your job is to go bathe."

"Fresh meat—"

"The stream is nearby; you aren't to go any further."

"Uncle—"

"Eddi, you reek of death and smoke. Your wings have destroyed your shirt. It's hanging in tatters around you. We'll have to pack extra clothing for you." Edvern knew this tone, and it wasn't the time to argue with his uncle. He nodded, clutching the soap in his hands. Alaxen was right; his skin was blackened with soot. His shirt was in ribbons.

"Scrub well. I'd hate to have to come in and assist." The lines around Alaxen's eyes crinkled with amusement. "It's been some time since I've washed a wriggly boy."

An unbidden memory, one of the earliest ones he had, surfaced in his mind. Edvern had been two when his cousins decided that using their father's best ink to tattoo themselves was a fantastic idea. Disaster followed. When Edvern escaped his nurse and found them, Kendrick decided that dying his hair would be lots of fun and dumped a bottle of ink over his head. Horrified at the sight of his small cousin covered head to toe in red, Bastian tried to confiscate the inks. Which resulted in the brothers fighting.

Distressed by his cousins wrestling, Edvern cried, which alerted Aunt Thleah the boys were up to no good. At the sight of a small child covered in red ink, Thleah had screamed in horror. It had fallen to a grumpy Alaxen to scrub Edvern clean while Thleah chastised her sons. To this day Edvern could remember the smell of Thleah's favourite soap while he sat in the tub. He could still feel the washcloth as his uncle frantically tried to get the red out of his skin.

Rikar came home exhausted from a mission to find his son still red, the bathing chamber floor covered in bubbles and Alaxen fuming, elbows deep in the tub. His father had laughed himself silly.

Edvern had a rosy hue for a week.

Following the narrow forest path towards the stream, he allowed his power to flood in his veins. His skin prickled with heat as he peeled off his dirty clothes. The frigid water steamed, hissing as he sunk into the depths.

Skin smarting, Edvern trudged back up the path to the hut. While he bathed, a linen towel had been left with a clean shirt and breeches. Alaxen's doing.

The hut was quiet when he returned. He stepped past the selection of nobleman's clothes laid out. He swallowed a lump; it had been a long time since he had been allowed to wear something other than a uniform or rags. He longed to run his hand down the silks and velvets but restrained himself. He didn't want to dirty them.

Edvern turned away and slipped into the room where they had left Bea.

The old woman was slumped in her furs, one of her gnarled hands clutching Dirk's precious cloak, the other gently clasped by Alaxen. Her eyes were shut, her face relaxed. A smile curled on her lips, and Edvern wondered what she was dreaming about. The teacup and kettle were left untouched.

Alynta tracked his movements, her tail twitching.

"Is Bea ill?"

At Edvern's question, Alaxen's head snapped up. It was in this moment, looking at the strange pallor of Bea's freckled skin, that he knew.

"Bea?"

"She's gone," Alynta said, lifting her head to look at him with her wise lavender gaze. "I stayed so she wouldn't pass alone."

"Why didn't you heal her?" Edvern asked. The floor seemed to move underneath him. He'd only just had a conversation with her. She had sat on her furs like an empress, making all sorts of remarks. And now she was ... dead.

Alaxen shook his head. "I wouldn't dare."

"She looks ..."

"Not all deaths are evil," Alaxen said gruffly. He leaned forward, pressing his lips to her papery skin. "She's slipped away surrounded by warmth and safety. She didn't want healing to prolong her life. If I attempted to help her, I suspect she'd be very angry with me."

"It's better than what most of us can expect," Taseria said.

Edvern turned to see that the other tracker had come to lean against the door frame.

Alaxen looked back to the still form of Bea. Wrapping her tighter in her husband's cloak, he took her in his arms. He whispered the prayers for the dead and went outside. Edvern followed his uncle at what he estimated was a respectable distance. By the time his uncle had begun to build a pyre from the leftover firewood, Taseria had found a pair of candles.

Inspired by the memory of how fond Bea was of her tea and kettle, Edvern returned to the hut. He picked up the cold tea and went to the pyre.

"Peace, go with you," Edvern said, staring into the greying face of the old woman. Then, ever so gently, he poured the tea out onto the pyre. "Wherever you are, I hope Dirk greeted you. I know you missed him."

At Alaxen's nod, he touched his fingers to the wood and set the pyre alight. Together they watched the old woman burn.

Thunk!

Edvern swung the axe, the repetitive movement providing him with something useful to do. It had been two days since Bea's funeral, and their chopped wood supply needed restocking. His muscles screamed in protest, but he widened his stance and swung again.

Thunk!

The task also had the added benefit of drowning out Alaxen and Taseria's yelling. His uncle's stress and impatience were palpable. If she didn't ease up on her criticism and offer any solutions of her own, Edvern was sure Alaxen's temper would implode.

"Your overindulgence is going to get us killed." Taseria's voice sent a spike of anger up Edvern's spine. "Don't spend your efforts on the boy."

Edvern didn't hear Alaxen's reply, but he heard the door of the hut open and the sound of angry footsteps. He lifted the axe and swung, refusing to look behind him.

Thunk!

"When you're finished here, get started on the evening meal."

Gritting his teeth against the rising tide of his fury, Edvern didn't give her the satisfaction of responding.

Thunk!

"Your work is sloppy."

Edvern's grip tightened around the handle of the axe, his knuckles white from the pressure. He grunted and looked, unseeing, at the pile of wood.

Taseria sighed dramatically, turned and left him be. He was dimly aware of leathery wings unfurling as she took to the sky with Tynum.

Hefting the axe, he swung and, displeased with the split wood, swung again. And again. Until he lifted his head to scream.

The axe dropped from his fingers, and Edvern sat on the ground, cradling his head in his hands. Alynta padded through the clearing, three rabbits in her maw. She dropped them and came to sidle up to him. Without a word he grasped on to her fur and drew her close. Alynta huffed and laid her chin on his knee, lavender eyes staring at him adoringly.

"She is angry with me, not you."

Edvern startled. He hadn't heard his uncle approach. Much to his surprise, Alaxen joined him on the cold, hard ground. "What do you suggest I do?"

"Taseria's opinions hold little weight with me." Alaxen reached over Edvern's lap and scratched the underside of the dyrathakin's chin. "Do you trust me?"

"You know I do."

Considering him with his knowing gaze, Alaxen grunted. "Give me your injured hand. No matter what, keep breathing. This will hurt."

Alynta scrambled to her feet, growling and tail lashing. The fur of her underbelly glowed with fire, and the heat from her power radiated around them.

"Trust me ..." Alaxen offered his gloved hand. "The pain shouldn't last long."

Looking between his loyal dyrathakin and his stern uncle, Edvern made his choice. He nodded woodenly and gave Alaxen his damaged hand. His stomach still clenched every time he saw the stumps where his fingers should be.

Alaxen's answering smile did not reach his eyes. He took Edvern's hands in his lap and then removed his own gloves. Large, calloused hands clasped Edvern's. His uncle's skin was warm. "Your hand is cold. Best that we put some natural heat into your skin for this."

Alynta's fur was still on end, her ears to attention. Alaxen looked up at her, his smile twisting. "Your master is safe with me. The pain will not last."

"You hurt him, and I'll tear out your throat while you sleep," Alynta promised.

"Duly noted," Alaxen replied, taking out a pouch and tipping the half a dozen pieces of wood he had been whittling. They were small, oblong in shape, and when Edvern tilted his head ... bones. The parts were connected with mail, so they sat in two lines of three. They were different lengths ... They were ...

"Fingers ..." Edvern mumbled.

Alaxen nodded. "This hasn't been done for centuries. When I was a young man, I read of healers of the northern regions creating working limbs from carvings of wood."

Edvern's eyes were drawn to the wooden fingers. Protruding at their ends were pairs of spikes.

"Joining them to your flesh will be painful," Alaxen said, and his lips twitched. "For a man with your courage, it'll be a small thing."

"And will they work?" Alynta snapped.

"I dearly hope so."

"Do it." At Edvern's proclamation, Alaxen took up his hand and the carved fingers.

"I'll do this simultaneously. Deep breath."

Alaxen wasted no time. Edvern drew in a deep breath, and before he could think about what was about to happen, the spikes of the fingers were pushed into his flesh. There was a moment where instinct demanded that he struggle, but his uncle held him steady. His fire powers surged, wanting to rebel, to protect.

"Steady." Alaxen's mouth was close to Edvern's ear. When had he been drawn closer? "They're in. Relax your mind; it needs to join with your new appendages."

Gulping down breaths of cold air, Edvern fought to calm his racing mind. He could hear Alynta whining at his side. There was a heavy thump, and he was aware of Izorah and Lyrus nearby.

"It's almost over," Izorah said. *"Relax; lean into Alaxen's power. He's trying to guide you."*

Eyes squeezed tightly shut, Edvern squashed his growing panic, willing the inferno inside of him to quieten to a flickering flame. The moment he was able to do so, he felt his uncle's fingertips on his temples, his breaths against Edvern's neck and his power. Where Moira's power was insidious in nature, demanding and unrelenting, Alaxen's gifting was gentle. It was surrounding him, loaning him strength, whispering guidance.

The pain slowly receded, and exhaustion replaced it. In Alaxen's hands, Edvern wriggled his fingers. Five digits responded.

Alaxen huffed a cry of victory, releasing Edvern's temples. Opening his eyes, Edvern blearily looked up at his uncle's pale face. His lips were blue, his skin grey. He cried out in horror as his unyielding uncle collapsed.

Taseria returned to the hut to find Alaxen and Edvern curled up by the hearth, two steaming mugs of Bea's tea held in their hands. Once he had regained consciousness, Alaxen hadn't said much at all. He stumbled back to the hut with a concerned Edvern trailing him.

Alynta, sorry for her lack of trust, curled up against Alaxen's side, her head in his lap. Edvern had busied himself with finding them something to eat. Soon he had a plate of cured cheeses, pickled vegetables and dried ration biscuits. His uncle took the plate with a huff.

"I see you were successful," Taseria said. She sounded displeased as she glanced towards Edvern and then at Alaxen.

Still dumbfounded by his uncle's power, Edvern had been clenching and opening his fist when she came in.

"Worth it," Alaxen growled. His dark eyes were alight with triumph as he observed Edvern's wonder. He didn't look at Taseria.

Taseria frowned, crossing her arms against her chest. "You understand why I advised against …"

"A good night's rest and—"

"It might have killed you!"

Edvern's back straightened at Taseria's horrified tone.

"Nonsense!" Alaxen growled. He turned to Edvern. "Don't look at me like that. I know the limitations of my power."

"Giving him fingers, which he could live without, won't bring back Rikar." Taseria's cheeks flushed pink. "As much as I want your brother back …"

"Giving Edvern working fingers gives him his sense of independence, his pride. Blaming him for Rikar's lack of affections for you is stupid, Tas. It's frankly beneath you. Rikar made his feelings known."

Edvern stood, drawing back, not wanting to hear the rest of this disagreement.

"The moment Rikar brought his bastard home …" Taseria pointed her finger at Edvern, and her hand shook. "Some other foreign whore's child, he no longer wanted me!"

"We hid Edvern in the nursery nearly ten months before we announced him," Alaxen said. "Where you are concerned, Eddi had nothing to do with his father's decision."

"He was a newborn …" Taseria's face melted from anger to dawning horror. She turned away from Edvern, who was inching from the door, and back to Alaxen. "You ... you were using your gifting on him ... on a baby! Rikar and I were to be married. He hid his infidelity for that long ..."

Taseria's opinion of him, of the nature of his birth, did not bother Edvern. He had lived with the title of bastard for as long as he could remember. But his stomach curdled at the thought of his adoptive father bedding a woman like her. He shuddered, imagining what his life might have been like with a stepmother who loathed him. In refusing Taseria, his father had saved him from that fate. And yet his father never took a woman ...

Edvern rose from his place, wanting to be alone. His hand found the handle of the door, but before he could flee, his uncle's voice stopped him.

"I used everything within me to ensure Edvern stayed a newborn for the length of the time we hid him so Moira would never suspect where he came from. As for you, Tas, you proved yourself untrustworthy."

"I gave Rena one piece of useless information!" Taseria cried.

Alaxen stood, the grey pallor of his skin flushing to red. "In our world that could be death. He couldn't trust you after that. He had a *child*."

"I paid for that mistake thousandfold. After all these years of faithfully ..." Taseria pursed her lips, glaring at Alaxen. "Once you have your sons, Alaxen Tallermayne, I'll reconsider my position in your rebellion."

"Maybe as your general, I've already considered your position." Alaxen was calm. Too calm.

Taseria turned on her heel and marched from the room. Not trusting his own voice, Edvern stared up at Alaxen. Eventually he swallowed and asked, "Why didn't you tell her that I'm not Rikar's son? Why let her believe that Rikar was unfaithful?"

"If Taseria cannot accept you as Rikar's bastard, she won't accept you as a Nezahrian. Rikar feared she would be a danger to you."

"So in a roundabout way, it's my fault."

Alaxen snorted. "Taseria allowed herself to be swayed by Rena Hybeck. Rikar fed her information to see what she would do. Don't worry about Taseria. She's angry at herself. She failed."

"Did he love her?"

Alaxen returned to his cup of tea, and Alynta, who had been silently watching, wriggled closer to him. Large fingers ran over the dyrathakin's head. "More than life itself."

"And he gave her up."

"A rebelling Tallermayne needs to trust his woman." Alaxen's words echoed in his mind a warning his father had given him about Kirra Deltmine. No wonder his father hadn't approved of his fling with her.

"Taseria is a rebel too."

Alaxen smiled, but it was Alynta who answered. "The dragon rider woman was envious of you, Eddi. I'm wary of her."

Edvern silently cursed. The compulsion. It had taken everything from Rikar. He turned to go, to gather his own thoughts.

"Eddi," Alaxen called, halting him. "He was protecting himself as well as you."

CHAPTER 16

Plunder

MOIRA

Moira hated that Edvern had been right. The teal dragon, as beautiful and deadly as she was, was not large enough to bear her and the weight of the golden armour. Even though the flight distance between Gytall and Cynedir was not far, her creature's efforts were sluggish.

She dug in the points of her spurs, and the dragon wriggled and grunted. But the stubborn reptile lifted her head and beat her wings faster. When they landed, she would take a larger dragon for herself. The teal would be no good in a fight against Faelowyn.

Alaxen's defection had caused a rift in his ranks. He must have been planning his rebellion for years, working in the shadows. Many of his riders had disappeared.

Thieves, rebels and traitors.

They would die burning, begging for death before it came. She'd take their lovers and children. A harsh message would be sent to any who thought to defy her new order.

She was numb to what she knew had to be done. Blood meant nothing in this world. Not when they had so callously turned their backs on her. The remnants of her family would burn, and she would feel nothing.

Moira shook her head. Time was not on her side. She needed to consolidate her power. Cynedir had lost its lord. Alaxen, for all his faults and failings, had been charismatic enough to whittle her influence at his command post.

Moira would take everything from the spire city. Leave Cynedir a husk and build up the might of the spire in Navilla. A shame, but necessary, Moira thought. Cynedir was the most beautiful of the spires. Built from gleaming white stones, it rested on two islands. Its bridge was a feat of Aurelian architecture. The city also boasted the largest population.

The time for three spires in Aurelia was over. There was only room for one spire in her new regime. It would be her seat of power, where she would reign undisputed.

The beast beneath her rumbled in what might have been mistaken as relief as it banked, readying itself to land. The descent was swift, the landing clumsy. Moira struck the beast with the unforgiving handle of a dagger. With her expert aim, she hit the small vulnerable spot where the skull met the spine. The dragon emitted a strangled whine at the punitive action. Dragging its claws through the rock beneath it, the dragon obediently lowered itself.

Moira dismounted, ensuring her movements were dignified and graceful. She surveyed the damage to the enclosed bridge that connected the two spires of Cynedir and frowned.

"My Grand Lady!"

Moira turned, a harsh word already on her lips. She recognised the interloper as one of her own gifted spies, a young woman who had defected from Rikar's camp. She had been willing to testify against him at the closed trial. "What is it?"

"Our plans to infiltrate Irani have backfired." The spy bowed at her waist.

Moira swore.

"Our efforts did not go unrewarded. We have found evidence of Euquallian forces. Our king thinks he can stage a rebellion." The spy's lips twisted into a cruel smile. While Aurelia relied heavily on Euquall's imports, their king was stubborn. Despite being only a small country, their impressive fleet was the envy of the known world. The king of Euquall did not see King Oluvin as a monarch. Oluvin was a puppet who danced at her bidding. "Unfortunately for him, the Euquallians have refused and have pulled their weapons trade deal with us."

Clenching her fist, Moira wasn't sure how to feel about this news. The Euquallian king was a coward. "They don't want to find themselves in the middle of a civil war."

"The Euquallians have been imprisoned, and we all know how Empress Ionah feels about her homeland. She leads that emperor of hers around like a bull on a tether."

Moira exhaled, closing her eyes for a heartbeat to recentre herself. Euquall was not a priority. Not yet. "Are my grandsons alive?"

"Not for long. It seems Kendrick has been most industrious; this letter is labelled as copy seven. He's sending out letters asking for help. We've intercepted one. But his words condemn him." The spy produced a slip of parchment. Moira took it and scanned the contents. It was Kendrick's handwriting. That traitorous little bastard ...

The spires were under attack from the water wyrms. She did not have time to deal with Cynedir and Irani before flying to warn Lady Rena. Her time was running out.

"Make sure that letter finds its way into the king's hands."

If she couldn't get her hands on her own grandsons, she'd let King Oluvin have them. Perhaps it was better this way. No one could blame her for the king executing them. It would save some of the morale among the ranks.

Moira turned to sweep her gaze at her small escort of riders that had come with her from Gytall. Yahler had been suspiciously quiet during the conversation. Normally, he would have had something to add. "Bring me the most senior rider in Cynedir!"

Yahler inclined his head, his cold eyes drifting to Whilmana. He ran his tongue along his teeth. Like a bloodhound, he could sense death coming.

Moira gritted her teeth, biting back her scream of rage. While she had sent Yahler to get the highest-ranking officer, all he returned with was a grinning master at arms. The foolish man dipped his head in mock salute.

"Lady Moira, we were warned you were coming."

The traitors!

"Where are the dragons?"

"The young and riderless. Gone. Released them myself this morning to join the wilds." The master at arms shrugged his shoulders. "The dragons with riders also left."

"There was a statue of a dragon holding a green egg. Do you know it?" Moira asked. She could feel her blood boiling.

The man smiled. "Aye."

"Smash the statue. Bring it to me."

The smile widened, and the man shrugged again. "Can't. It was stolen."

"Stolen?" Moira shrieked with rage. Yahler reeled back, his ugly face twisting with a frown. The precious egg had been stolen, and no one had thought it important enough to report it to her. How could this have happened?

"There's no one left to fear you in Cynedir. You've no power here." The grin never left the man's face. "The water wyrms came and took so many of us in the night. Cynedir has already fallen. What is left of our ranks will join the rebels outright."

The man must have known that his defiance would be his undoing. Smirking, he lifted his chin in a silent dare. With a scream of rage, she swung her sword, decapitating him in one blow. She had expected a wail from a dragon, but there was none. He had freed his beast before confronting her, welcoming his death with open arms.

Kicking the head out of her way, Moira inspected the riders of Gytall. She would have loved to butcher the lot of them, but she needed numbers. It was unwise to kill every rider who had displeased her.

"The people are suffering, my lady." A young stable hand, brave enough to approach her, bowed low. "Water wyrms have killed many of the old and the young. Food is ..."

Moira paused to look at him. She saw the dark circles under his eyes, the grey pallor of his skin. He was much too scrawny for a boy his age.

"Shall we tell the people aid has come?" Hope still glimmered in the boy's eyes as he looked up at her. That was the trouble with optimistic people; they saw goodness where there was none.

"By sundown the people of Cynedir's suffering will be over," Moira said.

Relief blossomed over his face. It was so delicious to watch his expression fall as she lifted her bloody sword and pointed it at his chest. Running him through would be satisfying but wasteful. Something catastrophic was needed to pin the blame of Cynedir's fall on the Black Prince.

"Run, little rabbit," Moira said. "Run and spread the word to the simple people of Aurelia that the Black Prince came and stole our dragons. Cynedir burns. Its citizens are ash on the wind."

The boy's eyes widened.

"Run, and I'll let you live."

The boy did exactly what she expected. He turned on his heels and fled, leaving the fellow citizens of Cynedir to their fate. He had been courageous to approach her, but his bravery failed when she unveiled exactly what she was.

"Mount your dragon and burn the city. Kill everyone. My messenger is the only survivor," Moira commanded. She didn't bother turning to Yahler or Whilmana. She heard their murmured assent, their boots on the stone, their dragons spreading their wings ...

There she stood, watching as the great city of Cynedir caught alight. Before long the sky was thick with smoke. The screams of desperate and dying people filled the air. With the pungent smell of burning flesh in her nostrils, she bore witness to the beginning of the end of Ullryk the Liberator's great empire. Ash fell around her like falling snow, coating her hair. Beside her, her young dragon lifted her snout and bellowed. The cry echoed off the crumbling towers and the cold waters.

When the screams were finally silenced, she was left with the crackling of the fire. The world would burn at her word, and from the ash, she would make a new one.

Cultivating trust between commanding officer and his subordinates is the most efficient way to inspire loyalty among the troops. A good leader chooses those who serve under them wisely. Don't look for the cruel or callous. Look for those who the dragons love.

RIKAR TALLERMAYNE IN HIS LETTERS TO EDVERN, HIS SON

CHAPTER 17

Nezahrian Rider

EDVERN

Edvern leaned against the doorframe, observing as Alaxen prowled the tiny rooms of the hut like a caged mountain cat. They were no closer to finding a way into the palace, and Taseria found fault with everything. Her snide comments inflamed Alaxen's temper. Worse, her dragon, Tynum, snapped his jaws at Izorah for any perceived infraction. Where Izorah was happy to ignore the bad behaviour, Lyrus was less forgiving.

"There's plenty of work. Get off your lazy backside and contribute," Taseria snapped, storming through the front door. She kicked at Edvern's crossed boots, which he dodged.

Alaxen's pacing halted, the muscles in his jaw feathering. "Don't speak to him like that."

Taseria's lips curled.

"One might think I didn't cook breakfast or clean the dishes or haul water here to heat so you could bathe in comfort," Edvern snarled. "What intelligence have you brought from Irani? None. I suggest you get yourself and your dragon under control."

Taseria's eyes glinted. She turned to Alaxen. "Are you going to let the bastard speak to me like that?"

Alaxen didn't rise to the bait. He turned towards Edvern. "Go for a walk, relax, while Rider Taseria and I have words."

Balling his fists to his sides, Edvern would have loved to argue his point further. But he knew, whatever he might say or do, Taseria would never see herself as the one in the wrong. Words were wasted on her. If Alaxen's thunderous expression was anything to go by, he knew it as well.

Without looking back, Edvern opened the door and walked out before he said anything he might regret. Keeping to the shadows, he strode through the woods, his steps heavy and angry. Beside him Alynta prowled, keeping close to his side. Tynum had tried to chastise her, and the dyrathakin had clawed his face in response. Which had caused an awful row over breakfast.

"You're going too far." Izorah flew overhead, and he was thankful for her presence. *"Alaxen won't be pleased if you reach Irani."*

"With you guarding my back, who will dare approach me?" Edvern asked. "Besides, I am a man, not a boy."

Edvern's fingers slipped into his pouch. The egg was cool and secure at his side. Hidden beneath it was a thick gold coin. While Taseria and Alaxen fought, he busied himself rummaging through the spare trunks and found it. At the time he had thought that he might purchase a beer or three. His fingers recoiled from the coin as if it had burned him. A groan escaped his lips, his shoulders sagging. The dragons were relying on him ... and here he was thinking about his own desires. It was the behaviour of a boy.

"Eddi?" Alynta nudged his side. He was sure she could feel his self-loathing.

Swallowing, Edvern straightened his posture. His father had taught him that a man owned his failures, and so when he returned to the hut, he knew he needed to give Alaxen the coin. For now, he would put his skills to the test and find a way into the palace. Alaxen was determined once he had his sons to find his remaining general. He had sent Taseria scouting for Oskar, but there had been no sign of him, nor of any Cynedir riders. The silence worried his uncle. Without trained riders on their side, toppling Moira became more impossible. Edvern had heard Alaxen telling Taseria that with a force of riders, they might have something tempting to offer Raziel Yavari.

Edvern had been wary of asking his uncle about the conversation he had with his generals about a traitor in their ranks. He had hoped by Alaxen's order to find evidence that it was a minor inconvenience. But as Alaxen had told Taseria, even the most innocuous pieces of information could result in death. Or worse.

He understood his uncle's reluctance to act without evidence. Moira had given Rikar's execution order with very little information to convict him. Would he be tentative to kill if he was uncertain of guilt? Probably.

They needed Cynedir riders. Desperately.

By the time he reached the place where the trees became sparse and he could look out across the flat fields towards Irani, it was midday. Hesitant to leave the safety of the shadows, he remained in the shade. Above his head Izorah flew higher, her blue scales camouflaging her.

"Edvern, run!"

Edvern's head shot up at the warning cry. Silhouetted against the glare of the sun was another dragon. If Izorah thought he would turn tail and abandon her, she was wrong. Instead of fleeing, he took a few running leaps into the clear.

Alynta wriggled her hind quarters and was in the air, at his side in a flash of orange fur.

He didn't feel the burn through his shoulder blades as he tore off his shirt. Alaxen would not be pleased if he ruined yet more clothing. He was in the air in a matter of heartbeats, cursing that he had left his sword behind in his rush to get away from the hut.

"I said flee," Izorah rumbled. *"Not come this way."*

Edvern didn't reply. She knew his mind. Wings of fire beat hard, and he hoped against all hope he didn't receive attention from the village. He ascended into the sky, eyes pinned on his dragon. If anything happened to her because of his foolishness …

"I'm on my way." Lyrus' tone was short, and Edvern cried out in relief.

Reaching out with his senses, Edvern latched on to two dragon presences. A large male drake circled Izorah, with him a much smaller dragon. He felt the brush of a curious mind against his. This dragon was a stranger.

Moments later a large grey dragon with speckles of purple descended behind Edvern, taking him by surprise. Blank amber eyes stared in his direction without seeing him. Perched high on his head, a motley brown lizardling flicked his tongue. The rider on the dragon's back was a young woman with black braids, her fist closed around the hilt of a curved Nezahrian sword. She twisted in the saddle as Izorah swept behind her.

"What are you?" the lizardling chirruped. He whipped his slender tail around, flashing his fangs. As the creature shifted, Edvern saw that his wings were badly damaged.

"Why are you here?" Edvern shouted.

"Jirrah, you can't ask a dragon soul what they are!" the large grey rumbled. His voice sounded like thunder in Edvern's mind. He was old, but not quite as old as Kyros.

"Who are you?" Edvern yelled.

"We come looking for Lord Alaxen," the rider said. "Lady Moira has brought ruin to Gytall and has set the torch to Cynedir."

"Why should I trust you?" Edvern bit his lip. Cynedir had burned? What of Captain Oskar?

"I could ask you the same question," the rider snapped.

It was Lyrus' arrival that ended the standoff. Seeing the grey male, he gave a cry of delight. He swooped forward, then hovered, pressing their snouts together. *"Faer, scale-brother!"*

"Lyrus?" Edvern questioned.

"That's Lord Alaxen's dragon!" the rider cried. "Where is he?"

"This is Faer, an old and dear friend," Lyrus said. *"Jirrah is Faer's eyes, and Faer is Jirrah's wings. The rider is called Palea."*

Deciding he could trust Lyrus' judgement, Edvern retreated. Izorah and Alynta followed suit.

The lizardling shuffled forward, his tongue tasting the air. Edvern couldn't help but wonder if he liked what he scented.

"We should discuss this on the ground," Palea said. "You can lead me to Alaxen from there."

Edvern agreed, and without a word, landed. Faer followed, graceful and silent. Before Palea could dismount, Alynta was at the blind drake's side. She rested her forepaws on the belly of the grey dragon, tongue flicking and nose twitching.

Lyrus had been too excited over the arrival of the strange little group to stay still. Before Edvern could ask him to stay, he had darted in the direction of the hut. Which left him to awkwardly exchange pleasantries with Palea and her dragon companions.

"Will Alaxen be long?" Palea demanded. She cocked her head to the side, studying Edvern curiously.

"I don't think so."

"Did you steal your dragon?"

Edvern wanted to be outraged by such a bold question, but without waiting for an answer, Palea wandered away, turning her back on them.

"I like her," Izorah murmured. *"But she carries a heavy burden."*

Edvern had seen it, the way her hands trembled, the glassiness of her eyes. She wandered through the sparse trees like a lost soul, her fingers trailing over the bark. Pausing at a tree, she pressed her forehead to the trunk, her lips moving in a prayer.

Letting her curiosity get the better of her, Alynta crept forward, ears pricked up as she considered the newcomer.

Edvern watched from a distance, wondering where in Nezaha she was from. Her skin was a darker brown, and she was tall and willowy. Her thick, black hair was pulled back in dozens of braids, the ends held by wooden beads, some of which were carved with patterns. He wouldn't let her looks deceive him. Palea was not fragile. No doubt she could snap a troublesome man in half if pushed.

Palea caught him staring, and he felt his cheeks heat. Alynta snuck closer until she was a whisker's length away from the young woman.

"You have a dyrathakin." Palea's wry tone was clear it was not a question. Bending, she offered her hand to Alynta, and after giving her a good sniff, the dyrathakin allowed herself to be petted. "She's a pretty girl."

"Maybe I should add some beads to my tail," Alynta said thoughtfully. The dyrathakin reached back, plucking a feather from her tail, and offered it to Palea.

Edvern could see in the other rider's eyes she was stunned by the dyrathakin's behaviour. "She likes you," he muttered unhelpfully.

Palea took the feather and turned away, returning to her prayers.

Jirrah watched his human friend, shrugged and proceeded to fill the silence with all sorts of questions. No sooner Edvern fumbled over an answer, another was asked.

What happened to his finger? Did his flames burn or were they for show? Did he have a female to nest with? And most importantly, now that he had fangs, did he prefer raw meat?

It seemed the lizardling's questions and Edvern's muddled answers had the desired effect. Palea relaxed, chuckling as she shook her head at his antics. With the lizardling taking so much of Edvern's attention, he hadn't noticed her going to stand in the sun. Her brown skin glowed in the light of day. He could see the dusting of gold powder on her eyes and cheekbones. Palea was a woman of means.

"Do you understand the lizardling too?" Edvern asked.

Palea turned her face towards him, her eyebrow raised. "A silly question. No."

"Did you fly from Cynedir?" Edvern asked as Jirrah flicked his tongue aggressively in his direction.

"We had warning of Moira Tallermayne's arrival," Palea said, chewing her bottom lip. "Most of our host had left with ..."

"We left as soon as we got the news," Faer replied.

"Did many escape?" Edvern thought his question was reasonable.

Palea disagreed. "I think that's news for the general's ears. Who else is with you?"

"It was a bloodbath," Faer said.

Edvern decided to take the same tack as Palea, not letting her know Faer answered his question. "I think that's up to the general to divulge."

Far from being angry, Palea twitched her lips into a bemused smirk.

"Here's Alaxen!" Alynta wagged her tail, seeing Lyrus fly overhead. She ran to greet him as he jumped from Lyrus' back. As Edvern predicted, his uncle was not pleased with him. Dark eyes alight with rebuke, he stepped past Edvern and greeted Faer like an old friend.

"Palea ..."

"General." Palea grinned, her eyes wet with tears, and despite her words of deference, threw her arms around Alaxen's neck. "Missed you."

Edvern could not help the twist of jealousy coiling in his gut. Alaxen looked at her with unconcealed affection. Kissing her on both cheeks, he set her down. Traces of gold powder stuck to his beard. "Daughter of my heart."

Taseria, who had followed on Tynum, seemed most displeased. "Not another Nezahrian."

"Hello, Tas." Unconcerned by the other woman rider, Palea flicked her dark braids over her shoulder, her beads clinking. She beamed at Alaxen, turning her back on the flaxen-hair woman.

"Walk with me," Alaxen said, taking Palea's elbow.

Edvern was left behind with Taseria, observing as they walked ahead, plotting. By the time they reached the hut, a plan had been formed. So much for coming up with a cunning idea and impressing his uncle. It so happened that Palea had already scouted the town; the king's birthday gala was tomorrow night. Lords and ladies, as well as foreign dignitaries, had been arriving in Irani for the last fortnight ready for the event. Even better the revellers were all to wear masks to conceal their identities.

According to Palea, Bastian and Kendrick had sent letters to Cynedir, asking for aid. Captain Oskar planned to regroup and fly in to secure the capital, but she had not heard from him since he had left the spire. Anything could have happened.

"Tas, we need clothing that will get us into a masked ball. For your lack of proper planning and stupidity, you, Edvern, will chop wood." Alaxen pointed towards the collected pile of timber and the axe. Without waiting to see if Edvern would protest, he went into the hut, Palea at his side.

Cursing, Edvern realised he had left his shirt behind. He picked up the axe. Taseria stood outside the hut, her fists clenched. Alaxen's order had essentially blocked her from hearing what Palea had to say. Edvern swung down the axe, splitting the first log, keeping his eyes on his task, determined not to laugh at Taseria's thunderous expression. He lifted it again and swung.

Soon he was swinging to a steady rhythm. Despite the cold, sweat dripped down his skin. There was a sense of peace with the repetitive chore.

"Remember your place," Taseria said as she strode past him.

Edvern's rhythm was disrupted. He missed his piece of timber, the blade hitting to the side with a *thunk*. He lifted his gaze to hers. "The general gave you an order, Rider Taseria."

And with that, he hefted his axe and resumed his chore. Taseria made a disgusted noise before returning to her dragon's side. Edvern didn't watch her go.

Edvern straightened his ruby jerkin. His fingers trailed down the silver buttons as he observed Taseria while she prepared Tynum for the short flight to Irani. He had seen her conceal her weapon underneath the skirts of her copper gown. Her knives she had strapped to her thighs.

She was elegantly dressed, the collar of her dress a ruffle of feathers and a mask of a barn owl in her hands. To conceal her short golden hair, she had stolen a wig of fine auburn curls that bounced as she worked.

"Don't mind her." Palea leant over, whispering in his ear. "Bitterness is poison."

Palea's simple black gown glittered as she moved. The bodice and plunging neckline suited her willowy frame. Golden butterflies stitched with coloured jewels dotted the sheer fabric of her sleeves. Edvern felt a twinge of sadness seeing the gown; Larah would have loved to have the opportunity to sew a dress like Palea wore.

"She loved my da." Edvern turned away before Palea could see the pain in his eyes.

Palea sniffed. "I assume not enough to protect what he loved."

Edvern shifted uneasily.

"Taseria's and Rikar's whirlwind romance was a well-known scandal in Cynedir. The other riders still tease her mercilessly."

Edvern swallowed the lump, dismissing his thoughts of what might have been. "I feel sorry for her."

"You look nice." Palea reached out to him, her golden nails smoothing the dark cloak trimmed with the orange fur of a fox.

"How can I convince anyone I belong? Look at me." Edvern shook his head. What would Lyssandra think of him now? She had grown up around aristocracy, attending these parties. He was a fraud. While Rikar had cared for him and had taught him to dance, just in case, Edvern hadn't been exposed to polite society.

A heavy hand on his shoulder tore him away from his self-deprecating speech. Alaxen, wolf mask already in place, was dressed in a fine black suit. He looked like the god of death himself.

"Palea, go ready Faer. I want a word with Eddi."

Palea smiled, placing her lacy butterfly mask over her face.

Alaxen stepped forward, pressing soft gloves into Edvern's hands. "Remember who you are. Rikar's son, playing a Saemorish nobleman. Keep your head in the game."

"Yes sir." Edvern grimaced. His Saemorish accent was atrocious. He tugged on his gloves, pleased by the dexterity the magic fingers gave him. "I'll try not to talk."

"Weapons cannot be taken into the gala; we'll have to conceal them." Trailing his fingers over the sword at Edvern's hip, Alaxen grinned at the weapon. A tingling sensation ran down Edvern's thigh, pleasant but cool. "He designed your sword and engraved it himself. Do you know where the words come from?"

Edvern shook his head.

"I'm not surprised. Many falsely credit Ullryk, when in fact he quoted it from an extremely obscure letter from a Nezahrian father to his son, before the time there were dragon riders. 'With the heart of a dragon, take up your sword. Though I cannot go with you, let Qavi's eternal fire blaze through you. Light up the long night with courage'."

Edvern blinked, a lump forming in his throat. The sword had been a dangerous gift, and one of parting. He looked up into Alaxen's solemn face and knew this was Rikar's way of saying goodbye. At the time of the forging of this sword, his father had known his time was short.

"Qavi is the dark star. He has no light," Edvern murmured. "He cannot be seen."

Alaxen gripped his shoulders, fingers pressing firmly into the soft fur of his cloak. "Yet the lord of the darkest hour can be found to those who seek."

"I'm not sure I understand."

"Your father wants you to persist, be courageous and never give up."

Grasping the handle of his sword, Edvern resisted the urge to draw it. "That sounds like my da."

Alaxen inclined his head in agreement.

"Although, a fox?" Taking the mask from Alynta, Edvern stared down at the empty eye holes and the pointed ears. In Aurelian folk law, the fox was a creature of deception and trickery. A patron of thieves.

Alaxen snorted as Edvern attached his mask. "The devious, death and the just. How apt."

Alynta's tail lashed. "Orange dyrathakins are symbols of hope reborn." She turned to Alaxen. "Black dyrathakins were secret keepers, protectors."

Edvern swallowed, catching sight of Taseria watching them. "I don't trust her."

"Trust me," Alaxen replied, laying a gloved hand on his shoulder. "'Taseria has decided that once we have my sons and find Captain Oskar, she'll part ways with us."

Twisting his head around, Edvern asked, "Doesn't that feel a little suspicious?"

"Yes," Alaxen said, tone soft. "That's why I plan to severe ties at the ball tonight."

His uncle was planning on betraying one of his own riders! Edvern felt his eyes widen. Never had he thought that Alaxen would feel compelled to leave one of his subordinates behind. Had he found evidence that Edvern didn't know about, or had Taseria become too much of a liability?

Edvern found that he didn't want to know the answers. Leadership came with certain sacrifice and duties. Something his father said he could never truly appreciate unless he achieved the rank and was forced to make difficult choices. Grateful that he wasn't the one who had earned his uncle's displeasure, he inclined his head. He would trust Alaxen, even if he didn't have all the information.

CHAPTER 18

Dragon Flight

LYSSANDRA

Lyssandra was finishing lacing her court shoes when Prince Dalain entered the tent. She glanced up at him, admiring the crisp lines of his black shirt and the cloak of fur over his shoulders.

He stepped closer, holding a woman's mask out to her. "You look lovely."

"Praise is unnecessary." Lyssandra turned away, her skirts brushing against her feet. Lifting her hand to her hair, she checked once again that it was still tightly secured.

The empress' wine-red gown only required minor adjustments, so it hugged her body just so. Its low left her shoulders bare and her long neck on display. Biting her lip, she ran her shaking fingers over the gold embellishments.

"I don't have the right to wear gold."

"A beautiful girl deserves a beautiful dress." A sly smile lit Dalain's face. "No one will ever know it's you beneath the mask."

Lyssandra took the golden mask, tracing the swirls before lifting it to her face in resignation. In the past she would have scoffed at the two small antlers with flowers and berries.

Needing no instructions, Dalain stepped around her and took the ribbons to tie the mask into place.

"Mother is most impressed by the Saemorish tenacity to get involved with this subterfuge on Aurelian soil."

Lyssandra found it difficult to keep the pleased smile off her face. "I am a diplomat. It's within the realm of my capabilities."

"Stay focused on the mission," Dalain said. Lyssandra wanted to stomp on the prince's toes. She wasn't the one who needed reminders. "We find the Euquallian delegation and see if we can take the Tallermaynes prisoners."

"And once we have the Euquallians, then what?"

"Born on Euquallian soil, my mother is still their princess. She is keen to speak with my aunt, General Eupheana. The king of Euquall and my father aren't on friendly terms. But if we help Euquall, maybe my grandfather can be persuaded to help us. If Nezaha were to fall, my grandfather would only shelter my mother and me, even though I was not born on Euquallian soil, therefore not their princeling."

Through her training, Lyssandra knew much of this already. Hearing it again kept her focussed on her role.

"Would your father ransom the Euquallians back?" Lyssandra asked.

"He'd be a fool to try."

"And the Tallermaynes? What do you plan to do to them?"

"Whatever the emperor wills."

Lyssandra frowned. Unknown to the Black Prince, she had overheard the emperor and empress arguing about the worth of the younger

Tallermaynes. The emperor wanted to behead all Aurelians, while the empress wanted Edvern's cousins alive. She wasn't a fool to think that the Nezahrians wanted the Tallermaynes out of the goodness of their own hearts.

"Have you seen Markos?" Lyssandra changed the subject. She didn't want to talk about Edvern's family.

"Mother's ladies-in-waiting are pampering him," Prince Dalain replied. "His belly is full, and Lady Ustillian is reading bedtime stories until her voice is hoarse."

This time Lyssandra let the smile touch her lips. As long as little Markos was safe, she could revisit the problem of saving him from the Nezahrians later.

"I want you to know that I'm aware of your feelings for Edvern," Dalain said, surprising Lyssandra out of her reverie.

"And pray, tell me, what is it that I feel?"

Dalain gave her one of those long, lingering looks that told her that she was being rather dull. "You are fond of him," he said.

"*Fond*?"

A smile touched the prince's lips. "Yes, *fond*, and I won't stand in your way."

Lyssandra's cheeks flushed, but Dalain ignored that in favour of picking up a pale cloak trimmed with white fox fur. He placed it around her shoulders, and she drew it closer to her body.

"Nothing untoward happened," Lyssandra said. Inwardly she cursed her tone; it was a little too sharp. Such personal topics weren't discussed in polite company, but Saemorish diplomats used everything they had at their disposal to meet their king's needs. Including bedding whoever it took to get their way. Lyssandra wasn't chaste.

It was why she, a bastard-born princess, was given to the third son. There was an understanding that diplomats would have a secretive past.

Dalain's smile grew. "I didn't say it did."

"He's a ..." Lyssandra was going to say friend, but that didn't quite cover what she felt about him. "It's none of your business."

"No," Dalain said with an incline of his head. "But I'll withdraw my offer of a political marriage if it pleases you."

Lyssandra sat heavily on her pallet bed, the cloak pooling around her. Much of what happened was because Ellrahera had called off the engagement, had promised her to Edvern. And here was this prince saying he was willing to void the contract—for her.

"Your emperor ..."

"My mother has Father well in hand." Dalain smiled, his eyes shining wickedly. "He'll pose no problem. And if you are with him, you are still with a Nezahrian treasure, leaving me free."

"It would please me ..." Lyssandra said, her words fading in the space between them. She hoped that her next words would not cause offense. "To be free."

A soft smile curled on Dalain's lips. He inclined his head. "Then I release you from fulfilling your obligations."

Lyssandra looked away. She wanted to tell Dalain that she wasn't under any obligation to marry him. She hadn't been for some time. His gallant proclamation changed nothing. Yet his gesture was sweet.

"He needs allies in camp ..." It was a lot to ask.

Dalain crossed his arms against his chest, eyebrow quirking. "What makes you think I haven't been softening the blow that he is Aurelian-raised for weeks now?"

Lyssandra looked up at him, swallowing. "You'll be kind to him? He knows nothing of your language, customs ... He's ..."

"While my status may affect how I may or may not interact with him, I'll ensure he's well cared for." Dalain grunted, a curious expression crossing his face. "Father's presence in camp complicates matters."

Lyssandra looked down at her hands cradled in her lap. "How is Hedriel?"

"Still insisting he was abandoned," Dalain replied. "Of course, my father would never—"

"It's common for kings not to negotiate for hostages of lower status," Lyssandra said.

"Hedriel is the nephew of the Emperor of Nezaha. Born of an ancient and powerful line, a prince ..."

Lyssandra lifted her hand to forestall his next words. "Born to a father unworthy of his mother ... An inconsequential fifth child."

"Hedriel is young." Dalain shook his head. "Father loves him."

"An emperor's love goes only so far," Lyssandra said. "Were you not taught basic diplomacy?"

Dalain sunk onto Lyssandra's bed beside her, cradling his head in his hands. "I refuse to believe that my father left Hedriel in Saemore to die."

"My father, the crown prince, sent the messages himself." Konrad entered the tent, holding Antonella's hand tightly. Lyssandra took a moment to admire the cream dress trimmed with blue that her friend was wearing. "When Nezaha declined to engage with any talks, Hedriel's accommodations became more ... dank."

Dalain stared at Konrad with an expression that could only be described as somewhere between nonplussed and disbelief.

"We need to make ourselves ready." Konrad was unconcerned by Dalain's bewilderment. "Let's not bicker. Hedriel is a nephew, not a son. It was a sacrifice Nezaha was willing to make."

Dalain toed the ground, a grimace on his face. He straightened his jerkin, brushing away invisible specks from his cloak. He exhaled. "We should be off. I for one would like to see who the Aurelian dragons choose to ride them."

Faelowyn watched over the Aurelian dragons like a proud, overbearing matron. She kept Aerin in check on her right-hand side, nudging him back from the humans trying to do their jobs. Under her belly, Odharn took shelter, crooning and pressing himself closer to her side.

The squadron of Aurelian dragons who had defected from Moira's camp were lined up with Aerin, with Marsyna and Elisaria positioned behind the squad. Woe, a steel-grey dragon, was surrounded by a dozen royal guards. They were insisting on saddling the unhappy dragon. The beast blew hot air and shuffled backwards. Lyssandra could sense that despite the grey dragon's agitation, he was careful not to hurt any of the swarming humans.

"Force it over his snout. He's the tamest of the lot," one of the guards said, jangling what looked to be a bridle of twisted gold with bells and tassels. "Emperor Ze'hyrn demands his dragon is the finest in the skies."

"Force it on him at your peril." How Zanniel seemed to appear from nowhere in broad daylight, Lyssandra couldn't guess. But there he was, standing between the royal guards, stroking the scales of Woe's legs. "We must learn that dragons are not filthy beasts of burden as some might think, incapable of thought and feeling. The prestige of riding a dragon is an honour, royal-blooded or not."

"He'll learn to behave himself," one of the senior guards said through gritted teeth.

Dalain laughed, but Lyssandra wasn't fooled by the forced sound. The tension around the prince's jaw and the hard glint in his eyes spoke of his ire. "This dragon is only behaving because Raziel asked him to. Wouldn't want to be you if you push him ..."

"With all due respect, Your Highness …"

Dalain wasn't interested in what they had to say. "He's a dragon, not a warhorse. Do you want him to tip my father off his back once they are airborne?"

Codee, the yellow dragon that was a similar age to Woe, pushed his friend aside with his snout, blocking the grey dragon from the royal guards' view. The eldest of the squadron, a large red male, stepped forward and lowered his snout.

"Lord Balfar insists that if Woe is for the emperor, he'll be paired with the empress. He'll do so to ensure his flight brother is treated with dignity and not with human indifference." Raziel approached, waves of guards and soldiers parting for him.

"A wise man wouldn't antagonise dragons." Symmeon stood on Raziel's left, frowning at the royal guards. Stepping past Raziel, he offered his hand to Woe, who eyed him wearily and did not lower his snout. Instead, he shifted his weight, rearing his head back. "Their Imperial Majesties are not flying out today. Leave this pair alone."

The royal guards withdrew reluctantly.

Codex rumbled, lowering his nose so that he could peer into Zanniel's eyes. Nostrils flared as he scented the air around him, ruffling the spy's hair.

"Codex believes he is well-suited to Zanniel Oberion, our war wraith, as he is adept at flying great distances undetected." Raziel clapped Zanniel on the back, and Codex pressed his chin to the ground. "He would like to stay close to Woe if possible. They've been together since they were hatchlings. And you may call him Codee."

Covering his heart with his hand, Zanniel bowed his head, keeping his gaze steady on the dragon as he spoke. "I'll work hard to prove myself worthy of you, Codee."

Two other dragons joined the rumbling, and Raziel interpreted for human ears. "And Valtar has requested our Saemorish heroes, Antonella

Fenin and Konrad Stamos. Since Elisaria has a Saemorish rider, he'd like to test the mettle of Saemore too."

"Pardon?" Antonella asked at Lyssandra's shoulder.

"Valtar has requested two riders," Raziel replied with a shrug. "Apparently, he has a reputation for being greedy. And he's pointed out Antonella and Konrad are a mated pair."

Konrad, who had been content to be silent as he observed the proceedings, barked back an embarrassed laugh. At his side, Antonella nudged him in the ribs. Hard.

"And the last dragon?"

The final dragon was Gryph, a dark burgundy drake that was more aloof than his brothers. He tilted his head, a soft, rumbling purr coming from his throat. Closing his eyes, Raziel nodded, a smile forming on his face.

"Gryph would like the enemy of Bedvir, Symmeon, to be his rider."

Symmeon wasn't the type of man who was easily taken by surprise. She turned to see his eyes widen, his fingers coming to rest along the horrible scar along his throat. "You wily beast. You're the one who accidently interrupted your master, Bedvir, when he gave me this in Charkara."

Gryph rumbled again.

Raziel burst out laughing. "He asks you why you think it was an accident that he tripped up his rider."

Symmeon paused, biting on his lip. "Bedvir's dragon wants me?"

Peeling his lips back, Gryph showed his teeth, the muscles in his forelegs rippling as he crawled forward.

"He would like to remind you his name is Gryph, not Bedvir's dragon."

"Ah ..." Symmeon sauntered towards the dark red dragon. He reached out a trembling hand but stopped short of touching him. "Can't imagine Bedvir was a kind rider. I'll promise to treat you with respect if you don't tip me from your back."

Gryph lowered his snout, pressing himself against Symmeon's palms.

"He says don't give him a reason to kill you and you'll be fine," Raziel murmured.

Lyssandra choked.

"Woe and Balfar will stay behind to protect their Imperial Majesties and the camp," Raziel said, looking away from where Symmeon and Gryph slowly sidled closer to one another, both curious and wary.

Aerin huffed, and Dalain made his way to his dragon. The prince ran his hand down the large dragon's foreleg.

"Likewise, Marsyna will stay in the camp." Prince Hedriel stood by Marsyna's head, pointedly ignoring the royal guards that had been shadowing him all morning. Rumour had it he had argued with Raziel about coming and had been most put out that he would be returned to his mother's estate as soon as it was convenient.

Lyssandra gathered her skirts, not daring to look around at the others as they all mounted their dragons. Out of the corner of her eye, she saw Odharn squirming away from Faelowyn's shadow. His shoulders were drooped, his wing dragging on the ground. He looked the very picture of dejection. She wished she had the words to speak with the young dragon. But he had one wing, and in this situation, he would be a liability. Even Edvern would want to keep him away.

Odharn's eyes flicked up to Raziel. When the Black Prince shook his head, the green dragon slunk away, tail dragging behind him.

"He looks like a kicked pup," Symmeon muttered.

"I'm sure Faelowyn will spoil him with attention and food when we return," Raziel replied.

Under her thighs, Lyssandra felt Elisaria's muscles rippling as she unfurled her wings and lunged into the air. She swallowed an undignified scream.

Lyssandra allowed her mind to wander at the steady pumping of Elisaria's wings. They flew for what seemed like miles. She continued to drift in her contemplations until she heard Elisaria emit a low warning rumble. It was so out of character that she jerked back into reality.

"What's wrong?"

Symmeon's dark red dragon flew to her left-hand side.

"Wild dragons," Symmeon called. "Angry wild dragons."

"Wild dragons are Nezahrian, aren't they?" Lyssandra yelled back, hoping that whatever their alliances, the wild dragons were on her side. She looked to the looming shadows. Five dragons were speeding towards them, each larger than the last. The leader seemed to be a huge black drake, with eyes as silver as the stars.

"Mind your tongues," Symmeon murmured. "You don't want to provoke them."

"They're for Nezaha though, aren't they?" Antonella asked. Her voice had a shrill edge of panic. Lyssandra could see how tightly she held on to Konrad. Her friend buried her face into her lover's shoulder blades. Even though they were flying on the backs of two different dragons, Lyssandra longed to comfort her friend.

"Wild dragons were an old civilisation before the time of kingdoms," Symmeon said. "Just because they have made their home in our mountains doesn't mean they're allies."

Lyssandra felt lightheaded at the thought. Her clammy hands scrambled for purchase on Elisaria's scales.

"The presence of Aurelian dragons is likely to upset them."

Lyssandra wished she had the reach to punch Symmeon.

"How could they possibly know that ...?"

"Faelowyn is the only Nezahrian dragon," Dalain said. "Although they will not treat with humans, the wild ones have kept an eye on Nezahrian territory. We won't be able to hide from them that we have Aurelian dragons in our camp."

The dragons continued to approach. Raziel and Faelowyn pushed their way to the front. The leader of the wild dragons, the large black, was easily double Faelowyn's size. He roared at Faelowyn, and Lyssandra thought she saw the great female dragon wither.

Silver eyes full of ancient knowledge peered at each dragon in turn. Lyssandra thought she would faint from shock and wondered what poor Elisaria was feeling under the weight of his stare.

"Tyrbanath, the King of Air, the Song of Ages, sire of Faelowyn," Raziel announced.

"That's Faelowyn's father?" Antonella shrieked.

Dragon hearing must be astounding, Lyssandra mused. A dragon of dappled red and orange turned her large eyes in Antonella's direction.

"Amorith, Faelowyn's mother."

Lyssandra bit her tongue, swallowing her plea for Raziel to keep his knowledge to himself.

Tyrbanath bellowed, glaring at Faelowyn and Raziel on her back. His tail flicked back and forth, but he did not allow his dragons to approach. Lyssandra found herself exceedingly thankful.

"What do we do?" Lyssandra whispered.

"No sudden movements," Symmeon replied. "I never thought to see the wild ones so close."

It seemed as if the large black dragon was having a conversation with Raziel. Lyssandra watched as the Black Prince's fingers stroked comforting circles at the base of Faelowyn's neck. Muscles around his jaw feathered, and a range of emotions flicked in his eyes as long moments passed.

Finally, the Black Prince turned towards them. "Everyone land."

"I really must protest," Zanniel called out from Codee's back.

"Take our riders to the ground and keep them safe," the Black Prince continued.

There was no point arguing. If the wild dragons wanted them on the ground, the best course of action was to comply with their request. And since Raziel was the only one with them who could speak with dragons, they needed to ensure he was able to communicate.

Elisaria was all too keen to spiral into a sharp dive. Aerin surprisingly hesitated, hissing at the large black dragon. But Faelowyn snapped at his tail and forced him to do as he was told.

Lyssandra dismounted and found she was grateful to stand on solid ground once more. All they could do was watch in a detached sort of horror as two of the black dragon's company broke away to land on either side of their group. Although these dragons did not bare their teeth or growl, Lyssandra felt threatened. Wishing Edvern was with them, she lifted a hand to Elisaria's side and felt her dragon trembling. She was certain that he'd know what to do.

*The great dragons of the mountains, known for their power
and fires, were once the kings of all creation. Renowned for
their wisdom, the world was a place of order. Until mankind
entered the world.*

ANCIENT HISTORIES AND MAN

HAVEL

CHAPTER 19

King of the Air

RAZIEL, THE BLACK PRINCE

To any outsider, Faelowyn was the picture of calm. But Raziel felt the lingering touches of fear. It had been many long years since she had confronted her sire, Tyrbanath, the largest of all wild dragons. The last time they had seen him, she had been subjected to his stony ire after one of her sisters had attempted to contact her.

Even dragons were afraid of the unknown.

Tyrbanath did nothing for her as her mother, Amorith, chased her from his presence. Through the bond he shared with his dragon, Raziel felt her humiliation and longing.

"You are my family," Faelowyn's voice said through his mind. He could feel her shift under him as she peered at a dark grey dragon. The male stared back at her, flashes of red and gold among his scales. *"I need no other."*

Lies.

Raziel's palm pressed against her dark scales, his eyes briefly closing. He couldn't bear to feel her pain, but he carried the wound as if it were his own. When she had come to him, a beautiful black dragon wanting to join in the fight against the rebel Aurelians, he had never considered she had come without the permission of her great father. She had been exiled.

"You've not had any dragon ..."

"I have Odharn now," Faelowyn answered. Her head swayed to the side, eyeing her father, who curled his lips and snarled. After they had bonded, Raziel had learned that many years ago, Tyrbanath had been hurt by the Nezahrian emperor and decided his clan would no longer help humankind. This was revealed to him after a very angry Tyrbanath confronted him.

"Daughter." The weight of Tyrbanath's voice settled around the air like a heavy cloak. Bright silver eyes roved over Raziel, and he felt no more than a naked babe before such an ancient dragon. He braced himself and let Faelowyn decide on how she wanted to proceed.

"It's nice to see you," Faelowyn replied. Raziel was proud of the courage she was able to muster. *"Even under these circumstances."*

"These are not your lands," Amorith said. *"What are you doing here?"*

"War is on the horizon."

"War is always on the horizon," the dark grey dragon behind Tyrbanath said. Faelowyn tilted her head to the side to survey him curiously. She knew this dragon. He meant something to her.

"Yugrah, I was led to believe you were dead."

"Alive. Dead. What is the difference to you?" Smoke plumed from Yugrah; his lips curled back into a snarl. *"You abandoned us. My life or death is no longer relevant to you."*

"How can you say that?" Faelowyn reared back, her tail lashing the air. *"After everything we were? After the ransacking of our nest?"*

Nest? Shock coursed its way through Raziel's body, followed quickly by envy. Faelowyn had a mate. And he had never known.

"You left me alone to mourn!" Yugrah snarled. *"I'm no longer concerned with your affairs."*

"The Aurelian king is amassing an army. That should be concerning for all."

"Aurelia ... the land of healing waters. Ever our enemies and rivals." Tyrbanath was not pleased, and Raziel was happy they were far enough away that they would not experience the lash of his tail or the bite of his talons.

"Humans are the true enemy," Amorith said. *"We have our own spies within the Aurelian ranks."*

"Raziel isn't truly human," Faelowyn replied.

"They are," Yugrah said. He gestured lazily to the others on the ground. Raziel felt a rush of fear, taking in the two large dragons that penned them in on both sides. If Tyrbanath willed it, they would all be killed in a matter of moments. From the air he could see Aerin restlessly pacing, his broad dragon body only a pinprick. *"You may have forgotten your lost hatchlings, but I haven't."*

"I mourn still for all we have lost. But we aren't the only creatures under the Father Dragon that have lost," Faelowyn said.

"Your mind is polluted from spending so much time with them." At Amorith's stinging remark, Faelowyn drew further back.

"Humans have shown me both goodness and evil. I have seen courage and cowardice and loyalty and honour."

"Cuddling up with Aurelian dragons."

"Perhaps there isn't such thing as a Nezahrian dragon, wild dragon or Aurelian," Faelowyn insisted. *"Perhaps we're all the same."*

Amorith scoffed, but something like curiosity sparked in Tyrbanath's eyes. This surprised Raziel. Whenever he could coax Faelowyn to talk about her dragon kin, she always praised her mother ... but felt wary of her father.

"What do you mean by such a bold statement, daughter?"

Sensing that Faelowyn was unsure how to proceed, Raziel answered for her. *"It seems the Aurelians have a way of enslaving their dragons' minds. We have seen—"*

"The eggs, yes," Amorith said. *"They were originally meant for the Uhl'hari ... our spirit kin. The dyrathakins were creatures that could conduct and enhance powers. The control over the dragons was an unfortunate by-product. From the time of their creation, they were never meant to be in human or dragon possession."*

An interesting confession, Raziel thought, that a dragon would admit they were not to be in the hands of their own kind. By rights he should have been the guardian of the eggs as the Yavari, the military leader of the blessed ones.

"Kyros thought he knew better," Tyrbanath rumbled. *"He always had a high opinion of his abilities."*

Raziel had known that Kyros was an old dragon, older than Faelowyn. That he was known even to his wild kin was a surprise to him.

"Your brother thought that bonding himself to a lower born human, a servant of the royal bloodlines, was a brilliant idea." Amorith shook her head. *"My own hatchlings ... flying from the nest, spreading their wings against their own kind."*

Brother? Raziel felt a jolt of shock. How had he never known this?

"Mother, I didn't do what I did to spite you. I believe—"

"Both you and Kyros have severely injured me." Amorith was in no mood to listen to her daughter's excuses.

"Brother?" Raziel pushed into Faelowyn's mind. *"He was your brother?"*

But Faelowyn didn't answer. She gnashed her teeth. *"The Red Plague is dead. I hope you're happy."*

Tyrbanath reared his crowned head back, roaring to the skies. Raziel had spent his life with a dragon; he was no stranger to their moods and fits of fury. But seeing the largest dragon he had ever seen lashing out, bellowing like thunder, made him nervous. Dragons tended to forget that humans were delicate creatures. Although not entirely human, Raziel was still vulnerable.

"How?" Amorith had softened a little, and Raziel mused that perhaps dragon parents were similar to humans. One could be angry towards one's own offspring ... but Kyros had remained Amorith's son to the bitter end. It hurt the draconic matron to hear of her son's death.

"I tried to help. There were too many." Now Raziel could hear Faelowyn's grief and regret mixing with her dislike for the red dragon. Had it been there all along? And if it had, how had he missed it?

"How?"

"The Aurelian dragons attacked him," Faelowyn said.

"Enough!" Tyrbanath snarled, although there was no heat in his tone. *"He was dead the moment he was enslaved by the Aurelians."*

"He bonded with the Uhl'hari," Faelowyn said. *"Whatever his failings, he is responsible for the emergence of the Uhl'hari ... and by default the defection of the Aurelian dragons."*

Faelowyn turned her head to regard the Aurelian dragons down below. Even though they were just specks at this height, Raziel could sense their general unease. *"Our Aurelian dragons were ones that escaped and fled the towers. We expect more soon."*

Tyrbanath rumbled, eyeing the Aurelians with clear distaste. It would take more than his exiled daughter's word for him to consider them anything more than pawns or puppets.

"Why didn't you tell me about your family? Your children." Raziel's mind whispered his question privately into Faelowyn's mind, trying once more to breach the walls she had erected. He felt her recoil a little and the sharp slicing pain of heartbreak.

"Because that dream was gone. It was my secret to protect."

"Kyros was exiled because he bonded with Ullryk?"

"Ullryk was considered a man with minor abilities by his own people. Kyros bonded with him and proved otherwise. Whatever punishments the Nezahrian emperor piled on Ullryk's shoulders, he overcame ... They were not treated well. Kyros was officially exiled the moment they absconded to Aurelia."

"The more I learn ..."

"Not one of our kind is innocent."

"What is that?" The incredulous tone from Tyrbanath's low growl tore Raziel from his conversation. He had been so engrossed with Faelowyn that he had not noticed that the wild dragons' attention was no longer on him. He turned, the wind whipping his long hair into his face. He sensed Faelowyn's quiver and rumble of fear.

"The little fools."

Against the size of the wild dragons, Woe was small. He clutched a happily wriggling Odharn in his claws. His wings beat erratically. He had flown hard and fast to catch them. Large amber eyes burned with exhaustion.

"I'm flying!" Odharn cried, his four legs splayed and peddling in the air. Raziel took a moment to enjoy the expression of joy on Odharn's countenance. It had been decades since he had let himself feel the wonder of flight.

"If you're not careful, I'll drop you," Woe snarled with the effort of keeping himself steady. The younger dragon was not making his task easy.

"You've uttered the same threat the whole flight," Odharn replied. *"You haven't dropped me yet."*

Tyrbanath made to approach them, but Faelowyn found her courage and intercepted him.

"No!" Faelowyn barked, her tone sharp and sure. *"You'll bring them no harm."*

"It has only one wing!" the dragon behind Tyrbanath said, his chest rumbling with laughter. *"Look at it!"*

"His name is Odharn," Faelowyn rumbled, her head swaying from side to side. Raziel wisely held his tongue, not daring to point out that not long ago, she had not felt kindly towards the youngling.

"Green!" The younger male continued his cackling, glee lighting up his expressive orange eyes.

"He's mine!" Faelowyn snapped, watching as Woe reached them. With gentle claws Faelowyn took the small green dragon into her talons, relieving Woe of his burden. *"I'll tear you to shreds."*

The male checked himself, but the smirk on his face didn't disappear as he glanced sidelong at Tyrbanath.

"You took the chance from me to have a family," Faelowyn said. *"I made my own with Raziel and Odharn."*

"I see." Amorith's drawl told Raziel that she didn't see at all. Meanwhile Odharn continued to swing his legs, his one wing beating against Faelowyn's side.

The young male continued his chuckling. He shook his head under the weight of Faelowyn's glare. *"To think, our little Fae, a mother."*

Faelowyn rounded on him, her jowls snapping. *"It would be a miracle if any female dragon would nest with Prynn the Pompous!"*

"I have three hatchlings!"

"Enough!" Tyrbanath had had enough of the arguing.

"Who are your friends?" Odharn asked.

"Friends?" Prynn snorted, and a plume of smoke curled from his nostrils.

Odharn blinked, snout upturned to look up at Faelowyn. Raziel caught the playful smirk. *"Who are your foes?"*

Faelowyn seemed torn between demanding that Odharn be taken away and demanding he stay by her side. In the end it was Woe who broke the spell. When Tyrbanath made no move or sound, the steel-grey dragon decided it was safe to approach the wild ones. Cold silver eyes tracked Woe's progress, and Tyrbanath ignored Faelowyn's rumbled warnings.

"*Who are you?*" Tyrbanath growled.

"*I am Woe. I humbly request permission to return home.*"

The sky around them erupted into growls and rumbles. Woe calmly watched on, unconcerned that the wild ones might consider smiting him for his audacity. "*I remember a nest inside a mountain, where rock ran liquid and red,*" Woe said. "*I'm the only one of my nestmates to survive. I—*"

"*Did you take for yourself a rider?*" Tyrbanath demanded, his tone clipped and sharp.

Woe drew back, his wings trembling under the heated stare of the ancient dragon. "*My lord, there was no—*"

"*Did you take for yourself a rider?*" Tyrbanath repeated.

Raziel could only feel pity for Woe, observing as scaled lips frowned and his horned head dipped. "*I did.*"

"*Did you fly for the Aurelians?*"

"*My lord ...*"

"*Did you fly for the Aurelians?*"

"*I did, my lord.*" Woe looked so utterly dejected and defeated that Raziel wanted to reach out and run his hands down his warm scales.

"*Then you may not return.*" Tyrbanath's words were like a death sentence handed down.

Woe lowered his snout even further. Without looking towards Faelowyn or Odharn, he tucked in his wings and dived. He landed beside his brethren, the other Aurelian dragons crowding around him. Aerin's squad had formed their own family, away from the mountains where their eggs had been laid.

"*That was very unkind of you,*" Odharn said, rounding onto Tyrbanath, staring matter-of-factly into the aged dragon's face. "*Codex was also poached as a fledging from your nest. The others were mostly stolen eggs. Through no fault of our own, you reject us.*"

Silver eyes narrowed into hard, angry slits. *"I am Tyrbanath. I don't need to be kind. My sacred duty is to protect the dragons under my rule."*

"What about the young that you've lost?" Odharn said. *"He's one of you, and yet you deny him without considering what he's been through."*

"He flew with humans," Tyrbanath replied. *"His own words condemn him."*

"I think you most unwise," Odharn replied, ignoring the furious rumble from the much older dragon. *"You'd prefer your young to be slain rather than grow strong and find their way back home. Do you not know of the suffering our kind faces in Aurelia?"*

Unconcerned about the ancient one before him, Odharn loosed himself from Faelowyn's grip, beating his one wing frantically to get closer to the displeased Tyrbanath. He pressed his snout against the ancient one in a common gesture of kinship. Raziel drew in a deep breath. Underneath him, Faelowyn shifted.

"Did you not hear our pleas for help?" Odharn whispered. *"We called and called. And no one ever answered."*

"Why is it you have one wing?" An undercurrent of anger could be heard in Tyrbanath's cool tone. It seemed the ancient dragon did not wish to answer Odharn's uncomfortable question.

Odharn didn't hear it. *"I escaped the dragon's den."*

Tyrbanath blinked slowly.

"Humans cut the wings of dragons who are to serve in the dens," Odharn continued.

Tyrbanath reached out with his great claw and plucked the struggling Odharn up so that he no longer had to pump his wing up and down. The green dragon looked past the much larger male, boldly staring at the imperious Amorith. *"Hello."*

Tyrbanath turned sharply towards Faelowyn. *"See what happens to foolish dragons who trust humans!"*

"It was two humans who rescued me," Odharn interrupted, turning his head to look down at Lyssandra, who was a tiny speck on the ground. *"That girl there and ... and another friend. It's my turn to rescue him."*

"No," Faelowyn said, finally able to choke out some words. *"Your job was to stay in the camp."*

Odharn rolled his eyes, looking smug as he turned back to Tyrbanath. *"Old dragons are bossy."*

Prynn choked back a laugh.

"You escaped?" Amorith asked. *"How?"*

Odharn nodded. *"Lyssandra has magical powers. She broke the locks with apple seeds. We climbed up the side and ran. The old blind drake and my mother..."*

"Your mother?" Amorith slunk closer, her voice as soft as the morning wind.

"She didn't make it to the gates."

Raziel closed his eyes, pained to hear of Odharn's mother's fate. It was not lost on him his action was mirrored by both Tyrbanath and Amorith.

"We ran to the forests, and Eddi taught me to hunt ... and kept me safe. Alynta, the dyrathakin, was very good at fishing, and I was able to keep everyone warm."

"Survival against the odds." Tyrbanath nodded and turned away.

"Father, we're not your enemies," Faelowyn said. Perhaps this was the time to be bold. They still didn't know why the wild dragons were in Aurelia. *"We all want to see the dragon riders fall ... even some of the riders themselves wish it."*

"I'll ask again, Great One," Raziel continued, licking his lips, and his gaze speared Amorith and Prynn. "Let us go on our way."

Tyrbanath breathed in, looking part amused and part defeated. *"Our kind is ancient enough to feel war in the air. Lizardlings of the forests and water wyrms are stirring in the depths."*

"Will they help us?" Odharn asked.

Prynn barked with laughter. *"Our cousin dragons of water and ice, the patrons of Aurelia, have always been envious of air and fire. They would rather watch us drown than help us."*

Eyeing Prynn, Tyrbanath inhaled, running his tongue along serrated teeth. *"The Aurelian water wyrms will rise to battle their home's enemies in whatever form they believe they take."*

"Let's not forget the lizardlings' love of violence." Prynn grinned, showing rows upon rows of white, savage teeth. *"Lizardlings see humans as the enemy of the land and everything that is living."*

Odharn cocked his head to the side. *"Perhaps they can be persuaded to show mercy."*

"Like you came to persuade me, little runt?" Tyrbanath asked. Odharn wriggled in the ancient one's grip, flickering his tongue out playfully. *"You knew exactly who I was when you confronted me. I sensed it."*

Odharn paused, his tongue snapping back into his maw. *"You knew?"*

"You are either very brave or very stupid," Yugrah said, his eyes shifting back to Faelowyn. There was a sad solemnness to the male drake.

"I'd prefer to be known as brave," Odharn replied. If a dragon could blush, Raziel was sure the young dragon would be red to the very tip of his tail. *"If you won't help, then I was hoping you would not hinder."*

Tyrbanath growled.

Amorith eyed Faelowyn, something unspoken shared between mother and daughter. Then she turned her tail and flew away. Prynn followed her, and then after one last lingering glance, Tyrbanath released Odharn back to them, and he followed.

Raziel exhaled, his hands stroking Faelowyn's scales. They watched together as the wild dragons on the ground also followed Amorith. In silence they hovered until the wild dragons were specks on the horizon.

"Tell Woe to take Odharn back to camp and the emperor," Raziel snapped, hand running down Faelowyn's slender neck. "I don't fancy explaining to Ze'hyrn why his dragon ran off."

There was plenty of rumbling shared between the Aurelian dragons before Woe did as he asked, taking a squirming Odharn back to camp. Aerin joined him in the sky first, closely followed by Elisaria, then Gryph, Valtar and Codee.

Raziel dreaded to think upon the destruction coming their way. A storm was on the horizon, and he wasn't sure he was the one to weather it.

CHAPTER 20

Halsabith Reborn

MOIRA

There was something beautifully poetic about knowing that one's patience had yielded fruit. While Cynedir's ruins smouldered, Moira sent her riders to ascertain the whereabouts of the Cynedir riders. As she suspected, Alaxen's captains had sided with him. They had flown free, fates unknown.

The surrounding area around the spire gave little clues to where they had gone. Even a host of a dozen riders was difficult to hide. They couldn't have gone far without detection.

Whilmana and Yahler, she released on the outlining villages. They questioned men, women and children. When bribery failed to loosen tongues, she allowed her torturers to showcase their talents in a more practical manner. Pain only resulted in babbled nonsense and outrageous lies.

A simpler woman would have thought the process a waste of time, but Moira knew that riders of Cynedir would have gone to ground, hoping to wait her out.

It wouldn't be fire or steel that betrayed Alaxen's men, but their natural needs. Food, shelter and updated information were essential to their survival. They would be watching the skies, hoping to divine her movements. If the captains were truly stupid, they'd question the same villages she had.

In anticipation of catching them, Moira grounded most of the dragons. To the new masters, she gave very strict flight paths. If Alaxen's people were watching the skies, she could shepherd them into a better position to pick them off one by one.

The results took three days.

A villager, a middle-aged man with a balding head, came hobbling unexpectedly to her camp. Perhaps he thought if he was first to deliver his information, he would be seen as loyal. Or more likely he expected a reward.

"Bring him here!" Moira demanded after she watched the man struggle in her sentries' grip. Her guards were not gentle as they took him by his biceps and dragged him along the ground.

"I spotted them, milady!" the man cried, his large round eyes bloodshot and yellowing. "I saw 'em."

"Where?"

"Not five miles from here." The man gestured with his head, feet scrabbling to get underneath him.

"And their number?"

The man shuffled; his head bowed.

"How many of them are there?" Moira bellowed.

"I don't rightly know," the unfortunate man replied. "I can't properly count."

Moira clicked her tongue. "Run him through."

"Wait! Wait!" the man cried, his eyes bulging out further. "I can't count, but I'm mighty helpful with me herbs. I snuck in their camp and poisoned them."

"Poison?" Despite herself, Moira was intrigued. The villager didn't look like much, but he had a vicious streak.

"Yes, ma'am." The man nodded his head up and down, his movements strangely disjointed.

"Pray tell, my simple-minded friend," Moira purred, "what does your poison do?"

"Awful things to your guts. They'll be soiling their britches for days."

"Five miles?"

The man shrugged. "Around about that, I reckon."

Moira considered this news, lifting her head to catch Whilmana's eyes. This was it. They had the Cynedir riders where they wanted them. Once she was sure her torturer understood that they would move once it was dark, she turned back to the guards holding the informant.

"Strangle him."

"Milady! Milady!"

Turning upon her heel, Moira didn't look back on the pleading man. To do so would show weakness. She was the Grand Lady of Aurelia; compassion wasn't one of her failings. She was the uncrowned queen, and she would not have any cause to doubt her strength.

As the villager said, they found the camp of the rebels within the five-mile radius. From the air, Moira noted the neat organisation favoured by Alaxen and those under his command. The fire pit was in the middle, surrounded by the cook's tent and supplies. The officers' quarters were close to the supplies, while common riders had their smaller tents forming a protective ring around the camp.

It was late, and she couldn't detect any movement below. A nudge of her heels and a tug of the reins, and Moira's dragon banked. The camp was silent, but she counted eight sentries, their torches still burning.

Yahler brought his dragon level with her, his beady eyes glinting in the moonlight.

Raising her hand above her head, Moira enjoyed the quiet moment she knew all her riders' eyes were on her. She was the huntress, and her prey was beneath her, defenceless and unaware of their impending doom.

Her arm came down, and she was surrounded by the raucous shouts of her riders. Dragons bellowed, and from their bellies, they spewed their fire. Heat blistered through the air, and Moira could taste the steel and blood on her tongue in anticipation.

The screams did not come.

All around Moira: silence.

"You've been fooled," Fennix said, his voice clear within her head. She felt his arms around her waist as he tugged her closer to his chest, as he did in life. His cold breath ghosted over her cheek. *"I trained Alaxen for the day he needed to overthrow you."*

Anger snaked in her guts; she clenched her teeth, wanting to fight her way out of those phantom arms. Fennix might not be with the living, but he had found a way to torment her in death.

A cry rent through the air, wrenching Moira out of her horror. Head jerking up, she was in time to see riders of Cynedir poised above her force.

Yahler's dragon twisted around and up, thrusting himself headlong to meet the dragons of Cynedir. With a cry, Whilmana joined him. Moira could only watch in morbid fascination as the Cynedir riders ploughed through her ranks.

Into her power's waiting embrace, Moira sunk. She had delved deep last time she had killed dragons. This time she would sink even deeper. They said madness was inevitable if power was mined recklessly.

But boundaries were made to be broken. It was her power, and she was strong enough to fully grasp it. She would be the greatest queen to walk the three kingdoms. One by one each nation would be put to the torch until only she stood.

Lifting her hand, she concentrated on the nearest dragon, her fingers stiff and shaking with effort. The beast screamed with confusion as unassailable fear took hold. Fear wasn't enough. Hatred was a stronger emotion. The beast struggled with its own consciousness in midair, its rider helpless as the beast tore her from its back. Moira's body shook in ecstasy, relishing the rider's screaming pleas.

The beast's mind was broken. Bringing the rider to her maw, the dragon swallowed her rider whole.

Moira released her power, letting the creature to grapple with what it had done to its own rider. Laughing, she reached out for another, hatred flowing forth. This time she experimented. The dragon writhed, frothing at the mouth. It was stronger than her first victim.

Strong talons ripped at its own underbelly. It thrashed as it delivered its own killing blow. Moira fed it such self-hatred that it killed itself on the battlefield.

"Moira!"

Moira tilted her chin to look up. Above her, Alaxen's oldest friend, Oskar Hertforde, glowered down at her. His neatly trimmed beard and face were spattered with blood, and his sword, infused with his magic, hummed with an orange glow.

Moira reached out her hand to take a hold of his dragon, her mind racing for something truly terrible for the beast.

A thunderclap resounded around her, and a flash of golden light. Ears ringing with pain, she noticed she was all alone with her forces.

Swearing, she rounded onto Yahler. "Find him!"

"My Grand Lady," Yahler stammered, his face pale, "Hertforde used his power on us."

"As far as I am aware, he was only able to move himself and a small contingent." Whilmana joined them, her dragon sporting a terrible gash down its side.

Closing her eyes, Moira tried to push the fog out of her brain. She couldn't think. Couldn't remember the important information she should know about Hertforde.

"Instead of pushing himself to another location," Yahler supplied, his voice grating on Moira's nerves, "he moved us to another part of the country."

Moira's went dry. Oskar Hertforde had been secretly expanding his power too. Now she had no idea in what part of the country she was, and once she returned to the place of the battle, her enemy would be gone.

"He was always a hard one to pin down," Whilmana murmured.

"Wily or not," Moira said, her lips curling into a smile, "I look forward to catching him one day. His death will be delicious. For now, time to land and regroup."

Moira's dragon gratefully landed, huffing and puffing as she did so. The others of Moira's force swiftly followed. Looking around she saw that the

Cynedir force had done very little damage. Most wounds were superficial. They had lost two of their numbers.

While her riders took the opportunity to rest, Moira strode to the cover of the trees. Her skin felt unbearably tight on her body; it tingled with untapped power. A smile touched her lips, and she ran her tongue along her teeth, remembering the terrible things she could do with a dragon's mind.

"You have descended into darkness." Moira looked up, not surprised to see Fennix leaning against a tree only feet away from her. Dark eyes studied her, looking into the depths of her soul. He pushed himself from the tree, approaching her with a shake of his head. *"Such a waste, Halsabith."*

"You're dead," Moira reminded him.

Fennix smiled. *"Not as dead as you would like, my dear."*

"You betrayed me."

Fennix laughed. *"You killed our daughter and our son and seek the death of our other son. Who betrayed who?"*

"No." Moira swallowed, taking a step back. "Go away; you're dead."

"Tamah was your fault."

"No! The Nezahrians!" Moira clutched at the locket around her neck as if the piece of jewellery were the only thing from stopping her from spiralling out of control.

"The Nezahrians were the blade you used to kill Tamah. She would have never flown into that territory if you had allowed me to teach her as I taught our sons. If she had listened to her father … she didn't have to die that way."

"You're dead!"

"Lady Moira, who are you talking to?"

Moira spun on her heels, her eyes taking a moment to focus on Whilmana. She swallowed again, forcing her fingers to relax and let go of the locket around her neck. She'd be Halsabith reborn. She'd be strong, untouchable. Not even the warnings of the dead could reach her.

Forcing a smile on her face, Moira stepped out of the clearing. "It's nothing," she said. "Just practicing stirring the troops."

Whilmana dipped her head in acceptance, and together they left the ghost of Fennix Tallermayne in the clearing.

"Do you think you can turn your back on me?" Fennix's voice was a whisper in her ear. Ghostly fingers curled around her neck, tracing the chain of her precious locket. *"I'll always be a part of you."*

Biting down on her lip, Moira grasped at the chain. It was choking her. Holding her back from what she ought to be. Her fingers fumbled on the catch, her footsteps faltering.

"It's not too late," Fennix said.

Moira held up the gold locket, and for the first time since Tamah's death, the sight of it did not stir or grief or anger.

It was time to let Tamah go. Her daughter belonged to a time when she still had a glimmer of hope.

There was no prayer or words of remembrance for her daughter as she dropped the locket on the forest floor and walked away.

A smile curled on her lips because Fennix was wrong. It was too late for her. Darkness had always been her shelter when life's sorrows came her way. Within the shadows she had grown stronger, mightier than any other dragon rider. From the darkness she had come, and to the darkness she would return.

Chapter 21

Garden of Lights

Edvern

Through the unyielding leather of his fox mask, Edvern peered at the amassing nobles. Among the extravagance of the gentry, he felt woefully out of place. Women dressed in the finest silks and jewels flocked around aloof gentlemen who eyed the world as if it owed them a great debt.

Through the sea of milling guests, Palea swept through knots of the most influential men and women of the three kingdoms. She brushed through them, gentle as a summer breeze, leaning into groups to share tasty titbits of information. The women gathered around her, gossiping and arguing like barnyard hens. The men observed her, preening and vying for her attention.

Edvern watched as she approached him, his posture stiffening as she tucked her arm in his. She smiled coyly at a group of men, who scowled at Edvern. He clenched his fists. The thick parchment of their stolen invitation was damp with his perspiration.

"Relax. We'll be let in the palace soon enough, my dear." Palea's lips brushed against Edvern's cheek, her warm breath ghosting over his skin. A chaste kiss, but affectionate enough that some of the gentlemen turned away, looking for easier quarry.

Edvern swallowed, forcing his hands to relax. "I'd rather be thrown to rabid dogs."

"Relax," Palea repeated. "The rich are easily impressed."

"They're watching you." Edvern stood taller, letting his lips fall into an unnatural leer at a young man striding their way. The stranger eyed Palea hungrily. He caught sight of Edvern, checked himself and retreated to his jeering friends.

"You're scaring away my prey." The gold beads in Palea's braids gleamed in the torchlight as she tilted her head to wink at a man who was gawking at her. She grinned wolfishly, the affect disconcerting with her delicate butterfly mask.

Edvern lifted his chin, not allowing his gaze to settle on anyone. Surrounded by so many pompous fools, he felt his fingers twitch. He lowered his mouth to Palea's ear. "How I long to rob these idiots."

Palea's fingers lingered on his arm. "Maybe you'll get lucky tonight, Sir Fox."

The line of nobles progressed, and before long, a soldier dressed in the king's livery drew level with him.

"Papers."

Edvern relinquished the parchment, ignoring the bemused expression on the soldier's face at the crumbled invitation. Palea laughed, lifting her hand to Edvern's chest.

"My dear, you ought to whip that manservant of yours," she simpered. She turned to the soldier, the curve of her smile widening. "He, of course, refuses to listen to me."

"He serves my needs well," Edvern said, hoping that his reply would appease the soldier. "But he's a surly cur after a beating."

The soldier fingered the parchment, and Edvern flexed his new fingers under his cloak, testing their strength. They had been one of the most marvellous gifts he had ever received, and Taseria's continued remarks left him with a sense of guilt. Alaxen should not have spent so much time and effort pouring his healing into his hands. She was right; he could survive without his fingers. Alynta believed Edvern was ridiculous for having such thoughts and offered to tear out the woman's wig. He declined the offer of revenge. Alaxen was going to deal with her anyway.

"Everything alright, sir?" the guard asked. "You're looking a tad uncomfortable."

"Aurelian winters are nearly as inhospitable as its people. Are you going to let me in or not?" Edvern asked, drawing upon the memory of Lyssandra's voice when she wanted to get her way. In doing so his accent held a slight Saemorish lilt. She'd be impressed.

"I thought all the Saemorish diplomats had already arrived," the soldier said, eyes lingering on Edvern's dark hair.

"You heard wrong," Edvern replied, wishing it were Lyssandra who was on his arm. He missed her company.

"Begging your pardon," the soldier said. "Your companions are to see His Majesty, the king, in the morning."

Edvern smiled thinly, a little surprised to hear there was a delegation of Saemorish diplomats. Maybe Lyssandra was here. He tucked the information away for later and stepped past the soldier. The throng of nobles led him towards the famous gardens of Irani. It was tempting to look around for signs of Taseria and Alaxen. But with the crowd of nobles, servants and guards, it was next to impossible to do so.

"I'll see what I can find out," Palea whispered in his ear. "Head to the gardens; check the boundaries. Don't be obvious."

"I robbed Moira Tallermayne," Edvern murmured. "I know how to skulk."

Palea grinned at him, her dark eyes bright with amusement behind her lacy butterfly mask. She turned from him with a peck on the cheek. "Don't have too much fun."

Edvern watched her go. She disappeared into the night, melding effortlessly with the nobles. They parted for her, gentlemen and ladies alike turning their heads. Although she seemed to be unaware of the attention, Edvern was sure she was enjoying every moment. She belonged in their company.

Once she disappeared, Edvern pushed his way through the crowds. No one paid him any attention. The frosty air turned warm as he entered the inner sanctum of the gardens. Originally the palace had been Ullryk's summer house, a gift for his wife Saskah. The palace had been built around a large inner garden. Even after centuries, the power that kept the garden in perpetual summer remained strong.

Edvern sucked in a breath, taking in the silver lights hung in giant trees. Banners of burgundy and gold hung from evergreen branches. Little more than ghosts, dancers dressed in diaphanous gowns weaved between the garden paths. They mingled with the guests while musicians played flutes and lyres.

"Wine, my lord."

Edvern plucked a goblet of silver from an offered tray, his eyes on the beauty of the gardens and not the servant. He stepped forward, the rim of his cup going to his lips. He vaguely heard the servant chuckle at his wonder, but Edvern said nothing as the flavour of summer berries and honey danced across his tongue. Staring down into the dark wine, he noticed flakes of gold in his drink.

The sight of such unnecessary luxury made Edvern's insides freeze over. He resisted the urge to drop the goblet. Did the nobles not care about the number of lives that were lost each winter?

"My lord, are you well?"

Fighting to regain his composure, Edvern lifted his eyes from his goblet.

The servant eyed him suspiciously. "First time at court, my lord?"

"A shame to fill wine with gold," Edvern said, ignoring the question. "Expensive piss if you ask me. I wager one goblet would be a year's wages?"

The servant bit his lip, holding back a bark of laughter. After lifting the wine once more, Edvern forced himself to drain the goblet and return it to the tray. His stomach knotted as the warm alcohol ran down his throat. With a dismissive nod, he turned upon his heel.

Following the sound of laughter and music, he had the insane urge to join the revelry and forget the mission. Alaxen had ordered him to search the gardens, to test the perimeters. No doubt to keep him out of trouble.

"My lord!"

Every muscle in Edvern's body tensed. The servant rushed up behind him, holding the tray of goblets expertly so none of them spilled. It took all of Edvern's willpower not to run but to stand and look at the man.

"You dropped this, my lord." The servant offered Edvern a square handkerchief, shifting his weight. The scrap of fabric was soft and painted with muted colours.

"I didn't ..."

The servant lowered his head into a respectful bow. Before Edvern could think of a reply, the servant slipped back into the crowd, leaving him with the mysterious handkerchief. Pushing through the milling crowds, Edvern reached a lonely torch. He unfolded the fabric and lifted it to the light. Most likely it was a signal for forbidden lovers. With that thought came a twinge of guilt and loss.

The painting in verdant greens and vivid blues was beautiful. The exquisite garden and waterfall were overlooked by Aryis, the star lady of hope. She was embraced by her consort Qavi, the lord of the darkest hour, his form depicted as curling clouds in the night sky. Strange that such a keepsake was painted and not embroidered.

He lifted the handkerchief to the light to inspect it closer. Aurelian dragon riders had all sorts of ways to deliver secret messages. He hadn't expected to see a glyph, the one calling for help and warning of danger, hidden in the full moon.

Sucking in a breath, Edvern tore his eyes away from the painting, afraid that someone might have realised what his prize was. There were only two dragon riders in Irani that he was aware of.

Tucking the handkerchief into his boot, Edvern hurried to the gardens, hoping that he wasn't heading into danger. Without a backwards glance, he disappeared into the dark garden paths, the joyful music fading from his hearing. The king's gardens were extensive. It would take time to ensure he would not be ambushed once he found the waterfall. Curiosity tugged at him.

He followed each garden path meticulously, marking the types of partygoers, the number of patrolling guards and the direction he was moving in. Wild fruits grew beside stone paths, leading to narrow staircases.

Far from the music and the dancing, he found it. The thunderous waterfall overshadowed the gardens. The water fell in a cascade into a large, dark lake. A testament to the pride Aurelia felt at being a nation that embraced water.

The lights along the stone railings were lit, but there didn't seem to be another soul about. Cautiously, Edvern stepped closer to the columns of a balcony that overlooked the lake. In the flickering torchlight, the streaks of gold from the king's large fish darted in and out of the shadows.

Enthralled by them, Edvern leaned on the edge and peered into the water. He cried out in disgust, catching the long, sinewy, snake-like creature who weaved among the fish. It reminded him of his unpleasant encounter with the water wyrms.

"If you lean any further, you'll fall in."

Edvern whirled around, the hem of his winter cloak brushing his legs. A dragon rider, his golden hair shining in the light, leaned against a marble pillar. The long silver blade at his side lifted slightly, his face remaining in shadows.

"The king's eels are carnivorous," the rider said.

"That I believe," Edvern muttered, eyes turning back to the churning water.

"You weren't who I hoped to lure here. You're not a Cynedir rider."

Edvern remained silent.

"One might ask what nefarious plot you're up to." The rider took another graceful step forward. "Have you nothing to say, Sir Fox?"

"Kendrick…" It had been over a year since he had seen his cousin. Edvern lifted his hand to fumble with the lacing of his mask. "It's me."

"Edvern?" Kendrick blinked; the point of his blade lowered. He glanced over his shoulder, his face paling. "Keep that mask on! You need to leave. *Now*."

"We've come to rescue you," Edvern countered. "Your father is here."

"Da is here?" The hope on Kendrick's face hurt.

Edvern nodded woodenly. "Where are Bastian and your dragons?"

But Kendrick had questions of his own. "Did you get our letters? Is that why you are here? Is my father coming with his riders from Cynedir?"

"Letters? Cynedir?"

Kendrick's expression shuttered. He looked to be at war with himself. "Are the rumours true?"

Edvern wanted to scream. Why was Kendrick being so difficult? "Depends on which rumours you're referencing."

"You fled Gytall."

"It's true." Edvern shook his head, keen to get his cousins and run. The quicker they got out of the king's palace, the better. "We must find your father and go. I don't want to stay in this place any longer than necessary. We're—"

"Hyrin and Narani were both confiscated," Kendrick said. "If I leave, we'll be hunted down like dogs."

"You'll be cornered if you stay," Edvern said. "We'll find a way to free the dragons. We're running out of time."

"You're the one running out of time."

Edvern resisted the urge to punch Kendrick in the face. Why was his cousin being so obtuse? He threw his hands up in the air, biting out each word as he replied, "We're here to rescue *you*."

Kendrick swallowed, looking at Edvern's gloved hand. "Get back to the party. I'll find Bastian. Watch for my signal, and if everything goes to hell … duck for cover."

"I am *not* a child."

"You're surrounded in enemy territory." Kendrick was not impressed. In disbelief Edvern watched him striding away, hating that he was considerably younger than his cousins. How typical of Kendrick to boss him around with only half the information.

"We need to find your father."

"I need to find Bas … he's missing."

Edvern swore. "Why didn't you say that earlier?"

Kendrick looked over his shoulder at him, eyebrows raised.

"Fine, what do you want me to do?"

Kendrick tilted his head, looking Edvern's costume over. "You can dance, can't you?"

"Dance?"

"For blessed talons," Kendrick growled. "No one is looking for a thief and intruder on the dance floor."

"Your father sent me to the gardens," Edvern replied. He doubted that Alaxen was on the dance floor with some lady. "Not to prance around with the nobles."

"Keep watch and apprise my father of the situation," Kendrick said. "If all goes well, we'll disturb the king's plans for his Euquallian prisoners and dissuade the Saemorish in forming an alliance. Cynedir riders will be here soon to assist, I hope."

"Euquallian prisoners? Riders?"

"We're hoping to avoid bloodshed." Kendrick's smile was stiff. He was keen for action; he had been in exile for over a year. If tonight came to blows, Kendrick would be in the thick of it. "I don't have time for this. Do as you're told."

Edvern watched his cousin disappear into the dark of the trees, leaving him alone with the roar of the waterfall. He couldn't help but feel he was an unsuspecting mouse trapped in the scheming of others.

Turning on his heels, Edvern tugged his cloak tighter around his shoulders. Those in power might hold the best cards, but he was learning how to play the game well.

Making his way back to the gala, Edvern was careful to appear unhurried. He weaved among the partygoers, smiling and laughing. He took the gold-dusted drinks and turned his eyes to the sky.

Riders from his uncle's spire might be Alaxen's salvation. They might also be Edvern's doom. He needed to find his uncle, to make sure he was near when they appeared. But with the crowds of nobles and servants, it was an impossible task.

In among the swirling skirts, Edvern caught sight of a familiar form dressed in dark red velvet and gold. Lifting his latest goblet to his lips, the wine was tasteless on his tongue.

"Be ready." Edvern sent a hasty message to Alynta and Izorah, putting his goblet down on a server's tray as he waded through the crowds. His heart skipped a beat. He would know her anywhere.

"Lyss ..."

CHAPTER 22

Dance of Destiny

LYSSANDRA

Even in the depths of winter, the palace of Irani held a captivating mystery that the dour Gytall Spire failed to capture. At home among the sea of bright colours and jewels, Lyssandra weaved through an army of silks and velvets.

Empress Ionah's red dress constricted her. Sweat dripped down her spine. The king's garden was heated by an unnatural warming spell. Tilting her head, she pretended to study the lights in the trees that emitted a golden glow around the crowds. The celebrations were confined to a strict circular clearing. Guards were posted on many of the garden paths that led into the pitch black.

"Keep away from the shadows." Konrad bent his head, whispering into her ear. On his arm, Antonella waved her feather fan, her eyes on the groups of musicians.

"They'd be a good place to hide," Symmeon said gruffly behind him. He had decided that he would play the role of bodyguard for the two young noblewomen and suitor. It would give him the excuse to watch and not engage with strangers. It also meant that no one would pay him any mind. Despite herself, Lyssandra felt a little safer knowing he was close by. "Raziel's group would be through the western entrance by now."

"Smile," Antonella said, smacking Lyssandra's arm with her fan. "This is a party. And we got through the eastern gate without any problems."

"You've been to plenty of soirées." Konrad's voice was muffled by his mask.

"Let's find some cake," Lyssandra said, mustering her confidence and training. "I could do with a sweet."

Lyssandra touched her fingers to her own mask to ensure her face was still hidden. Standing among the throng, she thought the mission seemed suicidal. What were they hoping to achieve? Break into the king's dungeons and liberate the Euquallians?

She made her way to a server and grabbed a pastry and a goblet. The pastry was both tart and sweet on her tongue. Swallowing the treat, she paused, curious about the strange statues. While sculptures in Saemore were cut from white marble, the Aurelians seemed to favour a black stone that shimmered in the torchlight. She approached the effigy of a woman wearing flowing robes and was stunned by waves of heat coming off the stone. The details were extraordinary. Even the statue's long, flowing hair looked as if it were being teased by an unseen wind. Lyssandra almost expected the woman to draw in breath and greet her.

"Dragonstone. Its properties enhance the spells to maintain the summertime temperature."

A young man joined their group, his familiar blue eyes bright behind his fox mask. Lyssandra straightened, sucking in a breath. A quick glance at Symmeon told her that he had already deduced the young man's identity. The young man only had eyes for her. He offered his hand and bowed at the waist. "Might I spirit you away for this dance?"

"You may ..." Lyssandra's lips formed the words.

Soft leather gloves, which hid the injury she knew was there, squeezed her fingers and led her away. Hoping that Symmeon would not cause a scene, Lyssandra dared not look behind at her companions.

"The rocks are formed by dragon fire. It is an Aurelian way of showing wealth."

"Eddi," Lyssandra whispered. She took in the gentle smile and the soft, dark hair hanging in waves about his face.

His fingers squeezed hers a little tighter. "What are you doing here, Lyss?"

"I could ask you the same thing." Lyssandra looked over her shoulder at Antonella, who was coquettishly twirling her hair around her finger. Konrad looked amused. She could see him eyeing Eddi up and down. Symmeon was scowling.

"Do I need to teach him a lesson?" Edvern nodded at the Nezahrian general.

"He's with us," Lyssandra said quickly, placing a delicate hand on Edvern's arm. His muscles were coiled, ready to strike. She didn't like how her stomach cramped at the thought of Edvern coming to blows for her.

"It's not safe," Edvern whispered, leaning forward so his warm breath sent shivers up her spine. "Dragon riders are coming."

Lyssandra nodded, drawing herself closer to him as they joined the dancers. The music washed over her, and for just a moment, they were an ordinary couple. "It was a risk we took." That was when she noticed that Edvern's right hand now had five fingers, but there was something not right.

"Your hand—"

"A gift."

"You're healed? How?"

Edvern shrugged, lips tugging into a frown. "In a manner of speaking. It's not important."

Lyssandra shook her head, tucking Edvern's words away in her memory for later. She'd puzzle out the meaning when they were out of danger. "The Aurelian king is going to do something terrible."

"We're here for my cousins," Edvern said. "King Oluvin isn't any concern."

"You were spotted by a Nezahrian war wraith ..."

"He survived his little swim with the water wyrms then. Good." A vicious look of humour crossed the lines of Edvern's face. Glancing over his shoulder, he seemed to be contemplating his next move. "Kendrick suggested I get myself on the dance floor and look out for trouble."

"I thought I lost you," Lyssandra whispered, gathering her courage to inch a little too close for propriety. Alive and unharmed, he was with her. All she needed to do was to find a way to keep him safe.

Edvern's back straightened, his eyes darting to the side of his red leather mask. He chewed his bottom lip as his hands clasped around her waist and pulled her flush to him. "I didn't think you'd care too much one way or another."

"You're my friend," Lyssandra said, her head spinning as they swirled on the dance floor. She wanted to twist her fingers in his long hair, to bury her face in his chest and make reality go away. He was a mystery. Five fingers and his hair back to its long length unnaturally quick. There would be time later to hear his story. "I've been so worried."

"You worry needlessly. I am unharmed."

Lyssandra noticed how Edvern's eyes refused to look at her. He glanced over her shoulder and only relaxed once he saw they were out of the line of sight of Antonella and Symmeon. Konrad moved to flank them on the opposite side, Antonella trailing him. Lyssandra risked a glance, catching her cousin's eye. Well-trained at the Saemorish palace, Konrad was shadowing her. She pulled Edvern closer, resting her chin on his shoulder while staring at Konrad.

He's a friend.

The revellers danced around them, swallowing them up as they swayed in time to an ancient Aurelian tune.

Edvern's steps were fluid. Her skirts swept around her feet as he twirled her. He was alive. He was whole and ... despite herself she loved him. She felt him sigh softly, and she breathed in the scent of him. Fire and smoke.

"I'm sorry." She drew close to him, sensing his sharp intake of breath as she laid her palms against his chest.

Edvern's eyes were on the sky. He looked down at her, confusion written over his face. "I don't understand."

"I treated you poorly," Lyssandra said, and she dragged in a deep breath. "Talons knows, I'm ashamed that I tried to force you to come to Saemore with me to a life I know you would have hated."

Edvern was speechless. She could see it in his eyes; undoubtedly no one had ever apologised to him for the wrongs they committed against him. In some respects, she was glad that she had been the first. She could make everything right between them. She had to tell him.

"Edvern, I ..." Lyssandra reached up, brushing away a soft lock of black hair.

"You don't have to apologise. Not to me." Blue eyes filled with confusion and fear.

Lyssandra felt a flickering of annoyance at Edvern's interruption of her declaration. She grabbed his hands, squeezing his fingers. The digits on his right hand were wrong.

"Listen. Please. The Nezahrians are here looking for the Euquallian party and your cousins."

Edvern paled, and Lyssandra wondered how much he knew. His lips pressed into a firm frown, and then he spoke, his voice low and grave. "My uncle believes I'll be safe with the Black Prince."

"You'll not come to harm at the hands of Raziel Yavari." Throwing out all her training as a diplomat, Lyssandra decided to be direct with him. Edvern was a man who valued forthrightness and honesty. "But your other family members, I'm not so sure."

"Is he here? The Black Prince?"

Lyssandra nodded.

"I have to get my cousins out," Edvern said. He shook his head, taking her hand, and dragged her through the swaying masses. "Can I trust you, Lyssandra?"

Lyssandra did her best not to feel the sting of Edvern's words. He spoke as he saw fit, not seeing any reason to sweeten what he felt must be said. "You know you can."

Edvern's vivid blue eyes seemed to drink her in, taking in her ridiculous mask and her gown. He bit down on his lips, still chapped and sore from their misadventures. Lyssandra chastised herself for her longing to reach out and brush her lips against his mouth while he was struggling with his own inner turmoil.

"Eddi?"

Edvern startled, his hands searching for his pouch on his hip. Fumbling, he pressed the pouch into her hands. "Faelowyn is a wise dragon, I believe," he said, stepping closer and lowering his voice. "A gift from the Tallermaynes. A sign of good faith, if you will."

"Eddi ..."

"It's something of great worth."

Lyssandra took the offered pouch, opening the drawstrings. Nestled inside was a familiar-looking egg. Instead of the pleasant amber she had previously seen, it was forest green. Her hands trembled. "You're giving this to me? This is—"

"A dyrathakin egg ..." Edvern said.

"You're hoping this purchases your family their lives."

Edvern nodded. "I can't abandon them."

And despite having no family of her own, Lyssandra understood. For Edvern's sake, she hoped the Black Prince would too. Tying the pouch to her side, she could feel the glass warming through the leather.

"Tell the Black Prince that the dyrathakin eggs were giving Moira more control over the dragons. Without them ... this is our chance of toppling her. Alaxen has hopes of getting the last egg from Navilla. Riders from Cynedir have defected. Kendrick mentioned they were coming." Edvern's words came out in a rush, like he feared he wouldn't have time to convey all he needed to.

She observed as Edvern's piercing eyes dulled. He gave her a small nod, and she knew he was resigned to his fate.

"Cynedir isn't here yet. There'll be time to make an escape."

Edvern's gaze drifted over her shoulder. Was he looking for a last glimpse of his family?

Hand resting on the egg, Lyssandra considered her next words carefully. It would be no good to scare him off now. However reluctantly, he was close to agreeing with her. "Please consider handing yourself to the Black Prince tonight. Speak with him and make these requests to him. He respects honesty."

"You want me to yield to Raziel Yavari?"

"We're surrounded by his agents." Lyssandra took him by the elbow. "There's no shame in a tactical surrender."

Edvern opened his mouth to speak. His eyes refused to look at her. Whatever he was wanting to say was interrupted by a flurry of trumpets. He flinched, startling at the sound. Grabbing him, Lyssandra dragged him behind two taller noblemen who had stopped mid-disagreement. She turned her head in time to see Symmeon shadowing them.

Torches flared on a balcony, and a man dressed in blood-red ceremonial robes stepped into the light. He flung his arms wide, raised to the sky as the partygoers stopped to look up at him. All knees, with the exception of Edvern's, hit the ground, and Lyssandra's stomach churned.

The Aurelian king certainly didn't look like an imposing man. In the firelight of the sconces that burned on the palace walls, the red gems on his crown winked like pools of blood and highlighted the red tones in his hair. His face was gaunt, eyes sunken into his skull. The frown on his thin lips was ugly.

Lyssandra had a healthy amount of self-preservation. She had knelt when everyone else had. It was best to play along with these sorts of games. She would be unnoticed. But Edvern remained rigid, his knees locked, chin raised defiantly.

"Behold the fates of those who stand in the way of Aurelian progress." King Oluvin's voice held an unpleasant rattle. He was advanced in years and was weakening. Lyssandra didn't have time to contemplate the political implications that both Aurelia's and Saemore's monarchs' days were numbered.

Lifting a crooked finger, the king gestured to the gardens. As one, the expectant crowd turned towards the darkness.

At the king's ominous proclamation, hidden torches flared to life, and the darkness became light. Upon a high structure, built to look like an ancient Aurelian temple, lines of Euquallian prisoners stood gagged and bloodied. Dozens of the king's men surrounded them. Swallowing back a mouthful of bile, Lyssandra stifled her cry of horror and grasped Edvern's hand to tug him to a kneel.

"It seems the rules of diplomacy are changing." Antonella had somehow moved through the crowds to come beside her. She hid her furious expression behind her fan.

Lyssandra blinked, trying to make sense of what she was seeing. The prisoners were obviously the Euquallian delegation. But they weren't the king's only surprise. To either side of the line of prisoners were large flags, each covering a lump.

"Behold the might of Aurelia's throne." The king dropped his hand, and at the gesture, the flags were cut free.

Lyssandra found herself struggling to breathe, while Antonella groaned and turned her face away. Edvern's howl of rage broke her heart. His gloved hands trembled as he clawed at his cloak pin.

"Eddi!"

Lyssandra grabbed his sleeve, but he didn't react. His blue eyes filled with unshed tears as he stared up at the two dragon heads, their mouths agape and glaring down at the revellers. He wasn't the only one crying their outrage. For now, he was camouflaged among the crowd's shouting. She knew Edvern; he wouldn't be hidden for long.

"Eddi, kneel!" Lyssandra pleaded, knowing that it wasn't in Edvern's nature to do so. "Symmeon!"

Lyssandra frantically searched for her companions, only to find that Symmeon had been bailed up by a tall Aurelian dressed in black. The Aurelian leered behind his wolf mask, keeping his blade at Symmeon's throat.

"General Tallermayne," Symmeon purred. "Going to cut my throat?"

"Don't tempt me," Alaxen Tallermayne barked. "Where's Raziel?"

Symmeon's retort was lost by the presentation of the first prisoner, a woman wearing a plain cotton scarf around her hair. Clearly, she was an unfortunate servant of the delegation. The poor woman babbled into her gag, shaking her head as she struggled against her captors.

The crowd stilled; even Edvern was silenced.

A sword swung through the air, and the woman's muffled protests ceased. Lyssandra shut her eyes tightly, her ears catching the sound of the victim's head hitting the ground with a heavy thump. The guards threw her body over the side, and Lyssandra flinched, swallowing vomit.

"Monster!" Edvern's voice cracked through the crowd, resounding and clear as a warning bell. Despite the hammering of her heart in her chest, Lyssandra liked what she saw. Uncompromising strength.

"Of all the impertinence!" The king's eyes were feral, and spittle flew from his mouth. "Who are you to stand before your king?"

Edvern cocked his head to the side, a slight smile on his lips. There was little warmth to his voice when he spoke. "Apparently, the one willing to stand against a tyrant."

Fire licked up Edvern's feet and twined up his limbs. Before she could cry out, he seemed to glow in a halo of flames. His hands unclasped his cloak, and wings of fire burnt their way through his shoulder blades and clothing. His cloak pooled at his feet.

"Foul creature of the underworld! Cursed one! Guards! Bring me his head."

Edvern didn't as much as flinch at the king's command. The unsettling smile left his lips. "You've made a grave error, Oluvin."

The king made no reaction to Edvern using his first name. His stillness unnerved her. Calm could sometimes disguise the treacherous workings of a mad mind.

Desperate to find a way to help Edvern escape, Lyssandra looked around for the approaching guards. Apparently uncaring of his own approaching fate, Edvern seemed oblivious to the Nezahrians flanking him. She spotted the grim smirk on Dalain's face, and a shadow that could have been either Raziel or Zanniel weaved forward.

"Time to die!"

Lyssandra was jolted out of her search by the approach of a woman in an owl mask. She grabbed Edvern, wrenching him from Lyssandra's grasp.

"Taseria!" The Tallermayne general behind her was not happy.

Edvern snarled at the woman, freeing his arm. He bit down on her, blood trickling down his chin. In the past the two elongated canines in Edvern's mouth would have disgusted her, but Lyssandra found herself intrigued.

There was a flash of steel and no time to scream a warning. The woman grabbed him, hauling him off his feet, dagger at his throat. Edvern's hands groped at his hips.

"Behold the Tallermayne traitor!"

"Taseria!" Alaxen Tallermayne roared, throwing Symmeon to the ground. He ran forward, growling through his mask. His progress was halted by a dragon landing. Partygoers scattered like mice before a cat.

The dragon lumbered forward, maw open, ready to devour his prey. Edvern lifted his hand to the creature. It would be alright. Edvern could speak with dragons. The woman pressed the blade firmly against Edvern's throat, slicing the skin.

"Take your hands off him!" Alaxen screamed over the panic of the revellers. "Tynum, stand down."

Lyssandra's heart sunk. The dragon rumbled again but did not move.

Alaxen wouldn't reach them in time.

Remembering that she had vowed never to lose Edvern again, she grasped the only weapon she had. The pouch with the dyrathakin egg. "Touch him and die!"

She swung the pouch. The egg connected to Taseria's jaw, sending the woman sprawling across the ground. Edvern bounded to his feet, drawing a weapon seemingly from nothing. From where she lay, Taseria spat out two teeth, and glared up at Lyssandra.

Spinning on his heel, Edvern took Lyssandra in his arms, his sword crackling with fire magic as the woman's dragon lashed out. Edvern's wings of flame sheltered her as their feet left the ground. Fire danced around them, but they did not burn. The last few minutes had been a nightmare. Lyssandra tucked her face into his chest, taking a precious moment to breath in his scent of woodsmoke.

His power had exponentially grown.

"Ha!" Edvern's dark chuckle drew Lyssandra's attention to the ground.

A young Euquallian woman in a shimmering black gown pounced on Taseria. Long golden nails grabbed hair, and the wig tore from the attacker's scalp. Taseria screamed as the young woman kicked her feet out from underneath her.

Arrows flew around them. Looking almost apologetic, Edvern landed right beside Dalain and released her. Lyssandra's fingers fought to catch him, but he was gone in a flurry of flames.

"Palea!" Dalain cried, grabbing Lyssandra and thrusting her behind him. The woman in black turned towards him. She saluted, grinning, blood in her teeth.

Palea! The name resonated with Lyssandra, but she didn't have time to examine her memories.

Taseria seized her chance, swiping her blades against Palea's face. She disappeared under the belly of her dragon. Dalain and Symmeon charged forward to push the beast backwards. The green dragon snapped his jaws at them but shuffled to hide his rider from view.

"Palea, what are you doing here?" Dalain's face twisted in anguish.

Another dragon landed, his eyes glassy with blindness. Despite the many layers of her skirts, Palea ran towards the creature. While her beast held the other dragon at bay, she settled onto his back. A small, wiry dragon, wings twisted, stood on the large blind dragon's head.

"Palea, get down." Fury and fear mingled on Dalain's face.

Everything had happened in a matter of heartbeats. She glanced around. Where were Antonella and Konrad?

"The wall!"

Turning her head, Lyssandra felt her stomach lurch. The executioner had been looking to his king for his next command. A cry stuck in Lyssandra's throat as an elderly man's legs were kicked from underneath him. Pity for the stranger welled within her; she could see his hands shaking.

The sword poised over the neck of the elder man never had the chance to fall. From the shadows another warrior, faster and better skilled than the executioner, ran along the edge. Prisoners shuffled out of his way as the silver blade intercepted the killing blow. Three quick strikes, and the executioner was dead.

It had been some time since she had seen Kendrick Tallermayne, but she knew it was him. When he travelled to Saemore, accompanying his father, she had watched him from the shadowed alcoves as he trained with the swordsmen, shirtless and relentless. He possessed a natural feline grace, his poise as beautiful as any dancer. A second warrior joined, limbs more gangly, his strokes precise and measured. Guards fell away from the prisoners, scattering like leftover crumbs.

"Archers!" King Oluvin screeched. "Kill them!"

Kendrick moved through the maelstrom of arrows, seemingly untouchable. Lyssandra could see a shimmer of a shield around him. He moved like a man possessed.

Two blue dragons burst through the sky. The largest of the pair, darker but with a silver underbelly, bellowed at the sight of the two dragon heads. He landed with a heavy thump, his roar shaking the ground.

Edvern made it to the lighter blue dragon's back.

Lyssandra felt pressure in her mind from Elisaria. She sensed her dragon was scared but had been told to wait for the opportune time to reveal themselves.

I'm well, Lyssandra thought, wishing once again she had Edvern's connection to dragons.

Lyssandra didn't know where he had come from, but she was grateful for Zanniel turning up. His cheeks were splashed with blood, and he was grinning savagely.

"There's the dyrathakin," Zanniel yelled.

"Where?"

"On the wall."

Lyssandra tilted her head back, spotting Alynta, who looked much larger than when she last saw the fire fox. Her fur glowed a brilliant orange in the darkness as she mauled her way through the Aurelian guards.

"No!" Lyssandra screamed, catching sight of a silver blade in the dark. A knife sunk into Alynta's flank, and the dyrathakin howled in pain.

Grasping on to Zanniel's shoulder, she stood on one leg, hurriedly unlacing her useless court shoes. Then, barefoot, she gathered her skirts and sprinted through the crowd. There was no way that Edvern would want Alynta fighting for her life alone. She had to reach the dyrathakin.

The partygoers were only too willing to move out of her way as she darted through them. She charged forward, ignoring the cuts on the soles of her feet as Alynta yipped and attempted to retreat. She reached the stairs, still running as she grabbed a fallen soldier's sword.

She was screaming, Lyssandra realised, her sword raised above her head. Alynta saw her charge and ducked into the shadows. The soldier who attacked the dyrathakin leered at her approach.

Breathing in, Lyssandra drew on all her lessons in sword play and charged. The man, seeing only a girl in a red dress, underestimated her. She took advantage of his laxness, driving her blade against his. The clash of steel sent a jolt of pain up Lyssandra's arm, but she pushed her advantage, enjoying the moment when the man realised he had been beaten by a woman.

Putting one's sword through the throat of a dummy was vastly different than ramming the blade through real flesh and blood. Mercy wasn't something she was willing to give. She continued to press her advantage, sinking her blade into her opponent, then spinning to impale another, and another and another. Blood splattered over her cheeks, hair and gown.

Propriety be damned. They had attacked the dyrathakin, so they could die upon her weapon.

"Fancy meeting a diplomat here of all places." Kendrick Tallermayne's hand was on her shoulder, steadying her as she blinked. Their enemy lay dead around them.

"It's nice to see you too, Kendrick," Lyssandra murmured. Stepping back, she stared around at the still corpses, her hands shaking. Then she looked to the grim-faced rider. She remembered him as a young man who had always been eager for light-hearted antics. Now all signs of joy had been leeched out of his soul. He moved like a looming darkness, tall and handsome in his black leathers.

Lyssandra looked around again, her knees weak. "Call this renegade's diplomacy."

"Get your breath back," Kendrick said, his voice low and not unkind. "First kills are the hardest."

Lyssandra took a moment to steady herself, not bothering to tell him these weren't her first victims. From the shadows, Alynta padded closer, sniffing at the dead soldiers. She wrinkled her nose at their bodies and looked for Edvern in the sky. He was difficult to miss with his brilliant wings of fire.

High in the air, he had been kept busy by the king's archers.

Bastian came to join them, taller than his younger brother. He was a slim man with a brooding, serious face. He grunted, staring up at Edvern, then grabbed a bow and fired it on the nearest archer.

The archer was dead before he hit the ground.

"Bullseye!" Kendrick chortled, taking up a bow as well. He notched two arrows and let them fly. Each found their mark.

Bastian didn't react. He notched and fired. Notched and fired. Notched and fired in a steady rhythm. The expression on his face didn't shift. Not one of his arrows missed.

"Killing the king's lapdogs is boring me," Kendrick said.

Again, Bastian grunted.

"For my dragon!" Kendrick notched another arrow, and without any ceremony, let it fly. It found its mark, lodged perfectly in King Oluvin's throat. Lyssandra sucked in a surprised gasp, her hand flying to her mouth. The Aurelian king fell to the ground.

Dead.

Kendrick Tallermayne had assassinated the king of Aurelia. Lifting his face to the sky, the younger Tallermayne laughed. Enraged, the king's archers turned their arrows onto them.

Bastian snarled; with a gesture of his hand, the arrows were halted in their flight by a wall of wine. Tears of mirth ran down Kendrick's face.

"Ran out of water, brother?"

"Wine will do," Bastian snapped.

From the east came yet another resounding rumbling. Lyssandra had known when they had left Tacebia that Empress Ionah would come, if not for her sister, her people. She was a staunch patriot. The roar of Ionah's mount, Balfar, echoed through the palace moments before the emperor and empress burst onto the scene.

Momentarily stunned, those engaged with the fray froze.

Ze'hyrn's golden armour glinted in the moonlight as he charged into the chaos on the back of Woe. While Ze'hyrn flew high, Ionah wasn't a woman to keep to where it was safe. She guided Balfar to fly close to the wall and jumped to land just before Lyssandra. The Tallermayne brothers exchanged weary glances with one another.

"Welcome, Your Majesty," Kendrick said with a bow.

"Excuse me. The soldiers are swarming the stairs." Bastian stepped past the empress with a small dip of his head.

Ionah regarded the pair of them. Perhaps she was expecting monsters and not the enigmatic young men before her.

Desperate to catch another glimpse of Alynta, Lyssandra hefted her sword, looking around. The palace guards charged up the stairs, knocking over escaping prisoners. Soon they would be trapped.

Lyssandra knew the Aurelians feared that if they left one Euquallian alive, they would face terrible consequences.

Ionah's blade sung as she joined the fight to free her people. The empress moved with impressive speed and poise. Lyssandra protected her flank until she felt a sharp cut to her side. She screamed, the force of the arrow knocking her off her feet. Fortunately, she had only been nicked.

Kendrick came to her, a terrible, grim expression replacing his laughter. He helped her up, offering her protection while she gathered her wits. Making a gesture, he did not even look at the next volley of arrows as they crumpled.

They were pressed on all sides. Kendrick made another sweeping motion, and the swords before them were torn from their masters' hands by an invisible force. Sweat poured down his face as he bellowed, lifting the palace guards with his power and tossing them down the stairs.

The show of power was costly.

His skin turning a grey pallor, Kendrick looked to her, his expression stricken. His assassination of the king meant he was the target. The king's men wouldn't allow him to escape, and his chance of surviving this night was slim. Yet he had fired that arrow for his dragon.

Taking out the swordsmen allowed the archers to get between his defences. Bastian screamed a warning, but it was too late. Kendrick had exhausted his power with the strength of his display. Lyssandra was unsure if it was her imagination, but she felt the soft tendrils of the rider's magic fading away.

Arrows filled the sky, their enemies screaming their triumph. Abandoning his sword, Kendrick grabbed the empress' shoulders, turning her so that his unprotected back shielded her. He lifted his hand. Another shield, one made of Kendrick's rapidly depleting power, enveloped around her. Seconds later Lyssandra heard the deadly thwack of four arrows embedding themselves into Kendrick's body.

The empress was falling, Kendrick on top of her.

Kendrick!

Talons, Kendrick!

Lyssandra might have screamed. Not in anguish or fear, but in fury. He had saved her. Saved the empress of the nation that was his natural enemy. It wasn't meant to be like this.

Bastian roared with her. She sensed the ripple of raw power as a boundary of wine shielded them from the flight of arrows.

After scrambling to Kendrick's side, Lyssandra helped him roll off Empress Ionah. Blood frothed and bubbled on his lips as he smiled at her. Glassy eyes flicked towards the Nezahrian empress still sprawled on the ground, then to his brother's shield.

"Why?" Lyssandra whispered, dropping to her knees, ignoring the blood and gore. She lifted a shaking hand and swiped away the damp hair plastered to his forehead.

"Anything to be of service to a pretty lady. We're not all bad ... us Tallermaynes." The light in his eyes dimmed, and his lips tugged into a frown as he turned his face towards the dragon head on his left-hand side. "Oh, Father Dragon ... the pain. The pain."

Lyssandra's hands found his cold fingers, and she squeezed. She groped around for his sword. He shouldn't be without it in death. The empress knelt, placing the handle of his weapon into his hand.

"It's a good thing to die honourably," Empress Ionah said. She helped him bend his arm, pressing his sword to his chest. Kendrick's lips twitched as she stroked his hand. "Don't be afraid. Rest now."

Staring into Kendrick's face, Lyssandra took in his pale lips twisted in anguish, his eyes staring back at her, unseeing.

"I'm sorry." The words stuck in Lyssandra's throat. She stood, surprised that her legs could take her weight. All the while the green egg burned her through her dress, its burden heavy.

HAVEL

CHAPTER 23

Emperor's Arrow

RAZIEL, THE BLACK PRINCE

Raziel watched from the ground as Edvern burned across the sky. His heart leapt, relieved to see that he and his dyrathakin had made their transformation without his help. Dyrathakin and Uhl'hari would soon learn to siphon each other's power, to magnify what they were capable of. It had been many centuries since a dyrathakin hatched and bonded with an Uhl'hari.

"Praises be to the Father Dragon," he murmured, shock and awe keeping his feet planted to the ground. Sound ebbed and flowed around him, and it wasn't until a panicking man rammed into his shoulder that he snapped back into awareness.

Edvern was screaming for Alynta. He could feel it in the air, the Uhl'hari's distress and the dyrathakin's pain. Their bond was suffocating in its strength. Turning on his heel, Raziel pushed his way through any man or woman who barred his way to the dyrathakin.

Raziel's gut clenched with the all too familiar pain and worry. He knew from the timbre of Edvern's cries what he would see when he found Alynta, for he screamed as if his soul had been rent in two. She was hurt.

"Faelowyn, I need you." The heat of his dragon's answering fury filled his chest, so hot that he almost believed he could breathe fire. Nothing would stand in his way in getting to the dyrathakin.

Flames filled the sky, the searing heat of the dragon panicking the crowds. It had been years since he was a human on the ground while dragons flew overhead. He did not miss the helplessness.

Studying the dragons circling in the sky, Raziel was pleased to see their dragons were busy doing what they could to protect the humans on the walls. Rock and stone rained down as Aerin swooped and slammed his body into buildings hiding enemy humans. Above him, Codee circled, working with Alaxen Tallermayne to subdue another green drake. Valtar bellowed for his Saemorish riders—they seemed to have gone missing. Balfar provided cover for the wall, while Woe and the emperor kept their distance.

"Alynta. Come!" Reaching the wall, Raziel felt fury blaze within him. He hacked away at soldiers as Alynta hobbled her way through them, her tail lashing. Lavender eyes bright with awareness stared unwaveringly at him. She wasn't mortally wounded.

Barefoot, her beautiful gown torn, Lyssandra ran down the stairs. Without speaking he grasped the diplomat's shoulders. Tears streaked down her blood-spattered mask.

"She's hurt," Lyssandra gasped, her hand dropping to Alynta's head. The dyrathakin whined and limped forward. Her nose twitched, scenting the air, and her ears pinned back along her head.

Zanniel reached his side, sword outstretched to a shadowy figure creeping down the steps. Hands tapping on his thighs, Bastian

Tallermayne stared back coldly. The Aurelian eyed the weapon and batted it aside as if it were no more than a fly.

Zanniel lunged for him, but Bastian raised his eyebrows and stepped to the side. It wasn't often that Raziel saw his spy flustered. He reached out with his power, holding the Tallermayne in place.

Expecting snarling and cursing, Raziel was surprised when Bastian cocked his head to the side.

"That's enough, Zanniel." The empress stood behind Bastian, who inclined his head and let her through. "Bastian Tallermayne is our guest."

Bastian scoffed. "Guest indeed."

"Where's your brother?" Zanniel demanded.

"Dead." The word fell from Bastian's lips.

"Your dragon?"

"Dead." If not for the young man's trembling hands and spasming lips, Raziel would have thought him unaffected by reality. Bastian shifted, his gaze drifting to the decapitated dragons.

"Give me one good reason I shouldn't remove your miserable head from your shoulders." Zanniel stalked forwards.

"Perhaps you should." Bastian's breathing hitched, his stare never leaving the gruesome sight of the dragons' heads, as if he wanted to emblazon it into his memory.

Raziel was surprised when Ionah intercepted Zanniel. "Bastian is not to be harmed. Bind his wrists."

"Edvern wouldn't like this," Lyssandra said, watching as Bastian held out his wrists, his shoulders slightly stooped. Dalain had joined them, and it was he who stepped forward and bound the young Tallermayne's hands. "Edvern gave me a gift for Nezaha in the hopes you might show his family compassion. And considering what Kendrick did ..."

"Kendrick fought on behalf of his dragon, not a foreign queen," Bastian said. He lifted his chin, Aurelian pride still burning in his eyes. He wasn't defeated. Not yet.

"Kendrick died protecting Empress Ionah." Lyssandra frowned at him, enunciating her words for the benefit of the gathered Nezahrians. "And Edvern has expressed his wishes to ensure the safety of his family in the return of his surrender."

"Uhl'hari belongs to Nezaha, and he'll learn to do as he is told by his betters," Zanniel snarled.

"Edvern never did as Moira wished." Bastian's eyes returned to the silver blade at his throat. "What makes you think you can bend him to your will? Whatever he has given Nezaha to secure our safety, I doubt he's done so with permission."

Raziel lifted his gaze to search for the Uhl'hari. Edvern had managed to pull himself onto the light blue dragon's back. His fiery wings left trails of light. Bare-chested, he was vulnerable—most armour wouldn't allow for movement for his wings.

Elisaria greeted Edvern's blue dragon with joyful enthusiasm. In return the blue shielded her from incoming arrows from the Aurelians.

"Taseria!" Lyssandra spat, eyes filling with fury. She lifted her finger, gesturing to the woman who had grabbed Edvern in an attempt to hand him over to Oluvin. Taseria was astride her dragon, barrelling towards Edvern. Swallowing a snarl, Raziel followed her flight path, wishing he was in the sky to end the wretched woman's life.

He wasn't the only one who had marked her.

Alaxen's blue drake crashed into her roaring mount. The Tallermayne general was screaming at her, his words lost in the wind and battle. Raziel glanced between the pair. If his memory served him right, she was one of Alaxen's trackers.

"That betrayal hurts," Bastian murmured.

Talon to talon the dragons fought. Codee joined the fray, but Taseria's dragon was larger and near feral with rage. Sharp fangs found purchase in Codee's flank.

Zanniel made a choked noise of dismay, his blade dropping as he watched his dragon disengage. The yellow drake was having trouble manoeuvring to protect his vulnerable flank.

Alaxen's blue dragon came to the side of the ailing yellow. From above Elisaria dove down onto the neck of Taseria's dragon. Talons grappled with scales. It was only moments, and the green dragon was gone before Taseria could strike at her with a sword, but it was enough to tip Taseria's mount off course.

Alaxen had been watching, waiting for this moment. He stood upon his dragon, a soft power coating his hands, and leapt into the air. It took a brave heart and a stomach of steel to jump from one dragon to another. Landing safely on Codee's back, Alaxen pressed his palms against the warm scales. Raziel had seen Alaxen do it before, calm and assured. At his touch, the wound on Codee's side stitched itself together.

"A healer," Lyssandra whispered as if something had occurred to her. She choked back a gasp as Elisaria rounded Taseria and her dragon again, ramming her head into his hind quarters. Healed and angry, Codee twisted his head around so that Taseria was forced to retreat.

Zanniel grunted in agreement, lifting his blade once more as Alaxen Tallermayne jumped from his dragon's back to his own. Edvern's attempt to join his uncle was hampered by their own dragons. He roared in fury at them, signalling frantically to Alaxen. There wasn't time for Raziel to study their hand movements to ascertain their plan. But General Tallermayne made no attempt to attack or harm the dragons separating him and his nephew. Interesting ...

"Lyssandra, it's time to take out the egg," Raziel said. As a boy growing up in the temple at his predecessor's side, he heard all the fables. He had no doubt what the gift was that Edvern had given her, and that he'd unwittingly chosen the right person to give it to.

"What?"

"Take out the egg," Raziel said.

Lyssandra's eyes were full of doubt and a spark of hunger. Her soul knew the path set before her, even if she was not conscious of it. She obeyed, lips parting to question him.

Dyrathakins often came forth from strife, and they only grew into maturity when there was a great need for their powers to feed into their chosen Uhl'hari. It was one of the great mysteries of the dyrathakins.

Lyssandra kneeled on the ground, her hand shaking as she held the egg tenderly in her palms. He joined her, trying to give her a reassuring smile. The diplomat's fingers were icy, but at her touch, the egg was hot. The small creature inside was responding to the sense of fear and urgency of the one who held it.

"Come, little one," Raziel whispered. It should be impossible. Once the great rift between the nations occurred, Saemore lost their powers, and Aurelia would no longer bow. Nezaha was the only nation to hold to the old ways … from Nezaha the Uhl'hari were to come.

Sweat stung his eyes as he tilted his head to study the pained look on Lyssandra's face. She could feel the dyrathakin moving, reacting to her touch.

The ground beneath their feet quaked so violently that Zanniel lost his balance, and the empress grabbed Dalain to keep herself upright. Enraptured by the egg, Bastian didn't attempt to escape.

Cracks skittered across the surface of the egg; a small, quivering snout pushed through. Which was quickly followed by tiny wings, long, gangly legs and a tail. The newborn dyrathakin was damp and sticky.

"Wrap him up and keep him warm," Raziel said.

Eyes wide in wonder, Lyssandra tore her skirts and wrapped up the little creature. He lacked the vivid orange of Alynta. His fur was a soft brown with a tinge of green. Small twig-like horns were already growing from the crown of his head. Alynta was fire and wind; this little fellow was earth, the patron of ancient Saemore.

Some great work was happening. Saemore had an Uhl'hari. An earth dyrathakin hadn't hatched in nearly a millennium. The pair must be protected at all costs.

"Get her out of here!" Raziel bellowed to Zanniel. The pair of them might hold some enmity between them, but he could trust Zanniel's skills and abilities. He tore his eyes away from their small group, searching for Tallermayne.

Alaxen was on the wall, a body wrapped in his strong arms. The sound that came from his enemy was something he never wanted to hear again. Grief. Utter devastation. He had believed Alaxen a monster, and yet in this unguarded moment, he hadn't ever been more human.

"Balfar, get your rider!" Raziel turned from his enemy. Nothing could be done for the dead.

The ground quaked again. Balfar landed, sidling closer to both the empress and Prince Dalain. Dalain tugged a lax Bastian with him. The younger Tallermayne seemed unresponsive as his feet obeyed and he was forced onto the back of Balfar.

"Something else is coming," Lyssandra whispered, her soft voice gaining his attention.

"Lyss, get out!" Raziel snarled, annoyed that she was still kneeling on the ground.

"Something is moving in the depths of the earth."

Soil rose and fell, uprooting the stone path. Raziel had heard of the phenomenon, but he had never witnessed an underground dragon attack.

"Go!" Raziel screamed, throwing his hands in the air in front of Balfar. The old dragon snuffled the ground, sniffing curiously. Further mounds of dirt formed around them. Seconds later he recoiled, wings snapping open as he made a swift ascent.

Grabbing Lyssandra's upper arm, Raziel dragged her away from the shifting mounds. The ground continued to shake, and claws attached to lithe front legs raked through dirt and stone. Elongated snouts, rimmed with razor sharp teeth, emerged from the depths.

The lizardlings hissed in a symphony of displeasure. Sinewy tails whipped around, striking any unfortunate human who still lingered.

"Mistress," they called out to Lyssandra. "You have called for us."

"Not I!" Lyssandra cried, tucking the mewling dyrathakin closer to her chest.

Lizardlings were a notoriously aggressive species of dragon who lived in family groups. The lizardlings flicked out their long purple tongues. Tails lashing, they turned, snouts raised to the fighting in the sky. Their presumed leader, a littler larger than the rest, slunk forwards, his scaled lips peeled back into a leer. Luminous eyes fixated on Lyssandra, his slitted nostrils scenting her. "I taste filthy betrayal. For now, we feast on wretched Aurelian flesh, the subjugator of dragonkind."

"No!" Lyssandra cried, her hand outstretched.

Raziel laid a comforting hand on her shoulder. "We cannot stay."

Lyssandra made a strangled noise of protest, watching as an unfortunate soldier fell to the lizardlings. Sharp rows of teeth clamped around his thigh. It must have been painful, but the man gripped his sword tighter and swung. A mistake. More lizardlings joined the first until he was covered in them. The screams torn from his lungs were terrible as they ripped him apart.

Their attack moved on, although Raziel noticed they killed those who were armed, and frightened party guests, they harassed. He shuddered. Such cruel cunning from a small but fierce creature.

"No!"

At Lyssandra's cry, Raziel whipped around in time to see Taseria draw her bow, the string taut and ready. He cursed himself for losing sight of the traitor in the confusion.

Aerin swooped in, catching the thick arrow in mid-air, snarling and snapping the shaft with his talons. He dropped it on Taseria's dragon's head.

With a rustle of fiery wings, Alynta was gone from Raziel's side. The dyrathakin raced through the air and hit Taseria. Her long claws grasped the rider's face, pulling her from the back of her dragon. The fire fox was not built for withstanding a human's weight. The woman fell, which Raziel thought was the dyrathakin's intent. The body thudded into the dragonstone, bones shattering and blood pooling.

General Tallermayne's dark blue drake blazed across the sky, Alaxen lying low over his neck. His dragon showed no fear, no hesitation as he slammed himself against the side of the riderless dragon, taking his attention off Alynta. The two males fought.

Then Palea, sweet, defiant Palea, joined the fight. Her blind dragon snapped the neck of the other. Together, Alaxen and Palea watched their enemy plummet.

"That stupid man!" Lyssandra cried. "Don't shoot!"

It took Raziel a heartbeat to work out what the diplomat saw. The emperor raised his longbow, an arrow ready. A cry of horror lodged in his throat, too late to hail Faelowyn. She was too far away to prevent the arrow from finding its mark.

Ionah had warned him that Ze'hyrn wished to relieve Nezaha of the burden of the blessed ones. Born with limited powers that he had failed to cultivate, the emperor coveted those with strong giftings. He feared, above all, Raziel taking his throne from him. Never mind Raziel was born of dragons and was not suited to ruling humans. It was why Ze'hyrn had demanded a dragon of his own, despite hating them. The emperor might abhor dragons on principle, but he also lusted over the prestige of 'owning' one.

Edvern's wings of fire were a direct threat to him. Nezahrians who held to the old ways would celebrate the legend reborn. He would quash the hope of his people just to ensure he maintained power.

Raziel had heard the whispers, listened to Dalain's fears. To the emperor, Edvern was just a dirty Aurelian dog.

The arrow was loosed.

Aerin dove. His claws missed by a hair's breadth. Raziel's heart stopped, watching as the arrow found its mark, puncturing Edvern through the centre of his chest. Edvern slumped, grip loosening, and he fell from his dragon. His sword, bathed in fire, fell with him.

Faelowyn caught him neatly on her back, twisting abruptly to ensure the emperor would not get another clean shot.

Snarling in fear, her eyes rolling to the back of her skull, Edvern's dragon protested when Aerin intercepted her. Elisaria joined them. The last thing they needed was to injure Edvern's distressed dragon.

"His breathing," Faelowyn relayed. *"Hold on, I'm coming back for you."*

Gathering her skirts, Lyssandra screamed like her heart had been ripped from her chest. Zanniel caught her arm, trying to sooth her as Ze'hyrn took aim a second time. Woe banked, throwing the emperor's aim. Furious, Ze'hyrn struck him over and over with the shaft of his arrow. The abuse had little effect on Woe.

"Shall I splatter him?" Woe's voice was full of righteous anger.

"I ask you to please bear with it for a little longer," Raziel replied.

Clasping the mewling dyrathakin kit to her chest, Lyssandra hunched her shoulders as she wept, choking on Edvern's name.

A shadow fell over Raziel. Alaxen Tallermayne's dragon wheeled around. Faelowyn loomed over them. Ashen-faced, Alaxen did not falter before her.

"Black Prince!" he cried. "I'm a healer. Let me near Edvern. I can still save him."

Years of conflict had conditioned Raziel to give his enemies nothing. He had to bite down a stinging reply; Edvern's life was on the line. Alaxen had already proved his skill in healing Codee while in flight. If he wasn't already dead, a healer was the only chance he had.

"Talons!" Alaxen swore, obviously taking Raziel's hesitation as a denial. "Let me heal my nephew, you Nezahrian dog."

Their dragons would die if they stayed here. Lizardlings might be small in comparison to their cousins of fire, but they had phenomenal jaws. Once they latched on to their victim, they never let go. Thirty lizardlings could kill a dragon. There were hundreds of them tonight. And no telling if they would turn on them once all the soldiers were dead.

"Faelowyn, to me. Zanniel, take Lyssandra and *GO!*" He turned back to the expectant Alaxen Tallermayne. "Follow my dragon. This isn't the place to do a tricky piece of magic."

Lyssandra wasted no more time. She gathered her skirts, impractical for a fight, and ran towards the gates. Zanniel followed her.

Faelowyn huffed warm air at Alaxen's dragon, who rumbled in protest as she swept by to land. Three heartbeats were all it took to get himself onto Faelowyn's back.

"With me, Tallermayne. Let's go."

Faelowyn shifted, handing Edvern's limp body into Raziel's waiting grasp. While slim, he was a dead weight. Warm blood coated his hands, and he could only imagine the damage the arrow had done to Edvern's insides. He could only pray his enemy had the necessary skills and knowledge to fix him. He settled the unconscious Uhl'hari against his chest, wincing at the gurgling sounds as he fought for his life.

"Hold on," Raziel murmured, knowing Edvern could not hear him. "It's not that bad. It's not bad."

Swallowing bile, Raziel banished his worry. Ze'hyrn was emperor. If he were anything less, Raziel would have the authority to smite him. Alas, human politics deemed that he would not be held accountable for the near murder of Edvern Tallermayne.

But it wasn't the mortals of this world that Ze'hyrn had affronted. Justice would not be served by hands of flesh and blood. An Uhl'hari had been deliberately targeted; retribution would come.

What did Ze'hyrn believe about the tales of the ancients? Did he know or even care that in the sight of the immortals, he was a condemned man?

Eye witness
accounts-
leaf shape
scales
Lizardling by Edwan
Meet Kira midnight
Soak Aerins beef red wine try again

CHAPTER 24

Defiance

LYSSANDRA

Lyssandra's legs shook as she ran for the palace's front gates. In her arms the brand new dyrathakin trembled. She lowered her chin to him, meeting his too large eyes. Too afraid to stop running, she tightened her fingers around him.

"Please." The word fell from her lips like a prayer. Something she was unaccustomed to doing. She had been the fate-maker in her own life; she needed no one to forge a path ahead. This time she was powerless.

Edvern's new body was unearthly. His wings of eternal fire cast shadows and illuminated his face. Moira Tallermayne had been right to be afraid of her bastard grandson. Raised in Aurelia, he still had the might of Nezaha in his veins.

But it had been a Nezahrian arrow that had felled him.

She could imagine the sound of the impact as the arrowhead pierced his flesh, slicing through organs.

"Damn him," Lyssandra cried, choking back renewed sobs. Had she found him again, only to lose him?

The small dyrathakin mewled and lapped at her skin. She pressed him closer, hot tears streaming down her face.

The palace gates loomed ahead, and Lyssandra's feet pounded on the stones of the garden. She closed her eyes against the dawning understanding that she wouldn't have the chance to talk to Edvern again. He wouldn't see the second dyrathakin; he would never know what his giving of the egg had done.

"No!" Lyssandra dragged in a breath, her palms hitting the rough stone of the wall. She stared at the metal work of the gate, which had been left open wide.

"What are you doing?" Zanniel's large hands took her about her waist, forcing her to stand upright. "You must keep going."

Perhaps the dyrathakin sensed Lyssandra's general unease with the Nezahrian war wraith. The little creature wormed his way out of her grasp and bit Zanniel's arm. Tiny pointed fangs pierced the spy's clothes, and Lyssandra felt a savage satisfaction that was not hers wash over her.

Zanniel released her with a yelp, lips turning down in a scowl.

The dyrathakin looked up at the war wraith, his face twitching and lips forming a strange smile. With a long purple tongue, he wiped the blood from his teeth. Lyssandra grabbed him up, afraid that Zanniel might react poorly.

"He's already grown."

Lyssandra didn't have to look down to know that Zanniel was right. The young dyrathakin felt heavier in her arms. He wriggled free again, clambering up to settle around her shoulders, where his talons pricked her bare skin.

"We must continue."

They ran through the dark, Lyssandra trying not to think about all that had happened tonight. Where were Konrad and Antonella? Her stomach curdled. Were they safe?

She would have turned back, but Zanniel, sensing her thoughts, grabbed her bicep and forced her to keep going. This earned him a second bite. A smile touched her lips. She was grateful that the little creature was on her side.

They reached the town of Irani to find it on fire, which was unsurprising since the air was full of dragons. The lizardlings were now swarming the skies. No one gave them much attention as they ran. There were plenty of fleeing partygoers, their finery ripped and scorched.

A large dragonish shadow elicited new screams of fear around Lyssandra. As hard as it was, she blocked out the sound. Behind her, a dragon swooped and took her into her talons. Biting down her own yells, Lyssandra looked up and into glowing amber eyes.

Elisaria ...

Blessed mercies. Elisaria ...

If Lyssandra had been told a year ago she would be glad to see a dragon, she would have called that person mad. Now, encased in armoured scales and warm breath, she welcomed the relief that her dragon gave her.

Elisaria rumbled at her, the scales of her underbelly glowing. Then, very carefully, she set Lyssandra on her back. High on her perch, she watched Zanniel's dragon, Codee, swoop and gather up his rider.

The yellow dragon rose to fly level with her, Zanniel's face a grim line of determination. She had no time to contemplate the spy. Her dyrathakin leapt from her shoulders and scampered along the dragon's back. In the air currents, he flapped his wings and swished his tail. He yipped and howled in delight as the wind whipped through his soft brown fur.

"Faelowyn isn't far." Elisaria's voice was warm, rich and feminine.

Lyssandra stiffened, unsure if she was hallucinating or if the voice was real.

"We'll join you with your mate soon."

"Mate?"

"Do you not desire to make an egg with him in due course?"

"Egg?"

Zanniel shot her a suspicious look, and Lyssandra didn't blame the spy for his amused incredulity. She highly suspected she would have to get used to strange looks.

Lyssandra was the one to spot them first. Wings outstretched and neck arched, Faelowyn was a large dark shadow, Edvern on the ground in Raziel's arms. A smaller dragon, light blue, bellowed back at her, clawing the ground. Another, a navy dragon with a silver underbelly, stood alongside Alaxen Tallermayne.

"Land!" Lyssandra screamed, her hands beating on the scales of Elisaria's back.

"Already said I would." Elisaria scoffed, plumes of smoke curling from her nostrils.

Elisaria banked, and Lyssandra jumped from her back the second her claws touched the earth. She stumbled, her face hitting the grass as her legs failed to obey her. Refusing to feel any embarrassment, she pushed herself to her feet and ran, her dyrathakin bounding after her.

"Edvern!"

There he lay, arrow protruding from his chest. His skin was sallow and his breathing laboured. When he opened his eyes to peer at her, she could tell he was in a tremendous amount of pain. Instead of the vibrant blue she was expecting, they were a dull grey. Bloodstained lips attempted to tug into a smile for her, which faltered.

She fell to her knees at her friend's side, her hands grabbing for his. "Eddi ..."

"Don't tell me ..." Edvern's face spasmed. His eyes fluttered closed, his brow wrinkling as he fought to look at her once more. "You're worried ..."

Whatever Lyssandra might have replied, her words were interrupted by the calm, commanding tones of Edvern's uncle. "Let me approach."

Without waiting for a response, Alaxen left the safety of his dragon's side, striding across the distance. The blind dragon also landed with his rider. The lizardling dismounted also and curled up on the grass to watch the action.

Faelowyn growled, lips curling back to reveal her fangs, but Raziel laid Edvern's head down gently on the grass and stood. The black dragon stilled, her nostrils flaring at the Tallermayne general, who stared back at her, unafraid and unapologetic.

"Watch my back until it is done," Alaxen said to Raziel, falling to his knees. Strong fingers tapped Edvern's cheeks lightly. Edvern's eyes fluttered open.

Palea approached, throwing her useless butterfly mask to the side. Lyssandra sent her a questioning glance. Who was she and what did she have to do with Eddi?

"What have you got yourself into this time, Eddi boy?" Alaxen murmured. He supported Edvern's body with one arm, his free hand brushing through the sweaty hair plastered on Edvern's forehead. "Brace yourself."

Strong fingers took the feathered end of the arrow. Edvern's eyes widened. Dazed, he stared up into his uncle's face. "I'm sorry."

Palea knelt by Edvern's head. "That is some war wound, Uhl'hari."

Lyssandra's heart raced in her chest, ignoring the urge to demand that the other woman take her hands off Edvern.

Alaxen looked between the two of them and hesitated, the silvery-blue light of his power gathering in his fingers. She hoped that Edvern was numb to the pain, but she remembered reading somewhere that wasn't how healing worked ...

"Kendrick ..." Edvern fought to keep his eyes open.

"Kendrick's gone to be with his Nezahrian mother." Alaxen closed his eyes, grief transforming his features. "Talons damn me, I loved her."

A light touch on Lyssandra's elbow was enough for her to break her gaze. Zanniel shook his head. "You might not want to see this."

Lyssandra frowned at him. Edvern was her friend. She wouldn't abandon him. Not again.

The spy dipped his head in acknowledgement, then bent to hold Edvern's legs.

Alaxen took the shaft of the arrow, snapping it. On the ground Edvern screamed, his body lurching forward. Curled around Alaxen's drake, Edvern's dragon howled with her rider.

Lyssandra wanted to look away. To deafen her ears to Edvern's cries. She trembled, forcing herself to watch, to be strong and acknowledge the pain her friend was feeling.

Edvern lay gasping and shaking on the ground.

Alaxen's expression softened. He gripped Edvern's shoulder gently, waiting until his nephew's eyes met his. "Deep breaths. I'm here with you."

Lyssandra looked up, blinking back her emotions. She felt the weight of Elisaria's concern ... and the gentle sense of curiosity and wonder from her little dyrathakin. He sensed her worry in return and padded over to see what the fuss was about. She felt the press of his soft fur against her leg but didn't have the willpower to pick him up. She stood trembling, alone and afraid.

He mewled at Edvern.

Edvern's eyes fluttered open, and a weak movement of his lips was the only indication that he was still conscious of what was happening around him. He lifted a hand to the small creature, and the little dyrathakin's nose twitched, scenting him in return.

Lyssandra looked up again, noticing that many of the Nezahrians had landed in a ring around them. She saw the stony-faced emperor watching on, his golden armour in almost pristine condition infuriating her. Empress Ionah stood apart from him, her expression icy.

But Lyssandra didn't care about them. She didn't care about *any* of them.

Alaxen seemed to agree with her sentiment. He was aware of their arrival; she could tell by the tenseness of his shoulders. Instead of confronting his enemies, he whispered soft words to Edvern. Then with practiced gentleness, he slowly pushed the arrow through Edvern's chest.

Lyssandra could only imagine the slow and terrible torture of a shaft travelling through her body. Edvern lay on the grass and let it happen. She wasn't prepared for the amount of blood pooling out of the wound as the shaft was finally removed.

Alaxen clasped his hands to the wound, and she watched in amazement as it sealed over. It wasn't until Edvern's chest rose and fell in a steady rhythm that she allowed herself to hope. Edvern's eyes slid shut.

Alaxen rocked back on his heels, lifting his face to the sky and taking deep breaths of his own. She heard him mumble a prayer of thanks to Qavi, lord of the darkness, which was peculiar because he wasn't a deity for healing.

"What have you done?" Zanniel cursed.

Alaxen returned his gaze to Edvern's face. The colour was starting to return to his cheeks. "He needs quality rest."

"Move away." Zanniel unsheathed his sword and pressed the point into Alaxen's neck.

Looking along the silver blade, Alaxen raised his eyebrows at the spy. He leaned his body over Edvern, his powerful arms bracing against the ground. "No."

"No?" repeated the emperor, his golden sword gleaming in the coming dawn.

Palea stepped forward. "General Tallermayne has ever been my friend and my guide. He's not yours to command."

The empress held up her hand. "Palea, my love."

"Mother."

Mother?

"So you're a princess," Alaxen muttered, his expression darkly amused. "When were you going to share that bit of information?"

"I am a Nezahrian dragon rider thanks to you," Palea replied.

The emperor halted, turning his head to look at his serene wife. Lyssandra wasn't fooled. Empress Ionah was furious. The clues were there in her stiff posture and momentary narrowing of her eyes.

Dalain left the side of Bastian to come and embrace Palea. "Sister, my twinheart."

"General Tallermayne, release the boy into our custody and we'll make your execution swift." The emperor's voice was full of hatred, and he huffed as he watched his son and daughter greet one another.

Alaxen turned his face to stare at the royal couple. There was resignation in his dark, wise eyes. And steel.

"Shall I hand my nephew to the man who pierced him with an arrow?" Alaxen asked, eyes raking over Bastian to undoubtedly check his son for injury. "I'm not so hasty to sacrifice him for the comfort of a Nezahrian axe."

"Our Uhl'hari was shot down by Aurelian spies!" Lyssandra could hardly believe that was the narrative the emperor was going to tell. He was emperor; Alaxen was an enemy of his country. He would weave whatever tale he wanted, and the people would believe him. She looked to Raziel. His influence was the military, not the hearts of the people. He rarely attended court; the emperor had more sway than him.

"An Aurelian arrow?" Alaxen dipped his head, pressing Edvern closer to his chest. The muscles in his jaw clenched. "I'll not compromise my nephew's safety by handing him into the hands of the man who demands the heads of little children. To a known murderer."

"Aurelian dramatics." Emperor Ze'hyrn waved a dismissive hand.

"Peace could have been achieved with my father," Alaxen said. "But you lusted after blood and war. That day in Yrew, you saw your chance to rid the world of Fennix Tallermayne."

"Silence him!" Ze'hyrn barked, gesturing to his guards. "He's murderer of Nezahrian babes."

"Don't be foolish, Ze'hyrn." Empress Ionah held her hand up to stall the guards. "General Tallermayne has just lost his son."

"An Aurelian!"

Alaxen shook his head, turning instead to Raziel. "Vow to me, Black Prince, that you'll not harm Edvern or allow others to cause him harm."

Raziel didn't waste a heartbeat. He spoke before the emperor could interrupt. "Upon my dragon soul, you have my word."

"Then I relinquish custody of my nephew to you alone."

It was at this moment that Edvern groaned and opened his eyes. Colour rapidly returned to his pale cheeks, and he tried to rise from his uncle's embrace.

"He is awake. Step away!" Emperor Ze'hyrn took another step forward. "Or we'll smite your son where he stands."

"You'll do no such thing," Empress Ionah said. If the situation weren't so serious, Lyssandra might have laughed at how Emperor Ze'hyrn's head snapped around to stare at his wife. "Kendrick Tallermayne gave his life so I might live. So I have granted Bastian safety within Nezahrian camp. I extend this offer to Alaxen."

Edvern blinked, looking around at the gathered Nezahrians. His brow wrinkled in confusion as he looked at Lyssandra, searching for answers. Alaxen, she noticed, still had one hand on his sleeve.

"Uncle?"

"Listen to me. Raziel Yavari has given me his oath. I want you to go willingly with him," Alaxen whispered frantically in Edvern's ear.

"No." Edvern's voice wavered, and he shook his head.

"Eddi ..."

"Your uncle is a Tallermayne guilty of war crimes against Nezaha," Emperor Ze'hyrn barked. The empress' angry glare could no longer hold him back. His face twisted into a dark fury that frightened Lyssandra. In it she saw the death of Alaxen and Bastian. Edvern saw it too.

"Uncle, no!"

"Silence, dog. We'll see how brave you are when you face death upon the high peaks of Halvaine."

Alaxen barely reacted to the threat. He drew in a deep breath, his eyes on Raziel alone. His large hands covered Edvern's. "Let me go, Eddi."

Edvern released his uncle, only to jump to his feet and face the emperor. "I shall face judgement with my uncle." His wings sputtered and flared to life from his shoulders, warming the air with waves of heat. Lyssandra had no idea how fast Edvern could move. Despite nearly dying on the cold, hard ground, he managed to grab a blade off a flabbergasted Zanniel. She had seen defiance in the face of authority many times, but never had she seen a man so determined to make that authority step down.

"Don't be ridiculous. You were born of Nezaha; you belong to Nezaha." There was genuine fear in Raziel's tone. She knew as soon as he uttered those words, he made a mistake.

Edvern turned his eyes, smouldering with anger, up at him. "Nezahrian born I may be. But I'm no slave that you own me. I am Tallermayne raised, Tallermayne educated and Tallermayne trained. Under Aurelian law I was adopted into the Tallermayne family, and that makes me equal to a born Tallermayne. So arrest me for war crimes as well."

Raziel opened his mouth to speak, but Alaxen interrupted him, a pained grimace on his face. "Eddi, fall back ... Let me go."

"No!" Edvern yelled. "I've lost everything. I'll not lose you too!"

"I command it," Alaxen said. Lyssandra had to admire the calmness over Alaxen's features. "When I began the rebellion, I knew the cost. It took my wife; it's taken my sons ... My life is a small price."

"Father ..." Bastian stepped into view.

Hand still on the blade, Edvern turned pleading eyes towards Faelowyn. "Great one! You saw the neglect and suffering that Kyros experienced. I saw what they did to hatchlings and old ones in Gytall … They butchered dragons and riders. Moira is just as much a threat to us as she is to you. Your kin are screaming in Aurelia … The dragon Moira rides now …" Edvern's voice broke, overcome with emotion. "She begs for death … and poor Odharn. I lost him too! If you take my family from me, you lose me."

Faelowyn rumbled, turning her snout towards Edvern.

"Eddi … back down," Alaxen ground.

"Uhl'hari, you are to be sequestered to Raziel's tent. Faelowyn, our Nezahrian dragon, will fly you back immediately." The empress strode forward, ignoring her husband's furious glare. She glided across the distance, and Edvern couldn't help but stare. "Your uncle and cousin, we'll detain until such time we can interrogate them."

Edvern's light blue dragon snarled, baring her fangs.

"Don't separate a dragon from her rider," Bastian Tallermayne said.

The empress inclined her head. "I'll allow her to accompany her rider."

Edvern fisted his hand at his side, no doubt remembering the methods of Aurelian interrogation. When Alaxen made no further objections, Lyssandra took this as her cue to act. She slipped next to Edvern's side, taking his hand in hers. The small dyrathakin followed, sat and begged for a pat.

A smile curled on Edvern's face, looking down on the little creature.

From the greying gloom, Lyssandra saw the lavender eyes of Alynta. Slowly the older dyrathakin slunk forward, her belly to the ground. In her mouth she held Edvern's sword. It still burned with his magic but didn't harm her. The Nezahrians who had never seen her whispered and pointed as she padded towards her Uhl'hari.

Reaching out an offered hand, Alaxen crouched to the ground. "Alynta, come."

The dyrathakin didn't hesitate. She crept towards the Tallermayne general, her steps a little quicker. She dropped the sword at Alaxen's feet and rubbed her face over his chest. The dyrathakin was purring. Gently, Alaxen stroked his thumb between Alynta's eyes, and she melted into his arms.

"Let me take a look." Running his hands along the slender back of the dyrathakin, Alaxen's fingers ghosted over the fur matted with her blood. Blue light surrounded the sight of the injury, the dyrathakin whining and laying her head affectionately on Alaxen's shoulder.

"Are you finished fighting?" Alynta asked, turning to study the small dyrathakin kit, who was batting the ruined hem of Lyssandra's skirts. The two flying foxes scented one another, ears perked and tails wagging.

"Faelowyn, escort Edvern to camp and to my tent. His dragon is to follow you. The rest of us will finish our enquiries here."

Lyssandra squeezed Edvern's hand. "I'll go with Uhl'hari."

Edvern turned to look at her, his gaze still uncertain.

"It is good to have a friend at your side," Lyssandra insisted.

"The creature and the sword stay!" the emperor boomed.

"Who are you, human, to command me?" Alynta reared back, her hackles raised and her long black ears pinned against her head. "The sword is my Eddi's. I'll bite the first man who dares to touch it without permission."

The emperor's lips parted, shaking with fury. He tried to form a response. But Alynta was quicker.

"You harm my uncle, I'll do worse to you. Is that understood?" The dyrathakin shifted her gaze to Alaxen, appraising him for any injuries. The Tallermayne general stared back at her, clearly shocked by her declaration. She cocked her head to study Bastian. "He might be uncle's grown kit, but hurt him ... I'll shred your royal bedding before finding one of your kits."

Lyssandra had no idea that the dyrathakin was so prone to violence. She turned tail in the air and picked up the sword once more, then trotted to stand before Empress Ionah. "Are you the matriarch of these people?"

Ionah's eyes flicked to Raziel, then her husband. She inclined her head. "I am."

"Two of your people have been left behind. Their dragon would not leave Irani," Alynta said matter-of-factly. "The dragon said they were looking for a cohort of Saemorish diplomats."

Antonella and Konrad. There was a momentary flash of white-hot anger in Lyssandra's belly that the dyrathakin had gone to Ionah with this information and not her. The emotion soon dissipated when Alynta continued. "You must go back for them."

"Alas, we were forced to retreat."

"Some of the Euquallian delegation found safety in the gardens during the fighting." Alynta's lavender eyes glowed, her tail lashing from side to side. "Would you abandon them?"

"Empress, with your permission I'll go back to Irani to check the fates of our friends." Lyssandra squeezed Edvern's hand, hoping he would understand.

A smile tugged on Edvern's lips as he looked at her, his blue eyes dull with fatigue. He was leaning on her heavily, and she hated to leave him while he was so vulnerable.

"I'll accompany her," Palea said. The empress opened her mouth, a clear argument forming on her lips. But Palea continued. "The lady should have someone of Euquallian blood with her."

"Palea is a good ally to have," Edvern whispered. He staggered to the side, and from their contingent, Dalain made his way over.

Edvern steadied himself, eyes wary as he observed the prince's approach. Was he remembering their last encounter when he had attacked Dalain and been held at his own sword point?

"Dalain is trustworthy." Lyssandra used Edvern's closeness to her to their advantage, answering so that others would not hear. "He's been good to me and has promised to help you in the Nezahrian camp."

"If it is acceptable, Lord Uhl'hari, I will assist you to Tacebia, where you can rest."

Edvern swallowed, his eyes darting to his uncle, to Bastian and then the emperor. She could feel him trembling with what she could only describe as rage as he beheld the monarch's pristine armour. His injury had not addled his memories. Lyssandra could only imagine what it would be like facing the man who had callously shot you, knowing there would be no consequences for the attempted murder.

"Dalain is in a position to help you where the emperor is concerned," Lyssandra whispered in Edvern's ears.

Dalain shifted, a curt nod telling her he heard and accepted his role.

Edvern trembled, attempting to take a step. Gritting her teeth Lyssandra used all her strength to keep him upright. "I fear I require your assistance, my prince," Edvern murmured.

The pressure of Edvern's full weight was lifted from Lyssandra as Dalain took it upon himself. Edvern sagged against him, face grey. He'd been putting on a brave face for her, Lyssandra realised, standing so she didn't have to bear the burden of his body. She'd kick him for his stupidity later. First, she had to rescue Antonella and Konrad.

At her feet, her dyrathakin mewled. Without thinking, she picked him up and thrust him into Edvern's arms. "Since you have experience with dyrathakins, look after him for me."

As she suspected, Edvern's arms instinctively took the kit. The dyrathakin looked to Edvern, and Edvern looked to her, bemused. "He needs a name."

"Camyrs." With a long, parting look, Lyssandra turned and ran for her dragon, yelling over her shoulder, "For the Saemorish spirit of a bountiful harvest."

By the time Lyssandra mounted Elisaria, Palea was comfortably astride her blind drake, the lizardling perched and chirping what could only be assumed as orders.

Wind whipped around her as Elisaria took flight, ruffling her ruined dress about her legs. She turned to Palea, wondering what business, if any, Edvern had with a princess. Then she chided herself for such childish thoughts.

Closing her eyes, she tried not to imagine the terrible fate that may have befallen her friends amidst the carnage of Irani. There had been a time Lyssandra had dreamed of being the hero of her nation. Now she only wanted to save her friends.

Antonella and Konrad were alive; they had to be.

Hatching
Day Gifts
Alynta - beads for
tail
Camrys - bird bath
Gwyn - ball

Purchase Nezahrian Gold
Ring or necklace.

Reasons to
visit Sangell
- Warm
- No Nobles, No
Emperor
- Palea's
Summer House
- Beach

Camrys
Earth
Dyrathakin

Lyssandra
hates sand
- Palea will take
her shopping for
luxury goods.

CHAPTER 25

Tallermayne Secrets

RAZIEL, THE BLACK PRINCE

As Lyssandra and Palea departed to return to Irani, Raziel murmured a quiet prayer for the two young women and their dragons. Palea was just as stubborn as her twin, Dalain. He had spent many hours with them when they were children, training and tutoring them whenever the Aurelian raids were quiet. He had been grieved when Palea was assumed dead and had gladly taken Dalain under his wing. And here she was …

Never mind, Raziel thought. *There will be time later to process all that has happened.*

There was a surge of pride in his heart as Dalain took charge of the situation. The prince must be reeling in the return of his twinheart, yet he seemed unfazed as he escorted Edvern to Faelowyn.

Poor Edvern was ailing, his legs unsteady as he attempted to walk. Beside him he heard Alaxen's intake of breath as the boy stumbled again. Out of the corner of his eye, he studied the lines of worry on the Tallermayne general's face. The man cared. Deeply. The enemy he had thought to be bloodthirsty and callous was not as hardened as he had always believed. Tallermaynes were supposed to be emotionless and without compassion.

Unwilling to put Camyrs, Lyssandra's dyrathakin, down, Edvern struggled with one hand to mount. Symmeon strode across the gap, expecting that Dalain would require his help to assist the Uhl'hari, but Edvern flinched away from his touch, leaving his second-in-command to stand to the side, dumbstruck.

The soul touch. Raziel grimaced. It would take Symmeon time to earn Eddi's trust. If he even had it before.

Aerin, in a rare show of thoughtfulness, gave Edvern and Dalain a boost onto Faelowyn's back with his snout. Arranging himself on Faelowyn's back, Edvern lay against her neck, the little dyrathakin tucked under one arm. On the ground Alynta prowled, rubbing her head against Aerin's foreleg in silent thanks.

Dalain swiftly mounted, sitting behind Edvern, his hands awkwardly on the other boy's hips. The prince leant down, whispering in Edvern's ear. The Uhl'hari shook his head, his eyes sliding shut.

"Fly swift, Faelowyn," Raziel sent through his bond.

Faelowyn acknowledged his sentiments with the unfurling of her wings, her long neck turning to look at Edvern's blue dragon. She was agitated, and it was with some shock he recognised her as Rikar's. His spies had not seen her in the skies since the news of Rikar's arrest and execution. Separating a dragon from a rider they were fond of was always a bad idea. Especially if that dragon had already recently lost another rider. Some dragons did not do well with grief.

"We must get your rider to safety and rest quickly," Raziel said to her. *"Go with Faelowyn."*

"If she hurts him …" the dragon's voice warbled.

"I am not going to hurt him," Faelowyn replied waspishly.

The blue dragon recoiled from Faelowyn. Raziel could sense that underneath her fear and uncertainty around Faelowyn, there was determination. Although it wasn't a good to see a dragon so distressed, it gave Raziel hope to see that even though he had been bonded with his dragon a short time, Edvern's union with her was strong.

"Come, Izorah," Aerin said. He nudged the blue dragon, who looked back at Alaxen's drake. *"I'll go with you; the others will look after Lyrus."*

Lyrus, Alaxen's dragon, lifted his head, and Raziel was bombarded with pain from him. Had he been hurt? *"Go with your rider. I'll stay with mine."*

That was what the blue dragon had been waiting for; she said no more, spread her wings and leapt into the sky. Aerin and Faelowyn followed.

Alaxen let out a sigh of relief. But Raziel watched until the dragons were out of sight. He wanted Edvern gone for what he planned to do next. He couldn't have the Uhl'hari protesting and making further trouble.

"Woe, I need you to distract the emperor." Raziel's anger bubbled and boiled as he connected to the emperor's dragon. The steel dragon's spirit was shier than Faelowyn's. There was a vulnerability to him that saddened Raziel, although it was carefully hidden behind the drake's sass. His soul burned with grief, the loss of his nestmates and a deep sorrow that drew him to Codee.

"How long do you need?" Woe asked, seeming delighted with the prospect of annoying his rider.

"An hour should suffice," Raziel replied. *"Codee, see if you can give your rider a reason to be near the emperor."*

"We'll give you two hours," Codee said. *"Tell my rider to put his claw away and give me a scratch."*

"Watch this!" Woe cried, moments before he let out a pitiful howl.

Holding his right wing at an awkward angle, he limped, dragging his back leg along the ground. Curling his long serpentine body into a pathetic ball, he whined, loud and long. Terrified that his dragon was injured, the emperor bellowed for help. Perhaps if Ze'hyrn had the wits to look at his dragon himself, he would have known that Woe was performing. And perform spectacularly he did.

"Talons, have mercy," Balfar complained, lowering himself onto the ground beside the empress.

Raziel could not remember the last time he was so entertained. It was amusing to watch the young dragon howl and flap, shuffling away like a kicked dog anytime the emperor's men attempted to touch him. He was glad that a few had accompanied the royal couple on the backs of the dragons, as they provided more opportunities for Woe to create chaos.

"Oh, I hurt and I languish," Woe whispered in his mind, writhing on his belly and blowing smoke into the faces of the men. *"How long must I bear this suffering?"*

He would have to find some way to repay the grey dragon for his willingness to distract the emperor. Although Woe seemed to be thoroughly enjoying himself. *"Zanniel and Codee will help you keep your rider busy."*

On cue, Codee bellowed and thumped his way over to his 'injured' friend, scattering the emperor's men. Zanniel trailed him with a pained expression on his face.

"Get that beast away!" Emperor Ze'hyrn yelled.

"A thousand apologies, Great One," Zanniel huffed, with a deep bow. "But these two are brothers. Perhaps Codex will calm him."

In the end, the emperor was forced to allow the two dragons to stay together. This gave Zanniel the perfect opportunity to be the responsible rider and watch over them, and the chance to overhear if the emperor would make any of his plans further known.

Content that his players were in position, Raziel turned towards Alaxen. The general was sprawled against the warm side of his navy dragon, ignoring the drama unfolding. He stared at his hands coated with Edvern's drying blood. His dragon was huffing heavily, tail twitching. Alaxen brushed his hands over the soft belly of his beast.

Bastian stood close by, his arms folded over his chest, staring up at the sky. He swayed on his feet.

Alaxen lifted his gaze as Raziel made his way over, Symmeon shadowing his footfalls. Dark eyes watched their approach. Here was a man who was resigned to his fate. "Thank you for allowing me to heal Eddi," Alaxen murmured. He inclined his head but did not stand. "Will he be safe?"

"I'm well-practiced at defending myself against Nezahrian rulers who don't like the threat of outsiders." Raziel understood the concern. Alaxen did not look at him. His stare was only for the emperor and the empress.

"Emperor Ze'hyrn shot him," Bastian commented, pressing his palms against his trousers. Fingers tapped his thighs.

"Ze'hyrn is a fool," Raziel admitted. There was no harm in saying so; the Tallermaynes already knew that. "I'll ensure that Ionah has words to him about the political foolishness of murdering a Nezahrian icon. She is my preferred leash for the emperor."

"They'll make it sound like an accident," Bastian said.

Raziel merely nodded.

"Just like they'll say our deaths are an accident."

"Bastian, please." There was no shifting of emotion on Alaxen's face.

"They told Edvern what he needed to hear to get him out of the way."

Raziel held up his hand. "If we're to come to an understanding, we've limited time."

Alaxen nodded, the movement a little curt, and he sat up straighter.

"We need to regroup. Recalibrate ..." Bastian turned back to the sky, as if he was looking for something.

"You don't give orders here, swine." Symmeon's sword was in his hand in an instant.

Bastian didn't react to Symmeon's harsh words or his weapon. "I can't function without her ... I need her ..."

"I'd like to see you fix that, healer," Symmeon muttered.

"Nothing to fix," Alaxen snarled. He hauled himself to his feet, coming to stand close to his son. The words he spoke were low. Whatever he said calmed Bastian. His erratic movements stilled.

"Do what you must. I know what he is." The glimmer of Aurelian pride shone through Alaxen's eyes as he nodded at Symmeon. "I am ready."

"Nezahrian interrogations can be intense. Keep your mind focused on memories that will prove your intentions. Symmeon's power will seek out what it needs." Raziel thought it only fair to warn the Tallermayne general how powerful soul touch could be to someone who had never experienced it before.

"I wasn't one to think you would give up so easily, Tallermayne," Symmeon said. The luminescent blue of his power swirled around his fists. He approached the general. Alaxen watched him with an unconcerned air. Bastian flinched.

Raziel came around to Alaxen's other side so that Symmeon could share what he saw from his soul touch directly. Nothing in the smooth contours of Alaxen's face gave any evidence of his anxiousness.

Letting his commanding officer's power take control, Raziel grabbed Alaxen's left wrist while Symmeon grabbed his right. The general jerked back at the abruptness of his own swirling memories.

Despite Alaxen's calm exterior, his mind was a riot of emotion and memories. The grief clung around him like a second skin. Guilt coloured every memory. Experienced with Symmeon's power, Raziel could sense the magic having trouble sifting through the tide of memories to select

one. Consumed by the general's pain, he wanted to scream and leave the interrogation to Symmeon. But he knew he could not. Two witnesses were required under Nezahrian military law.

He gritted his teeth, thankful that Symmeon's power finally found a memory to grasp on to.

It wasn't a recent memory. Alaxen was still a boy, hurrying after a robed figure. He could almost smell the scent of human refuse and summer storms that hung heavy in the air as they stalked through winding alleys. They came to a house, the doorframe marked with a sprig of myrtle. The elder figure rapt on a door, and a pale-faced woman answered.

Eyes full of fear and hope stared at Alaxen. The woman opened the door further, asking, "Is this him? The boy?"

Young Alaxen shifted, darting a glance over his shoulder. A heavy hand clasped his arm, drawing him through the doorway. "My son, Alaxen. Show me the child."

The woman bobbed, scurrying through the impoverished home. She returned moments later with a small babe. Fennix Tallermayne drew his hood back and took the child, crooning and rocking her. The long dead dragon rider looked down at the babe, at the soft downy hair that framed two perfectly pointed ears.

"Must we do this?" Alaxen fiddled with a long-bladed dagger, sending concerned looks to the woman, presumedly the mother of the child. "She's so small."

"Do you know what happens to those with Nezahrian ears in Gytall?"

"I know, Father."

"Illusions can fail, but docking her ears will give her a lifetime of freedom."

Alaxen looked stricken. "I can't."

"You can," Fennix replied, his voice lowering to a pleasant rumble. "A great leader must be able to make difficult decisions. A little pain and a touch of your healer power now, and the child will never know. Otherwise, she'll taste death before her time, cast into the dark waters of the river."

"*I don't have your strength.*"

"*Then you must learn. One day when I'm dead and gone, you'll be the Grand Lord.*"

"*Tamah … Mother …*"

"*Your mother is without pity and poisons your sister. And your brother, talons bless him, claims that dragons talk to him. It's to you that I look for our future.*"

Alaxen looked at the baby who was cooing in his father's arms. "*This is about something more than this child.*"

"*Emperor Ze'hyrn refuses to listen to my offers of peace. His terms for Aurelia cannot be accepted. It's time you start learning the fine art of being a good man and leader versus Grand Lord.*"

"*Why can't we talk with the Nezahrians? Isn't she a blessed one? Couldn't we—*"

"*The emperor has demanded all the heads of all dragon riders, including every member of their families. Not even our small children will be spared from Nezahrian wrath. And the first head they want is Rikar's.*"

"*Rikar is just a silly boy,*" Alaxen said. "*He's fourteen.*"

"*The emperor insists I kill my sons. He has ordered a large population of Aurelia executed. And then has the audacity to demand the surrender of our rivers and fertile lands. All produce is to be given to Nezaha. We cannot treat with these terms,*" Fennix said. He handed the baby to Alaxen. "*The emperor and his Black Prince are unreasonable.*"

"*What is her name?*" Alaxen looked regretful the moment he asked the question.

"*Rosemary.*"

"*The fact you saved part Nezahrian babies by chopping off their ears, a heinous act, does not prove that you can be trusted.*" Symmeon's power was unique in that it had a voice. A discerning ear that could hear what it was seeking. Under its thrall, his emotions a storm around him, Alaxen could not resist or fight back.

Alaxen's stricken mind brought them a second memory, settling on a time where he was standing shoulder to shoulder with Rikar. They stood in silence, observing a small boy, about eight years old, struggling with a cranky black stallion. It was with some shock Raziel recognised the child as Edvern.

"Edvern's tutors tell me the boy is stupid. He can't read." Rikar sighed, glancing down at a beautiful book in his arms. "Master Petros had him in tears again over that ridiculous prayer."

"Hence the gift." Alaxen nodded at the book.

"My brother never fails to give good parenting advice." Rikar's fingers stroked the cover inlaid with dragons. "If we read every night together, surely it would help him. He's dreading his lessons."

"Petros is a fool. Panicking a child that needs patience does no good." Alaxen scoffed. "Edvern can read. His mind needs calm. Besides, his understanding of mathematical principals is far above his age."

"Found him under my bed last week," Rikar admitted. "Apparently, he corrected Bedvir twice in one lesson."

Alaxen laughed. "Little hellion."

The brothers' discussion was interrupted by the stallion's annoyed whinny. Rikar startled, ready to respond. But Alaxen held out his hand to stall him.

"Stop," Alaxen said. "He's learning resilience."

"He's struggling with that horrid beast of yours."

Alaxen gave his brother a withering look.

"He'll fall!"

"Stop being a mother hen," Alaxen said. "Let your boy learn."

The two brothers returned to silence until Rikar sighed heavily. "Does my son have permission to ride your horse?"

"He does not," Alaxen said.

Alaxen's mind stilled for a fraction of a second. Fondness for Edvern, for Rikar, washed over the general.

"We knew you helped Edvern. We don't care," Symmeon's power hissed. "You're giving us nothing."

There was a shift in Alaxen's emotions, a rallying cry to the challenge. They were wrenched from the pleasant memory of Gytall into a cold and damp cell.

Raziel could almost feel the agony of an exhausted war wraith who lay chained to a wooden table in the middle of the cell. Her long black hair was coated in sweat and grime as tears ran down her face. What was left of her clothing was torn, exposing her skin to her tormentors. Alaxen loomed over her, and he prepared himself for the onslaught of hatred he had for this Aurelian man.

Alaxen surprised him by drawing a blanket over the Nezahrian spy's body. He leaned over her, his large hand clasping hers. "I could heal you, or I—"

"Kill me." The woman licked her bruised lips, her body trembling.

Alaxen brought a cup of wine to her mouth, cradling her head so that she could drink.

"Why waste luxury wine on your enemy?"

"Everyone deserves a last drink and dignity."

"I'm afraid ..." Racking coughs left the woman breathless.

"Death comes to us all. I can ease your passing."

The war wraith rallied to finish what she was saying. "I'm afraid if I live much longer, I will break my oath to the Black Prince."

"You are strong and brave," Alaxen soothed. "I'll ask you no questions."

"You have those under your command who can force my mind ..."

"I'll not call for them," Alaxen said. "Not until you are dead and there's naught they can do."

"Kill Whilmana ..."

"Alas, not even I have the power to do that. Not yet." Amusement coloured Alaxen's tone.

The woman wheezed, her breath catching. She trembled a little, a smile touching her lips as she understood. "Thank you."

Alaxen returned her smile. "Sleep now ..."

And with that the spy breathed her last. Alaxen stood over her, bearing witness to her final moments.

"The lord of mercy strikes again."

Alaxen turned to face one of his officers. This hadn't been the first time Alaxen had shown mercy to an enemy. He had done it so many times that his officers had a name for him.

Lord of mercy.

"She's an enemy, Alaxen. Why didn't you use your power to make her heart stop?"

"Why?" echoed Symmeon's power. "Why show mercy?"

"Poison is gentle," Alaxen said, stepping out of the cell. "Kinder."

"We've seen enough. Let us go," Symmeon's power said.

But Alaxen's emotions were still strong, the current of them sweeping them away. Panic seized Raziel as the Tallermayne general fell apart around them. Intangible memories swirled past.

"Control yourself," Symmeon's power said into the storm.

Long moments passed, but finally Alaxen's mind grasped on to a memory and settled.

"Put a sack over my head." Rikar's face, bloodied and bruised, filled his vision.

Alaxen's pain buffeted his heart, accusing him of the worst of betrayals.

"Pardon?" Alaxen was shocked by Rikar's request. "No. It's a sign of a coward. I refuse. I'll not dishonour you."

"I know what kind of man I am." Rikar's hands shook, but there was a steel resolve in his eyes. "If Father's illusion over me fades when my body fails ... Edvern will be in greater danger. We cannot compromise his safety."

"Rikar..."

"I'm going to die, Alaxen," Rikar said. "You cannot stop that. Let my dishonour and death protect my Eddi. If Mother ever suspects I'm not her son ..."

Alaxen nodded wearily.

Rikar drew his knees up, his voice cracking with the next declaration. "I want to see Eddi."

"I can't bring him to you."

"I want to hold him one last time. Talons, when was the last time I told him I was proud of him? I'm going to die, and he won't know …"

"He knows."

"I want to see him." In the darkness of his mother's dungeon's, Rikar was breaking, his brother the only witness.

"I know."

The world dissolved around them. Rikar's dying screams still rung in Alaxen's consciousness. He turned from his brother's smouldering remains and grabbed Edvern. Rikar had no right to speak to or touch his son—but he still did. He held him upright as the young man collapsed in his arms.

Leaning against the wall, Alaxen held the shaking Edvern in his arms. "It's okay, Eddi boy, it's okay. He was so proud of you. Be strong now."

Edvern was still reeling when he was forced to leave to his exile in Cynedir. He left the boy tucked away somewhere safe in the spire, his father's dragon book on his lap. Then under the cover of darkness, he farewelled his sons and visited his spies in Gytall …

Alaxen's face was pale, tears running down his cheeks unchecked as Raziel came to. The way the general was looking at him told him he still expected to die, despite the promises made. Perhaps there was a part of the general that would welcome death. An uncomfortable thought; his enemy had been known for his tenacity. Reaching into the depths of Alaxen's soul, he saw him with more clarity. With heart shattered for himself, his family, dragon and country, he teetered above the abyss of brokenness.

The history between them was bitter, full of bloodshed and loss. They would never be friends, but Raziel could look beyond his enemy by virtue of his birth and acknowledge the man. Alaxen Tallermayne was flawed, had done terrible things. But then so had he.

"Wine, Symmeon."

"I don't need your pity." Alaxen's voice trembled, he sounded hoarse. He tried to rise, but Raziel held his arm to stop him.

Symmeon sneered, thrusting out a wineskin to Alaxen. The general looked down at it, brows raised. "Why waste wine on your enemy?"

Alaxen parroting the question of one of his war wraiths jolted Raziel. "A man who can show hospitality to a foe is a man I could learn to respect."

"Tell me. Did you enjoy it?" Alaxen grunted.

"No," Raziel admitted. "But I think our shared experience might mean we can come to a better understanding of one another."

Alaxen lifted the wineskin to his lips and drank deeply. The use of his healing power must have weakened him. He drank like a man dying of thirst. When the general finished, he smacked his lips, raised the wineskin and said, "Here's another little titbit for you. Another little secret of what house Tallermayne has done for you, Raziel Yavari. The mouse spying on you in the walls was Edvern. That boy heard every terrible threat you uttered against him, and to spare you trouble, Rikar stole that memory from him."

Raziel's memory took him back to the day he arrived in Gytall. To the knowledge he was being watched in the walls. He had assumed it was a Tallermayne trick, tried to have Moira's spy come and expose himself. It had been Edvern. He had told Rikar Tallermayne he would burn his son and enjoy his screams. Father Dragon above ...

"Edvern was well-known for his hiding spots. He once hid for three days from Master Bedvir to avoid a thrashing," Bastian said.

Alaxen laughed through his pain. Raziel watched as he fought to maintain control over his emotions. "It was Kendrick's fault."

"It was always Kendrick," Bastian replied blandly.

Father and son stared at each other in silence. Perhaps marking that their son and brother would no longer be causing mischief. Alaxen tore his eyes away from Bastian, his hand raising to cover his face as his shoulders shook.

"You have my sincerest condolences for the death of your youngest son. I assume you will wish to have the liberty of saying whatever prayers are custom to Aurelian people." The words seemed so inadequate as Raziel watched the man who was destined from the womb to be his enemy break.

In all his long years of military service, Raziel had seen many fathers grieve for sons and daughters. Alaxen Tallermayne was no different.

"It should have been me." Bastian shook his head. At his son's words, Alaxen forced himself to his feet, his strong arms wrapping his son in an embrace. "He was the better ... and now I'm a dragon rider no more."

"No. Don't say that." Alaxen's voice was filled with raw emotion. Here was a man stripped bare of all his titles and accomplishments. "Grieve for your brother, but please, don't say that."

A lump formed in Raziel's throat. He'd been given to the temple a few hours after his birth. His master, his predecessor, had chosen him. His soul had been melded to his and the Father Dragon to make him something more than human.

His predecessor ensured he was cared for, trained for military service and was strong. Kind words of encouragement were rare, while chastisement as a small boy was frequent. Everything done so that he might be the Sword of Nezaha. It seemed ironic blessed ones, those with tapered ears, were temple ornaments, believed to have no need of family.

"They were your dragons beheaded on the wall." Raziel could not imagine a worse way to lose a dragon. There was something within him that rebelled, that wanted to comfort his young enemy.

"Hyrin and Narani," Bastian said. "Brother and sister. Hatchlings of Lyrus, my father's dragon."

Raziel allowed himself to comprehend everything that had been said. "General Tallermayne, if you wish, I'll escort you somewhere private so your dragon and you may grieve together."

Alaxen nodded, downing the remaining portion of wine. "Are you like Edvern? Can you understand the words of dragons?"

Raziel nodded. He expected the general's request before he spoke it.

"Would you help me speak with Lyrus?"

The navy dragon closed his eyes, rumbling softly. Raziel approached and knelt by his face, pressing his hand against the strong jaw of the dragon. He looked Lyrus over. He was one of the healthiest dragons he had seen from the Aurelians. He sensed a strong pain within the dragon, the loss of his children, the love he had for his rider ... and despair he would not live to see a new nest with his chosen mate.

"Of course."

Before death takes me, I shall live the life gifted to me by the Father Dragon. I will burn bright upon this earth, for my adoptive country and the people who gave me sanctuary.

MEMORIES OF A VILLAIN

ULLRYK THE LIBERATOR

CHAPTER 26

Princely Ally

EDVERN

Edvern's stomach twisted into knots as he beheld Tacebia, the place that was to be his prison. Under his cheek, Faelowyn's scales were warm. She was a dragon responsible for many of the stories that surrounded Aurelian defeat, and he couldn't bring himself to speak with her. A number of times during the flight, he had fallen unconscious, a dangerous position for any dragon rider. But Prince Dalain's hands held him firmly in position.

The prince's grip tightened as Faelowyn landed in the middle of the Nezahrian camp. Eyes closed, Edvern could hear the startled sounds of soldiers that witnessed their arrival. He had never been given the opportunity to speak Nezahrian, and so he did not understand what was being said. He didn't care anyway.

Faelowyn snorted warm air, warning the milling soldiers to keep their distance. Strong claws raked the frozen earth, and she lowered her body for an easier dismount. All Edvern could do was open his eyes and stare at the never-ending sea of canvas tents and listen to the sound of men and women at work ringing in his ears.

They were in the very heart of the camp, where the largest tent resided. The black and crimson banners belonging to the Black Prince snapped in the soft breeze. Enough room had been made for the black dragon around the tent.

Izorah landed nearby, and her presence gave Edvern a measure of peace. The Nezahrians hadn't chained her. She could fly away if she needed. Although he felt very much like a prisoner, she was free.

"Eddi, come!" Dalain gestured to Aerin, who ambled closer to offer help. He dismounted first, landing on the snout of the strangely compliant dragon. He lifted a hand and gestured to Edvern.

Throwing his right leg over Faelowyn's back, Edvern let himself slip down her side. Dalain caught him before his knees could buckle, and Aerin lowered them to the ground. He planted his feet, widening his stance to appear stronger than he felt, and stared around the famous camp.

"Goodness. What happened?"

Edvern lifted his head. A boy ran toward them, nimbly jumping over tent pegs. He stopped before them, sweeping dark hair out of his eyes. He was well-dressed, and from Dalain's fond expression, a highborn noble of some sort.

"Father happened," Dalain answered.

Despite himself, Edvern's hands went to his wound, which of course had been healed and was no longer there. Curious eyes drifted over the dirt, blood and ruined clothes.

"I take it it didn't go to plan."

"An astute observation, cousin," Dalain answered wryly. "Hedriel, this is Edvern. Edvern, my cousin Hedriel."

"The Edvern? Tallermayne?" Hedriel's eyes widened, then further when he spotted Alynta observing him at a safe distance. "A dyrathakin? You found him then?"

"My cousin is known for his perceptive remarks." There was a teasing note in Dalain's voice. He nudged Edvern towards the tent. "Get some of my spare clothes, bedding and something to eat and drink."

Alynta prowled between Faelowyn's side and Edvern, a steely glint in her lavender eyes as she stared up at the black dragon. She pressed herself against Edvern's legs, her belly glowing a brilliant orange, the challenge clear: *don't touch him.*

Yawning, Faelowyn flashed her teeth and lowered her head to the ground, unbothered by the dyrathakin's threat. She closed her eyes.

Proud of herself, Alynta inserted herself between the princes and Edvern, her tail lashing.

Dalain winced at Hedriel's questioning gaze. Then the young prince's eyes darted to the little creature that had made his home on Edvern's shoulders. Camyrs uncurled and jumped, then landed on his feet and padded after Alynta. His nose twitched as he scented the older dyrathakin, his tail lazily wagging. Pouncing, he batted Alynta's nose and bounded to the side. Alynta's ears perked up. When he nipped at her tail, she gave chase. They hurdled over Edvern's feet. Stuck between the two playing dyrathakins, Edvern lost his footing, and Dalain lurched forward to catch him.

"You should rest," Izorah rumbled.

Faelowyn opened one eye, rising to stare at Izorah. When Edvern had met the black dragon at Mount Weirhelm, he hadn't fully appreciated her size. She loomed over Izorah, her scaled lips twitching. *"You'll go and stay at the edge of the camp."*

"I won't leave Eddi."

Edvern felt a fluttering of fear as the two female dragons studied each other. A snarl rippled up Faelowyn's throat.

Izorah's nostrils flared, her lips peeled back in a soundless growl. The hairs on the back of Edvern's neck rose. He could feel his dragon's simmering temper. She was tense, ready to attack. There were no words that the dragon could form to describe her fury and distrust. Fear roiled over the blue dragon, bleeding into the bond she had with Edvern. But she would not back down.

Edvern dove between the pair, hands outstretched as if by physical will alone, he could stop the warring dragons. Dragons lived in a culture steeped in the strongest vying for dominance, but he had no wish to see his dragon hurt trying to protect him.

"Izorah, please," Edvern said.

Izorah snarled, her jowls snapping at the larger dragon. *"Do you expect me to trust* her *with my rider?"*

"Izzie!"

"I promised Rikar that I would protect you."

"And you did."

"You were shot!"

"The blame doesn't rest on your shoulders." Pressing his palms to Izorah's scales, Edvern leaned into his dragon. He could feel her tension, the longing for her mate simmering under the surface. "Go, wait for Lyrus. He'll need you."

Aerin approached. He dipped his head respectfully to Faelowyn before turning a gentle gaze to Izorah. Edvern wasn't sure if he was impressed with the uncharacteristic behaviour or worried. *"Come. I'll go with you. My rider will protect your rider."*

Izorah huffed, disturbing the prickly grass under her talons, and nodded.

Displeased and defeated, Izorah looked Edvern over one last time. Then without looking to Faelowyn, she spread her wings and lifted her body into the air. Aerin followed. *"Sleep well, my Eddi."*

"Get inside the tent." The black dragon had a way of speaking that was imperious, expecting her every whim to be enacted on. Aerin had called

her the queen. Edvern wondered how right he was. *"I'll guard the entrance. None shall enter without my consent."*

Edvern regarded her, lips pinching together in a firm line. There was no point telling her that was exactly what he was worried about. He was the prisoner of the Black Prince.

Dalain tugged on his arm, and Edvern stumbled after him. The lighting in the tent was low when he entered. His feet sunk into thick carpet as he surveyed his surroundings. He took note of the war tables, desks with maps and parchments. Raziel and his generals met here for strategy meetings. He was quite literally standing in the heart of the Nezahrian war machine.

The dyrathakins returned, Alynta curling herself at his feet and the small newborn leaping into his arms. He settled, licking his fingers and curling into a tight ball so that Edvern had to use both hands to cradle him.

"Did you know?" Dalain asked. "That when you gave Lyssandra the egg, it would hatch?"

Edvern shook his head, feeling like his brain was rattling inside his skull. "I knew it wasn't mine. It stayed cold in my hands. I'm glad it hatched for her. I thought dyrathakins were for Nezahrians ..."

"Dyrathakins are from ancient times, appearing rarely." Dalain shrugged. "The little fellow judged her worthy. Truly, that is what matters."

Looking down at the little creature, with his soft fur and little twiggy horns, Edvern thought he was beautiful. His heart swelled with gladness, and he knew Lyssandra had a new loyal friend that would not leave her side.

She'd been the most beautiful woman at the ball. And when he opened his eyes after being healed, she looked like a warrior queen, her dark hair loose, cheeks smudged with dirt and blood. Her skirts, which were once fine, torn. Still, she held her head high. A woman of strength, who made his guts flutter thinking about how she had run to his injured dyrathakin. He was entranced like a moth to the flame.

"You should sit. Hedriel is getting you bedding." Dalain pulled out an ornate chair carved with dragons and mountains. The plush red velvet cushion was tempting.

Edvern gestured to his body, not letting his eyes linger on the dirt or his blood that coated his skin. "I'm filthy and bloody."

The smile on Dalain's face looked forced as he stepped forward and grabbed his shoulders. Before Edvern could protest, he was man-handled into a chair. "Be a good boy and sit."

Edvern watched the prince wearily as he went to a side table and poured two goblets of wine. Edvern's fingers curled instinctively around the stem of the goblet that Dalain thrust at him.

"Drink," Dalain said imperiously. "Are you hungry?"

"No."

Sipping the wine from his goblet, Dalain regarded Edvern over the rim. Edvern wasn't fooled. Dalain was gathering information as he observed him. To whom did he report?

"Do your wings of fire burn?"

This wasn't the question he was expecting. "No. They're warm."

"Can they bear the weight of another human?"

"I dropped one of your spies when I attempted to stop him from falling," Edvern said. "But I picked up Lyssandra at the ball."

"Very romantic," Dalain said drolly.

"Look, I ..."

Dalain took another sip from his goblet, his eyes alight. "Just saying, could be a manoeuvre to woo a girl." He put his goblet down with a definite clink. "I personally released Lyssandra from our engagement. She's very fond of you."

"Fond?"

"Fond," Dalain confirmed.

Edvern was about to open his mouth to question exactly what the prince meant when he was bowled out of his chair by streak of green scales.

Camyrs shrieked and wriggled out of Edvern's arms as a warm tongue lapped at his face, claws digging into the floor coverings as he was pinned down.

"Behave." Alynta crept forward, swatting the small dragonish snout. "Show some manners."

"Odharn!" Edvern cried, throwing his arms around the little dragon, all at once forgetting his princely audience and exhaustion.

"*Eddi!*" Odharn cried, flapping his one wing. "*I flew. I really flew … Woe took me to see the wild dragons, and I spoke with them.*"

"That sounds amazing," Edvern replied.

"He's become boisterous since Faelowyn decided to adopt him," Dalain said with a tight-lipped smile.

"The Black Lady of Dread adopted Odharn?"

"*She hunts for me.*" Odharn nodded his head, his long tongue lolling. "*She says I have lots of growing to do.*"

"*He never stops eating.*" Outside of the tent flap, Faelowyn sounded pleased.

Edvern was speechless and immensely grateful that another dragon had taken Odharn under their wing. This was how it should have been.

Camyrs padded along the table, scattering parchment in every direction. He leapt onto the war map and batted away the military figures. Tight-lipped, Dalain strode over to set the figurines to rights. At the edge of the table, Camyrs sat, his head cocked as he observed the prince's movements.

"Dyrathakins are naturally curious creatures." Edvern reached up to the table and snatched his goblet so he could take a taste. Closing his eyes, he savoured the tart flavours of Nezahrian wild fruits. He did not open his eyes …

"Are you sure you're alright? Do I need to get a medic?" a voice that was not Prince Dalain's asked.

Edvern's eyes snapped open, startled to realise he had fallen asleep where he had sat. His goblet, he was disappointed to discover, was gone. Hedriel had returned with half a dozen servants. Thank goodness the younger prince had the sense to bring bedding first. He lifted a hand to his chest. It had been a fatal shot. If he had been fully human, he was sure he would be lying dead. When Alaxen's power had flowed through him, it had been like an unrelenting river. Painful, but swift.

"I'm ..." Edvern was going to say fine, but he choked on the word.

"No medic," Dalain answered. "But he needs rest. He fell asleep in his wine."

Camyrs bounded along the table and into his arms. The little dyrathakin squirmed and licked his hands. Edvern brushed his fur back. He had fewer bone spikes than Alynta, but the ones he did have were hard like stone. Still curious of the small creature, Alynta came to his side. The two dyrathakins watched each other. Content that her friend was safe, Alynta dropped her chin to Edvern's knee, nose twitching as she watched Camyrs curl into a little ball.

Yawning, Edvern watched as the servants made quick work of assembling a cot for him. Despite his protests, both Hedriel and Dalain guided him to his bed once it was done. And then he was left alone with the dyrathakins and Odharn.

The cot that had been provided for him was large enough for a king, the coverings black and red velvets. Camyrs happily wriggled his way into Edvern's arms, while Alynta commandeered a pillow. Odharn lay down beside the cot and rumbled as he fell asleep.

As prisons went this one was the most luxurious he had experienced. The carpeted floor covers were beautiful. The furniture for the Nezahrian officers was all carved intricately with dragons.

Peeling off his gloves to stretch his fingers, he saw that even his knuckles were painted red with blood. Thankfully, Alaxen's magic fingers were undamaged. He unfurled his wings, and wrapping himself, Odharn, Alynta and Camyrs in his feathers, he lay down and closed his eyes.

*Emperors are rarely creatures that can be trusted. Absolute
power corrupts the mind, leaving space for selfish decisions and
greed. There's nothing worse than a powerful, greedy ruler.*

ULLRYK THE LIBERATOR
MEMORIES OF A VILLAIN

CHAPTER 27

Prisoners

RAZIEL, THE BLACK PRINCE

The Tacebia camp was in an uproar when they arrived with their prisoners. Raziel watched with barely concealed disgust as Ze'hyrn landed and paraded himself as a conquering hero. Faithful to her duty to the country, Ionah stood by her husband.

General Tallermayne said nothing as the emperor called forth some of his elite guard to take custody of their esteemed prisoners. The muscles in his jaw feathered, and he caught him looking to Bastian with fear in his eyes. The soul touch had given him some understanding of the man. What would it be like to sire a child and fear for them every day of their lives? Raziel couldn't imagine the torture.

"Until such time," Empress Ionah called out, "Alaxen and Bastian Tallermayne are our guests. They'll not be harmed."

Raziel looked at the people of his camp. He saw the mutinous expressions, the bloodlust and the need for revenge. When would it end?

Dalain walked through the throng of soldiers, coming to stand at Raziel's right-hand side. A quick glance in his direction was all that was needed for him to ascertain that Edvern was safe and hopefully resting.

"A Tallermayne laid his life down for the crown, and so we'll spare theirs," Ionah continued. Her gaze swept through the ranks of the gathering crowd. "For now."

Alaxen Tallermayne drew in a deep breath and exhaled. His stance shifted slightly, eyes darting back to Bastian. He nodded and whispered something to Symmeon, who shook his head. He was led away, the crowds parting before him. The Aurelian general would have to make do with the prisoner tents.

The empress watched the Tallermaynes depart, then turned to him. "I'll see the Uhl'hari now."

"He should not be disturbed, Great One."

The empress raised an eyebrow, but it was her husband who snapped, "You do not command my wife, Black Prince."

"Let him be, Ze'hyrn," Raziel replied, his throat tightening over the words he truly wished he could say. "The *unfortunate* injury was grave; his body is exhausted."

"He fell asleep upright in his wine, Glorious Father," Dalain said. Raziel noticed the clasped hands, a sign that the prince was shaking.

Emperor Ze'hyrn considered Dalain in silence, his eyes holding no remorse.

"Make sure he behaves himself," the emperor said. "Otherwise, he'll suffer the same as any servant of my household. I'll strap him to the whipping post and flay him myself."

"That won't endear you to the Tallermaynes," Dalain snapped. "Haven't you done enough damage?"

"Quiet, boy!" Ze'hyrn replied. "You will remember your place. The third born son—"

"Ze'hyrn!" The empress blanched, her usual tranquil demeanour fleeing the moment the words left her husband's mouth. Her children were her weakness. Dalain's fists clenched at his sides.

"You're going to fight me, boy? You're easily replaced."

Raziel thought he might be sick, seeing the fury in the emperor's eyes. He knew that he was capable of great violence, and yet Dalain did not back down.

"I'm more Mother's son than yours!" Dalain cried. "You chased off Palea and now ..."

"Palea whored herself to an Aurelian general," Ze'hyrn replied.

"Yet that Aurelian general obviously sheltered and protected her. She's a dragon rider. Perhaps he saw the strength in her that you were blind to."

"Tallermayne is filth. Palea is not my daughter."

Before Dalain could retort, Raziel grasped the prince's forearm and squeezed tightly. He was about to cross a line. Ze'hyrn was a man of passion and did not easily forgive. One of his younger brothers was sent to the front lines to die for besting him in what was supposed to be a friendly duel.

"Ze'hyrn!" A frantic expression filtered over the empress' face. "Please!"

"Palea is not my daughter!" The emperor's face turned a brilliant shade of purple. He turned to the pale empress. "Get your son into line, or you'll lose both of them."

"Ze'hyrn."

With a swirl of his cloak, the emperor stomped away, his royal guards pushing their way through the growing crowds.

Drawing Dalain closer to him, Raziel longed to whisper in the prince's ear that he had the power to protect him. Dalain's face was paling, watching the emperor's retreat with undisguised fear. He hadn't realised how quiet everyone was until the whispers started, sounding like buzzing bees.

"Enough!" the empress barked, her hands reaching out for her son. "Your emperor still burns with battle rage. No reason to fret. Our family is as strong and united as ever."

Dalain bit his lip, looking towards him.

"Raziel, I desire to cleanse myself of the filth of battle. Then once Uhl'hari has rested, we will interview him. Together, if that would put your mind at ease."

"As you wish, Your Majesty." Raziel made a sweeping bow, and the empress turned to leave.

"It's as you say. He's exhausted. He could barely stand up," Dalain told him, dropping his voice to a whisper. "He's not convinced of your good intentions. His dragon and Faelowyn had a standoff. I sent Hedriel to get him a change of clothes and something to eat."

Raziel was not surprised that Dalain had chosen Hedriel to gather supplies for Edvern, allowing the younger prince access to the Uhl'hari. There was something about Hedriel that put people under great stress at ease.

"Was he greatly distressed?" Raziel asked.

"Troubled, yes, but emotionally he seemed stable." Dalain laughed. "Odharn was very happy to see him."

Raziel let a smile touch his lips. "I'm sure he was."

"I can see why Lyssandra is so fond of him," Dalain commented.

Looking down at the prince, Raziel raised an eyebrow. "He's contrary, not likely to want to do what he's told without question. There's a boldness to him. Yet he's ..."

"The word Lyssandra used was 'sweet', according to, Mother."

"He's genuine. The new dyrathakin already loves him."

"If we use his charisma, let the people see his brash loyalty and gentle, bold personality, it could be used as armour to protect him."

"From your father, you mean?" Raziel asked.

Dalain nodded. "The more the people love him, the riskier it would be for my father to have him whipped or murdered. Creating a martyr is not good for the crown."

Considering the prince at his side, Raziel took his elbow, and they walked the camp together. They wandered through the tents in silence. He didn't want to return to his own war tent. A quick joining with Faelowyn told him that Edvern was very much asleep.

"You've a plan?" Raziel asked as they rounded the outer tents. Soldiers scattered before them, many knowing from living in camp that the Black Prince was owed space to have conversations in private. It was law in camp, one that all his people rigidly followed.

"Hedriel is beloved of the people. If he is seen as a 'close' friend of Uhl'hari, his popularity among our troops will rise." Dalain bit his lip, deep in thought. "I told Lyssandra that I might be limited in what I can be seen doing. But after today ... I think I might want to stay with you on a more permanent basis."

"Dalain ..."

"I don't want to return to the palace. Father already thinks poorly of me and ..." Dalain hesitated, cradling his head in his hands. "I can't pretend anymore. I can't. Don't ask this of me, Raziel."

"Your mother ..."

"If my mother loves me, she'll let me go."

Unbeknownst to Dalain, Raziel had this painful conversation with Ionah when the prince joined his army. The pain of losing his twin and the pressures of court had been a lot for him to handle on his own. While Dalain had matured under his leadership, Ionah swung between wanting to bring her son home and setting him free. Deep down Ionah did not want Dalain in the same city as his father.

"All I ask of you," Raziel said, measuring his words carefully, "is that you speak frankly with your mother before you make any decisions that affect your future. Write to your brothers, tell them what your father has done, counsel them to be cautious. Send your message with a trusted war wraith. I'll advise your mother to do the same."

"The emergence of Uhl'hari is a sign that Father's fate is to be dethroned." Dalain's face froze into an impassive mask, but Raziel could see the confusion and worry shimmering in the prince's eyes.

"Throughout history only one ruler remained on the throne, and that was because she repented. Your father is responsible for his own decisions."

Dalain nodded, something like relief on his face. His answer had given the prince some peace, and Raziel knew that he and Ionah were due for another very honest talk. Hopefully the empress was ready to let her son fly free of his father's net.

"I've got some good wine in my tent," Dalain said. "I think we ought to both wash away the grime of battle and take a nap while our Uhl'hari slumbers."

"A kind offer. Thank you, prince," Raziel murmured. He followed the young man through the camp, watching as he greeted soldiers working among the tents. When he had viewed Alaxen Tallermayne's memories, he had been glad that he would never experience the same sense of loss the general had.

Now the heat of the battle had cooled and the interrogations were over, Raziel realised he was wrong. He had thought that as the Sword of Nezaha, he was immune to paternal feelings. Although he had not sired Ionah's twins, he knew now what he felt was no mere fondness. He treasured the pair of them. It had brought him immense pleasure and pride, watching Dalain flourish under his command.

If anything were to happen to him ...

Nothing would, Raziel promised himself. Death would not have Dalain; not until he was old and grey and ready to surrender.

Her Royal Highness, Princess Fiora of Saemore, was said to be the most beautiful of King Jahon's sisters. The youngest by many years, she grew into a cunning hunter. It was during a conquest that she shamed herself. Nine months later she gave birth to a baby girl, malformed and father unknown.

THE ROYAL ANNUALS VOLUME 354

MASTER VIMBRYANT

CHAPTER 28

The Spider's Court

LYSSANDRA

Lyssandra took her time to study Palea astride her large grey dragon. The Nezahrian princess was as willowy as her mother, her dark hair braided and clasped with beads and jewels, gold cosmetics smeared on her brown skin. She was perfect, beautiful and graceful. She was also deadly; Lyssandra had seen her fight.

A lizardling, his wings bent oddly out of shape, perched on top of the grey dragon's head. He flicked out his long purple tongue.

"This silence is draining," Palea said, noticing Lyssandra staring. "I'm Palea, as you well know. This is Jirrah the lizardling and Faer, my dragon."

"Lyssandra, and my dragon is Elisaria."

"There," Palea announced as if it settled everything. "Now we're friends."

The silence returned until Lyssandra couldn't stand it anymore. "How did you meet Edvern?"

Palea gave her a sidelong glance. "Let's just say his curiosity got the better of him."

"You do know we're flying into danger?"

Leaning over the neck of her blind dragon, the princess grinned. "That's why we're flying together. If my father cannot stomach the sight of me, I still have Mother. I am her daughter, a woman of Euquall. A warrior."

Lyssandra wished she knew the feeling of being proud of one's mother. She swallowed, her eyes falling to Irani beneath them. Faelowyn had not transferred Edvern far from the palace before she had landed and allowed Alaxen to heal him.

"Take us down," she murmured, running her hands along Elisaria's scales. All her muscles tensed, her body preparing herself for what they might find on the ground below.

Rumbling, Elisaria banked into a languid dive, and Lyssandra closed her eyes against the harsh wind. This time when her green dragon landed, she did so gracefully. She opened her eyes and swallowed a mouthful of bile.

Throughout her life, she had witnessed the brutality of warfare. Little could prepare her for the ruins of the murdered king's palace. Faer landed behind them, his gigantic tail sweeping aside bodies so he could walk unhindered. Doing her best not to look at the scattered remains, she prayed Antonella and Konrad weren't among the dead. It was impossible to miss the singed bodies that had been broken and chewed after death. A wave of dizziness overcame her as her bare feet hit the ground. Lifting her hand, she allowed Elisaria to steady her.

The dragonstone statue of Saskah Tallermayne had been decapitated. Her head was left in a fountain that now ran red with blood. Soon the palace would stink of rotting flesh, and disease would follow.

Lyssandra glanced up and nearly lost what little food she had in her stomach. Upon the courtyard walls someone had taken the king's body and impaled him. She recognised immediately the emerald flag of Saemore pinned to the wall beside him.

"Can't say he didn't deserve his fate," Palea muttered. "But what do your countrymen have to do with this?"

Lyssandra shook her head. "I don't know."

It was Elisaria's distressed rumbling that broke Lyssandra's trance. She looked over her shoulder to see her dragon standing over the still form of Taseria's drake. Unsheathing her sword, Palea joined Elisaria at the scaled corpse. Chunks of hide had been gnawed away so that in some places, Lyssandra could see gleaming bone. "Lizardlings," Palea said, reaching out her hand to trace the air above the deep gashes.

The dragon's rider lay sprawled beside him. As Palea walked past her, she kicked her and spat upon her body, cursing in Nezahrian.

"I wish I had been the one to hit her. Her name was Taseria," Palea said. "Scheming, cowardly knave. For a woman who professed to love both Alaxen and Rikar Tallermayne, she was weak."

"I wonder," Lyssandra murmured, looking down at the still body. "Did she always have such a fickle heart?"

"We'll never know." Valtar stumbled through the courtyard. Dark blood clotted over his flank. *"They're in the ballroom. The palace is rigged. I cannot get to my riders without hurting them."*

Lyssandra considered the palace behind her. "What happened?"

"Nelly thought to check in with the Saemorish diplomats. Konrad followed her." Valtar swayed his head to and fro. *"I cannot speak with my riders, so they didn't heed my warning. It was a trap."*

"Nelly?"

"Antonella is such a mouthful, don't you think? We dragons will wait out here, ready to fly."

Faer sidled closer to Valtar. They greeted each other warmly, then allowed Elisaria to approach. Confident that the dragons would look after one another, Lyssandra drew her sword and moved cautiously through the courtyard. Weapon in hand, Palea followed. The small lizardling took up the rear, long, sharp talons clicking on the floor.

Lyssandra tried her best not to let her imagination distract her as they crept through the palace. Exchanging glances with Palea, Lyssandra considered the wisdom of splitting up. The signs of the attack were everywhere in the palace: bodies, torn tapestries and blood. An ominous silence filled the halls.

Slinking forward, Jirrah brushed against her leg. He tilted his angular head before disappearing into the shadows. Lyssandra felt sorry for any poor soul who came upon a lizardling.

Curiosity forced her feet to keep walking the desolation of the halls. Palea took her position behind and to the right of Lyssandra. Pausing by the ornate doors, Lyssandra studied the golden couple dancing together. Ullryk on the right, a crown of fire around his head, Saskah on the left, her skirts rippling in the wind. They were both young and barefoot. The golden forms of their dragons were spattered with blood.

"It was quite the scandalous love story," Palea whispered in her ear. "The love-conquers-all kind of tale."

At Lyssandra's light touch, the doors opened. She was not prepared for the scene in the ballroom.

Illuminated by flickering torches, the domed glass ceiling was alive with blues and oranges. At the bases of the great dome, a crisscrossing of golden ropes formed supports. It was from these supports that jars alight with swirling silver liquid hung at different heights. A second glance confirmed the liquid was on fire.

The moment Lyssandra saw her friend and cousin, she dismissed all wonder at the beauty in favour of studying them. Bound in the same golden ropes and on their knees, Antonella and Konrad stared at her with horrified eyes.

"Antonella!" Lyssandra screamed, running forward, sword in her fist. She'd cleave in two any enemy who harmed her friend.

"Stay back!" Antonella yelled, shaking her head, her dark curls loose and coated with dust and blood. She had taken a beating; bruising marred her brown skin. Blood coated her lips.

As Konrad struggled to rise, an arrow thwacked the floor beside him. He dropped back to his knees, face twisting with agony as he did so. He was badly injured. Something was wrong with his leg.

Lyssandra's steps faltered as she remembered herself, and she studied again the room. Her mad dash had taken her to the middle of the swirling jars. Palea remained by the door, watching and weighing her options. She was glad the princess maintained her warrior's poise.

Swallowing back her cry of rage, Lyssandra looked towards the Aurelian king's throne. The arrow had to have come from somewhere. Where once King Oluvin sat was a woman. Her hair, black as midnight, was streaked with silver. Her green dress was tight and would have been beautiful if not for the sheer black overskirt embroidered with spiders.

Lyssandra took an involuntary step back. This woman would have been at the gala; she was still wearing her shimmering mask. The silver lines of the cobwebs caught the light of her lit jars. Lyssandra could even see the individual dewdrops on her face.

"Welcome, my darling." A shiver went up Lyssandra's spine as the woman spoke. "Don't you recognise your own mother?"

When she had been a small girl, Lyssandra had dreamed of meeting Fiora of Saemore, her mother. Their reunion would be sweet with tears, cake and presents. She had grown out of such dreams. The weight of her diplomat training shattering the vision into cold reality.

Lyssandra took a step forward and stopped.

"Lyss! Get out of here!" Konrad's voice cracked.

"Silence, fool!" Fiora's long, elegant fingers stroked the string of her bow.

"Mother," Lyssandra said, proud that her voice did not warble. She took the tone of a courtier discussing the season's fruit. "I was not expecting you."

"Who is your friend?" Fiora lifted her hand, gracefully gesturing towards Palea, who was stalking along the edge of the ballroom.

Lie, Lyssandra thought. *Make it convincing.*

"Only a Nezahrian war wraith. Nameless and easily forgettable."

Palea remained silent.

"Is that so? I think of Gradie Holstym often." Fiora laughed. Her lips, painted black and dotted with specks of silver, curled into a wicked smile. From her skirts, she revealed a man's handkerchief. She held it up so that Lyssandra could see the monogram embroidered in silver thread on the black silk. Minuscule spiders in blood red had also been added to the border.

"Would you like a memento of your father, child? I stitched this while I was pregnant with you."

Lyssandra stood frozen, her skin crawling with imaginary bugs and spiders. In her lifetime she had met many powerful people. Her mother's words were not to give her peace or closure. No, the opposite was true. Now she knew her father's name ... He had been real.

"Why don't you tell our little misinformed diplomat who Gradie was?"

"He was a war wraith," Palea whispered. She sounded shocked. "High profile. Raziel's favourite. He went missing ..."

"Bedded and shredded."

If Lyssandra weren't so frozen, she would have dashed up the dais and slashed her mother's face with her nails.

"They told me you were deformed," Fiora continued. "Taken from the birthing chambers the moment you breathed your first. I hear Alaxen Tallermayne was responsible for the removal of your ears."

Lyssandra swallowed again. She heard what happened to princesses that dared to birth little bastards. Fiora had famously been imprisoned. It was said it was because of her deep melancholy and madness. Faced with Fiora, Lyssandra doubted this was the truth.

"What's the matter, dear? Did you think you were Ellrahera's favourite because of your keen intellect? My sister was so disappointed when you showed little progress with your powers. How she screamed when Jahon released me from prison. That was the end for her. Jahon needed little prompting to command her to commit the final protocol."

"I have nothing more to say to you," Lyssandra said. She wasn't an unknown bard's daughter. They had known all along her blood held power. But they had thought her weak and unusable ...

"Indeed, we're as two strangers." Fiora dropped the silken handkerchief as if it were a dirty rag. Had the woman kept it all these years just to use it to torment Lyssandra if she was ever given the opportunity?

"What do you want?" If she let her, Fiora would verbally manipulate and control the situation.

"My brother Jahon has offered me a deal," Fiora said. She stood, her silken skirts whispering along her thighs as she walked.

"I guess it has something to do with the Saemorish diplomats' arrival in Irani?" Konrad said, biting out the words.

"Konrad, be quiet," Antonella whispered.

Fiora stalked across the floor that separated her from her prisoners. She raised her hand and struck Konrad across the face. The slap resounded around the room as Konrad crumbled, his weight shifting to his leg.

"The diplomats are my court," Fiora said. "All I have to do to win the crown is deliver the traitors into Jahon's hands."

Tilting her head up, Lyssandra looked up at the strange glowing jars. She gestured casually to them. "And these?"

Fiora smiled. "Why, my dear, Jahon didn't say you had to be delivered alive."

Lyssandra looked desperately around the room. Poison. It had to be. She was of no doubt that Fiora had already ingested the antidote to whatever liquid was in those jars.

Drawing in a deep breath, Lyssandra looked around again. Concentrating on the problem wouldn't help her find the solution. Ellrahera had been a firm believer that all situations would have a way for survival. Pity she hadn't found one for her and her disciples during the Black Prince's burning of Correllain.

She spied her solution at the foot of the throne. Fiora had been served a platter of fresh fruit: strawberries, plums and golden pears.

There was no time to worry about how much control she had over her powers. If she was going to be the master of her own fate, she needed to lash out with no warning. She felt her gifting move within, uncoiling like a slumbering beast.

The fruit exploded, roots growing at a tremendous speed, spearing the ground of the ballroom. The golden plate morphed and twisted.

Fiora whirled, staring at the remains of the fruit. The saplings grew, and Lyssandra lost what little control she had over her power. Her mother reached out and grabbed fistfuls of Antonella's hair.

Lyssandra screamed, and the whole ballroom reverberated with the strength of her cry. The branches of her quickly expanding orchard wavered. The roots uplifted from their foundations. Free of the ground, the trees moved forward with slow, clumsy steps.

Fiora cut one of the jars, releasing the poison as the glass shattered into shards. But her act of defiance wasn't enough to protect her from Lyssandra's army of walking trees.

Lyssandra continued to scream, her eyes tightly shut, her fists balled at her sides. She felt her power, sensed rather than saw the trees lumbering forward on their roots. They swung at Fiora. A terrible cry was followed by a crack. The strike swept Fiora off her feet, battering her into another trunk. The trees tossed Lyssandra's mother between them until all that was left was a bloody pulp on the dais.

Pain erupted from Lyssandra's shoulders; her teeth ached. And still the power flowed.

Lyssandra had no illusions that she was going to die.

CHAPTER 29

Royal Boon

EDVERN

Edvern's muscles screamed as he pulled himself upright. He blinked blearily at the masses of silken cushions and velvet coverings. Stifling a groan, he recalled the tart flavours of Nezahrian wine and one of their princes putting him to bed. His mind snapped into focus.

"Alynta! Camyrs!" The dyrathakins were gone. Lyssandra was going to kill him if her kit had gone missing.

"Calm yourself, Uhl'hari."

Edvern jolted, realising that he was not alone in the war tent. The Black Prince sat in one of his ornate chairs, Camyrs on his lap and Alynta leaning against his side. Long, deft fingers inspected her side where she had been injured. But it wasn't Raziel who had spoken.

A woman dressed in a simple black gown stood, the silk of her skirts pooling at her feet. Her eyes shimmered in the light of Edvern's wings, a hunger and curiosity in their depths. Her smooth brown skin made her appear ageless, but she must have been old enough to be his mother.

Edvern blinked, staring up at the spiked crown that sat among her dark hair. "Your Majesty."

"You must forgive us. Raziel thought it necessary to administer a simple herb to help you remain resting. Take your time."

"How long ..." Edvern closed his eyes, grogginess clouding his mind. "What's happening?"

Alynta padded over to rest her chin on the side of Edvern's cot. "Asleep long enough your body is rested and I'm hungry."

Edvern couldn't help but smile, his fingers tracing over the dyrathakin's forehead. Jealous of the attention, Camyrs jumped from the Black Prince's lap and joined them, butting his head against Edvern's hands.

"We must speak, Uhl'hari." The empress' gaze was drawn to where Edvern's sword had been lain across one of the strategy tables.

"Ionah, he is still recovering."

Edvern wished that the ground might open and swallow him whole. The Black Prince sat at his strategy table, one long leg draped over his knee. A glass of red wine, fruity and pungent, was cradled in his hands. Both the empress and Raziel had washed since the battle. They were refreshed and refined, while he was only in his trousers and boots, his wings fanning out behind him. Dried blood coated his skin. The empress turned to look at him, her brow furrowed.

"You may keep the sword. Everything else Aurelian on your person will be destroyed."

A lump formed in Edvern's throat. He knew he should thank the empress for her consideration but found the words would not come. Instead, he inclined his head.

"Rikar Tallermayne was a clever man," the empress said. "Did he know, I wonder, that his stolen child had fire powers, that he was Qavi blessed?"

"No." Edvern shook his head. "It's one of my greatest regrets, Your Majesty, that I didn't tell him about my fire when I had the opportunity."

"He knew," Raziel said gruffly. The Black Prince lifted his eyes to the roof of his tent, closing them as if in pain. "He knew, Edvern."

"Qavi is not light or fire …" Edvern protested.

A strange expression washed over the empress' face. "Your soul son needs an education into Nezahrian beliefs. His Aurelian—"

"I'll oversee his proper education," Raziel said. "But we cannot erase his time among the Aurelians, Great One."

"Come now, Uhl'hari, it's time to be honest with one another. My husband is still deep in his cups, celebrating his victory, and will not disturb us."

"*Victory?*" Raziel rolled his eyes, clearly disgusted.

"The sacking of Irani, the death of the king of Aurelia and having two Tallermayne prisoners is cause for my husband to celebrate for days."

Edvern pursed his lips but was unable to stop his incredulous laugh. There were times that he struggled to hide the nervous habit. He could almost hear his father's exasperated sigh.

"Forgive me for being blunt, Your Majesty, but I'm not inclined to, ah …" Damn it, what would Lyssandra say?

"I don't expect you to trust His Majesty, Uhl'hari."

"Shooting me in the chest without proper introduction did damper my opinion of him."

"You'll be walking a dangerous line," Raziel said. He shook his head, holding out his hand to Alynta. Without looking back at Edvern, the dyrathakin went to him.

"Faelowyn will take you to where we're holding Alaxen. Tell your Tallermayne uncle news of Eddi, now that he is awake."

"I didn't want to leave Eddi," replied the dyrathakin.

"I think hearing news from you, my dear, will ease Alaxen's worry more than hearing it from my lips."

Alynta glanced back at Edvern, then to the Black Prince.

"You'll always have access to your Uhl'hari," Raziel assured her. "No one will hinder your movements in the camp."

"Go," Edvern urged her, sensing this was a precious opportunity for him to hear news of his family from a trusted source.

Alynta padded towards the tent flap. There she paused, checking on him before she slunk through the tent flap.

The empress watched her go. Then once the bushy tail disappeared, she turned her shrewd eyes to Edvern. "My husband shot you because like most modern patriots, he does not trust the ancient ways."

"I assure—"

"I'm not finished, Uhl'hari," the empress snapped. "You're not human. You're not royal."

"Your Majesty, my only wish is to free the dragons. I've no interest in Nezaha."

"You speak rashly, Uhl'hari. Don't let the men hear you speak like that. Nezahrians are a proud people." Empress Ionah held up an imperious hand, continuing as if his words held no value. "You'll stay in Raziel's tent and accept your place at his side. Raziel's officers will provide you with protection."

Edvern opened his mouth. At Raziel's curt shake of his head, he clicked his jaw shut, biting back his reply. This wasn't the time to fight.

"You'll keep yourself out of Nezahrian politics, and once the war is over you will remain at the estates provided to the Uhl'hari. You will not come to the cities. The moment you get yourself involved in anything that gives the impression you are plotting against His Majesty, your life will be forfeit. For now, the emperor is appeased that you're content with a simple life out of the public eye."

Edvern blinked. "Why not banish me? It would be simpler for the both of us."

"The Uhl'hari are for the dragons," Raziel said. "They're the link between humans and dragons. Without them ... your presence in Nezaha will only bolster our country's strength."

The empress smiled thinly. "Try convincing Ze'hyrn of your good intentions. You need to be alive to be of any use for us. Farewell for now, Uhl'hari."

"Your Majesty."

Edvern was shocked when the empress came to stand over him. She reached out to him and tucked her hand behind the curtain of his hair. Running her fingers along the smooth ridges of his ears, she murmured, "A royal boon. Wear them. Raziel will assist you. Black Prince, ensure he is washed and dressed accordingly."

"Of course."

Two pieces of golden jewellery were pressed into his hands.

"Food from the emperor's table will be provided for you, Uhl'hari." Ionah inclined her head to Raziel, her taut lips tugging into a smile.

Together, the Black Prince and Edvern watched the empress leave. When she was gone, they stared at one another, neither one of them daring to move. Edvern held his breath, feeling conscious of his bare chest and dried, crusted blood.

"Come here."

There was little point in fighting, so Edvern moved to the Black Prince's side. He stood still as Raziel brushed his hair from his face. The Black Prince took the first piece of jewellery, and with a sharp snap, it attached to his ear.

Edvern studied the second piece in his hands. An ear cuff made of swirling gold tapered at the ends. A thin golden chain looped from the very tip to the middle. A second chain held a glistening red ruby.

Edvern swallowed, sure that he understood the unsaid message they gave. A sign of ownership. He belonged to Nezaha and to the emperor who shot him. At least if he had to run, he had something of value to sell ...

Raziel tilted his head and attached the second cuff.

"I'll say to you what my master told me," Raziel said, taking his shoulders. "You belong to no man. You're for dragons. Father Dragon willing, you'll outlive the emperor, and you'll learn to play the game well."

"Alaxen told me you are a Yavari, selected from the blessed ones to be the Sword of Nezaha, the military leader," Edvern said. "You're not human."

"Your uncle is well-informed." Raziel nodded to the side. "I'm long lived, both a spiritual and military leader."

"The soul touch showed me that I was taken from the temple," Edvern said. He paused, but Raziel waited for him patiently to continue. "Alaxen admitted you had chosen me. What am I?"

Raziel furrowed his brow. "Both Yavari because I chose you and Uhl'hari because Alynta also chose you. Very few Uhl'haris have walked this earth. A dyrathakin hatches when they sense their chosen one, usually in times of turmoil. Alynta and you have formed a bond where you may siphon your power between one another. You also have a greater right and responsibility to intercede between humans and dragons. The people will see your coming as a sign of favour, that the wild ones will return and Nezaha will be reborn into its former greatness."

"The wild ones left."

"We haven't had a successful Uhl'hari for nearly a millennium."

"What if I fail?"

"The wild ones are already returning. The Father Dragon knew what his plan was for you, it seems." Raziel smiled. "Now, let me see your hand."

Edvern curled his fists, wishing that he could hide them. It was childish and stupid; he knew what the Black Prince wanted. He straightened his spine and gave in to the inevitable, holding out his damaged hand with

Alaxen's magic fingers. He took another step forward, not wanting to be seen as timid, and placed his hand in the Black Prince's own.

"A marvel," the Black Prince murmured. He smiled up at Edvern, but there was a glint of viciousness in his eyes. "One day I'll tell you the story of what happens to a mortal who maims an Uhl'hari."

Chapter 30

Mother Dearest

Lyssandra

Lyssandra was sure she was going to die. Her vision swam as her head thrummed with pain. No matter how her mind screamed, she could not get her body to obey her and get to her feet.

Blinking through her tears, she saw the room slowly come into focus. The twisted trees cultivated by her power were now still, the glowing lanterns of poison swinging dangerously between them. And talons, feathers!

Long dark hair askew, Lyssandra upturned her face towards the glass ceiling, screaming. Two long stag horns protruded from her skull. She clung on to them, shaking her head as if to ease her torment.

She had murdered her own mother, a royal born princess.

Jirrah, the lizardling that had been guiding Faer, pushed his way into her lap. He was all sharp angles and sinew, but his attempt at comfort was appreciated. He pressed his bony head against her chest, crooning and chirruping. Before long she understood his words.

"Look what you've done, you magnificent creature. Even without your dyrathakin present to help siphon your power, you've opened the floodgates to your gifting."

"What am I?" To Lyssandra's ears she sounded pathetic. She craned her neck to look at the wings on her back. The feathers were earthy, coloured like a hawk's, and leaves and vines grew amongst them.

"Uhl'hari of earth," Jirrah replied matter-of-factly.

"Of course." A small laugh bubbled from her lips.

"Are you ready?"

Lyssandra nodded, brushing her sweat-soaked hair from her face. She gritted her teeth and stood.

"Lyss ..." Antonella's bruised face grimaced in pain as she attempted to haul Konrad to his feet. She seemed conflicted between her friend and lover. Wearily, Lyssandra attempted a smile. Konrad's leg looked broken; he needed Antonella's support.

"I'm fine." Lyssandra swallowed; her voice sounded hoarse. "We need to move before any more of the jars fall."

One jar would make them ill; dozens were deadly. It was not the slow and painful death that she'd ever imagined for herself.

At the golden doors, Jirrah joined Palea, his head cocked to the side. "Remember how you said there were Saemorish diplomats ... I can hear them coming."

"And we just killed their new queen," Konrad drawled. "What a shame that was."

"They're armed," Antonella warned, dragging Konrad to the door. Wordlessly, Palea took charge and wrapped her arm around his shoulder.

The Nezahrian princess might be slim, but she was strong. She marched them into the corridor.

"When the Aurelian king was killed and the lizardlings started killing … they retreated into the palace and butchered anyone taking shelter inside. They barricaded the doors until the lizardlings got bored and left." Antonella's voice cracked.

The sound of echoing feet, accompanied by angry voices, resounded in the hall.

"I count six," Jirrah said, a slow, cruel smile curling on his lips. *"Stay back."*

From the dimness of the palace corridors, six Saemorish nobles appeared. They stopped, taking in their battered prisoners and the lizardling. Two were smart and turned tail and ran when they saw the snarling lizardling. The other four grinned at one another, ready for a fight.

The hordes of lizardlings in the palace courtyards had been terrifying, but Lyssandra was otherwise occupied and hadn't stopped to admire their ferociousness. Breath caught in her throat, her first thought was that a single small lizardling with a rumpled wing would not be able to do much against four grown men.

Her feet rushed forward to help, a war cry on her lips. But Jirrah didn't require her help.

He lurched forward at an impossible speed, his talons skittering as he leapt to the wall, running vertically along the corridor. Long claws clamped around the throat of the first unfortunate man. A yank, and his throat was ripped out. He fell like a puppet whose strings had been cut.

Using his victim's shoulders, Jirrah jumped into the face of the second man. Claws found eyes, back, legs, stomach. And the lizardling was already on the third man, jaws locked around the face. A sharp tug and a snap, and this man dropped soundlessly.

The fourth and final man had time to flee.

Jirrah stalked along the corridor after him, belly low and a growl rumbling in his belly. A shout for help was all the man had time for before Jirrah caught him by the ankles and toppled him.

Facedown, the man tried to scrabble away, his fingers clawing at the slippery tiles beneath him. The lizardling languidly stalked along his back until he came to the man's head. Back claws punctured the spine, and the struggle ceased. Curling around the man's skull, front talons pressed into flesh and bone.

Lyssandra had to look away from the carnage, her empty stomach protesting against the sight.

"Lizardlings are mighty helpful to keep around," Palea said in the ensuing silence.

Bracing her hand against the wall, Lyssandra nodded. "Which way is out?"

"The Euquallians are still being held prisoner," Antonella snapped.

"And I need fresh air," Lyssandra replied. She bit back other words she would like to say, knowing she was angry and confused. "I need time to regroup, and Konrad needs somewhere safe we can look at his leg."

"We're not leaving them?" Antonella asked.

"No," Palea said. "Let's regroup and see if Faer has pinpointed the location of any Euquallian prisoners. This way."

Allowing Palea and Jirrah to take control, Lyssandra followed after them. No one had the desire to speak as they made their way from the halls. They exited the palace, stumbling into the courtyard to see that it was fuller than when they left it.

Along the outer walls were dragons of all sizes, colours and shapes, Aurelian riders standing proudly before them. In the courtyard was a bronze dragon, his rider a broad Aurelian man with tattoos winding up his forearms.

In his grasp he held the two Saemorish nobles who had fled Jirrah's wrath. Lyssandra watched as he lifted them both, giving them a shake as he questioned them.

"Oskar!" Palea cried in delight, the heads of the dragon riders snapping to attention.

Lyssandra could feel their curious gazes raking over her new body. Though no one spoke, she saw the questions in their eyes.

Dropping the two Saemorish men, Oskar left his bronze dragon to loom over them threateningly. Terrified for their lives, the pair remained still, staring up into the burning eyes of the drake, who flared his nostrils and huffed blistering air over them.

Oskar strode towards them, and his stern face blossomed into a smile at the sight of Palea. Konrad found rest against a wall as the Aurelian clasped arms with the Nezahrian princess.

"Palea, such good tidings to see you well," Oskar said, genuine warmth seeping into his deep bass. The smile dimmed as he looked away from Palea and to the gardens. The decapitated heads of the dragons kept his focus. "What of the Tallermaynes? Kendrick's letter summoned us here."

"Alaxen and Bastian were able to withdraw from the battle. They are guests with the Nezahrians."

Oskar drew in a deep breath. "Guests, I see. Kendrick?"

"He ..." Lyssandra said, opening her mouth, because if she didn't say something, she'd vomit. "He didn't make it."

Oskar swallowed, his dark eyes dimming. The news affected him. He looked her over again in an appraising manner, taking in her wings and horns. "Where?"

Lyssandra lifted a finger. "Near his dragon's head."

Orange light glowed around Oskar's fists. He turned on his heel and pointed at two of his riders. "Here," he commanded, curling his fingers. There was a flash, and the two riders now stood before Oskar. They didn't look at all perturbed that their bodies had been moved from one place to another within a heartbeat. It was an interesting power to have. Lyssandra wondered if he had used it in battle.

"Kendrick, our fallen brother, lies with the dragon's head. Build him a pyre so we might honour his life and death. It's what General Tallermayne would want."

Expressions grim, the riders nodded and slipped past Oskar, looking for suitable kindling. When Oskar turned back to them, tears shone in his eyes. "Aye, I'm going to miss that boy."

Silent tears trailed down Palea's face, smudging the makeup around her eyes. Lyssandra lifted a comforting hand but restrained herself from touching the princess.

"Alaxen had his nephew with him, Edvern," Oskar continued. "Do you have any news of him?"

"Injured but recovering," Lyssandra said, deliberately omitting that it was the Nezahrian emperor who had shot him. She wasn't sure what to think of these riders. Edvern had given her the impression that most riders wanted to see him dead. Alas, her tongue spoke before she could mull over her words. "Edvern believed Aurelian riders mean him harm."

"Edvern"—Oskar's voice dropped to a low purr—"was kept hidden in Gytall for most of his life. He has only just begun to experience Aurelia."

"They are the riders of Cynedir." Palea laid a hand on Lyssandra's shoulders. "These are the men and women who welcomed me into their ranks. I trust them."

"You mentioned a letter from Kendrick?" Antonella questioned from Konrad's side.

"Yes, he warned of the king's planned rebellion." The warmth leeched out of Oskar's eyes as he looked up at the wall to where the king's body had been pinned. "He also mentioned that Euquallians were imprisoned here. We came for our Euquallian friend but were unfortunately waylaid after the burning of Cynedir."

"You came for me?" Palea asked.

Oskar shrugged. "You want your people free, and we wanted our Tallermayne boys back. But when we arrived ..."

Lyssandra looked towards Palea. Obviously, the riders did not know she was the emperor's daughter, which, considering that Alaxen hadn't known, shouldn't have been surprising.

"We'll look after your injured here," Oskar said. "The Euquallians?"

"Our reports said they fled into the gardens," Lyssandra replied. "Maybe my Saemorish countrymen could give clearer directions."

The Saemorish noblemen sung beautifully without many threats having to be plied. Once she felt she had sufficient information on where to look in the ancient gardens, Palea prepared to set off. It shouldn't have come as a surprise that Antonella wanted to go with her as well. The Euquallians were Antonella's people.

The scent of burning flesh from the Aurelian funeral pyres was strong in the air when Konrad was gently carried and laid on fresh leaves. The Cynedir riders insisted that an area be cleaned before they looked to Konrad's wound.

Useless to help, Lyssandra sat herself primly on the edge of the fountain, turning her face away from the bubbling blood. Edvern hadn't had his wings on full display for the ball, she mused. He must be able to tuck them away. She closed her eyes, ignoring the siren call of sleep.

Her power writhed within her, and her skin tingled all over. The wings furled, the feathers soft against her back. The weight on her head dissipated as the horns disappeared.

"I'm not sure I'll get used to that," Konrad remarked, his face tight with pain as a healer, a pretty woman, poked at his leg.

"This may sting," she said in a sweet little voice as she pressed down on the jutting bone.

Konrad screamed like Lyssandra had never heard before. The healer's expression didn't shift as she applied two hands over the breakage. There were no words of comfort as the bone fused within his leg, the puncture site disappearing as if it were never there.

"The slight burn is the power fighting the infection," the healer said. "Would you like a drink of water?"

"Slight burn?" Konrad gasped, his face flushed. "And the water is fouled."

"Is it?" the healer asked, clearly amused. "Cloe, get our guest a drink."

Another young woman sauntered forward, hips swaying as she approached the fountain. She dipped her cup into the bloody water, her hand waved over the top and the red liquid turned crystal clear.

"Not drinking that," Konrad muttered.

"Here." Lyssandra held out her hand to the dragon rider, Cloe. "I'll test for my cousin."

A pleased smile spread over Cloe's lips as Lyssandra took the cup to drink. It was cool and sweet. It was safe to drink.

"Another, milady?"

Lyssandra nodded again. Once her thirst was sated, she helped Konrad to sit so that he could drink also. He was still sceptical, but once the cool water touched his lips, he drank like a dying man.

Together they sat and watched as Aurelian riders made ready and welcomed the Euquallians as Palea and Antonella ushered them from their hiding spots. The flow of Euquallians was slow at first, but as their countrymen were fed rations and given water and healers' attention, the stragglers approached.

The last Euquallian arrived back in camp with Palea and Antonella. From the moment this woman stepped into the courtyard, Lyssandra knew she was important. The riders sensed it too, many of them stopping their jobs.

Oskar stood from where he was meticulously cleaning Kendrick's sword to return to Alaxen.

"Imagine my surprise to find Aurelian dragon riders offering Euquall aid after your king kept us illegally imprisoned." The woman moved among the throng. Her diaphanous skirts, trimmed with gold, swayed as she walked.

A smirk played over Oskar's lips. "Princess Eupheana, always such a pleasure."

"General Eupheana," the princess corrected, her own mouth twisting into a wry grin. "It's good to see the Bull of Cynedir well."

Oskar pointed up towards where King Oluvin's body swayed gently in the breeze. "Trouble is brewing. Seems to me the general of Euquall might want to take advantage of the situation."

Eupheana turned her head to regard the corpse. "I can't say with any sincerity that I'm sorry to see the old bastard strung up."

"Mother came for you," Palea said. "Everything ..."

"Chaos happens in battle, niece," Eupheana replied, resting a hand on Palea's shoulders. Long golden nails glinted like strong claws. "A wise general knows sometimes a tactical retreat is necessary."

Lyssandra caught the gleam of understanding in Oskar's eyes the moment Palea had spoken. His lips formed a firm line as he said, "The Nezahrians are forming some response to Lady Moira's threats. You may want to hear what they have to say. Pitch Euquallian interests in the midst."

"I suppose you're going to help, Oskar?"

Oskar turned, gesturing to his dragons. "We'll already be returning some of the Black Prince's number to him. Our dragons can take a few more. Your sister, the empress, would be glad to see you, I'm sure."

"Ionah and I were close once upon a time," Eupheana said, her sigh wistful. "Alas, our father gave her in marriage, and the relationship between

Ze'hyrn and my father has cooled somewhat." Eupheana stepped past Oskar, looking down at Lyssandra. "I recognise you from the wall. You fought with the Tallermayne riders."

Lyssandra stood, doing her best to smooth down her ragged dress. Her wings had shredded the back lacings, and it was difficult to keep it from sliding down her shoulders. "Lady Lyssandra Stamos, Your Highness."

Regarding her coolly, Eupheana turned to Oskar. "A young lady should not be left in rags that could bring her shame and ridicule. Command your riders to escort one of my handmaidens to retrieve something from my chests. Ze'hyrn will not be kind if she's dressed in rags."

"You're most generous, Your Highness," Lyssandra murmured, watching as Oskar waved Cloe and the healer forward to escort the Euquallian handmaidens who had been fortunate to escape into the palace.

"Nonsense. I saw you fight for our people on that wall. Least I can do is give you something to ..." Eupheana waved her hand to emphasize her point. "Cover your body."

Lyssandra dipped her head. It would be wise not to tell the Euquallian general she was on the wall for the dyrathakin. Let her think her a more noble creature.

Ze'hyrn had proven himself to be a threat. A potential enemy. Whereas Eupheana was not shy to voice her dislike of the Nezahrian emperor. She would be an interesting ally to have against him.

Lyssandra needed all the allies she could get.

CHAPTER 31

Among Nezahrians

EDVERN

Edvern's first day of captivity consisted of being scrubbed and groomed. It was certainly an experience, Nezahrian servants bustling into the tent with warm water, towels and soaps. Most of them kept their gazes firmly averted. The moment they thought he wasn't watching, they observed. They spoke to him in clipped Nezahrian, but he could only shake his head. He suspected that not even servants would lower themselves to speak Aurelian.

It soon became abundantly clear that Empress Ionah was determined that he be stripped of everything Aurelian and presented as a young Nezahrian noble. As his brand-new boots were taken to be put to the flames, Edvern lunged and grabbed the painted handkerchief, thankful he remembered it in time.

Alaxen should have it. It was Kendrick's work, of that he was sure. Not his best painting, but it was something of his.

"*Ragtch*!" Edvern cried, pretty sure it was the Nezahrian word for 'no'. He had heard it multiple times as the servants hurried around him. Holding the scrap of fabric to his chest, he backed away. It was no mean feat to look intimidating in only one's smallclothes. "It's mine!"

The oldest servant stared with fathomless dark eyes, his gaze raking over every inch of Edvern's body. He held out a wrinkled hand, and when Edvern didn't immediately comply with the unspoken request, he wriggled his fingers. Cautiously, he handed the handkerchief over, which the servant inspected, holding it to the light and checking the stitching.

Biting his lip, Edvern watched on. "Give it back."

"*Ragtch*." Unfortunately, the man was military trained or knew of the secret messages that Aurelian dragon riders used. He spotted the glyph in the full moon.

"Seriously!" Edvern cried as the old man went to tuck it in his pocket. "Who am I going to signal here? I'm too well-guarded, and most Aurelian dragon riders will kill me on sight. Why do I bother? Are you even listening to me?"

"*Ragtch*."

Howling, Edvern turned away from the servant, his fingers curling into fists, his eyes stinging.

The old servant grunted, clearly unimpressed.

While Edvern was arguing with the servants, Alynta rescued the fur from Edvern's cloak, slinking from the tent without being seen. He received an image from the dyrathakin; she had taken it upon herself to build Camyrs his own little nest in Lyssandra's tent and the fur was the crowning glory of his bed.

Without speaking Edvern dressed in the clothing the old man handed him. Everything was black, down to the form-fitting trousers and sturdy boots. The clothing was all a fine make. When he threw the shirt over his head, the old man slapped his hands away as he attempted to tie the laces himself. He waggled his finger under Edvern's nose and gave him a sound tongue lashing.

"I don't understand you." Edvern shook his head miserably.

The sly glance from the old man to another servant was enough to tell him that they understood him perfectly. There was a part of him that wanted to scream and shout, to throw a tantrum and harry them out of the tent. But that was a child's reaction, and perhaps that was what they were expecting of him. He was a man now; he would prove them wrong.

"I've heard it said that Nezahrian hospitality is cold," Edvern said, watching the old man's hands as he tied the laces of the shirt. "Can't say I disagree."

There was a slight crinkling around the man's eyes, as if he wanted to open his mouth and argue. Edvern continued, "My father kept me in Gytall to hide me away from Nezahrian eyes. My experiences with Nezaha and my understanding of your culture are extremely limited. But I had a friend once. A servant boy. We stole scraps from the kitchens and played havoc in the servant tunnels. The older servants knew, of course, and did nothing."

The servant led Edvern to a chair and firmly sat him down. He closed his eyes as a comb was brushed through his wet hair.

"Quite a pair we made. The bastard and the Nezahrian slave. The only two dark-haired boys in the spire."

Experienced fingers rubbed hair oils, smelling strongly of herbs, into Edvern's scalp.

"We had our own little kingdom in the tunnels of Gytall. That was, until it came crumbling down ..."

Scissors were brought to his hair, trimming the ends.

"Of course, if it wasn't for Rikar, I would have shared his fate."

The pause was enough to tell Edvern that both of the servants were listening and invested in his story. He hadn't dared think about these memories of his childhood for years. The pain blossoming in his heart was unexpected. Hanging his head, he attempted to shield his expression from the servants. Loose fingers let go of his hair.

"What happened?" A soft question, uttered in Aurelian.

Edvern didn't feel the thrill of victory in getting them to speak to him. "We were punished for our friendship. And I no longer remember his name ..."

The servant boy had pissed himself when Moira caught him in the web of her power. He could still remember the way his father hauled him struggling from the stables, passing him to Bastian and telling them to run. For years he had blocked out the cries of the other child and his father's shouts for mercy.

Rikar had come to him that night in the nursery, when everything was dark. He had kissed his cheeks, beard wet with tears. For a fortnight he was kept unseen. It had been the first time he had told his father he hated Moira. When he was released from the nursery, he had marched straight up to his grandmother and told her to her face.

That was a beating that still lived in his memory.

He had been five years old.

"Uhl'hari ..."

"It was the only time I saw my father cry."

That was true. His father had wept as he had warned Edvern it was dangerous for the servants to be friends with him, and his father had sobbed as he was forced to thrash him. Better a thrashing from his father's hand than one of Moira's favourites.

Edvern sat in the chair in silence, staring out ahead of him, trying to conjure the other boy's face. It was impossible to imagine what he might look like now.

"You should eat, Uhl'hari," another one of the servants said as they finished grooming him. The man dared to lift a hand to Edvern's shoulder to squeeze. "Then you should sleep."

"I am tired of sleeping." Edvern huffed. "I'd like to see my uncle."

"Empress Ionah has denied this request already, Uhl'hari," the elder servant said. "What would you like to eat?"

"I am not fussy," Edvern replied. "But avoid pickled vegetables if you can."

The servants wrinkled their noses at him. "You eat from the emperor's table."

"Have Lady Lyssandra and Palea returned?"

"No, my lord."

Edvern clasped his hands in his lap. He glanced up at the eldest servant. "Do you know how long I'm to be kept prisoner?"

The servants exchanged uneasy glances; the older servant returned the painted handkerchief, setting it beside Edvern's elbow. Without any further words spoken, they both swept from the tent.

"I'll give you points for breaking the silence, and quite a triumph to have Ionah's own servants return your painting. It was quite a story."

Edvern started, his hands darting out for the handkerchief and tucking it into his tunic. He hadn't realised he was not alone with the servants. From the shadows of the tent, a man dressed solely in black and a dark scarf over his face appeared. It was with some humour he recognised familiar emerald eyes as the man who had thrown them off the bridge in Cynedir.

"It wasn't a story. It was all true," Edvern murmured.

The man sauntered forward, eyes glimmering over his mask. "That is what makes it so powerful. It was a clever choice to sway the servants into giving into your wishes."

"I have no wish to manipulate anyone."

"I'm Zanniel. I'm to be your shadow and protector. Along with Symmeon, whom you're already acquainted with."

"The war wraith."

Zanniel removed the scarf, the twisted smile on his face showing he was amused. "Yes, a war wraith, loyal to Raziel Yavari. Rider of Codex."

Edvern inclined his head, determined to keep this conversation civil. "Codee is a clever dragon; his instincts are impeccable."

"You've come a long way since Vancarde."

Edvern flinched, but he would not be wrong-footed. "And you're less wet than when I saw you in Cynedir. Thankfully, Alynta was thoughtful enough to fish you out of the river."

Something dangerous glinted in the war wraith's eyes. Edvern hoped it was grudging respect.

"I know you probably don't want to tell me ... but my uncle and cousin?"

"Still alive."

"For how long?"

Zanniel shrugged. "It seems that Raziel and Alaxen have come to an understanding of sorts. Your uncle and cousin were allowed time to mourn Kendrick. Private funeral."

"I should have been there!" Edvern flushed, feeling the heat rise to his cheeks.

"Emperor Ze'hyrn did not want his Uhl'hari near traitorous Aurelians."

"I don't belong to *him*!"

Snarling, Zanniel lifted his hand to warn Edvern. The volume of his voice had risen. The war wraith's eyes lingered on the golden ear cuffs, with their delicate chains and jewels.

"He shot me," Edvern hissed between his clenched teeth.

"Listen carefully, Uhl'hari." Zanniel entered the tent further, resting his hands on the table, and leant over so his nose was almost touching Edvern's. "The emperor announced that you were shot by an Aurelian rider. Nezahrians rescued you."

"That's not what happened."

"When the emperor speaks, the world listens. Not enough people witnessed what he did to be able to dissuade the army and common folk that their ruler is a liar."

"So I am now a slave to a man who tried to kill me?"

"No. You are Raziel Yavari's soul son. There are powers at play here, Uhl'hari, to keep you alive. And I'm one of them."

"Very well. Might I go for a walk?"

Zanniel seemed to consider him for a long moment. Then he nodded curtly. "A stroll might do you some good. Get the men used to seeing you. Come, there's something you might want to see."

Edvern wondered if Zanniel was a highborn. He seemed rather high-handed in his commands. Not wanting to waste his opportunity to leave the war tent, Edvern hurried after the war wraith.

They hadn't gone far before Odharn came bounding over to Edvern. Nearby Faelowyn watched on. A little further, Codex and Izorah observed. Edvern absently ran his hands down the young dragon's scales, staring out at his dragon. Izorah seemed unhurt, if uneasy. Stopping his fussing, Odharn scented Edvern. *"You smell like a rich man."*

"The empress was of the opinion that I stank."

Edvern was pleased to see that his off-handed remark earned him a chuckle from Zanniel. The war wraith could be charmed if he was careful. He glanced at his assigned shadow and wondered how quickly he could manipulate him into letting him see his uncle.

Faelowyn rolled to her feet, lumbering over towards Edvern. She lowered her snout, letting her warm breath wash over him. *"Do not think about it. Zanniel is stationed at your side for your safety."*

Odharn lifted his head towards the large black dragon, turning his slender neck up at her with reverence. Edvern was pleased to note that although still very scrawny, the little green dragon was in a better condition from the time he had last seen him. There had been a part of him that despaired that he would not survive on his own.

Odharn licked his chops.

"My belly is empty, great queen," Odharn said, his stomach rumbling to give credit to his claim. *"Take me hunting."*

Edvern felt a ripple of annoyance rush over him, quickly followed by pride for the little dragon. A hungry hatchling was a growing hatchling.

It seemed odd that he should feel also the emotions of dragons he was not bonded to.

"Thank you," Edvern said. *"For looking after Odharn. I thought ... I thought he was ..."*

Faelowyn cocked her head. *"Dragonkind should be thanking you, Uhl'hari, for looking after one of us."*

"Eddi?" Odharn looked back at him, looking guilty for wanting to cave into the instinct to hunt.

"Go," Edvern said with a smile, because it was right for a dragon to feel the urge to feed. It was good that Odharn had a dragon to care for him. It was exactly how the Father Dragon had intended it.

Zanniel walked shoulder to shoulder with him, mask around his neck. He had the uneasy feeling that the war wraith was taking him through the path of being seen by the soldiers of Raziel's camp, while shielding him from the royal guards. He saw no sign of the emperor's colours or men.

Most of those that they came across stopped to stare. He heard the whispers, all in the foreign language he didn't understand. Zanniel kept stride with him; from his expression he was clearly listening to the conversations around them, so Edvern kept silent.

They made their way to the outer tents, towards the stables. Edvern's heart leapt.

Prince Dalain was waiting for them, Aerin watching nearby.

"I heard you were on your way," the prince said in greeting.

"Can you speak with Aerin?" Edvern asked, curious to know if speaking to dragons was a Nezahrian thing.

"The skill of speaking with dragons takes something inhumane." Dalain was not put off by Edvern's clipped greeting. "One must have one's soul touched by a dragon to truly understand them. There are other ways for riders to learn their dragon's emotions."

"Of course." The more Edvern learned about dragons, the more he felt small and insignificant. "You must have made an impression on Aerin. I didn't think he would willingly attach himself to another human, not after …"

"He killed his last rider. It's a little nerve-wracking having him wanting to bond again." The prince's lips downturned into a frown. He glanced back at Aerin, looking like he was debating his dragon's motives for such a choice.

Aerin lifted his horned head, flashing his fangs with smug delight. *"I'm going to keep him wondering."*

Edvern snorted, shaking his head, and turned back to the prince. "Behave yourself, and I don't think you'll have to worry."

"He is quite moody."

"Kyros was considered moody and dangerous," Edvern said. "Dragons are sentient beings. Kyros had been mistreated for so long … but he responded well to kindness and a gentle hand."

Aerin snarled. *"Attempt to give me a belly pat like the soft Lyrus, and I'll bite off your arm."*

Dalain stared at his dragon with rising horror. The prince may not hear the dragons speaking, but he certainly picked up on Aerin's tense body language.

"The way to any dragon's heart is food," Edvern said. "Aerin loves a side of beef marinated in good wine."

"Traitor…" Aerin lowered his head, rumbling.

"I wonder how you became so wise since you were raised by savage Tallermaynes."

Squishing his first reaction of indignation and hurt, Edvern considered this statement. "From the time I could walk, I helped my father care for his dragon, Izorah. I was educated in the old Tallermayne practices even though most dragon lords and masters have abandoned them. He showed me ways to look after the neglected without alerting their riders. I was given time to learn each dragon's name and understand their personality. Rikar Tallermayne was the only father I have known. He brought me in and made me kin … The lack of blood ties doesn't matter in Aurelian tradition."

"As interesting as all of this is," Zanniel drawled, "if His Imperial Majesty wants you on display, then a display we shall make."

"Come." Dalain grabbed Edvern's elbow and dragged him towards a familiar black stallion. The animal lifted his head. He pawed the ground before he trotted over.

"Qavi!" Edvern climbed the fence and strode over to the stallion, leaving Dalain and Zanniel to follow in his wake. He ran his hands down the velvety nose, wrapping his arms around the strong neck.

"My father doesn't need to know the particular value of this animal to you," Dalain said, keeping pace. "Raziel kept your father's mount in the hopes he could return him to you."

Edvern swallowed the lump in his throat, burying his face into the stallion's neck. "I loved to ride. We'd pick the fastest animals in the stables and thunder through the forests and plains of Gytall. It was the closest thing to flying."

Edvern could not wait to gallop the stallion across the flat ground. He mounted without a saddle, his fingers twining in Qavi's long mane. He grinned foolishly down at the war wraith and the prince.

Dalain whistled, and a grey mare came obediently trotting towards him. He, too, mounted without a saddle.

Together they galloped free, Qavi leaping at the command. He heard Zanniel's stunned cry, and Edvern lifted his head to the sky, his hands coming free of the horse's mane. His fingers trailed in the wind; it coiled around him.

The stallion surged forward, Edvern feeling the powerful muscles working under his thighs. If the emperor wanted him on display, he would give the bastard a display.

Knowing he was safe on Qavi's back, he unbuttoned his shirt and let his wings of fire free. Sparks and flame danced around them.

Dalain drew level with him, and Edvern turned his head to grin.

Turning his mare's head and galloping away, Dalain cried, "Race you back to camp."

Qavi leapt to the challenge, hooves ploughing down on the green grass. For the first time in many months, Edvern felt the taste of true freedom.

*Navilla Spire is committed to the continuation of the
Tallermayne Dynasty. Research into new weapons against our
foes has continued day and night. We are close to something
truly remarkable.*

*LETTERS TO MOIRA TALLERMAYNE
FROM RENA HYBECK*

CHAPTER 32
The Third Spire

MOIRA

The rumblings of the squabbling dragons quaked the stones of Navilla Spire. Moira tugged at the reins of her teal dragon, who shrieked and lashed her tail. Her mount hadn't stopped complaining about a spiked bit that had been embedded into her flesh to inspire quicker obedience.

Sensing the teal dragon's weakness, Yahler's and Whilmana's dragons harried and bullied her from the flight where Oskar's power had dumped them. It was time to find a replacement.

Moira dismounted, her boots sinking into the soft earth. While the grounds on the southern wall of Navilla were open and flat for miles, it was still treacherous. The marshes prevented large armies from approaching on the land. To the north, the spire backed onto sheer cliffs. A fleet would have to brave the frequent storms that battered Navilla's shore. Isolated, Navilla had stood uncompromised for generations.

She ignored the shuffling of the novices who had been sent to tend to the dragons after their flight. "If you scratch my golden armour, you'll all pay dearly."

Fennix stood in his flight leathers, casually leaning against an open doorframe. *"There's no need for gold once you're dead,"* the spectre said.

"Shut up!" Moira gritted her teeth. She raised her hand to her hair and dug her nails into her scalp. It was getting harder to banish her late husband from her mind. Pain was the only thing that worked.

The novices exchanged wary looks. One brave boy left the main group to approach Moira's dragon. The creature hissed at him, peeling her lips back to reveal her fangs.

"Get on with it," Yahler growled. "Our own dragons require tending to."

Moira stepped away from her group of dragons, staring out at the open marshes of Navilla. The water of the marsh lakes was still frozen.

"Navilla Spire is glad to host you, Lady Tallermayne." Mistress Rena moved through the ranks of lesser dragon riders to come stand by her side. "Appropriate rooms have been made ready for your arrival."

Moira inclined her head. "War is on the horizon and will be on our doorstep. Preparations need to commence immediately."

"They've already begun," Rena assured her.

This news pleased Moira; she expected nothing less from Rena. The Black Prince wasn't the only one with spies. Alaxen and Edvern had been spotted together. She was no fool. Edvern knew of the eggs and their power. And if he knew, Alaxen knew. If they wanted the third egg, they would come to her. This would be the place of their final battle.

"Ensure the marshes are unstable," Moira said, unsure if she should tell Rena about the possibility of the water wyrms arriving. "Melt the ice."

"We do this routinely, Grand Lady, but I'll increase the frequency. I've something to show you. You won't be disappointed." Rena bowed her head, smiling in her self-assured way. "If you wish to replace your dragon, perhaps we can use it as a test subject. Let's not waste the scale and flesh we have."

Keen to see the Mistress of Navilla's new advancements, Moira nodded her agreement. Rena had an insatiable thirst for knowledge and worked tirelessly to discover ways for her riders to manipulate their powers.

"I've seen no evidence of your supposed barriers," Moira said. "I find myself dissatisfied."

Rena raised an eyebrow and gestured with one hand. Small beads of blue sparks became visible. "There is water within the air. The beauty of this defensive system is that it's invisible to the naked eye. My lady, you could pass through unhindered because I allow Tallermayne blood entry."

Moira frowned. "So Alaxen could ..."

"When news of Alaxen's treachery reached us, my mages made a few nasty little tweaks. You and your company were granted free access. To cross the line, Alaxen and any others will have to willingly shed Tallermayne lifeblood."

"And if they attempt to cross injured?" Whilmana joined them, her arms against her chest. Moira's interrogator did not like Lady Rena. The feeling was mutual.

"The blood must be willingly sacrificed. And then ... death will follow."

"A Tallermayne has never committed suicide," Yahler said, spitting on the ground. "It's the ultimate act of cowardice. The souls of those guilty are turned away from the eternal light of the Father Dragon."

Whilmana didn't look convinced.

"The enemy would have to know about the barriers and how to drop them," Rena said. "Who's going to tell them?"

Whilmana scoffed, turning her body to stare at Moira's teal dragon, who lumbered forward, blowing steam.

"The barriers were built to last for centuries and allow entry to our future Grand Lords and Ladies … We weren't given much warning about Alaxen's betrayal." Rena swept her long hair over her shoulder.

Sneering, Whilmana shook her head. "I saw betrayal months ago."

"Enough!" Moira snapped. "Please, demonstrate. It's cold out, and I would like a hot meal."

"If your dragon was to fly through with no rider, it would demonstrate the power of the boundary lines." Rena gestured for two riders to mount their dragons. She lowered the barriers with a hand gesture to let them through, and they turned and waited. "Yahler, mount your dragon and chase the teal through the barrier. She'll be fine to leave. But coming back …"

Yahler cracked his knuckles, grinning like a mad man. He jogged back towards his dragon, the sea of witnesses parting to leave his dragon space to fight and bully the smaller teal.

Unwilling to stay and play the victim, Moira's dragon bellowed and pulled herself free from the novices holding her. She madly flapped her wings and soared upwards.

"Yes!" Yahler cried with relish. He had reached his dragon, and with a shout full of bloodlust, they were airborne after the teal dragon.

It was as Rena said. The teal dragon flew past the barrier, unharmed. Yahler stopped short, his dragon's jaws missing the teal's tail by a hair. He banked and swooped around to watch what the teal dragon would do next.

The two Navilla dragons were ready on the other side. They lunged for the teal as she tried to dive between them in a desperate bid for freedom. But they were fresh, and the teal was tired from her flight wearing her golden armour. They were faster.

Her way to freedom cut off, the young dragon flew quickly towards the barrier, as if speed could save her. Moria could feel the crackle of power the second her dragon hit the barrier, which flashed crystalline blue.

The shrieks of terror were like nothing Moira had ever heard in her life. The dragon's wings stiffened and shook until her whole body convulsed. Unable to keep herself aloft, the dragon plummeted with an ear-splitting scream and landed with a crunch of bones.

On the ground the teal continued to quiver and shake uncontrollably.

"So, it comes to this," Fennix whispered in her ear. *"I cannot save you."*

I never wanted your saving, Moira thought. *Only power. Power is the only force in this world that will ensure I'll never hurt again.*

"Was your so-called power worth the price?" Fennix asked. *"Was it worth Tamah's life?"*

Yes. Because it was true. Any price was worth true power. Even the life of her beloved daughter.

Yahler landed, shaking his head with an elated grin. "Smells something terrible. What's for dinner?"

A smile touched Moira's lips as she turned away from the sight of her dragon. "Let's find me a new dragon."

CHAPTER 33

Wind and Fire

EDVERN

Edvern was bored. Lyssandra was somewhere out there playing dragon rider, while he was confined to certain parts of the Nezahrian war camp. Raziel had made it quite clear that he must be accompanied anywhere by Symmeon or Zanniel. And under no circumstance not to visit his Tallermayne family. It wasn't safe. Not yet.

It was boring living in a camp where most people refused to speak Aurelian. Many seemed too afraid to even attempt to approach him. He sighed heavily; it was the price of being some sort of Nezahrian relic.

To keep himself busy, he sorted through a case that housed bottles of ink. Not only did Raziel have the standard colours used in military maps and campaigns, but he also had a collection of rare colours. Golds, silvers, three different purples and a shimmering blue. Zanniel glowered from his corner as Edvern helped himself to parchment and started illustrating. He drew Alynta, belly aglow in the Kyros' funerary pyre. On another piece he drew Odharn curled around a campfire, his one wing outstretched. Feeling particularly rebellious he drew his father astride his war horse. The only colour he added to the picture was the red of his cloak.

"You're wasting resources," Zanniel said.

Edvern looked up from his latest picture of Izorah and Lyrus flying together in the night sky. "Would you prefer I escape?"

"They aren't your possessions for you to use as you see fit."

"Fine." Edvern slammed his hand down over the picture. He scrunched it in his fist and lobbed it at the war wraith, who sidestepped. After pushing his chair back, Edvern left the strategy table and stood by the tent flap.

Heavy rain had settled in overnight, making it impossible to go and visit the horses or rummage through the weapons tent.

The silence stretched between them. Edvern closed his eyes, listening to the driving rain.

The tension was broken by Alynta bounding past him into the tent, Camrys on her tail. Leaving puddles in their wake, the two dyrathakins tumbled around on the floor. Camrys nipped at Alynta's back legs as they darted under the tables. The older dyrathakin swiped at him playfully. He yipped and dashed round the circumference of the tent twice.

"At least some of us are having fun," Edvern commented.

Alynta padded over to him, pressing her wet snout to his cheek. "Camrys is excited. Lyssandra Sharp-Tongue is back."

Bolting upright, Edvern looked to his bonded familiar and then at Zanniel.

"No," the spy said before Edvern could even ask. "Wait here until we know it's safe."

Alynta tilted her head, staring at the war wraith, her lavender eyes questioning and curious. The younger dyrathakin stopped by the spy, sat on his haunches and clambered up his leg.

The surprise on Zanniel's face was obvious, but he stayed standing at attention. The small creature came to sit along the spy's shoulders. He batted Zanniel's cheek with his paw, claws retracted.

"Please, my human would like to see him." Big emerald eyes opened widely.

"Your mistress can come here," Zanniel said, clenching his jaw.

Camyrs licked his cheek. "Please."

"It's not within my authority."

Edvern glanced down at his fingers, considering a flicker of a plan. He had told Raziel he would not be a prisoner.

He turned, tilting his head to the side. The strategy table was full of gathered intelligence, which was priceless information for their fight against Moira. Raziel's bedding was too personal. Zanniel's uniform might cause injury. He settled on a side table with a pitcher of wine. It was two or three paces behind Zanniel. Perfect.

Breathing in, he gathered his power and exhaled. When he was ready, the table erupted into flames. Taken by surprise, Zanniel shouted, turning on his heel.

Edvern clenched his fist, extinguishing the flames. "I'm getting stronger, Zanniel. Take me out to her. Camyrs needs her."

"If I find myself in trouble because you ..." Zanniel lifted a finger. His face fell into an expression of resignation. "Don't leave my side. And tell Faelowyn to inform Raziel of your intended actions."

Edvern stared back at the spy. Compromise. His life would now be full of them. He nodded his assent and closed his eyes to reach Raziel's dragon. He sensed her standing out on an open field, her wings outstretched to protect Odharn, who played happily at her talons in thick, gooey mud.

Zanniel threw Raziel's oilskin cloak over Edvern's shoulders, with an exasperated shake of his head. Edvern ignored him, glad that he didn't have to insist further to go and see Lyssandra.

Picking Camyrs up so that the dyrathakin would not end up coated in muck, Edvern swept out of the tent. Through his thick gloves he could feel the frantic heart of the dyrathakin. Camyrs was excited to reunite with Lyssandra. He stroked his hand down the dyrathakin's back. The poor little mite hadn't much time with her since he hatched out of the egg.

Throngs of soldiers joined together in the rain, making their way to the open field north of the encampment. All around him, Edvern heard voices speaking rapidly in Nezahrian. He wished he understood enough to listen. He might have enquired with Zanniel, but he didn't want to waste any time.

When he entered the field, Edvern was disappointed to see that the emperor and empress were there. Looking distinctly sour, Dalain stood at his father's right-hand side. Stern and uncompromising, Raziel stood to the empress' left.

Most of the dragons of the camp had joined the force. The majority kept to the outskirts, but determined to look threatening, Emperor Ze'hyrn had his dragon standing behind him. To the untrained eye, the steel dragon looked reasonably tamed, but he could see the fury in the twitch of his tail.

Faelowyn was unconcerned by the lines of soldiers. She parted them with her bulk to come to the Black Prince's side. She lowered her slender neck, nostrils wide and luminescent eyes peering at the humans milling around.

Dalain broke away from his father and came striding over to them.

"Hail, Uhl'hari." The prince inclined his head. "It does me great joy to see you well."

"Your Highness," Edvern muttered, aware that Dalain's words weren't for him but the soldiers surrounding them. It was a verbal warning that he, the prince, had accepted Edvern and held him in some sort of esteem.

Staring at the amassing Nezahrian army, Edvern could not hide his bewilderment. Dalain cleared his throat and pointed to the far side. Alaxen and Bastian stood between half a dozen royal guards. His stomach dropped; his uncle looked stricken. Although he had been too young to comprehend the true pain of death, he had seen his uncle's grief when his aunt had died. Bastian stood, silent and watchful, beside his father.

"I'm confused. Are we going into battle?" Edvern swallowed, refusing to meet Dalain's gaze. Talons knew he would have trouble killing his own countrymen.

"No. Word has reached us that Alaxen's Cynedir riders met with Palea and Lyssandra in Irani. They're coming to treat with us," Dalain said.

It was almost with a look of pity that Faelowyn turned her head towards Alaxen. Lyrus and Izorah stood guard at this uncle's shoulder.

Damning the consequences, Edvern marched across the field towards his family. Zanniel might have expected this move; he heard the impatient sigh. He raised his chin as he made his way through the lines of men. Passing the emperor and Raziel, he pointedly did not hesitate or stop.

It was only until he stood before Alaxen that he halted, breathing heavily but relieved to find himself with his family.

"You are a stubborn one, my Eddi," Izorah said fondly. *"I knew you'd come."*

"Uncle, I ..." Now that he was standing before Alaxen, Edvern wasn't sure what to say. There were so many emotions and thoughts swirling around in his head, it was difficult just to select one.

"Alynta has been very kind, providing us with updates on your wellbeing," Alaxen replied. He looked up, taking in the sight of Zanniel no doubt standing a little too close. "We meet again, young man. A word of advice, if I may. Edvern is like a young drake. Once he gets something in his head, he's going to find a way to do it."

"Noted," Zanniel replied dully.

Edvern huffed. "And Bas? Are you well?"

Bastian's thin eyebrows knit together.

Laying a hand on his eldest son's shoulder, it was Alaxen who answered. "We're being treated well and are included in talks to form an alliance."

"If we can keep the emperor out of our talks," Bastian muttered, tapping his fingers against his thighs. Something he did when he was anxious.

"Ah, good." There were so many eyes on them that Edvern felt everyone was expecting something from him. "I ... I have something for you, uncle. I left it in the tent. I'll find a way to get it to you."

Zanniel had the audacity to raise an eyebrow when Edvern looked to him for help.

"It's just a painted scrap of fabric ... one of Kendrick's." Edvern watched Alaxen's face crumble.

"I'd be ..." Zanniel paused, frowning at Alaxen. "Pleased to ensure your uncle receives it from my hand."

"Thank you." Edvern exhaled, grateful that the war wraith understood his need. He had been barred from Kendrick's simple funerary prayers, but in this way, he could demonstrate to Alaxen that he stood with them.

"You need to return to the Nezahrian side," Bastian murmured. "The Black Prince is signalling you."

"No, I ..."

It was a tired smile on his uncle's face that stopped Edvern's protests. "Edvern, we relinquished Aurelia's claim over you. It's time."

"Goodbye then." Edvern turned to go.

"Eddi ... in whatever capacity I can, I will fight for you," Alaxen said. "I'm sorry I didn't sort Taseria out sooner."

Looking back over his shoulder, Edvern smiled. With head still high, he made his way over to Raziel's side. Unfortunately, his eyes met with the emperor.

"You've upset my master, Uhl'hari. You've my thanks." Lifting his snout to the sky, the emperor's dragon tensed. *"I'm Woe."*

Edvern bit back a bark of laughter, earning him a glare from Raziel.

"Uhl'hari, stand straight. Unfurl your wings and let the Aurelian dogs see what we have on our side." The demanding tone in the emperor's voice was enough to make Edvern bite down hard. He balled his fists to his side. He was not a prisoner.

He felt his power coiling in his belly, a sour bile fighting to get free. This man had shot him, and now he was expected to obey wordlessly. A wind, wild and rushing, filled the plain. Some of the horses spooked their riders, fighting to keep control. It buffered at the emperor in his golden armour.

Raziel's hand was on his arm, squeezing so hard that Edvern was sure he would bruise.

"Don't snap," Zanniel hissed behind Edvern. "Do as you're told, or it might mean your uncle's head. Talon knows I don't need you going on a murderous rampage."

I'd eat the pompous idiot before he touches General Tallermayne. He'd become dragon dung, Woe said, shifting.

"You'll do no such thing," Faelowyn chided. *"All that metal would give you a terrible tummy ache."*

With some amusement, Edvern noticed that Raziel was having trouble keeping a straight face. Was this what his life was going to look like? Listening to dragons' sass and pretending that he couldn't understand their conversations?

Taking heed of the warning, Edvern unclasped the oilskin cloak. He folded it slowly and handed the bundle to Zanniel. His wings unfurled, and the cold rain dripped down his feathers of fire. The wind died to a faint echo.

"Chin up, boy. Don't cower so." The emperor glowered at him, cruel eyes glinting as he gripped on to the handle of his sword.

"He doesn't yet know that your power of wind is manifesting," Raziel muttered, drawing Edvern to the side while the emperor barked loud orders to his royal guards. "Play the game. Keep it hidden."

Without a word Edvern lifted his head, staring defiantly back at the emperor. His hair plastered to his forehead and his feathers drooped, he was hardly impressive.

"The fool thinks we are a bauble to dangle in front of his enemies… to gloat for his own glorification." Woe yawned noisily, swishing his tail to make the royal guards jump back. Then he curled up on the ground like a cat. *"Not to mention, these are dragon riders under Alaxen's command. It takes a lot to impress them."*

"The Uhl'hari are not for humans to command," Raziel said lightly.

"You'll find, *Black Prince*," the emperor replied, "when he's in my military camp, he belongs to me."

"Forgive me, Your Majesty." Edvern was stunned to see Raziel bow his head. Then the Black Prince looked to him, a cold fury in his blue eyes. It was a game. And to survive, Edvern had to learn to trust the man who had lived centuries among these people. "It's not in the nature of dragon souls to bow to a mortal man."

"Then ensure he learns." The emperor took a step forward, his eyes glinting. He had to get out of the Black Prince's camp, out of the way of the emperor's gaze. All of his instincts were screaming this man was a danger; he would be a fool to ignore it. Already an attempt on his life had been made.

"Prince Hedriel and his useless beast shall squire for Edvern Uhl'hari."

Hedriel appeared from nowhere, his characteristically smiling face a welcome sight in a sea of warriors.

Approaching Edvern, Hedriel bowed. "At your service, my lord."

Edvern choked back another laugh, his mind blank. He knew he ought to say something to greet the prince, but he was at a loss. The young prince seemed to understand Edvern's uncertainty. Without being told, he nodded and stood with Zanniel.

Symmeon joined Raziel, briefly catching Edvern's eye. He spoke in the Black Prince's ear, then at Raziel's nod, took a step back.

"The Aurelians will be landing shortly," Raziel announced.

"Do not embarrass me, lizard," the emperor snarled, looking up to where Woe had made his bed. "I'm tired of your drama."

"Drama ..." One amber eye opened, a sly grin growing on his face. *"I can show him true drama."*

It seemed that Edvern wasn't the only one struggling to hide his mirth. He heard Prince Hedriel sniggering and the soft whoosh of air escaping his lungs as Zanniel elbowed him.

For his part, Woe opened one eye, lifted his tail and passed wind. *Loudly.* He then closed his eye and started snoring.

"Talons." Symmeon choked, his whisper carrying. "What have the kitchen staff been feeding him?"

"Dragons' stomach tracts can be delicate. Perhaps, Your Imperial Majesty, allowing your dragon the freedom to hunt and catch his own fresh meat would settle his stomach." Raziel's bold-faced lie was delivered so smoothly that Edvern nearly believed the Black Prince. Nothing was delicate about a dragon. Especially their stomachs.

The emperor's face flushed puce, and Edvern was sure that the monarch might self-combust. His angry outburst was halted by the riders of Cynedir appearing on the horizon.

A bronze dragon landed first, a familiar face dismounting. Orange power hummed through the air with Oskar's presence. He was prepared for a fight. The bronzed dragon looked askance at Woe, who was smiling in his 'sleep'.

"Lord Tallermayne." Oskar came to stand before Alaxen. He knelt, laying a sword atop his two palms.

Breath caught in Edvern's throat, understanding hitting him. Oskar had retrieved Kendrick's sword. Tears pricked his eyes, and he felt Hedriel's hand clasping his shoulder.

"My lord, I bring you the sword of Kendrick Tallermayne and news that his body and the remains of our dragons lost in Irani were properly burned and mourned."

Fingers trembling, Alaxen accepted the sword, bringing the handle to his beating heart so the blade ran vertical down his body. The warrior's prayer slipped from his father's lips, Oskar's own deep voice joining with his, Bastian's too. Edvern whispered the pieces he could remember.

Silence followed the prayer until Alaxen nodded, thrusting the blade into the ground. "It is safe," Alaxen declared.

One by one the riders landed, dismounting and coming to stand at attention at the legs of their mounts. They saluted Alaxen, not the emperor.

Edvern turned a concerned glance towards Raziel, gauging his reaction. But the Black Prince's face was impassive. The emperor, on the other hand ...

And then he saw her, standing with Palea.

Lyssandra.

Drenched from head to toe, she had never been so alluring. The simple black gown trimmed with tiny golden flowers clung to her body as she stomped towards Alaxen, uncaring of the mud splattering the bottom of her skirts.

Palea and another brown-skinned woman trailed her, calling her name.

"You knew. You bastard, you knew all along!" Lyssandra's voice cracked with emotion. Her whole body shook as she rounded onto Alaxen. As far as he knew, Alaxen didn't know who she was. That belief was soon shattered when his uncle spoke.

"Perhaps a little context, Lady Stamos." Edvern had to give it to Alaxen. His cool expression never wavered, despite the angry diplomat stalking towards him.

"You knew what I was! You were the one pulling the strings, manipulating Moira and Ellrahera ... the Nezahrians."

"I'm afraid you give me too much credit."

Lyssandra howled then, wings a mottled brown and black bursting from her back. Green vines twisted around the feathers. Most surprising and fascinating of all were the antlers protruding from her scalp. Edvern had to wonder, were they heavy?

Squealing in delight, Camyrs wriggled from his grip and bounded towards Lyssandra. Mud sprayed behind the little creature, and with a mischievous grin at Zanniel, Edvern used Camyrs' escape to excuse his leaving the emperor's side. He caught the little creature, careful to keep his paws away from his clothes.

Alaxen took a step back, his dark eyes glinting. "That I did not know," he said simply, taking in Lyssandra's form.

"Ah, your dyrathakin," Edvern said lamely, blinking in awe of Lyssandra. Was it rude to reach out and touch her feathers or her antlers?

At once Lyssandra's face softened. "Cam!"

Edvern handed the wriggling dyrathakin over.

"Perhaps, Lady Lyssandra, Lord Alaxen and yourself might have a private conversation a little later where you might be able to air your grievances in peace."

Clearing her throat, Lyssandra didn't seem to have the words to answer the empress. She brushed her hand down her clothing and attempted to smooth her hair back. She seemed lost for words.

"Zanniel, the cloak!" Edvern turned and beckoned to the war wraith.

The spy's lips twitched as he stepped forward, the neatly folded oilskin cloak in his arms. "You're becoming more imperious by the moment, Lord Uhl'hari," Zanniel muttered.

Edvern didn't care. He took the cloak and threw it over Lyssandra's back. "My lady, no reason for us both to be cold."

Still trembling, Lyssandra blinked at him. She was upset, the glassiness in her eyes betraying her. Her wings tucked closer to her body as she tugged at the cloak. Her wings had destroyed the top of her dress, which would become problematic if she didn't learn to control her powers. He wasn't sure if he was the best one to help. He glanced to Bastian.

His elder cousin had phenomenal control over his power. He had taught older riders than him the same discipline. Maybe he'd be willing to assist

Lyssandra. He couldn't imagine her lack of control would be pleasing to her.

"We've come under the banner of Alaxen Tallermayne in order to treat with you," Oskar said. Edvern noticed the look of relief on his uncle's face as his officer spoke. "We see our general is well."

"There's nothing quite like Nezahrian hospitality." A woman, who on closer inspection could have been the empress' twin, stepped forward. She lifted her hand in greeting, and Edvern caught the glimpse of sores around her wrists. She'd been a prisoner.

Turning his head, Edvern inspected once more the rows of dragon riders. Euquallians were dotted among them, eyeing the gathered soldiers wearily.

"Sister," Ionah said. "What a delight to see you."

The stranger smiled in response, flashing her teeth. She spoke with rapid words, the sounds foreign to Edvern's ears. The empress' eyebrows rose as she serendipitously looked at her husband. From his baffled expression, he didn't know what was being said either.

Alaxen's lips quirked into an amused smile, and Edvern could truly feel how small his world had been growing up. That his uncle understood what was said and was sharing a knowing glance with Bastian irked him.

"What news do you bring, Oskar? I know that Cynedir burned," Alaxen asked, when silence followed.

Shifting on his feet, Edvern wished that he might sink into the shadows. Had there ever been a more awkward meeting of allies?

"Raziel, I must insist these men and women bend their knees." The emperor narrowed his eyes, the muscles in his neck bunching. It must be infuriating for the most powerful man in the kingdoms to be treated so rudely by others. Perhaps if the emperor weren't so self-righteous and demanding, he would have commanded more respect.

"As a solider of Aurelia, a father to an Aurelian daughter, I'll not bow to a man who has demanded the children of Aurelia be put to the sword."

Oskar looked between the fuming emperor, the Black Prince and then to Alaxen. At Alaxen's nod he turned his body to address both Raziel and Symmeon. "It is true. Moira burned the whole city. From what we can tell, she left a sole survivor to spread her message."

"The message, sir rider?" Empress Ionah asked, her voice soft.

"My lady ... queen." Oskar dipped his head into a polite bow. He stood a little taller as he regarded her. "We have news spreading of a monster the Black Prince has created who did this. We aren't so stupid to believe it ..."

Silence followed as Oskar looked over Edvern with his wings of fire and then to Lyssandra. The flames around Edvern flared for a moment, hot and wild at being called a monster. He controlled himself quickly, running his tongue nervously along his teeth, feeling the point of his fangs.

"Truth be told, they don't look much like monsters to me." A boy, who couldn't have been more than twelve, had wriggled his way through the ranks. A tattered dragon rider's cloak many sizes too large draped around his shoulders. "They're just humans with extra pieces."

"That's enough, Ramm." Oskar affectionately ruffled the boy's hair and tugged him closer to his side.

"Water wyrms have devastated both Cynedir and Gytall. The Aurelian people would be on edge," Edvern said. "Doubt I'll be too welcomed."

"People are suffering and desperate," Ramm said. He turned and nodded back to the Aurelian riders. "We're mostly curious. We want to know, what are you? Some kind of birdman?"

"He is Uhl'hari," Zanniel said sternly.

Ramm cocked his head, apparently unimpressed by the war wraith.

Edvern sighed. "I suppose birdman is rather apt."

"No one believes any of the tales Moira has spread," the boy whispered.

Alaxen cleared his throat. "Cynedir has burned, Moira's spreading lies. Anything else you'd like to add?"

"We had a skirmish with Moira after the burning of Cynedir. Her powers have changed into something dark and dangerous. Our spies have ascertained she's heading to Navilla, and Rena Hybeck may have some new weapons she has developed to use against us."

"Been going mad. Murdering sages and librarians," Ramm added with an enthusiastic nod.

She knows about the egg, Edvern thought, trying desperately to get Alaxen's attention. But he couldn't voice his thoughts. He didn't know if the power of the egg being common knowledge was a good idea. What if the emperor took the last dyrathakin egg for himself?

Catching Bastian's eye, Edvern took a chance. Lifting his fingers to his ear, he signed, "Listen."

Bastian inclined his head and signed back, keeping his hands close to his thighs. "I hear."

Edvern's heart thudded, and he signed quickly, "She knows egg." A firm hand gripped his, and it took all his willpower not to struggle out of Zanniel's grasp. He had done his job. Hopefully, Alaxen would understand the message.

"While this is all fascinating," the foreign woman said, "I, as my father's voice, would like to speak with General Tallermayne, the Black Prince and our esteemed emperor and empress in private about Euquall's potential involvement."

"Of course, sister," Ionah purred. "I'm sure you'll find my royal tent to your exacting standards."

The pair of royal sisters sauntered off, the emperor and his guards following behind. Alaxen clasped Oskar's hand and heartily clapped him on the back. No words passed between them. Perhaps when one fought alongside their friends for so long, words were unnecessary. Bastian leaned in and whispered Edvern's message. Alaxen's eyes narrowed, and then he nodded. He trailed after the royals, head high and stride unbroken.

"It was foolish for you to signal General Tallermayne in front of the emperor," Raziel whispered in Edvern's ear.

"I warned him that Moira knows about the dyrathakin egg. We won't have the advantage of surprise," Edvern hissed back. "I don't want the emperor to have that knowledge."

"Wise," Raziel muttered. "Next time it would be far safer to talk to me. Your loyalty no longer belongs to Aurelia."

"Yes, sir."

"While I'm cloistered away in these discussions, Hedriel will escort you to our tent. Zanniel and Symmeon, watch the Aurelians. Make sure they don't start any issues with our men."

Extinguishing his flames, Edvern furled his wings against his back. Lyssandra did the same, adjusting the oilskin cloak. Camyrs was happily tucked under one arm.

"The emperor's tub was brought into Raziel's tent. Would you like to freshen up? You must be exhausted."

Lyssandra's haunted eyes met his. "Oh, Eddi, you have no idea. But first there are some people you need to meet."

Taking his hand, she turned and gestured. The brown-skinned woman who had approached with them but had been respectfully silent stepped forward. Then a tall man who Edvern vaguely recognised from the ball.

"Edvern Tallermayne, I presume." The woman smiled slyly, looking very much like a cat that had cornered a mouse. "Antonella Fenin, Saemorish diplomat, *very* good friends with Lyssandra."

Edvern bowed stiffly at the waist, murmuring what he hoped was an appropriate greeting. Antonella rose. She moved with the same grace as Lyssandra. Her large eyes swept over the man.

"You must be Captain Konrad Stamos," Edvern said. "I have been able to glean some information out of the Nezahrians."

The man inclined his head. "Perhaps I could interest you with a flight over Saemore where you can burn the palace there to cinders."

"He's joking." Antonella smacked Konrad's arm. But the light in the captain's eyes was serious.

"I'll see what I can do," Edvern replied, ignoring Lyssandra's rolling eyes.

"Why don't you go on ahead, Lyss," Antonella said. "Spend some time with 'my Eddi'."

Edvern was immensely pleased he wasn't the only one blushing furiously. He took Lyssandra's hand and tugged her through the camp, taking a route he noticed most men did not use but nevertheless led them straight back to Raziel's tent.

Behind them Hedriel whistled a merry tune. "I'll get you some dry clothes."

"That'll be appreciated. I can't stand being cold and wet a moment longer." Lyssandra ducked into the tent.

As she disappeared Hedriel grabbed Edvern's upper arm. "I've never seen her like this."

Edvern paused. "Who?"

"Lyssandra." Hedriel's grin was wicked when he stepped level with Edvern. "We've met on occasions."

"Of course." Another reminder that she was above his station. She rubbed shoulders with the rich and powerful. He had been tossed from his family like dirty garments.

"She loves you," Hedriel replied with a careless shrug. "She of course knows how to string along a man. It's all in the games that diplomats play. But you? You have captivated her affection. I wonder in what esteem you hold her?"

"Lyssandra is smarter than to get attached to a man like me," Edvern said.

"You're very quick to dismiss yourself," Hedriel replied. "You've a prince to be your squire after all."

Edvern raised his eyebrows. "To help or to spy on me?"

"The emperor was that transparent?" Hedriel winced, avoiding the question. "I suggest figuring out your feelings towards Lady Uhl'hari and making your intentions clear."

"All my intentions revolve around surviving." That was Edvern's first reaction. For him to have any type of future, he needed to live. "I'll worry about the future once I have one."

"It's never too early to dream," Hedriel said.

"The dead can't dream."

Hedriel sauntered forward, poking a bony finger into Edvern's chest. "I spent weeks in a Saemorish dungeon. If you were to ask me for advice, I'd say don't wait for tomorrow."

"Well," Edvern said slowly, hoping that Hedriel could hear his stern caution, "I'm not asking you for advice."

"A shame," Hedriel replied. He gestured to the Black Prince's tent. "I could be a friend."

Alynta lifted her head from the rug as Edvern entered. She stretched lazily, looking refreshed and warm. Perhaps his dyrathakin had been the wiser staying where it was dry. The dyrathakin looked towards Camyrs, who was scampering around Lyssandra's feet as she tugged at her wet hair.

She was angry. But not at him.

Slowly Alynta stood, picking Camyrs up by the scruff of the neck. *"I'll take him to Lyssandra's tent. A mated pair should have time alone."*

Lyssandra turned to watch the dyrathakins swiftly exit the tent, her eyes then wandering over to the large tub that had been brought into the tent. The servants had anticipated the need, and it was filled with steaming water. Soaps, hair oils and fresh clothes for Edvern had already been laid out.

"The emperor's tub is big enough for the two of us." Lyssandra chuckled, her dark hair swaying as she stripped.

Mortified, Edvern turned his face away. He had not expected the diplomat to be so bold.

"They're treating you like a spoiled prince," Lyssandra said, stepping behind a privacy screen that had been placed near the tub. The tightness in her voice betrayed how upset she was. He wondered what had happened and what he should do.

"You go first." Edvern grabbed the stem of a goblet and drank the leftover wine to give his hands something to do.

"Such a gentleman." Lyssandra sounded amused. She continued to strip, throwing her clothes over the screen. "Where's my drink?"

He turned to pour her wine, his breath catching at her sigh of pleasure as she stepped into the warm water.

Goblet in hand he made his way to the tub. Lyssandra watched him, her eyes still sad but hungry. She drifted her long nails over the water, creating ripples and spreading the smells of the fresh soap. Leaning her head back, she lifted her foot, and Edvern admired her shapely thighs. All he wanted to do was trail kisses along her skin. Would she like the points of his teeth? Some girls didn't mind a bit of biting.

"Were you happy as a diplomat?" Edvern asked, feeling a little hot.

"I thought I was," Lyssandra replied, closing her eyes. "I think I was deceiving myself. I don't want to talk about the past."

"Oh?" There was something about Lyssandra that flustered Edvern. He'd had his share of dalliances with the fairer sex, and it wasn't just her social graces. When he first came of age, before his father's betrayal, he had plenty of young minor nobles send their second born daughters his way. Bastian and Kendrick were out of their reach, but snagging themselves a bastard Tallermayne might be the badge of honour they needed to bolster their family's success. Edvern hadn't the heart to tell the girls that he wasn't the way to catch his grandmother's notice. Indeed, he had rather liked the attention.

"I was very worried about you," Lyssandra continued. Surprising Edvern, she stood, the water sloshing as she got out of the tub. He had expected her to linger, soaking up the bath oils and warm water. He stood, turning to give her privacy as she dressed quickly, stepping into a fresh pair of trousers and a shirt. She came to stand before Edvern, bending to brush a stray lock from his forehead. "I had such terrible nightmares about what you might have been through."

"I'm sorry …" Edvern's throat closed up, and breathing was increasingly difficult.

"No. I am sorry you had to fight alone," Lyssandra said. "The truth is …"

The Saemorish diplomat was babbling. Edvern cocked his head to the side, unsure of where this was going.

"The truth is I didn't realise what a friend I had in you until I lost you." Lyssandra straightened her shoulders, peering into his eyes with the stalwart confidence that was reminiscent of the diplomats of her country. Without breaking her stare, she grasped his hands, running the pads of her fingers over his skin. Gooseflesh rose to Edvern's arm, and he felt a cold sweat sweep over him. "I was rather foolish not realising it sooner."

"Lyss—"

"Edvern, I …" Lyssandra blinked rapidly. Her fingers trembled, but she tightened her grip and swallowed. "I've come to love you."

Edvern had heard of the phenomenon where all time stands still. But never had he experienced such pure shock that his lungs failed to fill with air. Surely Lyssandra had to be mistaken.

"You? Love me?" The notion was ridiculous. "Me? A drunk and a …"

Lyssandra leaned down so that she might silence him with her lips. She grabbed the hair at the nape of his neck and pulled him closer.

A shock of heat shot up Edvern's body, pooling in his stomach. Her free hand grasped the other side of his face, and she deepened the kiss. She nipped at his lips and pulled away, looking at him, her eyes ablaze. "I desire you more than anything I have wanted before."

Normally, Edvern was the bold partner. Never had a woman demanded control. Knees weak he groaned. He liked it.

Lyssandra's long, elegant fingers danced over the muscles of his chest.

"I want you," she whispered, her breath warm as her teeth nibbled on the lobes of his ear. He felt the sensual sting of her sharpened canines and shivered as pleasure raced up his spine. She brought him down onto his cot, and he lay there, helpless under her charms.

"Oh, sweet talons," Edvern said with a breath, clasping her around the waist. He tried to rise, to press her supple body against him, but she pushed him back down again. "Must you torture me so?"

Lyssandra smiled wickedly at him, her knees straddling his hips as she loomed over him. Her lips returned to his, and her tongue demanded entrance and obedience. Lifting his hands carefully to her waist, Edvern was happy to oblige her. Her hands were nowhere and everywhere at once.

"Lyss ... you don't know what you do to me, you wicked woman." He stared up her, feeling his fire curling within his stomach. He was burning from the inside out.

"Hush," Lyssandra whispered, pressing her forehead to his chest. Edvern could feel his heart beating erratically as her breath ghosted over his collarbone. "Let me have you this once."

"Do you think you can handle me?" Edvern replied. His fingers trailed their way up her spine, and she squirmed at his touch. His hands made their way to her hair, which he gave a playful tug.

"Take those gloves off," Lyssandra said. "Let me feel all of you."

"Hush," Edvern replied. He claimed her lips, intertwining their legs as he flipped their positions so she was now under him. "My turn."

CHAPTER 34

Entanglement

LYSSANDRA

Above her, Edvern was everything that Lyssandra had ever dreamed of. She felt a brush of heat, and gasping, pressed herself back against the covers. Wincing, Edvern shook his head. They were surrounded by his wings of fire. The feathers were hot, bringing a sheen of sweat to Lyssandra's skin.

"You're beautiful." Entranced, she lifted her hand to reach out and touch his wings. He moved them out of her range.

"Beautiful," Edvern spluttered indignantly. He scrunched his nose, bracing himself with her forearms. "Surely a diplomat of Saemore can come up with a more dignified adjective."

Lyssandra gestured to his feathers that were flicking between bright oranges, yellows and reds. "What would you prefer?"

"Magnificent ... regal ... hot. The list goes on."

"Would you settle for ethereal?"

In answer he lowered his lips to hers. He was an anchor, keeping her in the here and now. If he were hers, he would be steadfast. But she didn't have any right to him. The marriage contract between them had been another way to use and imprison him. It was not fair to ask him to allow himself to be coerced into a role he didn't want or ask for. He deserved the freedom to choose his own destiny.

She felt the sharp sting of his fangs before he pulled away, then pressed their foreheads together. A satisfied grin touched his lips, lighting up his face. "You're resplendent ... although I'll have to make sure not to lose an eye if I'm kissing you when you have horns."

"This isn't the time for talking." Swallowing, Lyssandra reached for him, stroking his face with her fingertips. The idea of confessing to Edvern her feelings had been terrifying. She owed him the truth along with his right to choose.

Kissing him was different to all the other men that Lyssandra had experienced. It was not an action expected of her to manipulate, nor did she want to lure him into her bed to satisfy herself.

When he took control, he stole the wind from her lungs. His gentleness made way for hunger and passion, and his grip on her was firm and commanding. Confident.

It was her turn to swoon under his spell.

She did not deserve Edvern's affection, nor did he owe her anything.

"Lyss, are you sure?" Edvern whispered, his breath caressing her cheek. "You think you love me?"

Lyssandra opened her mouth, ready to snap that of course she loved him. He was a damn fool if he thought she said words like those lightly. If said to the wrong person, they would be her downfall. She pulled away, and his grip on her loosened. Of course he would be suspicious of her. Given her training, she could hardly blame him.

"Yes, Edvern Tallermayne, I love you. You aren't required to reciprocate my feelings." Lyssandra paused for a moment to see what Edvern might say or do. "I wish you all the happiness in the world."

"All I know is that without you, I'd have no chance of ever knowing happiness," Edvern replied, his voice low and husky. "I'm a weak man, a prisoner of fate. Loving me may mean your death."

"Death is the only certainty in this world," Lyssandra said, fanning her hand along his bare chest. Edvern's lips quirked into a strange smile, which did not reach his blue eyes.

"Very true," Edvern conceded, and he inclined his head. He drew back. Lyssandra doubted that he was deliberately trying to look imposing. But with his knees on either side of her hips and halo of light surrounding him... Talons ... "I don't want to hurt you, Lyssandra."

He left the bed, turning away from her.

Biting down on her lips, Lyssandra tasted the coppery tang of blood. "Nervous of little old me?"

"A little ..."

"Take off those gloves," Lyssandra purred. "I want to feel your hands on my skin."

Edvern ruefully shook his head, his fingers fumbling with the pitcher and goblet. He attempted to pour them a drink. She noticed that he spilt a good deal; his hands were shaking. Her words hadn't been that sensuous.

He returned to the cot, two goblets in his hands. Lyssandra took the drink and placed it down firmly. Grasping his wrist, she bit down on the fingertip of his right glove. Edvern hesitated, a curious fear furrowing his brow. For a moment she thought he would stop her, but he seemed frozen.

"May I?"

Face turned away, Edvern slowly nodded.

Lyssandra moved her teeth from the glove to his neck. She nibbled his earlobe as she took hold of his glove and yanked.

"Who did that to you?" Lyssandra couldn't help herself. She sat up, taking in Edvern's discomfort.

Edvern was missing two digits. In their place were fingers of wood and metal. To her astonishment they curled alongside their flesh counterparts when Edvern made a fist.

"Alaxen made them," Edvern said.

That was not what Lyssandra had asked. She threw her arms around him. The fire of his wings sputtered. She raked her fingers through his hair. "Oh talons, I'm so sorry. When Raziel told me you had been taken by the Aurelians, I was sick with worry."

"I'm well."

"I nearly lost you!"

"I'm here now. Lyssandra, I—" Whatever Edvern was going to say was interrupted by the tent flap opening.

"I was under the impression the pair of you were putting on clean clothes. Not taking them off." Prince Dalain grinned at the pair of them. "Uhl'hari is still in his dirty pants."

The Black Prince entered the tent behind him. Lyssandra tossed her hair over her shoulder, meeting his gaze, his expression clearly saying she should know better.

Her fingers wrapped around the goblet and drew it to her lips. "Nothing happened. Edvern was a little warm."

Edvern choked on his wine, which he had raised to his lips. His uncle, red cloak snapping behind him, entered. Lyssandra raised her eyes to meet the man's glare, anger coiling in her gut, poised to erupt.

While Edvern caught his breath, the Black Prince raised his eyebrows at Lyssandra, pointedly staring at the way she was reclined on Edvern's bed. Then to Edvern, who was shirtless and flustered.

"It was all innocent," Edvern muttered.

"Mostly." Dalain hid his smile, obviously enjoying Edvern's embarassment. The Nezahrian prince clapped Raziel on the shoulder.

"Come now, uncle, I released Lyssandra from her obligation to me. I could tell she was besotted with Eddi the moment I met them at the river."

"Besotted?" Lyssandra asked, tilting her head indignantly.

"Painfully besotted," Dalain replied. "You've not fooled anyone, Princess. Except, perhaps, Edvern."

"Get up. Edvern, in the tub. Lyssandra, make yourself presentable. You wanted words with General Tallermayne; don't keep your guest waiting." The Black Prince was still not amused. He stepped around his strategy table, stooping to pick up a piece of crumbled parchment. His eyes lingered, his lips parting into a surprised smile. "You have talent." Raziel lifted his gaze towards Edvern. "It's the dragon sight. When a child is blessed with a portion of the Father Dragon's soul, reading can be difficult. But we make fabulous artists."

Edvern seemed to be at a loss for words.

Shaking his head, Raziel pressed the parchment onto his table, smoothing it with his hands. Lyssandra could now see it was a picture of two dragons. One a deep blue and the other a much lighter shade.

Under the weight of his uncle's gaze, Edvern shuffled and then dove among his bedcovers to retrieve a square piece of fabric. "For you," he said, thrusting it at Alaxen's chest. "I ..."

Edvern was engulfed in a strong one-armed hug, but the Black Prince's attention did not stray from the picture he was studying. Cocking her head to the side, she saw that Raziel was fascinated by a man on horseback, crimson cloak around his shoulders.

"Rikar ..." Lyssandra said. Edvern had been foolish enough to draw Rikar-bloody-Tallermayne.

"I'm sorry ..."

"No." Raziel stood, taking the portrait with him. He folded it and deliberately slipped it into the cushions of Edvern's bed. "It would be most unwise to keep this. By rights I should burn the evidence. But I know I can never take Rikar from you. Keep it hidden."

"Thank you." It was Alaxen who spoke, throat bobbing as he swallowed past what Lyssandra could only describe as sorrow.

"I never knew a father," Raziel said, vivid blue eyes staring at Edvern, as if for the first time seeing him. "It isn't the Nezahrian way. I was born a blessed one, taken into the temple and changed to this form by my predecessor. I grew up in the temples, surrounded by older men, taught and trained to be the Sword of Nezaha. It seems in his wisdom the Father Dragon had another destiny for you. You're perhaps the first blessed one in centuries to have been raised by a human father."

The Black Prince's eyes went back to Edvern's bedcovers where he had hidden the portrait of his enemy. "The Father Dragon gave Rikar a great blessing in giving you to him."

"He died," Edvern said. "I know that you rejoiced as he burned."

"I did. And I was a fool." Raziel exhaled, brushing his long hair back from his face. "I may be four centuries old, unlikely to die soon, but I know death is a beginning. Rikar gave himself for his son, and his soul is still burning bright."

Edvern opened his mouth to reply, but all that escaped his lips was a small sound.

"Death is not the end," Raziel said. "We're all the Father Dragon's creations; our souls he holds in the palm of his hands. Lady Lyssandra has been given one hour with the Tallermayne general. Dalain, come."

Alaxen Tallermayne moved around the strategy table, his keen eyes taking in the maps with their soldiers and neat piles of correspondence. Raziel swept from the tent, an amused Dalain at his heels. It was a sign of Raziel's growing trust that the general was allowed access.

"You mentioned that you wanted words with me, Lady Lyssandra," Alaxen said.

"I did." Lyssandra lifted her chin, watching from the corner of her eye as Edvern stood awkwardly to one side. She couldn't imagine that having a bath while she had this discussion with his uncle would be relaxing. "My parents. You knew exactly who they were."

"Were? She's dead then?" Alaxen let out a bark of laughter but composed himself quickly. "Forgive me, but that is a beautiful piece of poetry."

Lyssandra's eyes filled with unshed tears, and she dropped heavily in a chair.

After pouring a goblet of tart wine, Alaxen pressed it into her shaking hands. He gripped her shoulder, giving it a squeeze. "I'm sorry. That was ungentlemanly of me."

"She was horrible. Not at all what I imagined," Lyssandra murmured, pressing her head into her hands. "She killed my father, and I ... I killed her."

"My lady." Alaxen's voice softened as he came to kneel by her chair. "I'll tell you something that Rikar often told Eddi. You're not your parent's disgrace. You decide your own path to either honour or dishonour. Talons, look who I have for a mother."

Choking back a laugh, Lyssandra lifted her face and wiped at the tears forming in her eyes. She hadn't realised it, but she was mourning a woman who had lived in her imagination. The feeling left her hollow and irrationally angry.

Gently, Alaxen cupped her face in his hands. "Your Nezahrian father was a good man."

"Did you know him well?"

"No. No one knows a war wraith well," Alaxen replied. "His name was Gradie. Maybe in another life we would've been friends."

"You were the one who docked my ears, an abhorrent Aurelian practice." Lyssandra's voice tightened, as if a vice had clamped around her neck.

"I'm a healer. As terrible as the practice sounds, we saved innocent little babies," Alaxen said, dark eyes sweeping to Edvern. "It seems that I spared a few too many part Nezahrian babes throughout Aurelia. One day I came home to find a war wraith playing with my five-year-old son. He confronted me about my power, and in exchange for his silence, I pledged him one use of my power. Kendrick was quite enamoured by his new playmate." Alaxen grimaced. "He divulged all sorts of embarrassing family secrets, but nothing useful."

Lyssandra brushed her face with the back of her hand.

"What type of secrets?" Edvern asked.

"Hush, you," Alaxen replied, although his sombre expression shifted. The memory was a fond one for him. "I thought he would come to me one day with a mortally wounded companion to ... No. Gradie summoned me into Saemore, smuggled me into the palace and begged me to help a newborn girl that he needed to hide. I did as he asked. He died protecting you. Lyssandra was the name he had chosen for you."

"Did you tell the Black Prince that I'm ... that Gradie is my father?" Lyssandra asked.

"That's your truth to tell when you are ready," Alaxen said. "Gradie was a close confidant of Raziel. He'll want to know."

"And that was why you brokered the marriage contract for me and Edvern."

Alaxen scoffed. "You give me too much credit. Rikar was the master conspirator. Even in that jail cell, he was plotting for Edvern's survival. Perhaps he made a good choice with two blessed ones. You seem to *enjoy* my nephew, no?"

As he flashed her a smile, his pointed teeth on display, Lyssandra might have answered yes, she enjoyed Edvern very much. In fact, she would have preferred to be enjoying his delicious sharpness on her skin or his playful nips. He caught her looking, and his grin became devious, promises of pleasure and fire in his deep blue eyes.

"You wanted him out of the country." Lyssandra shook her head, hoping to dislodge inappropriate thoughts of what exactly she would enjoy doing to him later when they were alone.

"All these plots within plots make my head spin," Edvern muttered. "Moira decided that she'd murder me on Saemorish soil instead, take the gold and declare war."

"It left me and Donnell in a flurry of panic," Alaxen admitted. "If you don't have any further questions for me, General Eupheana of Euquall is keen on questioning Oskar about his powers. It seems she has a plan."

"I'm satisfied with your answers, General Tallermayne," Lyssandra said.

Laying his hand over his heart, Alaxen inclined his head. "Once the alliances have been properly drawn up, I'll make sure that you'll be appraised." He lifted his head and winked at Edvern. "Enjoy your bath and your lady." Edvern started to splutter a protest, but Alaxen stood and made his way to the tent flap. "As hard as it is to believe, I was once a young man very much infatuated with a young woman. Eddi, my boy, you've found your match."

Watching the general go, Lyssandra pounced on Edvern the moment he was gone. Edvern's lips were warm as she pressed her body to his. He trailed his hands down her side, slipping his fingers under her shirt.

"I'll have to thank your uncle for the prosthetics he made you," Lyssandra murmured, her lips peppering kisses down his throat. Hands on his chest, she pushed him towards the tub.

"You like them?"

Pulling his head down to hers, she kissed him, her teeth biting and pulling on his lips. She could feel his fire magic responding to her. Talons, even his magic yearned for her.

"I love them." She lifted his carved fingers to her lips and kissed them. "You're perfect."

CHAPTER 35

War Counsel

EDVERN

Edvern's head was still reeling with his rendezvous with Lyssandra when Alynta slunk into the tent. Camyrs bounded after her, batting her tail. The fire dyrathakin looked to where Lyssandra and Edvern lounged on the bed. Nimbly she leapt onto the cot and rested her chin on Edvern's chest.

Not to be left out, Camyrs joined her, nuzzling Lyssandra's cheek. The diplomat opened one eye lazily and pushed gently at the kit.

"Alynta, you're getting too big for this," Edvern muttered.

"We were sent to see if you had appropriate clothing on," Camyrs announced.

Lyssandra groaned, her face pressing closer into Edvern's chest. "Talons, no, I don't want to move."

"You have five minutes," Alynta said. "Alaxen sent me ahead."

Closing his eyes, Edvern moaned. He pushed the fire dyrathakin off his chest and rolled to his feet. There was a frantic search for clothes, for brushes and for Lyssandra to set the scene so it did not look like they were lounging in bed.

The dyrathakins curled up on Edvern's cot, watching the flurry of activity. When the Black Prince entered with several others, Edvern was pretending to study the map table while Lyssandra sat drinking wine at the other end of the tent.

Alaxen ducked his head to enter, his expression clearly showing that he did not believe the scene they had set.

Dipping his head, Edvern counted the number of people who accompanied Raziel. Immediately upon seeing him leaning over the maps, Zanniel made to stand at his shoulder. Symmeon followed closely behind Raziel, darting furious glances at Alaxen. His uncle didn't have everyone convinced.

The two princes, Hedriel and Dalain, sat beside Lyssandra, the younger prince warmly smiling at everyone.

Empress Ionah entered, accompanied by Palea and the other woman who had arrived with the Cynedir riders. Standing between the two older women, Palea seemed to glow. She caught Edvern's eye and came to his side.

"Edvern," she said, "I'd like you to meet my aunt, General Eupheana, princess of Euquallia and fifth daughter of the great king."

"Your Highness." Edvern swept into what he hoped was an elegant bow.

"Palea has told me of your adventures," Eupheana said, her voice soft and melodious. Not at all what he thought a general should sound like. "It'll be a privilege to host you in Euquallia once this time of fighting is over. I have a large home in Sangell to host you and your friends."

Edvern blinked, surprised by the invitation. "That is most generous, Your Highness."

Eupheana waved away his thanks. "Nonsense. A well-rounded man ought to see what the world has to offer."

"Not to put a sour note on introductions, but we need to make our move against Moira quickly." Edvern hadn't noticed Oskar enter the tent. His uncle's captain rounded the tables to come stand opposite him. He stabbed a large finger on the map, directly on top of Navilla. "Navilla backs onto the water. It's a great weakness."

"My dear Aurelian friend," Eupheana said, "I am the commander and chief of my father's navy, and when I say those straits are too dangerous to navigate this time of year ..."

"Where are your ships, sister?" Ionah asked.

Eupheana looked towards the tent flap. "Where is your husband?"

The empress' face was cold as ice as she looked towards her daughter. "Ze'hyrn has publicly called my daughter a whore of Aurelia ... He needed time to contemplate his words and will be indisposed."

"If that man makes a move to harm your children"—Eupheana stepped forward, her eyes aglow—"I'll make Father take them in."

"I'm not a stray, auntie." Dalain leaned back in his chair, boots on the table. His twin sister gave him an exasperated roll of her eyes.

"Where are the ships, Eupheana?" Raziel repeated.

Eupheana glanced towards Oskar, who was staring at her as if he expected an answer. She stood still, hands loose at her sides. "Do you really think you can do this?"

Oskar nodded. "All I need is the location of the ships, and time."

"You'll deplete your power." Alaxen shook his head. Obviously, he didn't like the formulating plan.

"With all due respect, General, I moved Moira's entire fleet of dragons across the country. Moving ships, while delicate, will not be a cause of concern."

Inhaling and closing her eyes, Eupheana succumbed to her inner battle. She loomed over the map, so close that Edvern could smell the sweet perfume of jasmine on her skin. Running her nail along the blue ink, she pointed to the western slip of land near Irani. The channels of Alvaraine were a safe place to dock ships. Alvaraine was land deemed useless, wedged between the Nezahrian boarder and Irani. The population was small, and Moira had very little reason to patrol that 'waste' land.

Oskar nodded. "I estimate it'll take us two jumps to move the ships into position."

"Moira will be looking to the skies for attack, not the sea." Alaxen came and leaned across the map. He pointed to a bay south of Navilla. "Station the ships here and wait. The waters are calmer here."

"The water wyrms," Edvern said, feeling he should speak up. "What will we do if they arrive?"

"Edvern's right. They've attacked Gytall and Cynedir," Lyssandra added.

Eupheana smiled, her eyes gleaming with delight. "Our harpoons will pierce any dragon skin if they are foolish enough to come to us."

"It's decided then," Oskar said with a confident nod.

"Payment for your rescue at Irani, although it came too late for many," Eupheana agreed. "Three days, and I'll meet you all on the battlefield."

"It should be noted that Navilla is the epicentre of Aurelian ingenuity. There have been rumours for months that Rena Hybeck has been working on new weaponry." Alaxen lifted his hand to his beard.

"More likely something to do with Navilla's defences," Oskar said. "Our spy reports have been sparse and lack detail."

"Likewise, war wraiths have not uncovered any solid intel," Zanniel admitted. "But that is hardly surprising when it comes to Rena Hybeck."

"Caution is always wise when flying against Aurelians," Raziel commented. "We'll concentrate on turning dragons against their dragon riders."

"Getting the third egg should be a priority," Edvern argued. "That's what she's hoarding behind those walls. She knows they're important.

Once we have the third egg, most, if not all, control of dragons will be lost to her."

Alynta's ears perked up at the mention of the third egg. "If she loses the dragons, she loses the battle."

"And the riders of Navilla?" Alaxen asked.

"If they fight against us," Raziel said, "they die."

The tactical talks went into the night, Edvern attempting to follow along and make well thought-out observations. By the time Eupheana and Oskar disappeared in a flash of orange light, he was ready to fall back into his cot.

He watched as one by one their party left the tent, stepping into the night. All was quiet until he heard the dragons arrive. Without looking to Raziel, who was reading an old report by the candlelight, he stood and went outside.

Izorah had curled her body so that her scaled side touched the canvas of the tent. Odharn was at her feet, gnawing on a large bone. As Edvern went to say his goodnights, Faelowyn landed. She huffed at the two dragons sitting in her space. Opening one amber eye, Izorah wriggled and made room for her. A smile tugged on Edvern's lips as the black dragon made a dramatic show of joining them.

"You're going to have to learn to share," Raziel said, coming to stand at Edvern's elbow.

Faelowyn lifted her snout, flaring her nostrils at Edvern. *"Hurry up and earn Raziel's trust and get granted your own tent so I can have my spot back."*

Edvern lifted his hand out to her. In the past he would never have dreamed to touch the Black Prince's dragon. She watched his hand, lips twitching. Izorah raised her head, ready if anything should happen. Her head cocked to the side, and she scrambled to her feet, looking up.

"Faer," Izorah said. *"I wonder what he wants."*

"Faer?" Faelowyn asked. She lifted her snout to the sky, and Edvern was struck by the waves of pain he felt crashing over the black dragon.

Raziel clapped him on the shoulder as he stepped past to go to his dragon, who ignored him.

Moments later, Palea's blind dragon, Faer, landed in the space that Izorah had made for him. He yawned widely, tilting his head in Faelowyn's direction, his sightless eyes unnervingly looking just to the left of the black dragon.

"It cannot be." Every muscle in Faelowyn's body was taut. She lowered herself to the ground, creeping forwards as if the grey were at risk of flying away. She blew warm air over his scales and shook her triangular head. *"It cannot be."*

Lifting his snout to touch Faelowyn's, a gentle, familiar greeting among dragons, Faer spoke quietly. *"Hello, Mother. I thought I should make myself known to you."*

"You died ..." Faelowyn muttered, the muscles in her forelegs tensing. *"You fell out of the nest ... gone ... your egg."*

"Yet here I am, Mother. Whether you accept me or not, that's your decision."

Faelowyn seemed to be in shock. Raziel had reached her, and she still had not responded to his touches on her scales. *"I would have thought I'd know my own young ... How ... how did you end up in Aurelia?"*

Faer rumbled, a shiver running up his spine. *"Tyrbanath sent me."*

"My father?"

"Palea went to Tyrbanath, and I intervened so that she'd not be eaten. She convinced Grandfather that having a spy within the Aurelian border could only benefit them if a tremendous war broke out. I was sent with her to Cynedir, the blind, useless grandson. It's a very long tale. Do you wish me to go?"

"Stay. Please." Faelowyn shook her head, her belly resting on the ground. She stared down at Raziel. *"I think I'd like to go somewhere quiet."*

Raziel murmured to Faelowyn. When he finished, she stood, spreading her great wings. She took to the skies with Faer trailing her. Together the Black Prince and Edvern watched them go.

"Get some rest," Raziel said, turning to go back into the tent. "Tomorrow will have its own problems."

Edvern bid the dragons goodnight, his hand going to the golden ear cuffs. Soon he would confront his grandmother, not as an Aurelian but a Nezahrian enemy. He had left Aurelia as a nobody and would renter a non-human entity. A creature from fables.

Raziel was right. Tomorrow had its own problems.

CHAPTER 36

Beginning of the End

LYSSANDRA

Three days later, Lyssandra stared at her reflection in the wash basin. Dressed in the finest armour that Raziel could find, her hair had been bound tightly in braids and pinned to the crown of her head. Today was the day they would fly to war. She could feel her stomach churning and her mother's cruel words ringing in her ears. Perhaps she was looking for the validation she had missed as a child. Or the knowledge that someone of her blood would grieve if she fell.

Lifting her hand to her head, Lyssandra let her fingers run the length of her antlers. The armour had been adjusted to accommodate her wings. She'd have to stay in this form until the fighting was done. It was too difficult to undress to unfurl her wings, and it also lacked dignity.

Edvern, the lucky bastard, could burn through his clothing.

"You're stubborn as your father."

Lyssandra started, spinning on her heel. Empress Ionah stood on the threshold of her tent. She was dressed in soft trousers, a long overcoat of black on top. Upon her head was a spiked battle crown. Lyssandra wasn't surprised to see her in scale mail, or the long, heavy sword strapped to her hip. She was Euquallian, a daughter of a once fierce kingdom.

"A foolish man he was, but he was good."

"I gathered that was the case," Lyssandra murmured, turning her face away. She'd been too afraid to ask questions when she had told Raziel, and the Black Prince's expression had shattered. But she had heard what was not said. Gradie, her father, was respected and loved.

"He would be proud of his stubborn, strong-willed daughter."

Lyssandra turned back to her mirror, readjusting her bracers. "Or he would be ashamed?"

"I think not." The empress looked her up and down, her thin lips pinched into a firm line. "You were born a daughter of a disgraced Saemorish princess, a royal diplomat."

"That is no longer true." As Lyssandra spoke those words, she felt a sense of freedom and relief. She had thought that becoming prime diplomat and serving her king and country would be the pinnacle of her life. Under the impression that it was her destiny, she had studied and toiled. She lusted over position and power ... Now she no longer wanted those titles. "I'm a dragon rider, like it or not."

"You look positively deadly," the empress said. She stepped forward, grasping her chin and raising it. "A beautiful, avenging princess. Keep your head up, girl."

"Yes, Your Majesty."

"It is the strength of your conviction and courage that will forge you into a formidable woman."

Lyssandra wordlessly nodded, her mouth dry.

The pressure on her jaw constricted a fraction. Empress Ionah's eyes were ablaze with such a strong fervour, Lyssandra almost believed her. "You love our Uhl'hari of fire."

"Dearly," Lyssandra said, exhaling. Because it was the truth. Plain and simple. "I'd do anything for him."

"Fight hard today. Win the people of Nezaha's hearts, and you'll be able to keep him and yourself safe."

Lyssandra blinked.

"He's a *sweet* boy," the empress said. "Just like you told me the day we met. But he's a defiant creature and will not be easily tamed by my husband. I wouldn't have a fire Uhl'hari any other way."

"Edvern deserves freedom. He's faithful and unwavering in his beliefs ..."

"Edvern, as fire and wind, is a dreamer." The empress nodded. "You're the daughter of earth; an Uhl'hari that traditionally is more practical. Your diplomatic skills will be valuable in keeping you both safe. He will need you."

"Whether he wills it or not, I am with him."

"How I envy you, Uhl'hari. You'll make each other strong. He the vision, you the guide." The empress nodded, releasing Lyssandra's chin from her tight grasp. "Remember, the emperor may use the populace to wield his power, but they can also be used to manipulate him."

"We'll win the hearts of the Nezahrian people today." Lyssandra vowed she would use all of her intelligence and training to protect herself and Edvern.

"Gradie's daughter indeed." A smile touched the empress' lips, the light failing to reach her eyes. She lingered for a heartbeat, her mask of regal indifference slipping to reveal a deep sorrow. And then, just like that, the empress was striding out of her tent.

From her cot, Camyrs yipped at her. She shook her head, picked him up and slung him over her shoulder. She had spoken to Raziel about her dyrathakin. These strange creatures of legends did not do well when separated from the one who hatched them for any length of time. And neither would she. He was a siphon of her power, a living and breathing being that had the potential to magnify her gifting.

It was possible that if she used an outburst today, he would snap from his cublike state to adult.

Edvern confirmed that this was what had happened with Alynta. Through the act of providing a funeral fire for a dragon, both she and Edvern were changed.

She strapped on her sword and looked one last time around the tent. What her future would hold, she had no idea. Would she return to this place or go somewhere else?

Antonella met her in the open field where the dragons lined up in squadrons. She was dressed for battle, her tight curls pulled away from her face. Grinning, Lyssandra noticed that she now had emerald beads in her hair. Likely Princess Palea's doing. She had seen them speaking yesterday.

"Edvern is looking particularly handsome ..." Antonella nudged Lyssandra's ribs and nodded at where the object of her desire stood with his dragon. It was a tactic to get her thinking about other things. One she appreciated.

Lyssandra's body flushed as she remembered the heat of his skin against hers. His apparent sweetness contrasted sharply with the fierceness of his kiss when he took control. He was her walking contradiction. She wanted nothing more than to march over to him. Whether to apologise profusely for her presumptions or to passionately kiss him, she wasn't sure.

"It's almost as if his Nezahrian clothing was made for him."

Lyssandra had of course noticed that unlike his Aurelian kin, he was no longer wearing a cloak. Instead, his wings of fire fanned out behind him. His clothing was all black and fitted to the Nezahrian style. She noticed the Black Prince's badge embossed on his pauldrons. It seemed that the Nezahrians had thoroughly laid claim to him.

Good. The people needed to see him belonging to them rather than their ancient foes.

Over the distance that separated them, their eyes met, and Lyssandra looked away in haste. She felt her skin heat and her stomach flutter. The blue dragon at Edvern's side nudged him playfully, indicating her large head in her direction. Edvern seemed morose, and after dipping his own head, he stared in the opposite direction. The faraway look on his face told her he was communicating with dragons, and so Lyssandra forced herself not to be too upset. He had a job to do.

The Black Prince noticed her also. He studied her with those impenetrable eyes of his and nodded.

"Bastian is an interesting character," Antonella said. "He's flying with us."

"I think Bastian needs some foreign support against the heat of the Nezahrian hatred of him."

Lyssandra caught sight of Bastian and Konrad. The Aurelian dragon rider seemed emotionless and immovable. She studied him closer, worried that he seemed too calm. On the other hand, Konrad seemed to be in good spirits, even though Bastian was valiantly ignoring him.

Palea's dragon, Faer, walked among the dragons of his order, the princess at his side. He nudged dragons of all shapes and ages into ranks, flapping his wings and blowing hot air. The lizardling, Jirrah, sat proudly on the grey drake's snout.

"I'll see you after the battle?" Lyssandra asked. She hugged Antonella quickly and walked away. The longer she delayed, the harder it would be to say goodbye.

She approached Elisaria, who observed her with quiet confidence. Her tail flicked side to side. *"I'll look after you, mistress."*

Lyssandra lifted her hand with a sigh and brushed her fingers along the hard scales of her dragon. From her armour, Camyrs peered out at the amassing army. His long purple tongue gave Elisaria a lick. "You stay close to me." Lyssandra dropped a kiss to the furry head, his twiggy horns brushing against her cheeks.

Rumbling, Elisaria nuzzled Lyssandra's side.

"Are you ready?" Edvern stood before her, his stance awkward. His eyes darted to her dragons as if he was worried. He stepped closer, ruffling the fur on Camyrs' head, his frown twitching into a smile.

Nodding, Lyssandra stepped closer to him, pressing a firm peck on his cheek. "Come what may, I love you, Edvern Tallermayne."

Edvern took her gloved hand, raising it to his lips. He kissed her knuckles, and she wished his teeth were grazing her neck instead. "I ... I've never felt this way before," he murmured weakly. "My guts feel like they are revolting to escape ... and ... I care for you. Deeply. More than anyone."

"It's okay," Lyssandra replied, fighting the smile tugging on her lips. He was struggling to find the right words. He loved her. He said the words with each of his reverent touches and each of his acts of thoughtfulness. When he had come out in front of the whole Nezahrian army, defying the emperor to give her Camyrs, he'd been saying, *I love you*. It was Edvern who had put an oilskin cloak around her shoulders to shelter her and cover her torn clothing. She didn't need to push him. In time Edvern would realise he'd been saying the words all along.

"Edvern!"

Edvern jumped, startled when Zanniel called his name. He smiled apologetically, his head bobbing in a clumsy nod as he ran back to his dragon. She watched him go; the spy leaned in close to speak into his ear.

Oh yes, she was deeply in love with Edvern Tallermayne.

Elisaria unfurled her wings, beating them enthusiastically. The draft earned the green dragon the attention from the gathering Aurelian dragons. They lifted their snouts to the sky and roared a warning for their enemies. Today they would not back down. Today was the beginning of the end.

CHAPTER 37

War Flight

EDVERN

As Edvern reached Zanniel, Lyssandra's dragon started a flurry of sound from their small army of dragons. He paused briefly, glancing over his shoulder. Lyssandra was staring at him again, that strange hunger glinting in her eyes.

"You mustn't allow yourself to be distracted. Not today," Zanniel admonished. Annoyed, Edvern opened his mouth to argue, but the spy continued, "Clear head today. Go home tomorrow."

There was little that he could say to that. He shot another look over his shoulder to stare at the Saemorish diplomat. His heart sunk as he watched her stroke the snout of Elisaria, quietening the green dragon, only for Aerin to start a bellow.

Edvern fidgeted with his wooden fingers, testing their strength as he found himself doing when he was bored or anxious. Out of the corner of his eye, Zanniel watched with a frown. As he expected, Raziel had risen early to confer with his generals, leaving him alone with the spy to ready himself for war. Edvern was lost. A stab of longing struck him as he turned his thoughts of Lyssandra to that of his countrymen. He cocked his head to study them, lines of men and women donned in crimson cloaks. The Aurelians had not dared to approach him, not one, but it was their language and words he understood. Not those of the Nezahrian camp.

The energy surrounding the Aurelians shifted abruptly as Edvern studied them. Alaxen entered the field. His uncle lifted a glove hand in greeting, which Edvern returned, but surrounded by his riders clamouring for his attention, it would be impossible for Edvern to get near him.

Alaxen's attention was demanded from his riders, but Edvern lifted his hand to sign a message anyway. "Fly hard. See you at home base."

Alaxen may not have been watching, but a subordinate at his side had. He signed back, "Careful. Come home alive."

Edvern swallowed painfully, not expecting a reply. The man nodded and leaned to speak into Alaxen's ear. His uncle's head shot up, his dark eyes pinning him. He lifted his hand and made his own sign. "Be at peace. Live well."

"I know what you're doing," Zanniel said in his ear. "If today goes well and Moira is toppled, our Aurelian friends will be left in their homeland. They can sort out their own mess."

Edvern closed his eyes, understanding what remained unsaid. His Tallermayne family would be set free, and he would be taken into Nezaha. Alaxen had no idea if they would get a farewell.

Around them men shouted and parted as Raziel and Symmeon entered the field. Swords were drawn and clapped against armour. The Aurelians had agreed reluctantly to transport some ground troops on the backs of the dragons of lesser ranks. Some dragons had escaped Cynedir with no rider ...

Stopping by Lyssandra, Raziel drew her close. They spoke a few words before he approached to where Zanniel and Edvern waited. Hedriel pushed through the ranks of men to walk by Raziel's side.

"The more tasks Raziel gives Hedriel, the less time he has to squire for you," Zanniel said. "The less information he has to invent for his uncle."

Edvern snorted. It was true. For a 'squire', Hedriel had been absent frequently. Although he did enjoy the quiet afternoons with the younger prince as he attempted to teach him a Nezahrian strategy game.

"I want to be able to say goodbye," Edvern said as Raziel came for him. "Properly."

"Of course." The Black Prince looked down at him. Then slowly he lifted his hand and signalled Alaxen. "Down with Moira. Freedom for Aurelia."

Alaxen replied, "Down with Moira. Peace for Nezaha."

His uncle wasn't the only one who had seen the sign. Many of his riders had. They shuffled, eyes flickering between Alaxen and the Black Prince. Nezahrians had witnessed it too, and although they couldn't translate the meaning of the signs, the intent was clear. Alaxen and Raziel were a united front.

"Let Edvern signal to Aurelians," Raziel said to Zanniel. "It reminds our people that our fire Uhl'hari has a proud Aurelian heritage. If we do not accept the Aurelians, we will fall back into war and bloodshed. This battle is the opportunity for peace on many fronts."

And that was that. Edvern had to have faith that the Black Prince would hold to his side of the bargain.

"Keep close in formation," Raziel continued. "Zanniel and Hedriel will fly close to you. Symmeon and Palea will flank Lyssandra. Dalain will guard the emperor and empress. The Aurelians will carry as many men as possible for ground support, just in case."

At his side, Alynta leaned in. Raziel dropped to his knees. "As for you, little lady, keep moving and stay close to your Uhl'hari."

Alynta's nose twitched in response, and she lifted her paw to his knee. "Always."

"It's time to go." Raziel looked over Edvern's shoulder to where the emperor and empress were holding court. "Stay out of the way of any archers."

Edvern followed his gaze with a frown. He nodded. If he were hit in the middle of battle, his chances of survival were slim.

Finally, content with the formation of the dragons, Faelowyn lumbered over. She lowered herself, and Raziel mounted with the practiced ease of centuries. Mirroring the black dragon, Izorah also lowered herself. Edvern climbed onto her back as he had seen his father do on multiple occasions.

A dragon army becoming airborne was quite a sight. Woe and Balfar spread their wings first, taking the emperor and empress to the front of their host. Edvern and Raziel flew behind. The air became thick with the heavy sound of thrumming wings, cries of dragons and calls from riders.

Ahead of their fledging army, Edvern didn't have the luxury of studying their forces. He kept his eyes trained ahead and maintained his posture.

He might have kept himself rigid, but his mind returned to the image of Lyssandra prepared for battle. Her long black hair was braided artfully into a crown upon her head. Like most dragon riders, she was dressed in full leather armour. Her Saemorish friend Lady Antonella was at her side, and Lyssandra didn't look up at him as they spoke softly.

She had said she loved him. And he had been too damn scared to say the words back, afraid that if he did, he condemned them. What if he said those words and one of them died today? It was too late now. He was an utter bastard.

"You're a fool," Izorah told him mildly.

Edvern hummed in agreement. He was a coward. Strange how his heart had changed. He couldn't imagine life without her. When they had first met, she had been bothersome, entitled and opinionated. Now he wanted to steal illicit kisses from her, to listen to her amusing anecdotes and hear her laugh. To run his fangs down the pulse of her neck ...

Thinking about Lyssandra Stamos was torture. He knew the expectations on unmarried diplomats from Saemore, and he was not part of that lifestyle. Marriage was not a choice for her. It would need to be approved by the Saemorish king, or would the Emperor of Nezaha have a say ... or Raziel?

Edvern's stomach lurched. The future, if he was lucky enough to survive, seemed far away and frightening.

Izorah did not offer any more wise quips as they flew, and Edvern was glad of the reprieve. Most of the riders and their dragons were silent. Death on the battlefield was seen as inevitable among the Aurelian riders, especially those born of lower ranks. Many of them would not see the day when Moira Tallermayne was defeated.

The spire in Gytall had been a prison in the landscape of Edvern's life. Navilla was commanded by Lady Rena Hybeck and had become the epicentre of war and innovation. Gytall had been an oppressive tower, a powerhouse of political manoeuvres, while Navilla was a fortress to hold secrets close. Her walls were twice as thick and protected by a barrier that was flame resistant.

Wriggling his fingers, his wings flaring behind him, Edvern wondered how resistant they were.

The rumours of new weapons were nothing new. Rena Hybeck was known for her experimenting. They'd have to take care when they took the walls.

Moira was ready for them. She was in the air, riding a new dragon, a large female with bulging red eyes filled with madness. Edvern couldn't help but think of the teal dragon who had begged for death. Wherever she was, Edvern hoped she was safe.

A legion of Aurelian dragons flew behind Moira.

They hovered in the air, the two armies facing off one another. Edvern thought he would be overwhelmed facing his first dragon battle. But a calmness washed over him.

War was sometimes a necessary evil. Moira had used the Aurelian system to not only oppress humans but also dragons. The time of her power and those like her had to end.

"What are we waiting for?" Edvern leaned over his dragon's neck.

"Moira hesitates ... and I don't know why." Raziel turned to Alaxen, who had approached. "What do you think, Tallermayne?"

"She wants us to go to her." The sight of Raziel looking to Alaxen was startling. If he had been told a year ago that his Aurelian uncle would fly beside one of Nezaha's most notorious warriors, he would have thought the world was ending.

"Advancing is a bad idea." Bastian, with Antonella and Konrad, followed his father.

"I'd listen," Konrad said. "Moira is a crafty foe."

"We can't hover here all day," Edvern replied.

In the end the decision was taken away from them. Edvern spotted the war machines first. He could only stare in shock, mouth dry, and point.

Bastian's jaw dropped, his wide eyes darting to Alaxen. "She's built them."

If his own overactive imagination hadn't frightened him, his cousin's rapidly paling face would. He studied the machines. There were dozens of contraptions built from the hardwood trees of the mountains. Gargantuan crossbows, half as long as a large drake.

The sheer weight of the dense hardwood would injure and down a grown dragon. It was not feasible to grab and fly off with the weapons. Teams of dragons would be needed, and they didn't have the number of dragons to disable them.

Notched into the crossbows were shafts that seemed longer, thicker than what Edvern had expected. Moira had a dozen men and women manning each weapon.

The chains cranked back, and the first spears were loosed.

Izorah swept to the side, Faelowyn pushing Valtar out of the way. Their lines were scattered with very little effort from the forces of Navilla.

Enraged by the onslaught, Aerin bellowed, eyes rolling back. He bared his teeth and flew forwards. Edvern caught sight of Dalain holding on for the life of him, screaming against the wind.

Moira continued to watch, a strange, sinister smile on her lips. Something was wrong ... She was a spider sitting in the middle of her web, waiting for her trap to spring.

Marsyna, Hedriel's young dragon, panicked and flew after Aerin, crying out for him to return to her. Edvern caught a screamed warning in his throat as Elisaria and Lyssandra lunged forward to catch the young dragon.

He twisted around on his dragon, yelling at Zanniel, "Get the prince."

Hedriel's dragon was much too small to directly confront most of the dragons. Both of them lacked the experience of taking the front lines.

Aerin got within ten feet of Moira, who still hadn't moved, before he seized up ... His wings shuddered, and his body convulsed. Ripples of blue power shimmered and crackled around the jerking dragon. Edvern smelt the scent of cooking scales.

"Dalain!" Raziel screamed.

Blood poured from Aerin's open maw, and Edvern feared that he would choke. Unable to fly, Aerin tumbled from the sky. Dalain was silent as he fell.

Marsyna was flying lower ... Prince Hedriel jumped from the safety of her back to catch Dalain. Time stood still, and Edvern could have sworn Dalain tried to push his younger cousin back to safety. Marsyna, being smaller and more agile than a fully grown dragon, twisted back on herself. She caught Dalain in her back talons, but Hedriel she clipped with her swaying neck.

Edvern could imagine the sickening crunch as Hedriel hit his own dragon's armoured spikes and fell like a stone.

"Go!"

He broke the lines. Izorah dived. The wind stung Edvern's eyes; he couldn't see through the tears. He knew before Izorah pulled up and her wings brushed the ground they had been too late.

Faelowyn, who had the greater experience and speed, got to the broken prince first. As the black dragon soared upwards, Edvern caught sight of the limp prince. His neck was broken. He had been dead the moment his body collided with Marsyna.

Nezahrian poets in the past said that the cry of a dragon who lost a rider before their time was a terrible thing to hear. Marsyna's wails tore at Edvern's chest. He had not known the prince well; but an Aurelian dragon had loved him.

The wails turned to fire and rage. And Edvern's heart shattered in his chest.

"Marsyna!" Edvern's cry came too late.

Marsyna charged forward, slamming into the same resistance that Aerin had run into. Poor Dalain remained dazed in her back talons. She convulsed, her tail lashing the air around her.

Ignoring the swearing emperor, Woe sped forwards, old Gryph going with him. They took her hind quarters and dragged her away from the barrier.

Ze'hyrn's attention was not on the dead prince, but on his own son. Perhaps the battle brought out his paternal instincts. When Woe gently took Dalain from Marsyna and went to hand him to Symmeon, the emperor screamed, "No. Give me my son! Give me my boy!"

Woe obeyed, and Gryph ushered Marsyna away, Balfar and Valtar providing them with cover.

Dalain lay shocked in his father's arms, the emperor tapping his cheeks to rouse him.

As Woe flew close by, Edvern half stood on Izorah's back. "Your Imperial Greatness. Take Dalain to the ground!" he screamed, hoping that the emperor would see sense.

"Aerin is still alive. I'll keep his rider for him. We're needed up here!" Izorah may have sounded calm, but she was anything but. Under Edvern's thighs she trembled with fury.

Edvern could have laughed. It shouldn't have come as a surprise that if any dragon could have survived that fall from the barriers, it was the bull-headed Aerin.

"Fire!"

Enraged by the battle, Balfar roared at the enemy's cry. Edvern's head snapped up. The Aurelians were now coating the head of the spears with tar and setting them alight. Balfar's large body provided a shield for the still stunned Marsyna. He wouldn't leave the younger dragon vulnerable. But if he didn't move, he would be hit. And the empress was on his back.

The empress was pure rage. She rained down curses on Moira for the death of her nephew and for the son she now feared for. But there was little she could do with the barrier between her and the enemy.

Izorah roared, speeding past Faelowyn. She raked her talons against Marsyna's hide, pulling her away from the line of fire. Snorting plumes of ash and smoke, Balfar dived. The spear missed, the dragon catching it. He lifted it up to the empress, who threw it back at the barriers ... Edvern felt the flames singeing his hair.

Afraid that the weight of both him and another dragon was too much for Izorah, he spread his wings and leapt into the air.

One glance to the side, and Edvern was satisfied that Marsyna had been escorted down. He banked, pushing power through his shoulders down to his fingertips. As he approached the magic defences of Navilla, he could feel the warm trickle of blood running down his nose. He ran his hand along the barrier and was rewarded with an erupting inferno. His power pulsed and burned, turning orange to bright blue. But no matter how much power he fed the barrier, it remained.

On his tail were Zanniel and Palea, their respective dragons covering him as he burned with fury.

A rushing wind tore through him, and he remembered Zanniel saying he was the Uhl'hari of fire and wind. This untested gifting collided with his flames, spreading the inferno at a terrifying speed. It tore through the barriers, buffeting unsuspecting enemy dragons on the other side. It wasn't enough to kill, but it unsettled the lesser trained enemies. Some were even unseated from their dragons.

"Edvern!" Zanniel yelled over the roar of battle. "Conserve what you can!"

"He's right." Palea drew her dragon close to him. The lizardling clicked his long talons in disapproval at him. "We have to get these barriers down."

"Any ideas?"

"My aunt's fleet," Palea said, her face covered in ash and soot. "They've not turned up."

"I'll go with you!" Zanniel said. "Something might be stopping them!"

"Go! Go!" Edvern screamed, turning to look back at the fiery barrier. Every man and dragon were needed for this fight.

Everywhere he flew, Alynta shadowed him. It was her strength that allowed him to fly without break or rest.

Still Moira continued to watch him with the disconcerting smile of hers. Every time she lifted her hand to signal the loosing of another weapon, Edvern thought he would be physically ill.

All round their Aurelian dragons swarmed the barrier, looking for any weak points. Younger, nimbler dragons took the front rows, while older dragons spotted missiles. The stalemate seemed to last for hours. Numbness swept through Edvern. The dying roars of the injured blurred so that he didn't know if the sounds were imagined or not. He was lost in a fog of blood and horror.

That was until he heard Lyssandra's scream reverberating around the battlefield. Her cry awakened him from his nightmare. He darted into action before his distressed mind could truly comprehend what was happening. Lyss had lost balance on Elisaria when her green dragon was hit in her hind quarters. Camyrs, her dyrathakin, squealed and flapped his wings so that he was free of the struggling dragon.

The spear in Elisaria's side was not life-threatening, but a fall for Lyssandra could be if she couldn't catch herself. Had she flown under the power of her wings unassisted yet? It was a stupid oversight.

The green dragon tried to twist around to catch her rider, but the length and weight of the spear made her clumsy.

Edvern forgot all fatigue as he spun and dove towards his Saemorish friend. He grabbed her ankle desperately, his wings of fire beating to keep him aloft. His second hand, his right with his magic fingers, grasped her knee. It was inelegant, but she was alive.

"Put me down!" Lyssandra screamed, dangling upside down in his grip.

Edvern blinked. If he readjusted his grip, he might drop her. His fingers dug into her flesh harder, his knuckles turning white. "I'm not going to lose you!"

"This is most improper!"

Perhaps it was the adrenaline running through his veins, or the stress. But Edvern could not help but laugh. "I think we've well and truly surpassed proper protocols. Flap."

"What?"

"Flap your wings!" Edvern cried through gritted teeth. He waited until she righted herself, his grip slick with his sweat. Once he was sure she was settled, he released her ankle.

Feeling Camyrs' claws on the bare skin of his back, Edvern gritted his teeth. He could feel the fear and worry radiating off the little creature, so he didn't rebuke him. Camyrs scrambled down Edvern's body and leaped into Lyssandra's outstretched arms. His long purple tongue lapped her cheek.

Edvern stared back at her, realising how much he would have grieved if she had been dashed upon the ground. He knew his feelings had shifted, but he had no idea the strength of his emotions for her. Not until the moment he thought he had lost her. His heart still hammered in his chest.

"Elisaria ..." Lyssandra murmured, brushing back stray strands of hair.

Edvern glanced down; Elisaria had landed safely. He could see her on the ground, snout upraised, looking for her rider. Aerin was at her side, ushering her to take cover, his side still bleeding profusely.

"Your rider is safe," Edvern sent towards the green dragon. *"Find a healer. Take Aerin."*

On the ground he could see Elisaria shake her wings. She limped along the ground, leaving a trail of red. Snapping his jaws and hobbling, Aerin followed.

"Elisaria! Eli ..."

Edvern took Lyssandra's shaking hands in his. "She's grounded for now. She's alive."

Lyssandra's lips wobbled a little, and he lent forward to press his against hers softly. His arms circled her shoulders, taking the burden of her weight while she collected herself. He understood the fear of one's dragon being killed. Camyrs pushed himself between them, his small body trembling.

"Eddi ..." Lyssandra still seemed dazed and confused. She wriggled out of his grasp, and he let her go reluctantly.

"This is not the right time ..." Edvern said, squeezing her hands. "But Lyss ... I don't want a future without you."

"He wants to make his nest with you," a nearby dragon said.

Edvern was mortified, knowing that Lyssandra could now understand the dragons.

"Nesting mates is serious business," the dragon continued. *"Nesting is forever."*

Lyssandra looked between the dragon and his Aurelian companion, one of Alaxen's favourites, then to Edvern. "Eddi—"

"This isn't exactly the time to discuss ..." the rider said between his gritted teeth.

Lyssandra grabbed Edvern's chin and pulled him closer, pressing her lips to his. The touch of her seared his skin, and the crackle of his fire powers blazed within him.

"There may not be another dawn for us," Lyssandra said, her hands curling around his neck. He felt her trembling, her extensive training unable to mask her excitement and fear.

"Then know this, Lyssandra Stamos. My life and death, I place in your hands." Edvern swallowed past all the nerves, past his feelings of rejection and shame. "Until my final breath, I'll battle all the kingdoms of the known world to be the one at your side. And if today is to be my last day, my soul will continue to sing for you in the next life."

Lyssandra pressed her forehead against his, her fingers gripping his skin. "I never suspected you were a romantic, Edvern Tallermayne."

"I hope I don't disappoint."

"Never."

He reached out and plucked a feather of fire from his wings. Delicately, he nestled it among her feathers. Today amongst her vines were thorns. "Now you have a part of me."

"Do I get one?" Camyrs asked, sitting on Lyssandra's shoulders and staring up at Edvern. "Do you love me too?"

Touched by the little creature's question, Edvern nodded his head and plucked a second feather for Camyrs. The dyrathakin of earth took it from his fingers, sniffed it and very carefully placed the feather of fire in his tail.

Edvern pulled away, painfully aware they were in the middle of a siege that they were losing. A wave of conflicting emotions washed over him. He wished to stay in the moment, and yet he wanted the battle to be over.

Edvern was of no doubt that they were at an impasse. Moira and her forces were safe, conserving energy behind a barricade while they were beating their wings, using energy and power they couldn't afford to spend.

The way in wasn't through brute strength. Stealth and finding the one weakness were what was required. When Moira exiled him, he had become a thief to survive and shame their ranks. If any had the skills needed, he did.

After pecking Lyssandra on the cheek, he turned sharply and dodged between their tiring dragons. He found Raziel and Faelowyn. The black dragon still cradled the lifeless body of Prince Hedriel. The Black Prince was staring ahead with sightless eyes at the burning barrier.

Symmeon stood beside his dragon, signalling Faelowyn to give him the young prince. He took the body gently and turned to go, only to find the empress standing only a few paces away. Without speaking she approached, pressing her index finger and tracing invisible runes over her nephew's lax face. She spoke a prayer in Nezahrian, and then when she was finished, she turned to Symmeon. "Take him to the medics. They'll prepare his body ready for his final journey back home to his mother."

Guilt tore through Edvern. There was nothing he could have done to spare Hedriel, but the feeling persisted, nonetheless.

"I don't blame the young dragon for what happened," Faelowyn told him. *"She had little experience of carrying and protecting a human rider."*

"She'll need your guidance," Edvern said gravely. He felt bile churning his stomach. Looking at the chalky face of the prince, Edvern thought he seemed to be younger than his sixteen years. Somewhere in the background, he could hear Marsyna's echoing cries. "And your kindness."

"We need to pull back," Faelowyn said.

Raziel nodded sharply; he seemed to be only half listening. "We need to draw the bitch out."

"Palea and Zanniel went in search of the fleet."

"The dragons on the ground have found Moira's young teal ... She's not in a good way. Perhaps she can help," Bastian said, coming up on the left-hand side.

Faelowyn had the faraway look on her face, and then Edvern sensed them. Wild dragons on the wind. Ancient, immensely powerful and angry. She turned to him. *"They're here to see you."*

"Me?"

"To see if you will fulfil the pact between man and dragon," Faelowyn said.

Edvern looked towards Raziel for guidance.

"You'll not come to harm at their talons."

"I don't know about the pact."

"They're here to see if you are a worthy emissary between dragons and humans. If they like you, they might fight with us."

Edvern waited on a burnt patch of grass for the wild dragons to arrive. The dour marshlands of Navilla did not provide a lot of cover, but Moira's riders did not fly further than necessary. They were content to stay behind their barriers, picking them off one by one. While Edvern stood in quiet solitude, he glanced towards Navilla, wondering what Lady Moira thought of the proceedings. Was she already celebrating her victory? The thought of her gloating and toasting to the death of his friends was painful. He clenched his fists at his side and was thankful when Alynta arrived.

He stroked his hand down her orange fur, his fingers coming away with clotting blood. She did not speak or share any imagery of what she had been through in the fight, but he sensed it all the same. He felt each moment she checked on a dragon only to find them dead.

Between their entwined souls, they shared their pain and heartache, and Alynta's bright fur glowed. Her wings and tail became tongues of fire ready to battle Moira once more.

Thankfully, it wasn't long before Zanniel flying across the sky heralded the arrival of Tyrbanath and his mate, Amorith. They had with them three other dragons. Edvern watched them land, marvelling at how much stronger and vibrant they seemed in comparison to the Aurelian dragons. Even Kyros paled to these dragons.

Hovering above Edvern's head, Zanniel cried, "Where's Raziel?"

"With the emperor, I think," Edvern answered. "What's happening? Where's Palea?"

"This isn't all of Moira's forces … The fleet … she attacked. Heavy losses!"

"Palea?"

"Fighting alongside Eupheana!"

Thank talons. Edvern watched Zanniel depart while the great dragons landed before him, the ground shaking under their weight.

Licking his lips, Edvern searched for the right words to speak to the wild dragons. But Alynta took over. She trotted over to Tyrbanath, bowing her head for a fleeting moment before raising her eyes.

"This is my Uhl'hari, Edvern. You may call him Eddi. You may not disrespect him."

It seemed ludicrous that a small, furry dragon would have the audacity to speak to the king of dragons in such a manner. Large dragon eyes studied the dyrathakin, then swivelled to Edvern, then back. The drake shifted, flaring his nostrils, and nodded.

"I will afford Uhl'hari the respect that he deserves," Tyrbanath said.

"I'm very pleased to meet you, King Tyrbanath." Edvern bowed as gracefully as he could manage.

"King is a foolish human title," the regal female dragon said. His heart skipped a beat; he hoped that these dragons would decide to help them. *"I'm Amorith. I wish to enquire after my daughter, Faelowyn."*

"Fierce as ever, my lady," Edvern replied. "She is much grieved for Prince Hedriel ... and his young dragon."

Tyrbanath's nostrils flared. He turned his crowned head to survey the damage on the battlefield. He remained silent, staring unblinking at the injured and exhausted dragons. He spotted Marsyna, who was still wailing for her rider.

"She is too young to fight," Tyrbanath said, his displeased rumble reverberating the air around them.

"Her rider was of age to her," Edvern said. "Lady Moira knows no mercy when it comes to hatchlings. She killed all those too young or too vulnerable to fight at Gytall and Cynedir."

"Poor child." Amorith stalked past Tyrbanath and across the fields. The Aurelian dragons who were able parted for her. Edvern watched as the large female crooned at the grieving Marsyna and then curled around her. A sense of relief washed over Edvern as the young red dragon quietened.

"She should still be in her mother's nest," an orange dragon said. *"We should take her home to the mountains."*

Tyrbanath sidled closer. *"The time to allow humans to intrude on our world is once more upon us. It is high time we intervene."*

Doubt gnawed in Edvern's belly. The wild ones had been absent from the world of humans for so very long. "What of our dragons? It is my understanding that you want nothing to do with them. I've heard what was said to Woe."

"This is why I might just like you, Uhl'hari. Such boldness to speak to me in this way."

"Truth might be unpleasant," Edvern replied. "But it is still the truth. Best to face it straight on."

"Indeed."

"I'm curious about this Woe," the orange dragon said. *"Ridiculous name full of negative connotations. To speak such evil over oneself is folly. Where is he? I wish to have words with him."*

Cocking her head to the side, Alynta considered the orange dragon, then turned to point with her snout. "Fighting with his pompous rider again."

Edvern followed his dyrathakin's gaze to see that indeed Woe was at odds with the emperor. He bit back a shout of dismay as the emperor struck Woe's face with the shaft of his heavy spear. Twisting his head away, Woe rubbed at his snout with his foreleg. The strike had cut the thinner skin around his eye, blood dribbling from the wound.

Edvern wasn't sure who was more stupid, the emperor for taking up a long spear to strike a dragon or Zanniel, now landed, who grabbed the emperor's spear to wrestle it from him.

Never far behind, Codee snapped at half a dozen royal guards who proceeded to slap his hind quarters with the flat of their swords. Both dragons were being extraordinarily patient with human foolishness. But it wouldn't take much to make them snap.

Edvern swore under his breath, already turning on his heel.

"I'll deal with this," the orange dragon said.

"Prynn ..." Tyrbanath rumbled.

"I'm just going to scare them."

Zanniel was pushed to the ground, tumbling so that the emperor stood poised above him with the spear held aloft.

As Woe roared, making ready to lash out with his tail, Prynn charged, his head lowered. The emperor was forced to stall the killing blow on Zanniel to face the irate dragon. It was all Edvern could do but watch. Above his head Tyrbanath sighed loudly. *"Why did the Father Dragon bless me with such dramatic sons and daughters?"*

The royal guards left Codee's side to attack Prynn. Codee, known for his protective nature, stepped around them, placing himself between the wild dragon and the royal guard. Prynn, however, shoved him out of the way and roared in the faces of the guards. One by one they tumbled onto their backsides before the dragon's fury.

"You'll show your emperor the proper respect, dragon!"

"Wild dragons do not recognise the sovereignty of humans," Prynn rumbled, the meaning of his words lost on the emperor.

It was Zanniel, still prone on the mud-streaked ground, who answered the emperor. "Great One, that's not one of our dragons. He's wild."

Edvern knew that dragons could be gentle, but he wondered how Zanniel felt the moment Prynn reached out and grasped him in his talons. The war wraith wriggled and squirmed in the grip, his face paling. *"I'll be taking this human with me. If I decide to take up my human collecting hobby again, he'll do splendidly."* The orange dragon turned his face towards Codee and Woe. *"This pair are also coming with me. This grey one, yes, I believe he's my lost egg."* He lowered his snout, growling into the emperor's face, spittle and foam frothing on his teeth. *"Mine. Don't touch."*

Even if the emperor could not understand the words of dragons, the message behind Prynn's growls were clear to everyone. Gulping, the emperor had to concede defeat as Prynn prowled away, barking for both Codee and Woe to follow him.

Poor Woe looked so baffled by the turn of events that he stumbled after the orange dragon without protesting.

Tyrbanath made a sound in his throat as Prynn returned to his side with two sheepish Aurelian dragons on his heels. *"You don't have a lost egg, son."*

"The humans don't know that," Prynn said, tilting his head back to look at both Codee and Woe. He placed Zanniel on the ground to stand beside Edvern. *"I'll think I call him Kaida. A good, proper dragon name. A word meaning 'found'."*

A strangled sound came from Woe.

"Woe is not a suitable name for my son," Prynn said. *"Pretend or not."*

"Very well, Kaida and his friend are your responsibility," Tyrbanath grumbled.

Prynn just smiled wickedly at his father.

Seeming satisfied, Tyrbanath turned back to Edvern. *"Where were we? Ah, yes, you are the difference and the bringer of change. We cannot ignore the coming of Uhl'hari. You are both man and dragon soul. A gift, a mouthpiece from Father Dragon. You and I'll come to a solution."* Tyrbanath raised his head to the sky, taking in the sight of a dragon with two riders. Valtar.

He landed beside Edvern, dipping to allow Antonella and Konrad to jump from his back. The wild dragons seemed amused, tittering at Valtar's cleverness in choosing a mated pair for his rider. Antonella said nothing but touched Edvern's elbow lightly to let him know they had news.

"The lizardlings will come to see their risen Uhl'hari ... Water wyrms, as sly and treacherous as they are, will come out of curiosity. Battle enthrals them, and the possibility of all three Uhl'haris is intoxicating." Tyrbanath lowered his snout, giving Konrad a curious sniff. *"This one smells of strange fire. Ask him about it."*

"My experiences with water dragons and lizardlings aren't favourable," Edvern said, eyeing Konrad. The Saemorish captain did smell odd. "The last dyrathakin egg is behind the barrier."

"But Edvern, the water wyrms have come to our rescue," Antonella said. "We've just flown over our fleet. They've injured many of Moira's dragons. Did you know they can leap great distances from the water?"

"Ask him about his odd smell," Prynn asked. He, too, sidled closer, nostrils flaring.

"The fleet humans have a weapon that shoots fire!" Valtar said. He nudged Konrad playfully, and the Saemorish captain stumbled. *"My rider is a natural."*

Konrad looked to Edvern for translation.

"The dragons are curious of the new weapons and your smell."

Uncertain, Konrad bowed low to Tyrbanath. "It's a long, heavy metal pipe. They use a special powder and set it alight."

"It's very loud," Antonella said. "Konrad is a very good shot."

Konrad blushed.

Prynn turned to his father. *"I must see this!"*

"Patience, my son. The barrier must crumble first," Tyrbanath said. *"I foresee it will fall to another to do so."*

Turning, Edvern looked back at the ferociously burning fire. He had poured everything he had into it. And yet it held. There had to be another way.

"Who will take the barrier down?" Even as the words fell from his lips, Edvern knew he didn't want to know the answer.

"He will make himself known at the right time."

*The great dark star, Lord Qavi, was the first example to
mankind of sacrifice. In the ancient days he was a mighty
celestial being. Praised for his golden light, he was the day star
that brought light and warmth to the land.*

*When the evil days came, Lord Qavi was not content to bear
witness to the destruction of mortals and dragons alike.
Surrendering his powers, the sun was born, and the great lord
stepped on the earth for the first time. The being of light became
the lord of shadows, of the hidden hope that can be found in
humankind.*

*To this day, not many humans have the courage to willingly
lay down their own life in service of their country. Such men
should be remembered and honoured.*

ANCIENT HISTORIES AND MAN

HAVEL

Chapter 38

Antonement

Raziel, The Black Prince

Raziel wanted to hate every hair on General Tallermayne's golden head but found the emotions difficult to stir. His old enemy, his rival, landed nearby, studying the battlefield with such anguish that he knew he no longer despised the man.

Like himself, Alaxen Tallermayne had been born into his position. He survived with the path he had been given to walk.

Bastian Tallermayne knelt by the teal dragon, his fingers tapping against his thighs. The dragon's dull eyes blinked open to stare up at the young man. She moaned pathetically and shifted. "She's lingered too long," Bastian said, reaching out a hand to touch the dragon. He seemed afraid to do so.

Lyssandra stayed a little behind the group, the dyrathakin wriggling in his mistress' arms. He jumped free and padded to the quivering mess of burnt scales. The teal dragon's injuries were so terrible that there was very little left of the membranes of her wings.

"I know you can understand me," Bastian said, his hand still hovering. "We're not here to hurt you."

"Camyrs ..." Lyssandra called, reluctant to allow him near the dying dragon.

The young dyrathakin looked back at her, hesitated and padded closer. He whined and sat on the cold, marshy ground. "She's held off death for days. She needs to speak to us."

Alaxen speared him with a questioning gaze, but Raziel ignored him. It would be a mercy to slam his sword to the hilt into the dragon's chest and be done with it.

The injured dragon did not desire his mercy. She groaned again, lifting her chin. Her time was near; she ached for her suffering to be over. But not yet.

"I must speak with you," the teal said. Her voice was a pained whisper, and Raziel felt pity that she had suffered in her death throes for so long. *"Don't pity me. I have fought long and hard to ensure my last moments matter."*

"I'm listening, daughter of air," Raziel said.

"Lady Tallermayne has an egg behind those walls. You must get it."

"We know this information already, little friend." Through the bond they shared, Raziel felt Faelowyn's regret. They should have fought for the Aurelian dragons and for the lost eggs sooner.

Tired dragon eyes closed and then reopened, staring intently at Alaxen.

"There's one who can open the warding, but it will cost dearly."

"Who or what?"

"One of Tallermayne blood," the dragon said. *"Lifeblood is key. It must be willingly given. I heard their plans. They tested their barrier on me."*

Raziel turned towards Alaxen, knowing his former enemy did not hear or understand the conversation. He could see it in Tallermayne's eyes. His enemy knew something was wrong. Perhaps he had heard rumours of his mother's innovations ... Perhaps he already suspected what must be done.

"Bastian, take Lyssandra and stay by Edvern's side," Alaxen said, turning towards his son. Raziel felt a moment of indignation that he would issue a command without waiting for him. But there was another part of him that understood.

If Alaxen had his suspicions, he was making a move to protect his son.

Bastian looked between them. He might be grown, but he had been taught from a young age to respect his elders. And his father was a lord and at one time, second to Moira.

It was Alaxen's next words that confirmed to Raziel that the Aurelian lord knew the depth of the secrets the teal dragon had told him. "I am proud of you, son."

Bastian nodded; his brow furrowed as if he was trying to solve a puzzle. It was Lyssandra who moved first, and he followed behind. She nodded to Alaxen and touched Bastian's elbow lightly; she understood the dragon.

Camyrs whimpered, his tail drooping.

"Come," Lyssandra commanded, leading both Bastian and her dyrathakin away.

"The news is not good," Alaxen said. "Your face is easily read, Yavari."

"The barriers ..." Raziel paused. Alaxen deserved to know the gravity of what he needed to ask. He was not ruthless enough to send the man in blind. Besides, he was Edvern's uncle. "The barriers can only be brought down by someone of Moira's bloodline. Blood must be spilt, willingly."

"Ah, death. I will go." Alaxen turned to place an affectionate hand on the snout of his dragon. "But not with you this time, my friend. Watch over Bas ..."

The low rumbling sound coming from the belly of the beast spoke of the drake's discomfort, knowing what his rider was willing to do. Aurelian people believed that death by suicide would condemn a person's soul for eternity. The sages in their temples would scorn Alaxen for his sacrifice. He would be condemned to never know light or peace. Raziel wondered at the state of the man's faith.

"Lyrus wants you to know he'll stay by Bastian's side, and ..." Raziel swallowed, almost overcome by the weight of the navy dragon's emotions. "He loves you."

Alaxen's eyes filled with silver tears, his face crumpling. But behind his dark, stern eyes, there was determination. "And I love you with all my being, Lyrus. Don't mourn me for too long. I am not afraid."

Alaxen bowed his head, clasping his hands in front of him. He drew in a deep breath and murmured, "Rikar spoke with dragons."

Raziel felt a twist of indignation at the claim. "An Aurelian would never be ..."

"The real Rikar Tallermayne was murdered in his cot. To protect the murderer, Father took an a Nezahrian baby from docks of Gytall and illusioned him to look like his child. When Rikar was sentenced to die, he feared that the illusion over his body would fail once he was dead, revealing my father's deception. If Moira found out ... Edvern would have been in greater danger. So Rikar asked me to hood him for his execution, to hide his face. It was an act of selfless courage, to be shamed like that. Eddi should know."

"Rikar was Nezahrian?" Raziel brushed his hand through his hair. "I'll tell Edvern about the deeds of his father."

"Thank you."

If their situation were not so severe, Raziel might have laughed at the audacity of Fennix Tallermayne. How sweet to think that Moira raised a Nezahrian fraud.

"But you had this knowledge?"

"Kyros spoke with Rikar, and we later confirmed." Alaxen nodded. "It was Kyros who put it in Rikar's head that the weapon that Moira was sending him to destroy in Charkara had to be saved. We had no idea the wily old dragon had sent him to rescue a baby."

"Kyros ..." Raziel's voice lowered to a growl.

Alaxen gestured around him. "You can't honestly say that without an Uhl'hari that loved and honoured the dragons of Aurelia, that they would have been free. Would you have freed Lyrus or Woe or Izorah if you had the opportunity, or would you smite them?"

"He did what he felt was right, given the situation," Faelowyn said. She lowered her head. *"We also must accept some responsibility for the captivity of our Aurelian brethren."*

Over long years, Raziel had learned to trust Faelowyn's judgement. Although he could never accept that Kyros was good, he could acknowledge the strength of his soul son's affection for the brute.

"And knowing all this, you never turned on Rikar."

Alaxen smiled. "Rikar and I were close. That's why he trusted me with infant Edvern ... He knew my secrets, just as I knew his."

"*Your* secrets."

"There is something I'd confess before we assault the barriers," Alaxen said. He sighed, eyes drawn to the smoky sky. "I hope you would do the honour of speaking with my son. To explain to him his true history. Thleah, my wife, she didn't die of natural causes. My mother found evidence that she may have worked with Nezaha. In truth she was Nezahrian. Edvern wasn't the first baby born within the Tallermayne family to have the tapered edges of Nezaha's ears."

"Bastian. A blessed one?"

"Kendrick too." Alaxen nodded. "Thleah begged me to take Bastian to Charkara, to leave him anonymously. But I feared he would be slaughtered because of his Tallermayne blood, and I hesitated too long. And then Kendrick was born ..."

Raziel wanted to protest but found he couldn't deny the possibility of the Tallermayne boys being mistreated in their temples. Half Aurelian children were kept away from the 'pure' babes of Nezaha. Even if Bastian had been welcomed into the temple, his life would have been hard.

"Rikar had just found out about his parentage when he flew into Nezaha ... You've heard the stories how the other masters went against orders. He was a strong man. If he didn't want to help Edvern, he would have fought off the compulsion and left him to die. The dragons loved him. Izorah was smitten with Rikar. I might not have been able to talk with her, but she had picked her next rider in Edvern.

And Kyros, it didn't take too much to see Mother's dragon was tormented. Eddi soothed him."

"What is it you want, Alaxen?"

"I don't ask for your forgiveness, for I don't believe I deserve that. But Bastian, promise me he won't come to harm at your hands."

"Come what may, I will honour your sacrifice." Raziel inclined his head. "I'll support your son, the last Tallermayne, to my dying breath."

They stood together, standing vigil over the dying dragon, who struggled to her feet. Her head was bowed low, but she rallied what strength she had. *With your blessing, Black Prince, I'll go with him.*

Raziel opened his mouth, and before he could speak, Faelowyn granted the young one her blessing.

"Go in peace, General Tallermayne," Raziel said. "I for my part forgive you, and this is the moment I will remember you by."

There was calm acceptance to Alaxen Tallermayne that he couldn't understand. Together with the dying dragon, he headed to the wall.

Raziel unsheathed his sword and spoke to Faelowyn. "Rally the troops."

CHAPTER 39

Sacrifice

EDVERN

Edvern's soul tugged as Izorah returned to his side. She moved forwards, careful to keep her head lowered in reverence to the wild ones. Instead of greeting him as he expected, she turned her snout back to Lyrus, who had followed her. Riderless.

Where was Alaxen?

Tyrbanath's stern gaze took in first Izorah and then Lyrus. *"I pity you, son of fire; you've tasted what it was like to be a dragon bonded in a time where humans lived with us harmoniously ... and today that taste is bitter."*

"It is not pity I need," Lyrus replied, his voice a low purr. *"I consider myself the most fortunate of dragons."*

Alynta sat on her haunches, her long, bushy tail wagging. "It's time," she said, her lips parting into a wolfish smile.

Swaying his head side to side, Lyrus flared his nostrils as Lyssandra and Bastian joined them. *"There is a plan to take the wall. Bastian will fly with me."*

Nearly choking on the words, Edvern relayed the message.

Bastian's expression smoothed into a blank mask; however, Edvern saw the uncertainty. "But Father ..."

He could understand Bastian's shock. It was unheard of for a dragon to fly with one they had not bonded with, without their rider.

"I cannot accompany Alaxen in his task."

"Lyrus?"

The great dragon bowed his head, looking like the weight of the world was placed on his back. Edvern's next words were stopped by Lyssandra's hand on his elbow. She shook her head.

"Lord Alaxen made his wishes quite clear. The battle turns fierce, and my place is at his son's side."

Drawing in a deep breath, Edvern turned to Bastian. "Lyrus says he cannot be with your father, and Alaxen wanted him to stay with you."

"Then let it be." Bastian bit his lip, turning to look at their scattered forces. To Edvern's astonishment they watched as the injured stood and readied themselves. He could see the courage returning to them, and along with it, strength.

"The lizardling horde is almost upon us," Tyrbanath rumbled.

At Edvern's side Lyssandra stiffened. He could understand her hesitation. She had been on the ground, stranded and wingless when she came face to face with lizardlings for the first time. He had been soaring above.

"Thirty lizardlings working together can take down a fully grown dragon." Faelowyn, who had been busy organising the dragons into lines, approached. *"Father, I hardly dared to trust my instincts when they told me you were coming."*

"Daughter."

"Kyros always said you'd come back. He had faith that one day dragons would be free."

It seemed like a strange statement, but before Edvern could question it, the ground beneath his feet quaked. Lyssandra grabbed his hands, pulling him away from a forming hill.

"Lizardlings!" she hissed in his ear. "Watch their teeth and claws."

Edvern's stomach roiled at the thought of being torn limb from limb. Sensing his discomfort, Izorah growled, her belly aglow with flame. Lyrus joined her. Camyrs hissed.

"Enough, child," Tyrbanath rumbled. *"They are here to fight for us."*

"Bold statement, king of air," a wizened voice said. Edvern looked down to see a large lizardling emerge from the earth. His emerald scales were covered with soil, grass and weeds. Grumbling, the lizardling pushed himself further from his burrow. More lizardlings followed, and the cacophony of their voices made Edvern feel dizzy. He glanced towards Lyssandra; she had shifted her weight. Her dragon, Elisaria, came to join her.

"You have with you the Uhl'hari of fire and air," the lizardling said, his tongue flickering from his pointed mouth. The king of the earth rested his bulbous eye on Edvern, and he felt his shoulder blades tingle with the warmth of his power. The creature's stare turned to Bastian and then Lyssandra. *"And here is the Uhl'hari of the forests and the earth. Water, as usual, is the last to appear."*

"The Uhl'hari of fire and wind is the strongest," Tyrbanath said. *"From the dawn of creation, it has always been so. He will always come first."*

The lizardling king harrumphed. *"Water would rather wash away their kingdom and drown all her inhabitants."*

"We have dragons of air that require your certain skills of healing," Amorith said. She glanced at Faelowyn and took a small step forward.

Edvern bowed his head. "My lord, I would be incredibly thankful if you would assist my kin. There's been too much bloodshed."

"Aha ... the Uhl'hari seems to understand his place," the lizardling leader said, his tail languidly wriggling from side to side. The creature cocked his head. *"Maybe you should teach the dragons of air a thing or two. Very well, I'll assist, but for Uhl'hari and not King Tyrbanath's sake."*

"King is a filthy human word," Amorith snapped.

Cocking his head to the side, the lizardling chief licked his lips and made a parody of a bow. He and his clan members dispersed, humans scattering in their wake as they went to work. Edvern knew it was too much to hope that every dragon could be healed.

Moving forward on shaking legs, Marsyna presented herself to the lizardling king. *"Please,"* she said, her voice hoarse from her crying. *"My rider. I dropped him. I hurt him ... Is there ...?"*

"Blessed talons," the lizardling replied, flicking his tail. *"I'll have a look. Depends on how scrambled his delicate human brain is."*

Edvern had the terrible feeling that the lizardling was humouring Marsyna so that he didn't have to deal with an upset dragon.

"And my cousin, great king." Elisaria slunk forward. *"He's the one who helped us escape. He's the one who has taken care of riders when they become too demanding and cruel ... He killed my rider and set me free of her."*

"A murderer of riders, hey?" the lizardling leader said. *"I like the sound of him. Let's see what we can do."*

There wasn't time to contemplate the lizardling and the dragon; the waters around the battleground bubbled and frothed. Edvern felt the chill in the air drop. He tugged Lyssandra closer. The water wyrms were the least accommodating of the dragon types that he had met.

The water wyrms emerged in an eruption of cold water, and Edvern was glad that he stood well away from the banks.

"We have little desire to be here," the first water wyrm snarled. *"But the humans on the great ships wanted you to know water weakens the barrier."*

"This spire is built upon a large underground lake. Can that help us?" Tyrbanath asked. *"When the time is right, can we be assured that you and your kind will create enough of a disturbance to topple it?"*

"The waters care not for the sky, nor the land. We can get through the barriers just fine, perhaps with a ship or two on our backs. If you were to so kindly ask."

Tyrbanath's nostrils flared. He looked to Edvern, the ridged scales of his eyes rising. *"Very well. Cause as much damage as you can to the spiteful humans of Aurelia. Spare those that fight with us, and I'll be most grateful."*

"So very close. But you do not command me, Tyrbanath."

Alynta trotted forward and placed herself between the water wyrm and Tyrbanath. She glowered at the marsh water, her wings flapping. "Do it, you overgrown mealworm."

"Alynta!" Edvern cried, shocked by her rudeness.

But the water wyrm laughed. *"Get the barriers down, dyrathakin of air and fire. The humans on the ships would be slaughtered without their armies. I see that you've left the water dyrathakin's egg to rot. The powers of water always lie forgotten. Yet you cannot live without our abundance and gifts. Ungrateful…"*

Edvern could stand it no longer. "We're here trying to get the egg back! It's behind those stone walls."

"Indeed," said the water wyrm. His eyes flicked over Alynta, to Edvern and then to Bastian. *"If you fail to hatch the egg of water, I'll eat you."*

"You'll have to get through me first!" Izorah said, snapping her jaws. Lyrus was right behind her.

"How touching," the water wyrm said. He nodded to his clan, and they surged below the waters. Edvern watched the place where they had disappeared and hoped that if needed, they would help. He hated the idea of being uncertain if they could rely on them.

"We've found a way to take the barriers down." Raziel made himself known, bowing stiffly to Tyrbanath and then to Amorith.

"Our orders?" Bastian asked.

Raziel turned his face away, a grimace spreading across his lips. "Alaxen will fly out first. Bastian will fly with Lyrus behind Lyssandra and Elisaria. When the barriers fall, get inside."

"Where's my father?"

"He's …" the Black Prince paused, gazing out of the marshes and bloody field to the spire surrounded by Edvern's flames. "Preparing himself."

Edvern felt some great work was happening under his very nose. Just as confused as he was, Bastian looked to him. He could only shrug and mount Izorah.

"Are you ready?" Edvern asked, looking to Lyssandra and his cousin.

"As ready as I'll ever be."

"FATHER!"

Reflecting back on his cousin's alarmed cry, Edvern could only assume that Bastian had some sort of premonition of what was about to happen. Staring up into the sky swirling with smoke and fire and blood, he would never forget the sight that met him. Astride a small teal dragon, bedraggled, bleeding and dying, was his uncle.

"What's he doing?" Bastian demanded.

From all his interactions with the Black Prince, Edvern didn't think he was one for grand gestures—least of all an enemy rider. But he laid a comforting hand on his cousin's shoulder. "What he must. Go."

Bastian threw himself onto Lyrus' back. The blue dragon spread his wings and soared into the sky like an arrow. Instead of flying towards Alaxen, his rider, as his cousin demanded, he refused to listen.

Izorah and Elisaria drew level with Lyrus.

Alaxen drew closer to the barriers of fire. Beyond it, Navilla spire. What kind of plan was this?

"Lyrus, what are you doing?" Edvern screamed as the navy dragon flew wide.

"Protecting what is left of my rider's nest."

Up ahead, Edvern's fire and wind still licked the barrier to Navilla. They had not diminished. Indeed, whatever sorcery and power maintained Lady Moira's barricade was feeding the fire. Several hundred paces out, he could feel the flames beating on his skin.

"Uncle!" Edvern screamed, fearing his voice would be lost in the wind. "It's too hot!"

Alaxen looked back at him, then to Bastian. He lifted his hand in farewell and signalled one last word. "Proud."

Edvern's warning lodged in his throat, everything falling into place in an instant. In his horrified disbelief, he couldn't make a sound. He lifted his hands, fumbling the sign. "No. No. No."

"He gave me charge over Bastian." Lyrus' voice, full of sorrow and grief, rippled through his thoughts.

Edvern screamed, his heart full of the navy dragon's despair, which mingled with his own. It wasn't supposed to end like this. The sound of his cry alerted Bastian of the impending tragedy, and his cousin's ashen face turned towards his father, horror blossoming over his expression.

Edvern signalled again. "Please, no."

Alaxen drew his sword, and Edvern fancied he saw his uncle smile. Tears clouded his eyes as Alaxen thrusted his blade through his belly, a spray of red clouding his vision.

Bastian's voice joined with him. Edvern turned to see his normally poised and reserved cousin tearing at Lyrus' navy scales with his bare hands.

"Why didn't you stop him?" Edvern screamed at the dragon. "Why?"

Lyrus' answer was lost in the moment that the teal hit the barrier. The whole sky quivered on impact. Alaxen's body, along with the dragon, was consumed by the flames and power. Bastian screamed afresh ...

Lightning and thunder boomed around them, and the barrier fell, taking the wall of flames with it.

Izorah flew through unimpeded, Lyrus on her tail, followed by Elisaria.

Edvern's mind was numb. He was trying to fit all the pieces of the puzzle together. Uncle Alaxen, Lord Tallermayne, had committed suicide on the battlefield. Impossible. He had been told from boyhood that taking one's own life was a coward's way out—a blight and a shame unto the family. Alaxen would be turned away from light and peace in the afterlife ... his soul discarded.

Never had a member of the Tallermayne family committed such a crime. Not before Alaxen. He caught back a choked cry, fury coiling in his gut.

Alaxen wasn't a coward. Of that Edvern was sure.

He turned to look at Bastian, at his pale and wet face. He had quietened. Death was expected among the dragon rider ranks. One must grieve quickly and learn to move past the pain.

"He killed himself," Bastian croaked as Lyrus pulled level with them. The walls of Navilla Spire loomed ahead.

"No. The barrier needed Tallermayne lifeblood," Lyrus said, voice shaking with the conviction of his own words. *"Not suicide. He sacrificed himself to pave the way for us to have victory. I have faith that the Father Dragon was waiting to welcome him home. He would not suffer needlessly."*

Bastian swallowed, his throat bobbing with the effort.

"He's a war hero," Edvern said. "I'll honour him as such. The barrier ... it needed his lifeblood."

"Why his life?" Bastian screamed. "Why him?"

There was no more time to discuss the fate of one Alaxen Tallermayne. With a roar and rushing wind, the wild dragons flew overhead to beat them to the walls of Navilla.

The spears and weaponry hurled their way were useless against the wild ones. Watching the wild dragons land upon the walls was bittersweet. They had done it; they had made their way through the magical defences. All they needed to do was find the egg and kill Moira and her followers.

There she stood on the very top of her spire, surrounded by her top officers. Lifting his hand to them in mock greeting, Edvern swore that none of them would leave the spire alive. Here in the heat of battle, those responsible for so much death and pain in Aurelia were gathered together. That would be their undoing.

Moments later their trio of dragons landed, perching along the walls. Edvern kicked off, impressed that Lyssandra had already swung herself through one of the narrow slits that constituted as a window. He followed her and then turned back to help Bastian.

Edvern looked over his shoulder as he heard a battle cry from behind them. Their own battle legions were entering the fray. Raziel had been only seconds behind them, fighting off Moira's dragons so they might land safely.

The waters around the spire churned, and from the depths, perched on the backs of water wyrms, were the first Euquallian ships. On the prow of the closest one stood Oskar, his orange glow surrounding the ship.

Had he found a way for his power to work with the water wyrms? Along the deck he saw Palea standing with Eupheana. She threw herself onto her dragon, a curious long weapon in her hands. Her aunt mounted after her, and together they shouldered the long pole. They aimed. A boom and flying fire.

Delighted, Edvern laughed as the explosion hit one of the spire's walls, stone cascading down. They'd have to move quickly.

Alynta wriggled her way through the window. Her wings of fire illuminated the shadows around her. With her long, elegant legs and hunter's grace, she looked frightening.

Bastian, pale-faced, looked more determined than Edvern had ever seen him. "Any plans on how to kill Moira?"

"Slow?" Alynta said, ruffling her feathers. Her haunting lavender eyes flashed gold for a heartbeat. "Would you like first bite, human?"

Bastian's smile was full of malice. "It would be my honour."

"Plotting revenge is all very well and good," Lyssandra said, brushing down her leather armour. Edvern would have told her it was completely unnecessary, battles were messy, but he decided against it. She felt strong when she was in control and poised. He'd let her have those quirks of hers. "We need some type of robbery plan."

"It was meant to be this way," Alynta said. "Bastian and Lyssandra need to find the egg. We take the towers."

"The question remains how will we find the egg?" Lyssandra asked.

Alynta smiled, waving her tail behind her as she turned and trotted down the dark hallways. "You'll work it out."

*Likened to spun glass, dyrathakin eggs hail from otherworldly
gems. Lord Qavi blessed the red jewels of his crown with fire
and life, and so the first dyrathakin was hatched.
When Lord Camyrs of the Harvest and Lady Heleana of the
Waters joined Qavi, they also blessed their gems.
Each blessed stone was infused with the protection and sense of
their patron and would wait to warm for the right hands to
touch them. Dyrathakins will hatch under circumstances that
are dark and difficult.*

ANCIENT HISTORIES AND MAN

HAVEL

CHAPTER 40

Young Lord Tallermayne

LYSSANDRA

"Be careful." Lyssandra reached out and grasped Edvern's gloved hand as Alynta primly sauntered into the dark corridors. A tight smile touched his lips as he squeezed her fingers. She could feel the prosthetics under his gloves. Looking at Bastian, he nodded to his cousin and dropped to his knees beside Camyrs, who whined. The younger dyrathakin stared after Alynta, wanting to be with her, but pressed himself close to Lyssandra's legs.

"Look after Lyss for me," Edvern murmured, scratching Camyrs behind the ears, just the way he liked it.

"I will, Uhl'hari," Camyrs vowed, his long tongue licking Edvern's arm.

Straightening, Edvern unsheathed his sword and followed his dyrathakin into the dark. There was something horrible about letting him face danger alone. Lyssandra felt as though she were living in a nightmare. Edvern turned to look back at her, and she memorised the exact hue of his eyes. What if that was the last she saw of him?

"Are you well?" Bastian asked, drawing her out of her reverie.

Lyssandra startled, glaring at Bastian. He wasn't the type of man who often enquired on others' wellness. She nodded woodenly, biting her lips so that she wouldn't call for Edvern to come back. It would look foolish.

"I hate that he's going after Moira alone."

Bastian seemed unimpressed. "Edvern chose to go, just as Da decided—"

"Edvern lost another finger, and your father is dead." The words tumbled out from her lips, and she regretted them the moment she spoke them. "I am sorry, Bastian. I'm being selfish. Are you—"

"No," Bastian said with a shrug. He looked anywhere but at her. "No, I'm not alright. I lost my ma when I was young, Kendrick should be by my side, and Da ... my father ... Others have lost more than me."

"That doesn't take the sting out of your loss," Lyssandra said. She took a page from Edvern's book and unsheathed her sword. "Your pain is real."

"We should find the egg," Bastian said, his voice low and gruff.

Camyrs wagged his tail and padded off in the opposite direction. "This way."

"Well, it can't be too difficult, can it?" Lyssandra asked.

Bastian rolled his eyes, a frown tugging on his lips. "Grandmother is a wily woman."

"I guess they won't be anywhere convenient for us," Lyssandra muttered.

Bastian shook his head.

"You know your grandmother more than me," Lyssandra said. "Can you think of anywhere she would be likely to hide it?"

"Father disliked Lady Rena, and she loathed him," Bastian said. "I've never been inside this spire."

"Does your grandmother trust Rena?"

"Undoubtedly," Bastian said. "More than my father and uncle."

"I doubt she'd leave it with a dragon. Edvern has a way with them, and she was afraid he was taking the control from her," Lyssandra replied. She started walking, and a moment later, she heard Bastian's footsteps following her. "Moira isn't a stupid woman."

"Rena would be on the battlefield."

"An office would be too easy."

"What about her personal rooms?"

Lyssandra rolled her eyes. "Don't you think it would be too obvious?"

"Not if it wasn't visible or easily collected," Bastian said. "If it's in her personal rooms that solves the problem of trust, keeping it close at hand."

"Humans," Camyrs said. "Can't we just sniff out the egg?"

"You can track the egg?" Bastian asked.

Camyrs sat on his haunches and blinked up at them. "Can't you?"

"No." Lyssandra laughed nervously. Of course. The mythological creature she hatched had a way to find the egg. How positively inconvenient for Lady Moira. She opened her mouth to admonish her dyrathakin for not speaking sooner when the tower shook violently. She lost her footing, and she stumbled. Bastian caught her one-handed.

"I know why my cousin likes you," he said, pushing her back to her feet.

Lyssandra blinked. Her reply was cut off by a second tremor. When the quaking stopped, Lyssandra rightened herself and brushed fine granules of dust from her hair.

"Are you going to share your opinions?"

"Edvern was a flirt. Nothing kept his interest." Bastian eyed the ceiling.

"I'm fully aware of his past."

"He likes his women either cute but dangerous, or frivolous and trouble."

"Cute and dangerous?" The notion seemed preposterous.

Bastian nodded. "You're a pretty girl that can kick his ass if required."

"Ah ..."

"Many dragon rider men prefer their women docile and impressionable," Bastian said. "Edvern has never taken the easy route. He's attracted to trouble."

That was true.

Bastian's bored expression didn't change; he looked at her as if she were being incredibly stupid. "You like your men to challenge you. He's Rikar's son and stubborn."

Lyssandra hummed, flattening herself to the floor as the ground shook yet again. Camyrs dived under her arms. She had little knowledge of Rikar Tallermayne. Some called him a murderer and others a hero. There had to be some good quality in the man if he raised Edvern as his own, ruining his own reputation in the process.

With Camyrs leading the way, they had little difficulty in finding Moira's rooms. The earth dyrathakin scratched at the door until Lyssandra opened it for him. He bounded through, and she followed.

At a loss of where to look first, Lyssandra stood in the middle of the chamber. She had expected the private rooms of the woman who controlled a king and nation to be luxurious. Instead, they stood in a warrior's room. The bed was large with bundles of white furs. There was no dresser, just a cupboard for Moira's uniforms. She had bottles of wine on a table, along with a few thick military texts. The most expensive items were large candles set into crystal bowls.

"This does not look like a room with hiding places," Lyssandra said.

Bastian smirked. The anger he was feeling made his expression dark and ugly. "You'd be surprised. What do you sense, dyrathakin?"

Camyrs sat on his haunches. "It's here somewhere. We need to make a mess."

Sighing heavily, Lyssandra got to her knees to look for loose stones and other clever hiding spots.

Bastian had an entirely different idea of what might be considered a good spot to hide things. He went straight to Moira's cupboard and started shredding all her shirts, slicing up her leathers and even destroying her undergarments.

Lyssandra did her best not to stare, but she couldn't help but send glances his way every so often. Camyrs had come over to help, his sharp teeth ripping through satin and leather alike. There was a heaviness that had come over Bastian. His face was contorted with pain and rage. Deciding it was healthy for him to have an outlet for his ire, she made no comment. Better Moira's wardrobe than he hurt himself.

She found nothing on the floor tiles and went to the walls to tap on them to find hollow spaces.

Bastian took up the wine bottles and smashed them on the floor, filling the chambers with the heady scent of dark red wine. Lyssandra looked longingly at the wine. She could have done with a drink.

"Is all this necessary?" Lyssandra asked as Bastian picked up a crystal bowl that was full of sweet-smelling candle wax.

"Absolutely," Bastian said. "Grandmother was fond of her clothes, wines and candles."

He dropped the candle bowl onto the hard flagstone floor, and it shattered into a thousand pieces. He looked down upon it, and an intense sense of satisfaction filled his normally stoic face. He was pleased with his handiwork.

"The smells are confusing now," Camyrs said. He pawed at a candle with light blue wax. "Try all the candles. Maybe this one next."

Biting her lips, Lyssandra resisted the urge to give her dyrathakin a sound tongue lashing. Had the little critter known exactly where the egg was? She had been tapping on tiles and lying on the floor.

Bastian picked up the candle that Camyrs suggested. He smashed it against the floor, shards of glass spraying everywhere. Bending, he picked up the blue wax and drew out a dagger. Very gently he carved the wax away. Lyssandra watched the peelings of wax fall, and soon she saw the shape of a blue glass egg emerge.

"You found it," Lyssandra said, hardly believing her eyes. "Edvern's was amber. Mine green for earth."

Bastian held up the egg. "Blue for the waters of Aurelia."

"Let's go!"

But Bastian stopped by the door, cocking his head to the side as he lifted the egg to his ear. "The shell of the egg is warm … like it's trying to speak with me."

"Surely not!" Lyssandra said. This was more to herself than to Bastian. She rounded onto Camyrs, who wagged his tail. The blasted dyrathakin was grinning. "Did you know the whole time?"

"Know?" Bastian muttered. "Know what?"

Shooting a look at her dyrathakin, Lyssandra ran back to Moira's bed and grabbed a fur. "Congratulations, Lord Tallermayne. You're about to be a father."

Bastian looked to the fur bundled in Lyssandra's arms, then to the egg. If she weren't so frustrated, she might have found his expression of sheer panic funny. "I'm not ready for that."

Whether it was the Tallermayne lordship or fatherhood, she wasn't sure.

The glass egg began to shudder in Bastian's hands. "We're in the middle of a battle!"

"What better time to hatch?" Camyrs asked. His tail was still wagging.

Bastian placed the egg on the ground, giving it a curious poke. A small wing of wet black feathers punched through one side. He stepped back.

Time was running out, so the moment the little snout and two blue eyes emerged, she wrapped the creature up, eggshell and all. Thrusting it into Bastian's arms, she said, "Keep her close to your chest."

"She's wet and cold." Bastian held the baby dyrathakin to his chest, rubbing her sticky fur. "What are we going to do?"

"We're going to get her far away from this place."

The small dyrathakin cried out, mewling in fright as the tower started to sway. There was nothing for it. They ran.

Gwyn
Water
Dyrathakin
Side of beef for Aawin-
Wine for Dalain
EF
Pack extra bedding (and towels)
Prank for Bas (?)

CHAPTER 41

Untouchable

MOIRA

Fennix was with Moira as she watched her last child die. Ghostly hand reaching out for Alaxen, her husband stood aloof from her. This was the same as he had been in life. With her physically but emotionally removed.

His expression shifted from longing to sadness to rest upon a look of paternal love. No one had ever looked at Moira with such devotion, not even her own father.

Moira screamed with rage, knowing that a traitor was worthy of another's adoration and she ... she was not. If only she had never given Alaxen life. He'd stolen so much from her. He'd come into this world feetfirst and large, his skin grey. Labouring with him had nearly taken her life, but she had battled, hoping he might prove to have her strength. If she hadn't birthed and bled for him, she would have doubted the purity of his bloodline.

"Say something," Moira whispered to the back of her husband's spectre.

Slowly he turned, phantom eyes looking past her. Then he returned his eyes to the barriers. With the shedding of willing Tallermayne blood, the barriers spattered and fell. The flames ignited by Edvern dissipated, and the wind died.

Three dragons flew unhindered through the barriers. Alaxen's blue drake with Bastian entered their territory first, followed by Edvern and Lady Lyssandra. Clenching her fists, Moira resisted the urge to clutch at the locket around her neck. Only to remember she had abandoned it in the forest.

"You've become too greedy." Fennix's words to her were a quiet accusation. She swallowed bile. He had spoken those to her when he was alive on the night he had left for Nezaha to rescue Tamah. *"Your cruelty makes you blind."*

"There's nothing left for you here. Your golden son is dead by his own hand. A craven to the very end."

Fennix's low laugh was mocking. Stepping past her, he didn't dignify her with a glance. He moved through the ranks of her riders unseen. *"He grew to be a better man than me. You say I have nothing left, yet two of my grandsons still live."*

"One," Moira spat, uncaring that the riders around her exchanged wary glances.

Halting, Fennix looked out to the field. When he turned to look at her, his grin was full of malevolence. His body dissipated where it stood, leaving no sign that he had been among them. A chill ran down Moira's spine as his reply echoed in her head. *Two grandsons.*

Lady Rena stepped beside her. Moira started when she lay a hand on her shoulder. Her second stared out at the now wide-open air surrounding them. "They'll take the spire. What are your orders, my lady?"

For hours Moira had flown the boundaries of the battlelines. It was a miscalculation on her behalf, staying so long without a break. Her new dragon was fatigued and would not be able to fight the ailing enemy with the tenacity of a fresh mount. She looked over at the cool marshes, the bleak landscape littered with corpses of men and dragons.

She could hear the murmurs of fear rippling through her ranks. Madness was consuming her; she'd known it for quite some time. If the cost to dominance was her sanity, then that was the price she would pay. She turned her back on the battlefield to face her foes, her face still as stone. They would make their stand here, on the tops of the towers. The enemy would not penetrate their inner walls.

"Let them come," Moira replied, lifting her chin and baring her teeth.

Rena huffed, daring to voice her demands. "I'd like to take that foul winged Nezahrian traitor. I will dissect him in the name of research."

Moira lifted an eyebrow, knowing that some of her underlings would love to experiment on Edvern's inhuman body. She nodded. As long as Edvern's death was drawn out and painful, it made no difference to her. If her officers could learn anything from him, that would be a bonus.

"His fox dragon," Moira said. "I would like it for my zoo."

"It'll be done," Yahler commented from her other side.

"I'd have made it into a fur pelt," Whilmana grumbled. "Or crafted gems from her eyeballs."

"Get more of our dragons into the air. Concentrate your efforts on the Black Prince's dragon."

"Your will be done," Yahler drawled.

Confident that her commands would be followed, Moira turned and mounted her new dragon. The beast rumbled quietly and swayed her heavy head side to side. She prowled forwards, bent her legs and swept into the air.

If Edvern was searching for the egg, he would be bitterly disappointed. No matter the experiments done on it by Whilmana, it remained cold and unresponsive. Its ancient age was the only reason Moira hadn't thrown it into the watery marshlands.

While she hated the thought of losing the egg, she was more determined to keep her forces and weapons to a formidable size. The Black Prince's assaults and Saemorish cross words were not enough for her to abandon her idea of conquest. She would become empress ... She would rule over them all.

She lifted her eyes to the sky, signalling her most powerful. They would leave the apprentices and the small ones behind as bait. While they fought and died, she would move into a better position. This battle was not the end.

Her dragon swept around the spire, and she looked down at the battle. A grey dragon fought one of her large emerald drakes. He tore the hapless rider from the green dragon's back—the man died screaming. The emerald paused, shaking his horned head. The grey slammed him into the stone walls, shaking the tower.

Stunned by the blow and free of its rider, the emerald halted. It backed away from the grey and then tentatively stretched out its neck. Moira parted her lips, expecting the emerald to bite, but it merely sniffed at the grey.

The grey's rider, a young woman with black braids, leaned over the side of her dragon's neck, her hand outstretched. Nostrils still flaring, Moira willed the green to spew fire in the rider's face. No. He leaned in for a pat.

What was happening?

The dragons were going mad! The pathetic fools!

The grey nuzzled the emerald, and then the green dragon turned and attacked the rider on the back of another dragon. It was now attacking its own!

Roaring, Moira slammed her fist against the scales of her dragon. It grumbled in response, peeling its reptilian lips back to bare its teeth.

The grey heard her. He lifted his head in her direction. Upon his back his rider drew her sword, soaked in blood, acknowledging Moira's presence. "I am Palea, daughter of Ionah, and you'll taste blood before the day is through."

Moira's sneer only grew; she knew she was safe from her. As Palea's dragon charged, a second dragon, brown and raging, joined her.

The spire wasn't the only place Rena had laid her protections. Rena had been insistent that she also should have the lifeblood protection. At first, Moira had protested, thinking that hiding behind the magic protections was cowardly. Now she saw the wisdom. Alaxen had wasted his life on the spire. Now a second Tallermayne had to sacrifice themselves to get to her. It warmed her to think that if the enemy wanted to attack her, Bastian must die.

She was untouchable.

As the grey came closer, she felt the warm tingling that signalled the protections were working. The dragon shrieked in horror, his talons clawing at thin air.

Upon the grey dragon's snout was the ugliest lizard creature that Moira had ever seen. The lizardling erupted into angry flames and leapt into the air. The creature's wings were misshapen; it had no chance of flying.

The brown dragon bellowed, a deep, menacing bass, as he grabbed the tail of the grey dragon to yank him again. The brown's body hit the barrier protecting Moira, his rider toppling from the saddle. The rider fell ...

"Dalain!" Palea screamed, and Moira knew which rider she would kill next. If he survived the fall, she'd make the girl watch as she pulled precious 'Dalain' into small pieces. Her grey dragon ignored her screams for the other rider, blindly diving for the lizardling, yowling and screaming as he chased after the little fireball.

Moira cackled, watching the chaos as the brown dragon twisted, also making a valiant effort to catch his rider. Because of his large bulk, he hit the blind dragon, causing the grey to scream in confusion as he was swept off course.

Her eyes flicked to the rider, hoping to see him splattered on the ground. But she found him safe and well on the back of a yellow dragon, heartily clapping a war wraith on the back. Lucky bastard.

Her disappointment only grew when she stopped to compare her protection against what Rena had created for the spire. The grey dragon had not been debilitated by his brush against her barrier. While his movement was sluggish, he was not paralysed. Doubt gnawed at her. Damn Rena. Was her protection enough to kill any who tried to cross it?

Her breath caught in her throat as the grey dragon shuddered in midair, a scream of pain and confusion chilling the air. His wings seized, the muscles along his shoulders, rump and spine spasming. It would not be long before he plummeted, dashing himself and his rider on the cold, hard ground.

A shadow, dark and colossal, drifted over Moira. She wrenched her head back, staring at the gleaming underbelly of the Black Prince's dragon. There was another dragon, a charcoal grey, who escorted her. He had no rider. He was wild.

The air around them reverberated with his rumbling roar as he banked sharply to come alongside the ailing grey. His scales shimmered with gold as he offered a large leathery wing to steady the beast. It wasn't enough to keep the grey drifting.

The wild dragon grabbed on to the blind dragon, long talons burying into hard scales. Wings outstretched, this monster brought the injured one to a safe glide. It would have been a marvel to watch if they weren't foes.

Moira's dragon bellowed, not a cry for battle, but a plaintive cry of a much younger dragon. She went to dive after them like an eager hatchling, but Moira kicked her side. Her mount reared and bucked, and Faelowyn turned her attention to her.

The Black Prince's dragon was smart. She would not attack. Not when she knew Moira was untouchable. But the scheming glint in the dragon's eye sent a shiver of fear up her spine. For within those ancient pools, she saw death.

"You cannot touch me!"

The Black Prince's lips twisted into a disdainful hiss, his teeth covered in blood. His eyes, full of centuries of malice, glinted up at her. "I wouldn't be so sure of that! It was a pleasure killing Tamah, and it would be an absolute privilege to kill you!"

They were words of a desperate man, a man who did not want to admit that he had lost. Raziel Yavari had spent his long life defending Nezaha. Hopefully, he would live long enough to see his decrepit empire fall.

Moira laughed as the black dragon spewed fire at her. The flames dispersed, harmless. She was untouchable.

*Power given to create the sun in the sky, Qavi stepped onto the
earth with little of his light left. In pouring out the remainder
of his power to bless a mortal man, the first Uhl'hari burned
with holy fire. Qavi, once a great celestial light, was condemned
to darkness and shadow.
Camyrs, the spirit of bounty and harvest, and Helenea, the
lady of healing water, were persuaded to raise up other
Uhl'hari. But through great sacrifice, the fire came first. When
the world darkens and hope is lost, fire will rise.
Uhl'hari are Qavi blessed. Hurt or maim Qavi's chosen, and
he'll extinguish your last hope.*

ANCIENT HISTORIES AND MAN

HAVEL

CHAPTER 42

Qavi's Blessing

EDVERN

Edvern's sword hissed and smoked, the naked blade pulsing with the strength of his power. Among the throng of the enemy, he burned like wildfire. His steel carved his way through to the very top of Navilla Spire, and the stones ran red with blood underneath his boots.

Face wet with sweat, he reached the top of Navilla Spire. He paused to take in the fierce battle, chest heaving with adrenaline. The air hummed with the sound of steel, the coppery tang of blood taunting his senses. The moment the barriers fell, their soldiers had swarmed the spire. Everywhere he looked, bodies lay forgotten while the right to life was fought above them.

Below them, Euquallian ships moved around on the backs of the water wyrms, booming with the firing of their weapons. The air was full of flashes and smoke.

In the confusion of battle, it was easy to forget what one was fighting for and give into bloodlust. And so Edvern took a moment to steady his heart rate, remembering who he was and why he was fighting.

Seeing Whilmana tossing aside a young novice steeled his resolve. He charged, his cry for vengeance changing into an inhumane shriek. Whilmana had no time to respond. Blade sizzling, Edvern impaled her through the belly. Yanking his weapon back, he didn't watch her fall. Instead he turned to the next of his foes.

Cowardice was as easy as bloodlust to fall into. Yahler, Whilmana's close companion, fled as soon as he saw Edvern's charge. Leaping forward, Edvern had never felt more powerful.

He kicked Yahler in the back, his boots forcing the air from his enemy's lungs. Yahler sprawled, clawing the ground. His screams for his allies melted into cries for mercy. No one turned to him or took heed of his pleas for help. Edvern raised his sword and swung, putting all his strength into the blow. Yahler's head rolled along the ground.

Spattered in blood, Alynta bounded through the knots of fighting humans. She looked a fright, but her eyes glowed. The ground beneath them was soaked with gore and blessed by Edvern's fire.

A woman's body exploding caught Edvern's attention. Looking through the haze of red, he spotted Lyssandra running onto the roof, her blade crackling with green light. Slashing through the foes in front of her, she screamed as a rider kicked Camyrs' hindquarters.

Retribution was swift. Alynta growled, and jumping, she latched on to the man's throat. She wrenched her head and tore at skin and muscles.

Bastian joined them, a tiny black dyrathakin tucked under one arm, sword swinging with the other. Two of Moira's riders thought to take him from opposite sides. In response, Edvern pivoted, sweeping his hands in an arc. Flames licked the stones, climbing up the legs of Bastian's would-be opponents. They died screaming, wreathed in fire.

Edvern surged forward, biting back his questions. He needed to get closer to Bastian to help him protect his mewling dyrathakin kit.

Another person exploded, red mist filling the air.

"He had seeded fruit for breakfast," Lyssandra said, her wide hazel eyes taking in her gruesome work. If they weren't in the middle of a very serious battle, he might have laughed.

Lyssandra's mouth opened, just as a wind gust nearly tore him off his feet. The force grappled with his wings; he furled them at his sides with a grunt.

Hearing Lyssandra's scream, he turned to see Bastian's boots disappearing over the edge. There was no time for thought or planning. He was running and diving after his cousin. They plummeted together, Bastian just out of reach.

The fall was quick, but until his dying day, he would never forget his cousin's wide eyes or the frightened dyrathakin in his arms.

Hitting the water was like being impaled on thousands of iron spikes. He must have gained strength since his last unintended dip. Holding his breath, he battled to get to his cousin.

Bastian's eyes were closed. Whether the force of the fall had rendered him unconscious or he had given up, Edvern didn't know. The small dyrathakin, a murky black under the water, squirmed free, and her tongue flicked over Bastian's face. It was enough to make him open his eyes.

His cousin flailed, his arms pushing him towards the surface. The dyrathakin followed him. A simple gesture, illuminating the depths, and Edvern could see his cousin was breathing under the water.

It might have been the end of their little misadventure. But underneath them the waters churned. Catching sight of the sharp fins and scales, he screamed, allowing water to rush in his mouth and nose. From nowhere, a water wyrm cut through the depths, grabbing on to Bastian's boot and diving.

Bastian made a quick gesture with his hand. A bubble lifted Edvern up from above, pushing him to the surface.

The water buffeted at him as he tried to follow. His path was stopped as a water wyrm twisted into his path, bursting the bubble. Edvern's hands hit the scaled back, and he was rising above the waters. On the banks of the marsh, Izorah was waiting for him. After grabbing him in her jaws, she dropped him on the cold, muddy ground.

Firm hands pushed him into a kneeling position as he coughed up water. "What do you think you were doing?" Raziel was at his side, patting his back as he coughed up cold, dirty water.

Lifting a shaking finger, Edvern pointed at the churning water. "The third dyrathakin."

Raziel followed Edvern's gesture, gaze hardening. "Stay here."

What Raziel thought he could do, Edvern wasn't sure. "Black Prince ..."

"Impatient, contrary bastards," Raziel muttered. He shuddered as one of the weapons on the Euquallian ships boomed, the fiery missile hitting an unsuspecting dragon.

There was something to be said for a person who was unswervingly calm in stressful situations. Raziel's acceptance that the water wyrms were going to cause chaos and possible harm to their own forces melted away some of Edvern's panic.

The waters continued to froth, shards of ice rising to the surface. The sail fins of the water wyrms rose and twisted. And on the back of one of them was a very miserable Bastian. Edvern couldn't help but gape at the scaled wings and sharp fins on his cousin's forearms.

The water wyrm drew close to the bank and flicked Bastian on the ground. On his hands and knees, the new Uhl'hari gasped for breath.

"My dyrathakin, you overgrown earthworm, where is she?" Bastian coughed up water, glaring at the water wyrms.

The water wyrms hissed at him, their tails and fins thrashing on the surface of the water. And then Edvern spotted her. The little black dyrathakin was no longer little. In a blink of an eye, she had grown into maturity with her Uhl'hari.

She paddled her way to the bank, clawed herself up onto the ground and pushed her way into Bastian's arms with her nose. She turned and hissed at the water wyrms. "Gwyn."

"Calm yourself, water Uhl'hari. She's the daughter of waters and strategy, your companion."

Bastian blinked. "There must be some mistake … I am not Nezahrian."

The water wyrm snickered. "Humans always think they have all the answers."

"You almost drowned me," Bastian shouted.

"Uhl'hari tend to show themselves when they are under duress," the water wyrm said. "We helped the process along."

"Helped the process?" Bastian mumbled. "*Helped it along?*"

On the surface of the lake, the water wyrm hissed and laughed. "If you didn't die, why are you complaining?"

Bastian clinked his mouth shut.

"If the dyrathakin eggs have hatched, doesn't that mean the dragons are free of Aurelian control?" Lyssandra asked, lifting her eyes to the sky. Camyrs crept forward, ears pinned back to sniff at the water wyrms.

"Oh, they're free." Oskar dismounted his bronze dragon, jumping from his back and landing heavily. Hefting one of the Euquallian weapons onto his shoulder, he took aim. "Let's see how you like the taste of powder, Rena."

Edvern didn't have time to clap his hands over his ears as Oskar fired on the Lady of Navilla. Dragon and rider were gone in a flash.

"Mighty useful weaponry," Oskar commented. He returned his weapon to position and aimed again. "Very entertaining."

"Oskar ..." Raziel didn't finish his warning.

Oskar fired, aiming for Moira. The terrifying flare was swallowed up by a blue flash. Moira was protected. Looking contemplative, Oskar glared at his weapon. "Need another plan," he muttered.

"Moira's forces are being decimated elsewhere," Lyssandra said, laying a consolatory hand on Oskar's shoulder. "Her people will find little mercy in the flames and claws of those they enslaved."

"If the dragons are free, why doesn't Moira's dragon kill her?" Bastian grumbled, struggling to get to his feet. "She's flying around in circles."

"Moira is protected, even from her own dragon," Raziel said.

"We have to do something," Lyssandra replied. "She can't fly in circles forever."

"Take your dyrathakins into battle with her," the water wyrm said. It grinned, looking amused.

Raziel turned towards Edvern, then Lyssandra and Bastian. "Do as he says."

"About time." Lyrus landed. His navy scales were covered in soot and blood. Whatever action he had got himself into, he had been busy. Izorah and Elisaria flanked him. *"Let's go and eat some Aurelian."*

Bastian's eyes bulged.

And Edvern knew that his cousin heard his dragon's voice for the first time. Lyrus had been waiting for it to happen ...

Shaking, Bastian stood and stumbled over to Lyrus. "You'll have me?"

"In the ancient days, sometimes a dragon would take the son after the passing of his father," Lyrus said. *"We have both lost. But together we can make our own family."*

Edvern spread his wings and took flight. Izorah met him in the sky, but he did not mount her. They could work in tandem; she was better able to fight at his side rather than his beast of burden. Alynta led the dyrathakin, flying wide.

Edvern didn't know what the water wyrms were up to, but he was sure they had an ulterior motive. He could only pray he could trust them.

Moira's dragon saw them coming. She bucked, throwing her weight around violently, trying to dislodge her rider. To hold on to her misbehaving mount, Moira drew her sword and impaled it into the spine of her dragon.

"Help!" the dragon cried, her red eyes rolling back in her skull. *"Help! Help!"*

Raziel joined them in the air, yelling in Nezahrian. From his tone it was a string of curses. Edvern flew above while Moira was busy with the Black Prince. If he could get onto the dragon's back while she was distracted ...

Edvern grit his teeth. His instincts told him that if Tallermayne blood could dissolve the spire's barrier, then Tallermayne blood would destroy Moira's protection. He might not be Rikar's by blood. But Tallermayne lore considered an adopted child taken willingly was the same as blood. He could be enough ...

"Edvern! Wait," Raziel cried against the wind. "I know what you're thinking. Wait. *Please!*"

"Listen to him," Alynta said through their connection.

Instinct warned Edvern to obey. He turned to look into Raziel's face. The Black Prince's expression crumbled. "You're not Tallermayne blood ..."

"Adoption—"

"Rikar wasn't Tallermayne."

"No ..." Edvern had expected some desperate statement to get him to fall into line, but this was a surprise. His jaw worked, but he could not formulate a proper response.

"He was a Nezahrian foundling that Fennix used to cover up his son's murder."

If Moira had unwillingly taken in another woman's child and raised him ... Rikar could not be a Tallermayne. Rikar was a fraud. By extension, he was a second-generation imposter. He had never had any right to the name Tallermayne.

His blood wouldn't be enough.

But blood was needed. The only one left was ...

"We can't sacrifice Bas!"

"We made a promise to Alaxen. For him, we'll protect his last son. We're looking for another way," Faelowyn said. *"Our long years have taught us that in being patient, we can find weakness. There are always holes in magic defences that can be exploited."*

"You knew." The knowledge that the Black Prince had known Alaxen's fate prior to it happening felt like a betrayal. Edvern couldn't explain why. The pair of them had been enemies.

Raziel's expression was grim, but he nodded, confirming Edvern's suspicions. "Alaxen made his choice. I honour that. We'll take the spire, and we'll take our time to work out how to kill Moira, I promise."

"You knew he was going to die! To condemn himself to an eternity of darkness."

Grief was an angry monster, and she threatened to crash over Edvern, to drag him down into the cold depths where he could not fight his way free. He could feel the tightness in his chest, the haze of panic and fury.

"Eddi," Raziel said, holding up his hands. "That's nonsense. I know the mind and soul of the Father Dragon. We come from him, and you'll learn in time. In Nezaha we believe a man who gives all for the ones he loves gains a great reward. The Father Dragon will receive your uncle with open wings. Wherever Alaxen Tallermayne is, he's not in torment."

"I want to believe you," Edvern replied, his voice thick. "But look all around us. There's so much pain."

"And yet in the darkness, there's always a spark of beauty."

Edvern looked over the battlefield. The lizardlings swarmed enemy riders, tearing, biting and scratching. Those unfortunate riders who hit the water were then taken by the water wyrms.

Euquallian ships shot dragons from the air. Blood rained from the sky.

It was terrible; it was brutal …

But Raziel was right. He looked further afield. To Marsyna cradled close to Amorith's side, to Woe, now Kaida, walking shoulder to shoulder with the wild ones. There were soldiers and medics helping their fellows. In the air, dragons rescuing dragons of violent riders. And then there was Lyssandra, smeared with blood but smiling softly at her dyrathakin. Edvern's hand dropped to his side, his fingers brushing through Alynta's matted coat.

At Raziel's nod, Edvern followed him around the swamp marsh. The Black Prince led them wide to a quieter patch of sky so they might consider their positions. When Edvern tilted his head to the side, he could still see Moira wheeling around on her dragon. He strained his hearing and almost laughed aloud.

"What a strange dragon," the large wild dragon with dark grey scales said. He moved his languid neck, the fires of battle illuminating flecks of oranges and reds among his scales. *"Her name is Imarni. She's saying she'll fly around in circles until she plummets to the ground."*

"She's giving us a chance to kill Moira," Elisaria said.

The grey male dragon moved closer to Faelowyn, his snout touching her in an affectionate greeting.

"Yugrah …"

"I hope, Fae, that we can both forgive ourselves for our mistakes. Maybe we will fly once more together," Yugrah said. *"Imarni says she doesn't have long. The wound is deep but has missed severing anything that would severely compromise movement."*

"Aurelian dragons are taught to ignore injuries for as long as possible," Izorah added.

Lyrus lifted his snout, scenting the air.

But it was Elisaria who spoke. *"It'll be the exhaustion that kills her."*

"She needs to land," Faelowyn said.

Yugrah shook his head. *"Imarni refuses. Not until her rider is dead."*

Alynta peeled back her lips and growled. Blood and saliva mixed into her coat. "If she falls, she won't do anything to save Moira. Not the way that Kyros saved Edvern."

The dragon underneath Moira rumbled and shuddered with the effort to keep herself in the air. The instinct to survive was strong in dragonkind. It would be easy to wait for her to spend all her energy and plummet, taking Moira Tallermayne with her.

But that wasn't Edvern's way.

As sure as he felt his own heartbeat, he felt this dragon's pain thrumming through the air. He sensed hatching in a cold nest, an ill mother unable to look after her young. Her nest mates dying either from neglect or the cruelty of humans. Determination ran through her memories. Determination to live, to fight to see another day.

Self-hatred was there. A disappointment of what she had become and a desire to be free. He felt the ebb of Aurelian control and the suffering that went along with fighting it.

Moira's dragon rumbled again.

"Grandmother! Imarni wants to know if you feel death coming," Bastian called out. He fanned out his wings, displaying to her what he truly was.

Moira's eyes glittered with foaming hatred.

"You're of course welcome to jump from your dragon's back and save us the bother of killing you," Lyssandra said. She mounted Elisaria, tucking Camyrs before her securely.

Edvern's smile grew wider. When they had first met, he thought she behaved like a spoilt princess. Now she looked every inch a fierce warrior queen.

His smile faltered when the dragon underneath Moira dropped. He could see the Grand Lady holding on for dear life. He only cared for her dragon.

"We have to do something!" Bastian hissed at his side.

It would be easy to convince Bastian to attack Moira, to sacrifice himself to be able to harm the Grand Lady before her dragon failed. It would be wrong to exchange his for the dragon's life. Both deserved this opportunity to live.

He needed to save both.

What if he approached Moira not to kill her but to free the dragon? Would her protection affect him if he had no designs on harming her? It was a foolish idea. He could hear Alynta protesting in his mind. Something had to be done, and quickly.

He spread his wings and left the safety of Izorah's shadow. The blue dragon cried out in shock, but he couldn't risk her life. He kept his blade sheathed at his side, but shocks of power licked on the palms of his hands. Stretching out his arms, he met the barrier with fire.

Just as the barrier around the spire had done, Moira's protections burst into flames. It was weaker. There was pain, blood running down his fingers, to his elbows to his shoulders. But Edvern gritted his teeth and pushed a hand through the barrier.

Blood poured from his nose, and he was sure his ears were bleeding too. His whole body seared with pain. His screams echoed in his ears.

Alynta was screaming as well. Edvern sensed that Izorah had stepped in, penning the dyrathakin away. He was thankful that his dragon knew him so well that she understood he needed Alynta safe more than himself.

"Imarni!" Edvern yelled. "You must hold on."

Edvern's head throbbed with the pressure of his power ... his vision blacked. But he held.

"Let go," sobbed Imarni. *"I'm doomed."*

"No." Alynta had broken free of Izorah. She came around the other side, clawing and snarling at the barrier. Through their bond Edvern could feel her pain. But he also felt the barrier weakening. Alynta sensed it too.

The sky lit up with lightning, followed by a crack of thunder. The skies opened, and torrents of rain fell. Edvern thought he saw a blue flash among the red of his flames.

Bastian was shouting, his words lost within the thunder ... and a second grown dyrathakin, one with black fur and wings of water, weaved through the falling rain. She was stunning.

Through the heat of battle, Gwyn had grown even larger than Alynta. Her power mingled with Bastian ... He couldn't see his cousin, but Edvern could certainly hear the cries of shock from Moira.

Green light joined the blue, the air quaked and Camyrs joined the fray. His thin, twiglike horns were now longer and sharper.

The three dyrathakins joined with one another, the lights alternating between each one. Red. Blue. And green.

The barrier shuddered but held fast.

Edvern felt hands upon his shoulders. He was kept upright by another.

"Water ..." Bastian's voice was in his ear. "The barrier is further weakened by the storm ..."

"It's not enough!" Lyssandra's voice seemed far away.

"Imarni," Edvern slurred. "It's time to go for a swim."

Moira screamed and cursed as the three dyrathakins and her dragon brought her down towards the ground. They came down slowly, each dyrathakin supporting Imarni.

Through the haze of his pain and confusion, Edvern saw the water wyrms in the freezing river. Eyes of cold blue and silver watched them, silent and still, waiting for their prey.

"Do not hurt her dragon!" Edvern called, or he thought it was his voice.

The water wyrms swayed their head side to side. *"Never,"* they vowed.

Imarni's claws entered the river, the water dragons shifting underneath her to cradle her gently. Feeling the exhausted dragon's body slump, Edvern was touched by the gesture, for the water wyrms weren't exactly known for their kindness.

The sputtering of Edvern's fire was quenched. For a moment he felt a spark of fear as he was submerged. But a water wyrm lifted him up so that he stood on the surface.

There were many horrible ways to die. Edvern himself had witnessed his share of violence. His father had been bathed in flames, Prince Hedriel had fallen from the skies and Uncle Alaxen was forced to make the decision to take his own life.

Edvern panted from the cold, his hearing failing him as Moira was thrown from Imarni's back. The water churned around her, but her flailing limbs soon disappeared. Before he could think of the wisdom of his actions, he was running and jumping into the depths after her.

He found her struggling in the cold, dark marsh waters. At his command, his power leapt, and his hands wrapped around her throat. Wings of fire flashed blue, tendrils slithering down his arms.

Eyes wide in terror, Moria wriggled helplessly in his grasp. His grip tightened, and the blue power crept into her nostrils. The most powerful woman in Aurelia opened her mouth to scream under the water, blood pouring from her eyes. Even in the haze of the water, he could see his power lighting up through his enemy's body. She stiffened, and Edvern couldn't let go.

A cloaked figure joined them. Long, elegant fingers gripped Edvern's wrists. He looked up into a masked face and could only see eyes that burned with fire. The black cloak swirled around the stranger, fanning out to become large dark wings.

"Vengeance is mine."

There was no mouth slit in the mask, but Edvern heard the voice as clear as if they were having a pleasant afternoon tea. The voice was kind and coaxing.

"Let go, my son."

Edvern's hands fell away, his body bound to obey. He sensed rather than saw the cloak figure smile at him. Then the invisible smile faded into fury, which burned cold and hot all at the same time.

The whites of Moira's eyes were wide as long figures grasped her chin. She writhed, the touch excruciating. Her skin peeled from her bones; her lips opened in a wordless cry. She was consumed within moments. There was nothing left. Not even flecks of ash. Her existence had been erased.

Eyes of burning flames turned towards Edvern once more. The being reached out, and Edvern flinched. *"Lord Qavi."*

"Do not be afraid, young dragon soul." Qavi, the lord of the darkest hour, herald to the lady of hope, floated beside him. A phantom hand ran down Edvern's cheek. The touch was gentle, warming the flesh of his face. *"To say I have no light is foolish. I've enough to protect my chosen."*

"Why have I not seen you before?"

"I'm the lord of the darkest hour. My power, my hidden hope, is strong in the dark. I was always with you."

Edvern shook his head, and Qavi drew closer, pressing his forehead against his. He had seen dragons show this sign of kinship, but never a human. *"Let me give your troubled heart some knowledge to give you hope. Your father knew my name. He called upon me, asking for hope. And I answered and gave him you."*

"He's dead."

"He's home." Small tendrils of sparks wove between the dark feathers of Qavi's wings as he spoke. *"Your uncle too, Blessed One. Now it's time for you to live."*

Whatever force was keeping Edvern's lungs from exploding lifted. Panic of drowning nearly overwhelmed him, and he clawed his way to the surface.

From underneath him a water wyrm cradled his body, easing his way through the water. He felt himself slip, his consciousness ebbing and flowing. He was aware of pointed teeth, growling and a creature pulling him free. Hands were under his armpits, dragging him in the cold, wet mud.

"It's done." Dazed, he lay on the field of battle, his vision slowly clearing. Alynta was curled against his left side, Lyssandra on his right. His heart swelled as he saw her next to him. Her face was bruised but her lips smiling.

From her wings she took a feather and tucked it within his wings. "Now you have a piece of me too," she said, brushing her lips against his. She lifted her delicate hand and caressed his cheek. "It's done," Lyssandra whispered, a tear tracking down her cheek. "It's done, you stubborn bastard."

Qavi
Lord of the darkest hour.
The dark star.
Lord of Shadows

CHAPTER 43

Anniversary

EDVERN

One Year Later ...

As the dawn sun rose over the walls of the keep, Edvern rose from his bed. In silence, he and Alynta made their way into the stone courtyard. Today marked the one-year anniversary of the battle of Navilla Spire. While Nezahrians did not hold to the same traditions for the dead, he decided he would observe the teachings of his father's people.

It had snowed during the night. Snowflakes covered Edvern's hair and lashes with a fine powder. His boots sunk into the snow as he walked in the solitary courtyard of Raziel's palace. There were no Aurelian temples in Nezaha, but the Black Prince had gently suggested the courtyard as an appropriate place for him to hold vigil.

Statues carved from black dragonstone lined the square yard, radiating heat. They shone in the sun, reminiscent of the statues of riders and dragons in Aurelian temples.

"Father Dragon, hear me," Edvern murmured. He blinked up at the sun, whispering the prayers for the dead, which he had practiced in the privacy of his room. Alynta joined his prayers, her voice a little more fervent for Alaxen. He let his hand rest on her head, knowing that she missed his uncle, who she had claimed for herself.

Lavender eyes glanced up at him. Without a word, she padded over to a frozen fountain at the centre of the courtyard. She sat beside a stone bench, her head cocked to the side. A smile tugged on Edvern's lips as he joined her and knelt. This would be his altar.

Tugging his winter cloak tight around his shoulders, he glanced up to see that Izorah had come to perch on one of the thick walls.

"I'm proud of you, Uhl'hari," Alynta said as Edvern finished his prayers.

Edvern had been naive when he had declared everything done on the battlefield. In truth, victory was the beginning of the journey towards peace. Centuries of bloodshed and distrust could not be swept away after one triumph. It would take his lifetime.

"And me?" Camyrs scampered into the courtyard. Snow dotted his fur coat where he had evidently been rolling in the soft snow drifts. Edvern grinned, opening his hand to Lyssandra's dyrathakin, who although was now the largest, craved the most attention. Camyrs came to him, eager for an embrace.

"This is serious business," Alynta told him sternly. "It's been a year."

"It's okay," Edvern said. "Saemore has their own traditions ..."

"I'll stand with you, Uhl'hari Eddi." Camyrs tilted his head, snow dropping from his horns. He startled and yelped, sniffing at the snow.

Alynta shook her head at him. She had become quite a mother hen to the younger dyrathakins. Gwyn drove her to the point of madness with her boundless energy.

Kneeling at the fountain, Edvern drew out a set of candles. They were more expensive than the lonely one he had lit for his father in the temple. Last night he had left supper early to sit and carve names into the wax. One for Kendrick, Alaxen and Hedriel. He drew on his power, and with a soft exhale, he lit the wicks without lifting his hands.

Staring into the dancing flames, Alynta pressed her body against his, and Camrys rested his snout on Edvern's shoulder. He stayed until his muscles were stiff and a resounding roar interrupted him. Glancing up, he caught the sight of two dragons, one black and one navy.

"Bas ..."

An Aurelian rider had never stepped foot in the Yavari stronghold. This was most irregular. Further bothersome, Raziel had been summoned by the emperor in Halvaine. Why had he turned back?

Faelowyn's mate, Yugrah, dipped through the clouds, flying close to Lyrus and nipping playfully at his mate's tail.

"He thought he should commemorate the life of his father with his only remaining family."

Edvern jumped, and turning, caught Lyssandra's eyes. He had not heard her approach. She was on her knees too, her long, unbound hair drifting in the breeze.

"You don't need to do this," Edvern said.

"It's important to you, so it's important to me," Lyssandra replied. She stood, brushing the snow from her knees. "I won't ask you to give up your Aurelian heritage. No matter how the Nezahrian emperor begs me to. Raziel is of the same mind."

Edvern grimaced and turned to glare at the candles. It had been a major point of contention for the lords of Nezaha. His lack of knowledge of the Nezahrian language and his name had been debated in the capital for weeks.

While the emperor's court gossiped and argued about what his fate should be, Raziel had sequestered him in his own palace away from the capital. Yaryn was isolated from the larger cities of Nezaha. Most days he flew with Izorah and Alynta over the wide fields and through the barren mountain passes. He ought to spend his time learning the language of his heritage, as Lyssandra pestered him to.

"Finding acceptance in Nezaha will be difficult."

Lyssandra brushed her hair away from her face. "Power is shifting. The people are demanding peace. They are tired after centuries of war. If he wants to stay in power, the emperor needs to listen to their needs. Otherwise ..."

While Dalain's elder brothers were open and welcoming, the emperor had only expressed his disdain for Edvern. Much of Nezaha's history was based on the right of the Uhl'hari to mediate between humans and dragons. His first month in Nezaha had been suffocating. Many dignitaries wanted to see him, speak with him and touch him. Everything he did was monitored and reported back to the emperor. It was a relief when Raziel brought him to Yaryn. Symmeon was posted as his guard, and Zanniel still ghosted his steps when he wasn't away on Raziel's business. Which was quite often, as the emperor hadn't forgiven the war wraith his interference with Kaida on the battlefield. Poor Zanniel shouldered the blame for Ze'hyrn's loss of status as a dragon rider.

Gwyn bounded into the courtyard first. "Found you!" she cried, tackling Edvern to the ground. Bastian tutted, following her into the courtyard at a solemn pace. He did not seem shocked by Lyssandra's attendance. He moved forward, drawing out his own candle and setting it beside Edvern's.

"I'm sorry the service is small." Edvern pushed Gwyn off his lap and lit Bastian's candle with a swish of his wrist. His cousin knelt.

"Why?" Bastian asked. With a gentle gesture of his hand, he quietened Gwyn. "I think this is what Father would have wanted. Us together, still family."

There they stayed, kneeling in the snow. Edvern felt his thighs cramp but was unwilling to move until Bastian had finished his own vigil. When Bastian stood, Edvern turned to find Raziel had joined them.

"I thought you went to Halvaine."

"I found that I preferred to be here with you, honouring the noble dead, rather than at Ze'hyrn's side. And Bastian needed an escort to be here today." Setting down another lit candle, the Black Prince let his gaze linger on the one for Hedriel. "You've observed the year of mourning, Edvern. It's time to begin your new work. Bastian has already begun."

"I am most grateful, Black Prince." Bastian inclined his head, his shoulders drooped. Of all the kingdoms, Aurelia was the one who had suffered the most in the aftermath of the battle of Navilla. He worked himself to the bone to protect his countrymen. It would be several more months before Aurelia was stable.

Following the battle, the people were starving, and those who remained loyal to the memory of Moira were intent on terrorising the smaller villages. The lack of food and essential supplies meant violence erupted all over Aurelia. And it fell to Bastian, with Oskar's help, to find a way to provide for his people and settle the politics.

Bastian sucked in a breath, holding it as if the act would give him the strength and courage to continue. "There is no royal family in Aurelia. Likely a republic will be formed."

"Nothing you can't handle, Senator Tallermayne," Raziel replied. "The rebuild of the new capital of Cynedir is something to be marvelled at."

Bastian shook his head at the praise. "It took too much time to find and dismantle all the dragons' dens."

"But it is done." Odharn padded forward. The young dragon did not like the cold, and Edvern was touched that he came out to join them.

"I do have some good news," Bastian said. "I had one of our healers look over the drawings you sent us, Edvern. She convened with others, and they believe it could work."

"What would work?" Raziel asked, suspicion clouding his expression.

"A prosthetic wing for Odharn," Edvern explained. "I thought it might have been a flight of fancy. I've been studying Izorah's movements for months to better understand the mechanics of flight."

"A prosthetic? For me?" Odharn cocked his head to the side. *"You mean I will fly."*

"Not for some time." Bastian frowned. "Due to the nature of the procedure, the healers want Odharn fully grown. The wing is situated near the spine. They have one chance."

"They're going to build an adult wing?" Lyssandra asked.

"With some minor adjustments to Eddi's plans," Bastian said. "They've started on some prototypes."

"But I will fly?" Odharn asked, quivering from his snout to the very tip of his tail.

Bastian nodded.

With a cry of delight, the little green dragon flapped his wing, dove and dashed into the snow. He gambolled a lap around the courtyard, the three dyrathakins joining him in his excitement. He stopped before Raziel, eyes bright. *"Are Mother and Father here? I must see them!"*

Odharn had managed to not only convince Faelowyn to look after him, but also her mate. Edvern was not quite sure how he had managed to convince the proud wild dragon to share his kills. Yugrah denied it, of course, but he always left the choice meat for the younger dragon.

"They're waiting for you."

Wagging his tail, Odharn approached to snuffle at Edvern and then bounded away.

Edvern offered his hand to Lyssandra, wishing they were alone so he might steal a kiss. She had been busy with the Saemorish throne, trying to patch relations between her king and the Nezahrian emperor. Hedriel's mother and siblings might outwardly support their emperor, but they made their displeasure of the Saemorish king known. It was causing a diplomatic nightmare.

He knew that Lyssandra was feeling alone; Antonella and Konrad did not have the protection of being Uhl'hari. In Saemore they were criminals, and therefore it was unwise for them to return. They had boarded Eupheana's ship in the summer to explore Euquall. Konrad refused Raziel's offer to join his army. The young captain had had enough of bloodshed.

"The dragon kin are waiting for us to take our place," Lyssandra commented. She stepped past Edvern, and he admired the way she moved.

Raziel inclined his head. "It's the way of dragons."

Edvern grimaced. The Black Prince was right. Both Lyssandra and Bastian had begun making political changes to their kingdoms while he hid away in Yaryn.

"Fear not, blessed one," Raziel said, seeing the expression crossing Edvern's face. "Tyrbanath is a mighty ally, and he happens to like you."

The Black Prince's statement was debatable. Tyrbanath had made grumbling complaints, demanding that Edvern journey to meet with him. It seemed the ancient dragon wanted him to learn at his talons instead of humans. There was a part of him that longed to step into their caverns of liquid fire. The siren calls of the volcanoes terrified him.

"Fire will not consume fire," Faelowyn said. Edvern looked up to find her huddled next to Izorah. After the pair of female dragons came to an understanding, they had become friendly. Meanwhile, Yugrah had been spotted flying the skies of Aurelia, visiting Lyrus.

Edvern shook his head. "Have the lizardlings made contact?"

"They wish to keep communication to a minimum. They've promised a plentiful harvest the year that King Jahon dies. They have it in their heads that Konrad is the next king," Lyssandra said.

Bastian raised an eyebrow. "I'm not sure how they want us to achieve *that*."

Lyssandra threw her hands up. "They're impossible!"

"You're a Saemorish diplomat. You can do difficult things," Edvern replied with a grin.

Lyssandra shot him a withering look.

"And the water wyrms?" Edvern asked.

Bastian shrugged his shoulders, a curious frown tugging on his lips. "They haven't travelled far from the coast since the battle. Raziel's war wraith, Zanniel, has reported that they are shadowing my movements."

"Good, they're watching you," Raziel said.

Bastian frowned, his brow furrowing in confusion. "They were leaving impossibly large rocks in Cynedir on the shore, presumably for the rebuild. In the spring some followed trading ships. Younger, smaller water wyrms were spotted herding fish into nets in remote villages."

"It seems Lyssandra and Bastian have found a way to please their patrons. But I'm no match for the emperor."

"Dalain's letters have given us assurance his elder brothers will support you at court," Raziel said.

"Is that why you took him into your army? So that you'd have royal sanction?" Edvern asked. Both Dalain and Palea had refused to return with the emperor's men to Halvaine after the battle. They made a new home for themselves in their aunt Eupheana's palace in Sangell. Edvern was under the impression that Ionah stayed with her husband to keep the twins safe.

"Ze'hyrn has made life in the capital difficult for years." Raziel shrugged. "His sons no longer feel safe, and the court is on the edge of a blade."

Edvern looked back at the lonely candles. They snuffed out in the gentle breeze. "I don't think I deserve any of this."

"You aren't emperor," Raziel said. "That's a human title. You'll be Uhl'hari … a man with a dragon soul to lead a people with heritage that stretches back to the dawn of time. It's the emperor, or empress', task to listen to the will of dragons, to find the harmony between our kinds. Our people deserve a man who can hear the dragonsong. They deserve more than a bitter and empty empire."

Edvern looked up to the sky, watching as their dragons played above. A smile touched his lips; he had fought for this future. It was done. The assurance that the resurgence of dragons and mankind had been restored. Dragons were now respected, not beasts of burden. The legacy of pain and suffering was dead.

"You once told me that there were consequences to harming an Uhl'hari," Edvern said. His mind went back to the murky depths of the frozen swamps, his hands around Moira's neck and the strange, cloaked figure. "That's why Qavi stopped me from killing Moira? And is that why Ze'hyrn's court is teetering on failure?"

Raziel inclined his head. "Justice belongs to Qavi."

"Why would Ze'hyrn risk shooting me? It must be more than fear of a risen relic."

"The oldest stories speak of Uhl'hari of fire rising when Qavi is displeased. You were the first sign he was moving in the world again; the wild ones were the second sign. History has taught us that when dragons start to meddle in human affairs, the rulers of that time find themselves displaced."

Edvern considered Raziel's words. "Ze'hyrn was already condemned before he shot me?"

"No. I sent counsel to him when you were found to make changes in his reign. He didn't want to listen." Raziel shook his head, an annoyed frown on his face. "There was an empress that did not lose power when Uhl'hari rose. She worked with the Uhl'hari, diligently making necessary changes, and Qavi spared her. If Ze'hyrn listened …"

"Ze'hyrn is responsible for his own doom," Lyssandra said. "Aurelia has already fallen. It's a question whether it's the Saemorish or Nezahrian throne that falls next."

Fire was Qavi's blessing, and so Edvern would move into his future. "It's time I go to Halvaine. One last warning before I go to Tyrbanath."

"Eddi, the emperor does not wish to see you in Halvaine. He will not listen," Raziel warned. "Be aware that Qavi is an immortal celestial spirit. How and when he'll act is unpredictable. Ze'hyrn may rule for many years yet."

Confidence surged in Edvern's heart. His hand lingered over the sword at his hip, the one commissioned and engraved by Rikar Tallermayne. He sensed a tugging on his soul, an assurance that this was the move that Qavi wanted him to make. It was time. "No, Raziel. I'll meet my role, *with the heart of a dragon*. Ze'hyrn is a mortal man who has proved himself fickle and weak."

"Your will be done, Uhl'hari." Raziel bowed his head. "Come what may, we're with you."

Edvern's life had been smeared with loss and darkness. Through it all, he had journeyed from boy to Uhl'hari. He'd been crushed and crippled with self-doubt, yet he still stood tall. When he thought he had walked his path alone, he had never been abandoned.

"You've the support of the Aurelian senate," Bastian said, lifting his hand to cover his heart. "Although our government still flounders. Take Oskar with you, cousin. He can move you both out of Halvaine quickly if need be."

"What happens when Ze'hyrn falls?" Edvern asked. "What of the Nezahrian people?"

"Believe it or not, the world will keep on turning. Another will take his place." Tucking her arm in his, Lyssandra leaned in close. Her lips brushed over Edvern's cheeks, and a thrill of pleasant warmth pooled in his stomach. "I'll be by your side."

"Tyrbanath, for all that he is a bag of hot air, is wise. He'll help guide you, Eddi." Raziel let his hand drop to his side, his fingers brushing through Alynta's fur.

"I know the lizardlings don't want a lot of contact. Perhaps, Lyssandra, you might gently appraise them and enquire how they plan to convince Konrad to take the crown," Alynta said.

Camyrs sighed dramatically. "Tullsullah is such a dank, miserable forest for a colony."

Lyssandra pursed her lips, her expression sour. "I started this journey thinking I would find a way for my people to have dragon riders. Oh, the irony that the lizardlings have given a partial answer."

"What is it?" Edvern asked.

"They want the people of Saemore to vote to put Konrad on the throne, and they'll remove the curse from the land. People will be born with powers once more. Would Saemore have the Gravedigger King and drought, or a king crowned by dragons?" Lyssandra shook her head. "I don't even know how I'd conduct a vote without having my head taken off my shoulders."

Raziel huffed. "I suggest you call your cousin here to meet with the lizardling chief. They'll want to crown him first, before human hands."

"We shouldn't wait for the water wyrms to approach us," Gwyn added. "We should go first, ask them what they want from us."

Bastian nodded his assent.

Edvern looked around at his companions, pride swelling in his heart. Change had already revolutionised their kingdoms, and more was coming. Although he did not know what the future held, peace swept through him.

The future, although unwritten, wasn't something for Edvern to fear. He was the author of his own fate, not a foolish man with a crown and a quiver full of arrows. The sun had set on Ze'hyrn's crumbling empire. From the ashes a new kingdom would rise. Despite the pain that hounded him through life, he walked through the darkness and stood an overcomer in the light. He was Qavi's blessed and chosen. He had lived to see the dawn, to see hope resurrected within human and dragon alike.

And it was beautiful.

You've reached journeys end. I am eternally grateful for all the readers taking a chance on me.

If you enjoyed the book why not help an author out and leave a review on Amazon or Goodreads?

 amazon.com/author/kjburrage

goodreads.com/author/show/22623993.K_J_Burrage

Character Guide

Humans

Adelia Valynt (AY-dee-lee-yah   VAL-int) – Fennix Tallermayne's first love, rival to Moira Tallermayne.

Alaxen Tallermayne (AH-lax-en   TAL-ah-main) – a dragon rider lord; elder brother to Rikar and uncle to Edvern. Lord of Cynedir Spire.

Antonella Fenin (AN-tow-nel-lah   FEN-in) – a young diplomat stationed in Correllain.

Aryis (AIR-iss) – the lady of the dawn. Star of hope, used as navigation by Aurelians.

Bastian Tallermayne (BASS-tin   TAL-ah-main) – eldest cousin of Edvern Tallermayne, son of Alaxen. Dragon rider.

Bea Hillyard (BEE   HILL-ee-ard) – an elderly widow of Gytall, husband was a dragon rider called Dirk.

Bedvir (BED-veer) – a dragon master of the Gytall Spire who is known for his cruelty.

Dalain (DA-lain) – the third son of the Emperor of Nezaha, the prince to whom Lyssandra Stamos was betrothed.

Edvern Tallermayne (EDD-vern   TAL-ah-main) – the male main character, a disgraced bastard son of Rikar Tallermayne, a dragon rider.

Ellrahera (ELL-rah-hear-ah) – the Prime Diplomat of Saemore, sister to King Jahon of Saemore.

Eupheana (YOU-fee-nah) – Empress Ionah's sister, a general of Euquall, a fierce warrior and mistress of the king's fleet.

Donnell (DON-ell) – one of the captains at Cynedir Spire known to be loyal to Alaxen Tallermayne.

Fergus Kalbrynt (FER-gus   KAL-brigh-nt) – One of Alaxen Tallermayne's loyal captains, uncle to Kirra Deltmine.

Fennix Tallermayne (FEN-icks   TAL-ah-main) – Lady Moira's husband, the grandfather of Edvern.

Fiora Stamos (FIGH-or-ah   ST-am-os) – Lyssandra's mother, a disgraced Saemorish princess, called also the Spider of Saemore.

Gradie Holstym (GRAY-dee   HOL-st-im) – a high ranking war wraith that disappeared, reported to be Lyssandra's father.

Hedriel (HED-re-al) – a nephew of the Emperor of Nezaha, a minor prince.

Ionah (EYE-oh-nah) – the Empress of Nezaha. Dalain's mother, second wife to Emperor Ze'hyrn.

Jahon (Jah-hon) – the King of Saemore.

Kendrick Tallermayne (KEN-dr-ick   TAL-ah-main) – Edvern's younger cousin, son of Alaxen Tallermayne.

Kirra Deltmine (KIR-rah   DELL-t-mine) – a dragon rider novice that Edvern had an affair with. They share a friendship.

Konrad Stamos (Con-rad   ST-am-os) – Lyssandra's cousin, a captain of the guard and Crown Prince Torsten's bastard son.

Larah (LAR-ah) – a pretty seamstress of Gytall, whom Edvern had an affair with.

Lyssandra Stamos (LISS-an-dr-ah   ST-am-moss) – the female main character. A young diplomat stationed in Correllain, under the care of Ellrahera.

Markos (MAH-cos) – a small boy that Raziel Yavari rescues from the palace in Correllain.

Moira Tallermayne (MOY-rah   TAL-ah-main) – the Grand Lady of Gytall Spire, head of the dragon riders, who rules with an iron fist. Edvern's grandmother.

Nabert Valynt (NAH-bert   VAL-int) – the old cantankerous librarian of the Gytall Spire.

Oluvin (OL-u-vinn) – King of Aurelia.

Oskar Hertforde (OS-car   HURT-ford) – one of the captains loyal to Alaxen Tallermayne, stationed at Cynedir Spire.

Qavi (Qah-vee) – the lord of the darkest hour, the dark star. He can be found in the dark before dawn. Herald of his wife Aryis. He is the lord of those holding onto hope in the darkest of times.

Palea (PA-lee-ah) – a Nezahrian dragon rider, loyal to Alaxen.

Ramm (RAM) – a young Aurelian who escaped Cynedir with the dragon riders.

Raziel Yavari (RAY-zeel   Yah-var-ee) – the Black Prince. The champion of Nezaha and their only dragon rider.

Rena Hybeck (REE-nah   HIGH-beck) – the lady commander of Navilla Spire in Aurelia.

Rikar Tallermayne (RIGH-car   TAL-ah-main) – a disgraced dragon master. Edvern's father.

Saskah Tallermayne (SASS-car   TAL-ah-main) – the wife of Ullryk Tallermayne the Liberator, who always flew against the Nezahrian Empire. Ancestor of Edvern.

Symmeon (SIM-me-on) – once a noble of Charakara, he worked himself up the ranks of the army to become one of Raziel's most trusted generals.

Tamah Tallermayne (TAM-ah   TAL-ah-main) – daughter of Moira Tallermayne. Her favourite child.

Taseria (TAZ-er-ree-ah) – a dragon master under the command of Alaxen Tallermayne, Cynedir Spire. She is known for her skills in stealth and tracking.

Thleah Tallermayne (Th-lee   TAL-ah-main) – wife of Alaxen Tallermayne.

Titas Reinhard (TIE-tas   RIGH-n-hard) – A elderly general of Vancarde, Edvern serves in his household.

Tobin (T-oh-bin) – a young dragon master. A rival of Edvern's.

Torsten Stamos (TOR-stin   ST-am-os) – Crown Prince of Saemore, Konrad's father.

Ullryk Tallermayne (ULL-rick   TAL-ah-main) –A common man who defected from the Nezahrian Empire with his dragon and established the dragon riders in Aurelia. Edvern's ancestor.

Whilmana (Will-ma-na) – Lady Moira's head interrogator, known for her unfeeling façade. And getting anyone to talk.

Yahler (YA-lah) – A dragon master who works closely with Moira's interrogators, known for enjoying causing others pain.

Zanniel Oberion (ZANN-neel   OHH-ber-on) – the mysterious potter of Vancarde, who helps Lyssandra.

Ze'hyrn (ZEE-h-rin) – the Emperor of Nezaha.

Dragons

Aerin (AY-rin) – a large brown dragon, known for his large build and nasty temper. Bonded with Tobin.

Alynta (AY-lin-tah) – a dyrathakin, a small fox like creature, with the power to breath fire. Bonds to Edvern.

Amorith (AM-or-ith) – Tyrbanath's mate and queen of the wild dragons.

Balfar (BAL-fah) – an older dragon that was included in Aerin's ranks.

Codex/ Codee (CO-dex   CO-dee) – a younger yellow dragon that flew within Aerin's squadron. Close to Woe.

Crytheisi (CRY-thee-see) – a young teal dragon that Moira takes as her own, chosen for her vibrant scales.

Elisaria (ELL-eye-sah-rah) – an emerald dragon who escapes from Aurelia. A younger cousin to the vicious Aerin.

Faelowyn (FAY-low-in) – a large black female dragon. The faithful companion to Raziel Yavari, the Black Prince of Nezaha.

Faer (FAY-er) – an old blind dragon, whose rider is Palea.

Gryph (G-riff) – the eldest dragon in Aerin's squadron. Bonded with Master Bedvir.

Imarni (IMM-ah-nee) – a second dragon Moira Tallermayne flies into battle.

Izorah (ISS-or-ah) – a light blue female dragon. Bonded with Rikar Tallermayne.

Jirrah (JEER-rah) – a lizardling with twisted wings, who is the eyes for Faer, a blind dragon.

Kaida (KAY-da) – a new name given to the dragon called Woe.

Kyros (KIGH-ross) – a very old red dragon. A large male that was once Moira's favourite. He is bonded with the Grand Lady.

Lyrus (Lye-riss) – a large navy dragon with a silver underbelly. He is bonded to Alaxen Tallermayne.

Marsyna (MAH-see-nah) – a small red female dragon, still very young. Sister to Aerin.

Odharn (ODD-hahn) – a small green dragon with one wing, who escaped the Dragon Dens.

Pyrnn (PR-in) – a wild dragon, Tyrbanath's and Amorith's son.

Tyrbanath (TEAR-ban-nath) – king of the wild dragons, called King of the Air, mate to Amorith.

Valtar (VALL-tah) – a dark red dragon, a seasoned veteran within Aerin's ranks.

Woe (W-oh) – a younger grey male dragon. He had been stolen from wild dragon's nest as a young hatchling. His nestmates all perished. He renamed himself Woe. Original name is unknown.

Xyran (ZIGH-ran) – a large silver male dragon who had bonded with Fennix Tallermayne. After his master's death, he refused to be bonded to another.

Yugrah (YOU-gra) – a large dark grey wild dragon, once was Faelowyn's mate.

Location Guide

Alvaraine (AL-vah-rain) — a strip of land, largely inhabited between Aurelia and Nezaha. Not heavily patrolled.

Aurelia (AW-ray-lee-ah) — a kingdom and homeland of the dragon riders. A country that is a collection of many islands connected by trade bridges.

Charkara (SHAR-car-rah) – mountainous holy city in Nezaha. Twenty years ago, the dragon riders of Aurelia attacked with heavy casualties.

Correllain (COR-rell-lain) – the city of diplomats in Saemore. Where Ellrahera and her young diplomats reside and train.

Cynedir (SIN-ee-deer) – a dragon rider city, which includes one of the three spires. Seat of power of Lord Alaxen Tallermayne.

Dead Man's Folly, Mt Willahal (WILL-ah-bal) – an encampment of Lady Moira's dragon riders troops.

Euquall (EE-quoll)– a small independent kingdom, known for its trade and gentle magics, who likes to stay out of the conflict.

Fahlore Forest (FAR-lor) – a forest that borders Saemore, Aurelia and Nezaha. The Aurelians believe it to be haunted.

Fraehiln (FRAY-hill-n) – **a** town in Aurelia.

Gytall (GIGH-tal) – a dragon rider city, which includes one of the three spires. Seat of power of Grand Lady Moira Tallermayne.

Halvaine (HAL-vain) – capital of Nezaha and ruling seat of her emperor.

Hemmryn Vale (HEM-rin) – a small border land town in Saemore.

Irani (EYE-rahn-nee) – the City of Eternal Summer, where the king of Aurelia has his palace.

Navilla (NAH-vill-ah) – a dragon rider city, which includes one of the three spires. Seat of power of Lady Rena Hybeck.

Nezaha (NEE-zah-ha) – the old empire, protected by the Black Prince and said to be the birth place of dragon kind.

Saemore (SAY-more) – a kingdom known for it's fertile lands, said that dragons and magic abandoned their lands.

Sangell (SANG-gell) – capital of Euquall, a port city.

Tacebia (TASS-cee-bah) – the encampment of the Black Prince's forces.

Talsullah (TAL-sa-lah) – a dark forest that borders Saemore and Aurelia. Lizardlings were spotted here.

Tarramine (TAH-rah-mine) – the capital city of Saemore. Where King Jahon resides.

Valley of Yrew (U-roo) – a lake district in Nezahrian territory where Fennix Tallermayne was killed.

Vancarde (VAN-car-dee) – a border town of Aurelia, known for its population of artisans and military folk. One of the few towns not fully in dragon rider control.

Weirhelm, Mount (WIER-helm) – a large mountain on the border of Saemore and Aurelia.

Yaryn (Yah-rin) – the traditional landholdings of the Yavari.

Acknowledgements

I'm eternally grateful, to you, dear readers, for taking the chance on a small independently published author. Although this isn't my first series, every book comes with many hours of blood, sweat and tears. Without a readership, there would be no books.

I'm so fortunate to have a fantastic working relationship with my editor, Katie Wolf. She's not only edited by work but has taken time to speak with me about my concerns, questions and fears. The last year hasn't been an easy one, and the road to getting this series written and edited has been full of obstacles. Her guidance and advice has been invaluable.

To my beta readers Holly Cline and Janine Burger, thank you for all your hard work and dedication reading and reviewing both Traitor's Pyre and Renegade's Diplomacy in the manuscripts draft formats. I appreciate all the feedback.

Another great big thank you needs to go to Chicklen.doodle on IG who has done the covers. She's taken my scribbles and created a masterpiece.

Finally, to those that have helped with life as a single mother – allowing me to be at events, (or provided support at events).

I look forward to continuing the journey with you all!

About KJ Burrage

KJ Burrage currently calls tropical North Queensland, Australia, home. She has been developing her craft since she was ten years old. Alas, the original floppy discs from 1995 have disappeared!

She lives with her three young daughters, an exuberant pug-cross and a cheeky blue parrot.

Growing up she had grand visions of becoming CS Lewis. When she grew up a little more, she decided she was going to be JRR Tolkien. Now, she's learnt to be proud of her own voice and the pen name KJ Burrage is perfect for her.

She has a Bachelor Degree in Primary Education with a major in literacy and worked as a primary school teacher. She has also been a co-owner of a laser engraving business.

Life can be unpredictable (and unfair). After the sudden and tragic death of her husband, she returned to her passion of the written word.

You can read more at www.kjburrage.com.

facebook.com/profile.php?id=100071328683512

instagram.com/kjburrage_author/

tiktok.com/@kjburrage_writes

goodreads.com/author/show/22623993.K_J_Burrage

amazon.com/author/kjburrage

https://twitter.com/KJBurrage

Also by

Hungry for more?
Why not check out these titles?

The Dragon's Heir Trilogy
Son of the Crown
Prince of Scales
Herald of the Dragon King

Fantasy Standalone
Fires of Retribution

(Note Fires of Retribution is set 3000 yeas before Dragon's Heir Trilogy. Both projects can stand on their own and be read in any order. Although, an eagle-eyed reader might find some interesting connecting bridges.)

Dragon Soul Duet
Traitor's Pyre
Renegade's Diplomacy